A STOLEN KISS

"Why didn't you tell me about your betrothal?"

Slane looked away. Why did he feel guilty, as if he had betrayed her somehow? The thought was ridiculous. He had no allegiance to this woman, only to his brother. "It wasn't important," he said defensively. "Our relationship . . . yours and mine . . . is nothing more than it seems."

"I guess I was mistaken," she whispered.

Slane saw the way her lips trembled, the way her throat worked. "I never intended to hurt you, Taylor," he said quietly.

"No, it just seems to work out like that."

Her eyes were large and the deepest green he had ever seen. The candlelight shimmering around her head made her almost angelic. Unbidden, his fingers picked up a lock of her hair, and it curled around his knuckles. "My God, you are beautiful."

"You'd better get away from me. Very far away," she advised. "I'll bring you nothing but trouble."

Slane nodded. "Very far away," he echoed. But he lifted his hand to rub it along her jaw, over her cheek. Then he found himself leaning his arm next to her head, his lips mere inches from hers. Her sweet breath fanned his face.

She looked up at him. So beautiful.

He lowered his lips to hers. . . .

BOOK YOUR PLACE ON OUR WEBSITE AND MAKE THE READING CONNECTION!

We've created a customized website just for our very special readers, where you can get the inside scoop on everything that's going on with Zebra, Pinnacle and Kensington books.

When you come online, you'll have the exciting opportunity to:

- View covers of upcoming books

- Read sample chapters

- Learn about our future publishing schedule
  (listed by publication month *and author*)

- Find out when your favorite authors will be visiting a city near you

- Search for and order backlist books from our online catalog

- Check out author bios and background information

- Send e-mail to your favorite authors

- Meet the Kensington staff online

- Join us in weekly chats with authors, readers and other guests

- Get writing guidelines

- AND MUCH MORE!

**Visit our website at
http://www.zebrabooks.com**

A KNIGHT
OF
HONOR

LAUREL
O'DONNELL

Zebra Books
Kensington Publishing Corp.

http://www.zebrabooks.com

ZEBRA BOOKS are published by

Kensington Publishing Corp.
850 Third Avenue
New York, NY 10022

First Printing: September, 1999
10 9 8 7 6 5 4 3 2 1

Printed in the United States of America

To the true joys in my life: John, Brynn, Jason, and Taylor.
Always follow what's in your heart.

And of course, to my husband, Jack.
Without your help I could never write these wonderful stories!

Dear Reader:

I'm so happy that you've picked Taylor and Slane's story to read. Taylor has turned out to be one of my favorite heroines. She's feisty and strong-willed, and she wields a sword as well as any man. A mercenary who lives on the streets, she has come to think very little of honor. She does what she has to to survive. Slane, on the other hand, truly is a knight of honor. He is gallant and chivalrous. He's the type of hero ladies think of when they think of medieval knights. How can a mercenary and a knight of honor get together? Well, you'll have to read *A Knight of Honor* to find out!

I love to hear from my readers, because their opinions mean a lot to me. So please drop me a line at PO Box 7241, Algonquin, IL 60102.

Or visit my Web site—*Lady Laurel's Castle*—at: http://members.aol.com/laurelodon/ and let me know what you think. You'll also find free previews, reviews, and reader comments on my other books. Please stop by and join my mailing list for a chance to win free autographed books, cover flats, and more!

Thanks again for letting *A Knight of Honor* take you away into a wonderful world of adventure, medieval pageantry, and love.

Laurel O'Donnell

PROLOGUE

England—1340

Taylor Sullivan wondered if her mother had gone mad. No one in her right mind would be wearing a bright vibrant smile like the one that lit her mother's lips, not in a situation like this one. How could she smile in the face of such unspeakable horror? Taylor wondered frantically. Her own body shook with fear. She had to clasp her small hands tightly in front of her so her mother wouldn't see her fingers trembling with terror and misery.

The black gown her mother wore contrasted sharply with her pale alabaster skin, making her flesh look almost ghostly white. Her brown hair was tied back tightly into a thick braid that hung down the length of her back, dangling to and fro as she walked toward Taylor.

Dangling like a rope.

Taylor dropped her chin to her chest, unable to look at her mother's radiant face.

"Oh, darling," her mother murmured and reached for Taylor's hands. "Why such a sad face?"

Suddenly unable to control herself, Taylor hurled herself toward her mother, flinging her arms around her mother's shoulders and hugging her as tightly as she could.

With a startled laugh, her mother returned the embrace.

Taylor squeezed her eyes shut against the tears that burned there.

Her mother stroked her hair calmly, reassuringly. "Don't worry," she whispered. "He'll come for me. I know he will."

Taylor pulled back to look into her mother's blue eyes. They were glazed and had a faraway, dreamy look to them. The blissful smile Taylor had seen on her mother's lips when she first stepped into the room returned.

"He won't let me burn," she went on, even as the reflections of the room's candles dancing in her eyes tortured Taylor with a vision of the terrible things to come. Her mother turned to the window. She placed her palms on the cold stone ledge of the windowsill and stared out into the early morning sky. "We love each other far too much," she whispered.

"Father?" Taylor wondered, a weak hope in her question.

Her mother laughed softly. "No," she said.

Taylor heard the door opening behind her and turned to see two guards standing in the doorway. To a child of twelve, the two burly men looked like armor-plated giants. The light threw deep shadows across their faces, transforming them into gruesome masks that made Taylor think of the ogres in the tales her mother had once told her.

"It's time, m'lady," one of the ogres called, his voice gruff and menacing to Taylor's ears.

Taylor's desperate gaze turned back to her mother. Her time was running out. She had to stop this. "No!" Taylor cried out, finally finding the strength in her voice. "They can't do this!" She grabbed her mother's arm, pulling her deeper into the room.

Her mother touched her cheek softly. "He'll come," she reassured her and gently pried Taylor's small fingers from her arm. Then she stepped past her daughter, moving out the door.

Taylor watched her mother's straight, tall form and wished that she could feel the confidence that her mother voiced. Then the two brutes stepped in behind her mother, forming a massive wall of muscled flesh and cold steel. A sinking feeling grabbed hold of Taylor and pulled her deeper into despair. She followed the procession into the hallway. There was only one chance. There was only one man who could stop this.

Taylor turned away and ran down an empty hallway, fully aware of the blossoming sky as the sun chased the darkness from the land, fully aware that the sun's rays heralded her mother's doom. She couldn't make her small slippered feet move fast enough over the stones of the corridor. Her silk dress wrapped around her legs, inhibiting her hurried steps.

Finally, she halted before a closed door. Her fear rose like a tidal wave to battle her resolve. But like a brave knight, she fought down her dread and lifted a hand to push the door open.

The room was dark except for a lone candle on a desk. Taylor took a hesitant step forward. She made out the shadowed form of a man sitting behind the large desk.

The man slowly lifted his dark eyes to her as she entered.

The wavering flame of the candle threw slashes of reddish-orange light over his face, casting demonic shadows across his brow.

Taylor knew that she could not give up, despite every one of her senses telling her to run, beseeching her not to incur his wrath. "Please," she whispered. "Show mercy."

The man leaned back and his eyes disappeared completely into the darkness. After a long moment, he rubbed his palms over his eyes. "I loved her, you know," he murmured. "I gave her everything. Everything she ever wanted." He shook his head, his gray hair swaying around his shoulders with the movement.

Taylor thought she saw a sparkling in his eyes as he lifted his head to gaze at the ceiling and she wondered if they could be tears.

"This I cannot forgive," he groaned. "There will be no mercy."

"Please, Father," she whispered, barely able to contain the terror she felt.

Her father suddenly looked older than she had ever seen him before; the wrinkles on his brow, the lines around his mouth—all seemed to darken and deepen. "There is no such thing as true love," he murmured. "Remember that, daughter."

"But Mother—" Taylor managed in a whimper.

He rose and moved to the window, where the sun was just beginning to peer over the horizon. The morning's light splashed him in a bloodred wave. A sudden breeze from the window lifted his cape about his shoulders and the cloth fluttered behind him, making it look as if he had suddenly sprouted wings. "Will burn in a few minutes' time," he said flatly.

Taylor reared back. He was so cold. So uncaring. How could he say he loved her mother one moment and then sentence her to death the next? She straightened her back and glared at him, trying desperately to keep the pain from showing on her face.

She had failed. She had not been able to change her father's mind. In the distance, she heard the drums and their foreboding rhythm begin. She had to hurry. It was starting.

She started for the door, but his voice thundered across the room. "You will remain with me," he commanded.

"No," Taylor gasped. She had to say good-bye to her mother.

"You will stand at my side and learn what infidelity leads to."

Taylor felt her insides twist. Her blood pounded in her ears, drowning out the drum roll. "Please, Father," she begged.

"You will stay," he told her in a voice that could not be disobeyed.

For a long moment, a strange hush blanketed the castle. And Taylor's heart. She thought of disobeying her father and racing out of the room to be with her mother, but never in her twelve years of life had she defied him. Years of strict discipline prevented her from doing it now.

She silently begged God to spare her mother. She prayed that her mother was right, that "he" would come for her. She desperately wanted to believe what her mother believed. She desperately wanted a knight in shining armor to race to her mother's rescue and snatch her from the flames to which her father had condemned her.

Her mother's words rang through her mind: "He won't let me burn." Hope ignited in Taylor's breast. Her mother had so much confidence. Could she be right? Would he save her?

Taylor raced to the window, to her father's side. But her

frantic gaze wasn't on the courtyard, where the horror of her mother's execution was being played out. Her eyes searched the lowered drawbridge and the road beyond for the knight. The knight of honor who would rescue her mother.

But the road and drawbridge were empty. Silent.

"We love each other far too much," her mother had said.

Taylor glanced expectantly at the empty road, waiting for her mother's rescuer.

And waiting.

Her father's confession echoed in her mind: "I loved her."

And waiting.

"There is no such thing as true love." Suddenly, Taylor understood her father's words. And with the comprehension came a chilling realization.

There would be no rescue. Her mother would burn. A panic filled Taylor so completely that she trembled helplessly. As black smoke and dark orange flames spiraled up to meet the dawning light's rays, a scream rent the silence.

Suddenly a triumphant burst of flames sprang high into the dawn sky, its hungry tongues licking the fading night. To a terrified child, it was the face of death. Taylor fell to her knees, burying her face in her hands, her own agonized cry replacing her mother's suddenly silent one.

Jared Mantle cursed. What was England coming to if it allowed a fine woman such as Lady Diana to be put to the flame?

Diana was one of the most compassionate women Jared had ever known. Years ago, she had found him beaten and near death at the side of the road. She had taken him to

Sullivan Castle and nursed him back to health. Then she had asked Lord Sullivan to retain his services. It had taken ten long years of hard work after that, but Jared had finally reached the rank of captain. He had trained most of the men that now kept the castle secure. Few of them, if any, could best him in combat.

Now, after fifteen years of loyalty and devotion, Jared found himself back where he had begun. Alone. He rubbed his short beard. Oh, he was certain Sullivan would keep him on, but he could not stay where they would burn a kind, generous woman. Jared shook his head sadly. Besides, it was time he sought his fortune before he could not lift a sword.

He strapped on his belt and his scabbard, and he glanced one last time about the room. He pocketed the measly coins he had saved in his service to the Sullivans and headed for the door, stepping outside into the night.

The moon was a mere slit in the dark sky, a narrowed eye watching his departure. He moved deeper into the courtyard.

Suddenly, Jared tensed. Instinctively, he knew someone was there. He pulled back into the darkness and watched with curious eyes as a silhouetted figure sneaked into the empty courtyard. Huddled and tentatively watchful, the figure moved swiftly from shadow to shadow to the outer gates.

Jared's eyes narrowed and he moved silently across the yard, his large strides taking him to the figure, whose back was to him. "Late for an evening stroll," Jared said quietly.

The figure whirled to stare at him. Green eyes flashed defiantly up at him. The girl swung her clenched hand behind her back, concealing something in her fist.

Surprise jarred him as he stared down at the girl. Even with her face concealed beneath a velvet hood, he knew her instantly. Diana's daughter. What would a young girl be doing out this late? he wondered to himself. And without a chaperon.

"Don't try to stop me!" she snapped.

For the first time, Jared noticed the sack slung over her shoulder. She started to turn away from him, but he caught her wrist, pulling her hand out of the shadows. The ring on her finger shone in the night's blue light. Two crossed swords with a large S in the middle were etched into its surface. He raised his eyes to hers. Had the girl stolen the ring?

Taylor raised her chin and her eyes narrowed. "It was my mother's," she said imperiously.

He glowered at her for a long moment. "Running away?" he asked.

"Leaving," she insisted.

"With no one to watch over you? No guards?"

"I don't need a guard!"

He pondered her words. He could see traces of her mother in every one of her stubborn movements, the worry beneath the defiance in her eyes, the resolution that set her shoulders. She was so young. So young and so inexperienced. He glanced at the gates. The world outside would eat her alive.

"Where are you headed?"

Taylor paused for a long moment. She glanced at the wooden gate, then up at the walkways surrounding the castle as if they held the answer. "To London," she finally replied.

He grunted softly. She had no idea what she was getting herself into, what kind of people waited to take advantage of a twelve-year-old-girl. Most likely she would end up a prostitute. Or dead on the side of the road without her rich velvet cloak. He briefly wondered if she had even thought to pack any food. He glanced at her out of the corner of his eye. *Well, I owe my lady that much,* he thought to himself. "That's where I'm heading," he said. "Can you use the company?"

CHAPTER ONE

Eight Years Later

Slane Donovan dismounted in front of a small shop and tethered his black warhorse to a nearby tree. Woodland Hills was a simple town. There was only one shop to buy supplies in and this was it. The sign hanging from a weather-worn wooden pole jutting out from the building's thatched roof creaked as it swayed in the easy breeze. He glanced up at the charred words burned into the wood.

Benjamin's Goods

A prickling at the back of his neck caused him to look away from the sign toward the shop's open door. A small girl stood in the doorway, watching him with large brown eyes. Slane grinned and patted her head as he entered the shop.

The interior was dark except for the area lit by the flaming hearth burning to his left and the entranceway lit by the sun behind him. After his eyes adjusted to the gloom, Slane noticed a man sweeping the floor near the rear of the shop. When he heard Slane enter, the man stopped his work and looked up, clutching the broom handle with both hands. "Good day, sir," he greeted. "What can I do for you?"

"You must be Benjamin."

Benjamin nodded. "That I am. Are you needing supplies?"

Slane glanced around at the various tables that filled the room. Piles of dull-edged daggers, rusted knives, maces with chipped handles, and numerous other weapons filled several tabletops. Other tables held cooking utensils or farming tools. Shelves lining the wall held foodstuffs of all kinds, dirt-caked vegetables, trenchers, a few strips of salted meat. "I just need some information," Slane said.

Benjamin began sweeping again. "Nothing comes cheap these days, sir."

Slane sighed and pulled out a gold piece from the pouch at his waist. "I'm looking for a ring," he said. "Two swords crossed, and an S on it."

The man's eyes lit up at the sight of the coin. He reached for it, but Slane pulled it back.

"Have you seen it?"

"Yes," Benjamin said eagerly. "Not two days ago. A woman wore it."

"Did you see which way the woman went?" Slane asked.

"She rode off to the west. Near as I can guess, she was heading toward Fulton."

Slane nodded and handed the man the coin. Benjamin greedily snatched it from Slane's fingers. Fulton. That was only a day's ride. He turned and moved to the doorway.

He caught the small girl staring at him and her eyes went wide before she quickly pulled back out of the doorway. Slane grinned. He strolled out the door and moved toward his horse.

The soft tread of a child's footsteps followed him. "Did she do something bad?"

The girl's small voice caused Slane to turn. "No," he told her.

"Then how come you want to find her?" she asked.

Slane smiled and knelt down to the child's level. Her eyes were large and brown and innocent. "I'm looking for the ring."

"Oh."

Slane ruffled her hair and turned back to his horse. He swung himself up into the saddle.

"Like those other men this morning?"

Slane froze. "What other men?"

"Some other men were asking about the ring and the lady this morning," she said. "One of them was real mean—the one with the hair on his lip. I didn't like him."

"Corydon," Slane hissed, staring off down the road. When Corydon had won lands that bordered Donovan and Sullivan lands five years ago, Slane himself had approached him in peace, seeking to secure friendship with his neighbor. But Corydon had scoffed at his efforts and attacked his party. Two good men had been killed that day. Slane could still hear Corydon's laughter.

And now he had actively begun to accumulate an army of men. Enough men to lay siege to a castle. Slane knew he had precious little time to complete his mission. Corydon's appetite for new lands was insatiable.

Slane returned his gaze to the small girl. She couldn't have been more than four, but she was obviously smart beyond her years. He bestowed on her one of his most beguiling smiles. "Thank you, m'lady," he said. "You've been very helpful."

She put her small hands to her mouth and giggled.

Slane spurred his horse and the large animal fell into a trot and then a full-out gallop. With Corydon so close, he knew there was no more time to waste. He needed help. He needed experienced trackers.

The arm slammed heavily down upon the table. Cheers broke out around the room, echoed by groans and finally, what Taylor liked to hear the most, coins clinking together. She watched Jared rise from the table, a victory smile on his bearded face. His brigandine armor shifted with his movement, the leather shining dully in the fire of the hearth as he reached his full height. Taylor looked at the fire for a moment, at the snaking, whipping flames, then she quickly turned away.

Jared's opponent in the arm wrestling match, a taller and heavier man, rose from his seat, rubbing his arm. Taylor froze for an instant, her hand moving inconspicuously to the hilt of her sword, but when she saw the defeated man's shoulders slump slightly and his head hang she took her fingers away from her weapon. A smile curved the corner of her lips. He would be no trouble. There had been many a time when she and Jared had to leave an inn fighting. Most men were not easily parted from their hard-earned coin.

Jared clasped a few arms and slapped a few backs.

Most of the gambling men found it distasteful to give up their coin to a woman, and Jared was busy speaking with the patrons and his opponent. So Taylor and Jared had found it best to employ a man to collect their winnings. Taylor leaned against a wall at the rear of the tavern, scanning the room for the shady little creature. She had found it best to remain discreetly separate from the patrons, keeping an eye on Jared's back.

She spotted Irwin slithering from person to person in the dark room, collecting the coins that glinted in the torch light when they fell into his open palm. The way he held his hands curled into his chest, the way he scurried, reminded her of a rat. Keeping her gaze on him, she reached down to the table before her and grabbed her ale. Irwin held out his hand to the next man, who deposited two coins into his open palm with a grimace and moved away. Taylor lifted the mug to her lips, but paused as she watched Irwin's eyes shift left and then right. She knew what he was going to do even before his small hand dipped into his pocket and came up empty. Her green eyes narrowed and she threw back her head to drain the mug of ale.

By the time Irwin finally scurried up to her, Taylor was on her second ale. A grin spread across his rodentlike face as he produced the coin-filled pouch, chuckling gleefully, "We emptied their pockets!" He dropped it onto the table and the coins clanked heavily as they hit the wooden surface.

Taylor scooped up the pouch. She weighed it in her hand for a moment and was gratified to see Irwin's smile slip a notch. She tied the strings around her belt, watching him. "Nice doing business with you, Irwin," she said and took a step past him.

Irwin moved to block her path.

Her eyes slowly shifted to him.

"My payment," he whined. He extended his hand, palm up.

"You know, Irwin, as I see it, you have two choices. You can try to get your payment from Jared, but he's a smart man and all he would have to do is look in your eyes to see how you cheated him." She watched Irwin's face turn from gray to white. But he recovered quickly.

"Cheated him? I am a man of morals. I would never—"

"I *saw* you, Irwin."

He sputtered for a moment, his hands twitching nervously. "It was a mistake, a misunderstanding!"

Taylor nodded. "I know. And I sympathize with you. But I'm afraid that Jared is not the forgiving type. Do you know what he did to the last man he caught with his hand in our moneybag?"

Irwin shook his head, his black eyes wide, anxiously awaiting the answer.

"He followed him out into an alley and—well, the poor soul was never seen again. My guess is rat food."

"Rat food?" Irwin echoed.

Taylor nodded. "Not the forgiving type."

"You—you said I had two choices."

"Well, yes. You can take what you have . . . and disappear."

Irwin did not move for a long moment. Taylor was sure that she saw his little nose twitch. "But . . ." he finally protested weakly.

Taylor held up a finger, halting his objection. "Rat food," she reminded him.

Irwin shuffled his feet. "I see your point."

"And next time," Taylor murmured, leaning toward Irwin, "be sure that no one is looking when you steal."

"Sully!" Jared called.

Taylor turned to see Jared making his way through the crowd of well-wishers. He stood a foot above her, his bald head shining in the torch light.

"The ale is on me tonight!" he called out to her.

Taylor nodded. "I thought as much. Irwin here—" Taylor turned to Irwin, only to find him gone. A smile lit her face. "They don't like to get caught."

"God's right hand! Another one?" Jared roared. "Good help is hard to find these days. How much did he take?"

"Not enough to make a dent in the profits you brought in." Taylor hefted the bag in her palm. "It looks as though we'll sleep in a bed tonight!"

Jared dropped his head, seriousness washing over him. He took Taylor's arm and steered her to a private corner of the common room. "We can't keep on like this, Sully," he murmured. "We have to find work. A few coins from wagering won't see us past a night."

"You worry too much, my friend. I'm sure the morning will bring better luck *and* a paying fare. Just watch." She turned to move back into the crowd, but Jared caught her arm.

"If nothing comes on the morrow, we move north. Agreed?"

Taylor sighed. She didn't want to go north in search of employment. It was too close. Too close to what she had been avoiding all these years. She clenched her teeth and pushed away the unpleasant memories that threatened to take hold of her senses.

Jared shook her arm. "Agreed?"

Taylor pulled free of his grip. "Agreed," she reluctantly assented, then turned and barreled through the rowdy patrons and out into the night air.

North. She glanced up at the stars and suddenly their glistening brilliance shimmered, transporting her in time. Flames roared before her eyes. A horrible scream filled her ears. She quickly shook her head and marched around a corner. She paused to take a deep drink of ale. It slid over her tongue and down her throat, washing away the memories.

"It's dangerous for a woman to walk these streets alone," a voice called out.

Taylor groaned, immediately recognizing the voice. Usually when she told the vermin to stay away, they did. But it looked as if Irwin wasn't as bright as the rest. "Irwin," Taylor murmured and spun. "I told you to take what you have—" Her voice faded. The firelight shining through the tavern window illuminated three men standing in the alley before her: Irwin and two burly others. *So,* Taylor thought, *our little rat has friends.* She leaned against a crate that lined the dark road.

"I'm not satisfied with the payment I received," Irwin said.

"I could have guessed," Taylor murmured, lifting the mug to her lips.

"And now I want it all."

Taylor swallowed the ale in a surprised gulp. "All? Aren't we getting a little greedy, Irwin?"

He shrugged his scrawny shoulders. "If I have to get my fair payment this way, I might as well take it all."

Taylor dropped her chin to her chest, sighing. "I suppose I can't talk you out of this." Part of her didn't want to. Her hands itched for a little swordplay.

"Oh, your tongue is witty, but you'll need more than that to change my mind."

Taylor set her mug down on the crate, careful not to spill its contents. Then she straightened up and faced Irwin. "All right."

Irwin's beady black eyes widened. "You will give us the bag?"

Taylor chuckled in disbelief. "Not a chance, Irwin," she said. "If you want the bag, you're going to have to take it."

Irwin's companions laughed lasciviously.

The half moon that lit the sky cast a bluish glow over the alley, allowing Taylor to see her opponents as they approached. They were both big men dressed in soiled breeches and ragged tunics—one with a long, dark, unkempt beard that reached almost down to his stomach; the other missing two teeth. They moved slowly and laboriously. Taylor was certain that their bulk would be more hindrance than help in their actual fighting.

"Get her," Irwin ground out between his teeth.

"Tsk-tsk, Irwin," Taylor admonished. "You're not the one doing the dirty work. Give them a moment to think. Here, gentlemen. Let me make this easy on you. One of you go to my right, the other to my left. Try to surround me."

The two men cast speculative glances at each other before doing what Taylor told them.

"What an ingenious plot!" Taylor laughed. She continued to face Irwin, keeping the two men in her peripheral vision. Suddenly, the men acted. The one with the beard rushed her from her right while the other man charged from her left.

Taylor feinted back and then stepped forward. The two men knocked shoulders, the man without the teeth falling onto his buttocks. Taylor whirled in time to see the man with the beard stomping toward her. She heard a movement behind her and brought her elbow back sharply into Irwin's ribs, then danced two steps out of the bearded man's path.

"If this is the best you've got, you might as well leave now," she scoffed.

She stood two steps from the wall, able to see all the men. The man with two missing teeth climbed to his feet. Irwin stood beside the bearded man, his arm wrapped around his stomach.

The man with two missing teeth drew a small dagger.

All the amusement Taylor had felt up until now disappeared. When weapons were drawn, it was no longer a game. Now, it was a fight for her life. She eased her sword from its sheath.

The men halted for a long moment.

"She's a woman! She doesn't know how to use it," Irwin reassured the men. "It's just for show."

"Then you come and get it, Irwin," Taylor invited. "I'll put on a show for you."

Irwin swallowed hard. "This is what I'm paying you for," he said to the men. "There are two of you . . . and one of her."

The man with the missing teeth came forward, rage in his dark eyes. She had somehow insulted him and his anger was burning. He would fight irrationally. Every instinct told her to fight her way free and flee. But painful memories still lingered like a glowing ember inside her. She needed to bury them again. She needed a fight.

The gap-toothed man approached steadily. Taylor did not move back until he lashed out at her. She ducked and whirled away, but he followed her, dogging her steps. She caught one of his swings with her sword, and the dagger bounced harmlessly off her blade. He kept at her, and she moved carefully within the small space of the alley, biding her time. Finally, he foolishly waved his weapon by her face and she took advantage of the moment. She reared her head back from the sharp edge of the dagger as it swept just beneath her chin—and thrust forward with her blade at the same time. She had meant to wound him enough to scare him, but the idiot stepped into her swing. The sword hit flesh and for a moment everything froze.

The gap-toothed man's dark eyes went round with surprise; his mouth went slack with shock. His dagger slipped from his fingers and it clattered against the ground.

Taylor pulled her sword from his torso and turned.

The fist that slammed into her face sent her reeling to the ground! Her head spun fiercely for a moment and her cheek throbbed with a pulsing, biting pain. A kick to her side spun her over onto her back. She lay with her eyes open, gasping for a breath, unsure whether the white blotches that flared before her eyes were stars in the night sky or patches of pain clouding her vision.

A dark, twisted face suddenly appeared above her, a face covered with dirty hair and picked-at scabs. She felt hands shaking her shoulders. She saw lips moving and heard unintelligible sounds. Then two savage punches knocked her head back and this time she knew the flashes of white filling her vision didn't come from the heavens above.

She lay still for a long moment, her cheek pressing against the dust and dirt of the road. Slowly, the stars swimming before her eyes faded and the world came back into focus. She saw a splash of moonlight washing over her mug, which had overturned in the battle. Her eyes followed the thin stream of ale as it dripped down to the puddle below.

The bearded man's words cut through her fogginess. "Had enough?"

"You spilled my ale," Taylor groaned. She was rewarded with a brutal kick to her abdomen.

As she lifted a limp hand to ward off any more blows, she heard laughter.

"You were right," Irwin whispered in her ear. "That was a good show."

Their shrill laughter faded into the distance.

Taylor lay in the road for a long time, watching the growing pool of ale on the ground, wishing that the pounding in her head would stop. She tasted blood in her mouth; her tongue traced a gash on her lip. She forced herself onto her back and lifted a hand to her throbbing left cheek. She knew that it would swell and bruise before the morning. She closed her eyes, taking stock of her injuries. Stomach, side, but mostly her face. Her left cheek was by far the worst. The right cheek stung, but the ache was nowhere near as intense as the biting pain on the left side. Already she felt puffiness ringing her left eye. At least she didn't think anything was broken.

Her head pounded savagely behind her eyes and she rubbed her forehead with the tips of her fingers, unsuccessfully willing the pain to go away. She opened her eyes to contemplate the heavens and the God that had delivered her to such a fate.

That was when she noticed that her ring was gone! Her mother's ring! They had pried it from her fingers!

She tried to push herself up off the ground, but didn't make it past her hands and knees. "Damn it," she whispered, groaning as pain shot through every muscle in her body. She was in no condition to pursue the thieves, but she vowed she would have the ring back. Whatever it took.

She quickly scanned the alley, hoping that they hadn't taken everything. The man with the missing teeth lay sprawled not five feet from her. Her gaze shot past him, past her spilled ale, up the alley. Where was her sword? It wasn't what they had been after. Had they taken it to sell it?

She spotted her blade lying in the shadows against the wall of the tavern and breathed a sigh of relief.

The sudden clattering of hooves made her freeze. She crawled into the shadows of the tavern, hoping that whoever it was would not look into this dirty alley—and that it wasn't some wretched God-loving knight with a penchant for doing good. She was in enough trouble in plenty of towns as it was.

The horses continued past the alley without stopping. Taylor eased out of the shadows and took another look at the body only a few feet from her. The toothless man was definitely dead, his chest still and lifeless. Not the first man she had killed, and probably not the last. Unless, of course, she was caught here with his blood on her blade.

The dripping of her trickling ale caught her attention and she turned her head. Her mug rested on its side on the crate beside her. She reached up and grabbed it, then crawled over to her sword and took hold of it with trembling fingers. Kneeling, she resheathed the weapon, taking four tries to get it back into its scabbard.

She pulled herself to her feet, using the wall as support. Mustering as much determination as she could, she willed the pain away and straightened only enough to walk toward the tavern. Each step was agony; each footfall pounded through her entire body.

Finally, the open doorway of the tavern loomed before her. She stepped into the entryway and halted, leaning heavily against the wooden frame and closing her eyes against the throbbing pain that pierced every muscle in her body.

"Sully!"

When Taylor opened her eyes, she saw Jared sitting across the room between two buxom serving wenches. He jumped up and rushed to her side. Relief washed over her so completely that her shoulders sagged and her entire body started to go limp.

Taylor raised the empty mug. "I need a refill," she grunted before collapsing into Jared's arms.

CHAPTER TWO

Slane entered the Wolf's Inn, his blue eyes narrowing immediately as he assessed the main room. It was the kind of place that had trouble brewing around every corner, where pickpockets lurked in every dark shadow, where a killer could be bought for a shilling. Laughter and conversation rose and fell around him. A harlot seated near the door reached under a table and demonstrated her skills to an eager-to-learn merchant. Four armored men sat to Slane's right; all had the dull haze of too much ale in their red-streaked eyes. Most of the tables were occupied by solitary figures nursing their ales or filling their bellies with steaming vegetables and mutton. Nobody appeared to notice his presence, but he knew they were all aware of his entrance.

"What can I do for you, m'lord?"

Slane turned to see a short man standing beside him.

The top of his balding head barely reached Slane's shoulder. "I'm looking for a man called Jared Mantle."

The innkeeper chortled. "M'lord must understand that I can't just—"

Slane quickly produced a gold coin, silencing the man's objections. The innkeeper pointed a chubby finger in the direction of a back table, where two men were sitting. Slane tossed over the gold coin and moved through the room toward the table.

A lone candle illuminated the two figures in earnest conversation, one of them possibly a merchant—no self-respecting tracker would wear such gaudy colors, nor tie a yellow-and-red scarf about his waist. Slane's eyes quickly assessed the other man's well-worn leather armor and easy confidence, and he knew that this man must be Jared. He was much older than Slane had anticipated, but his age was probably a testament to his skill. He was still alive, after all. "Jared Mantle?" Slane asked.

The man raised his eyes—eyes that were suspicious and alert—to meet Slane's. "Who's asking?"

Slane swiveled his gaze to the merchant and then back to Jared. "Slane Donovan."

Jared's eyes narrowed slightly. "I'm Mantle. Do we have business?"

"I'd like to hire you."

"I'm in the process of doing the exact same thing," the merchant protested.

"I can offer you double what this man is," Slane said. "I need your services immediately."

Jared's eyes shifted to the merchant. "Can you better that?"

The merchant shook his head and rose from the table. "Perhaps next time," he murmured, casting Slane an irritated glance before moving away.

When Slane took the vacated seat, Jared asked, "What services do you require?"

Slane couldn't help but notice the skepticism in his voice. Had Jared had dealings with his brother, Richard? No matter. "I need you to find a ring."

"A ring?" Jared echoed. "What importance does a ring hold to you?"

"That is my concern. Can you find it?"

"What does it look like?"

Slane opened his mouth to respond when a woman slipped into the empty chair beside Jared. Annoyed at her presumption, Slane scowled . . . until he saw her face. It was covered in bruises and healing scabs. "God's blood!" he exclaimed. "Where did you get those injuries?"

The woman glanced over at Slane. The one eye that wasn't puffed closed narrowed instantly, and her swollen lip curled into a humorless grin. "A friend."

He stiffened at her cold tone. "If you'll kindly excuse us, we are in the middle of a business transaction. I'm not in need of your services."

The woman didn't budge. "If it's business, then you can talk to me as well. Jared and I are partners."

Slane darted a glance at Jared, who nodded, an amused look crinkling his eyes. "I'm only hiring you," he said to Jared.

"We come together or not at all," Jared replied.

Slane turned his thoughtful gaze to her. She responded with a chilly glare. He turned back to Jared. "Fine. But I don't intend to pay any more than I did before."

"For the work of two?" the woman objected.

Slane crossed his arms. "Take it or leave it."

He watched her shoulders sink as she sighed slightly and glanced at Jared, who nodded once. "What's the job?" she asked.

Slane leaned across the table. "I'm looking for a ring. Two swords crossed under an S."

Jared and the girl sat motionless for a long moment, then looked at each other. Suddenly, the woman began to laugh.

"What is so funny?" Slane snapped.

She met his solemn look with amusement. "This is going to be the easiest coin we've ever worked for," she replied.

Slane frowned quizzically. "You know where it is?"

She nodded and began to rise, but Slane grabbed her arm, halting her movement. "Look, woman. If you know where it is, tell me. We can begin and end your employment right here."

She hesitated for a moment, casting an unreadable look at Jared. "Sully," she finally said, her lips curving up in a grin. With her swollen lip, the smile was more grotesque than appealing. "My name is Sully, not woman."

Taylor leaned against a wall and crossed her arms over her chest as she regarded Slane out of curious eyes. What could he possibly want with her mother's ring? They had been traveling together for half a day now and he hadn't spoken one more word about it.

He glanced at her and she smiled brilliantly through her cut and fattened lips. He scowled and turned away.

At least he's consistent, she thought. Her gaze shifted to Jared, who was speaking earnestly with a large man—a man who was almost as tall as Slane but with a much less flattering physique. His belly flopped over his breeches; the muscles in his arms were slack. Jared had sensed he was the town gossipmonger the second he laid eyes on him. And as usual, Jared was right. The large man looked at her and smiled, then glanced back at Jared and spoke quickly to him.

Taylor shifted slightly. "This ring must be very important to rouse you from the comfort of Castle Donovan."

"Yes," Slane answered stiffly.

She cast him a wry look. It was like speaking to a wall. A well-muscled wall, with long, glorious blond hair, but a wall nonetheless.

Now Jared and his companion were heading over to them, Jared wearing the same exasperated expression he always wore when some man would insist on propositioning her. Taylor shook her head. They never learned. Or were there just too many to teach?

"He says he won't give me any information unless you bed him," Jared explained.

As a large, eager grin split the man's lips, Slane's eyes widened in outrage.

Taylor pushed herself from the wall, placing a hand on Slane's chest to quiet him. "I'm used to it," she said.

"You're not thinking—" Slane began, but Taylor turned her attention to Jared.

"You offered him a gold coin?"

Jared shrugged slightly. "Two," he said.

Taylor smiled at the large man. "You know, you're being quite unreasonable about this," she told him. "All we need is information. You've seen the ring?"

The man nodded. "I've seen it. But that's all you'll get from me unless I see some action."

"Action?" Taylor repeated. "Is that all you want?" She half turned to Slane, clenched her fist, and turned back to the man, ramming her balled fingers into his stomach.

The man doubled over. Taylor shoved the brutish lout

backward over Jared's carefully positioned foot and he slammed into the ground. Taylor whipped out her dagger and held it to the man's neck. "Is this the type of action you wanted?" she asked.

The man fought back the urge to swallow as Taylor pressed the side of the blade against his throat.

"All we want is a little information about the ring. I know that you'll be very accommodating, won't you?" Taylor eased the tip slightly from the man's neck.

"I don't want any trouble," the man gasped.

"Out with it," she ordered.

"They went toward Briarwood," he gasped. "I swear that's all I know. They rode north!"

Taylor paused for a long moment. She knew he was too shocked and scared to lie. Still, she liked the feeling of this slime groveling in the dirt. "Maybe next time you'll think before you insult a woman," she said and slowly stood up.

The man sat up, putting his hands to his throat, eyeing her with hatred.

Jared joined her, standing protectively behind her.

Finally, the man narrowed his eyes, stood and scrambled away.

Taylor's eyes gleamed with satisfaction.

"I bet you make a lot of friends that way," Slane said and moved toward the stables.

"No one needs friends like that," Taylor retorted, casting one last glance at the man's retreating back before following Slane.

"Good job," Jared congratulated as he trailed after the duo.

*   *   *

Slane rode behind Sully and Jared. His gaze lingered on the woman, this enigmatic Sully. Her long, braided black hair swung back and forth over her cuir-bouilli armor. The hard leather armor had been worked and shaped to fit her tiny figure. And the leather maker had done an admirable job. It fit her very well indeed. She wore black leggings beneath her armor. Black boots hid her calves. The sword strapped to her waist continued to catch his attention every time he glanced at her. He had rarely seen a woman with a blade and wondered how good she was at wielding the weapon.

It was a shame he probably wouldn't have time to find out. He turned his concentration back to his mission.

The Sullivan woman.

He was certain that once he found the ring, he would find the girl and his search would be over. He wondered what she looked like. Had eight years on her own taken their toll? Was she haggard and gaunt from lack of food and working too hard? Did she look older than her twenty years? He knew she had dark hair. But that was all he knew of her.

His eyes shifted to the two horses before him as one of the animals snorted. Sully smiled at Jared in a private joke and spurred her horse on to take the lead. Slane wondered if Sully and Jared were lovers. And if they were, how could he have let her get beaten like that? How on earth had she gotten those cursed bruises? Why, if Sully was his woman, he would never let anyone hurt her. He would kill anyone who laid a hand on Elizabeth.

He sighed slightly, thinking of Elizabeth waiting for him at her home in Bristol. He had sent word with his best man, John Flynn, that he would be delayed. He knew John would watch over Elizabeth and protect her while he was away. He wouldn't be long. Not with the best tracker this side of France in his employ.

Slane nudged his horse and took up step beside Jared, turning his head to regard the mercenary. He was indeed old. There were deeply shadowed wrinkles around his eyes and his skin sagged around his cheeks. He glanced up ahead at Sully. What could she see in this old man? What kind of pleasure could he show her? And then another thought occurred to Slane. Perhaps they weren't lovers. Perhaps their relationship was more of a father watching over a daughter.

"We're coming to Briarwood," Jared announced.

"Are you sure the ring is here?" Slane asked.

"Look," Jared said, "you're paying me to track. That's what I'm doing. I'll find the ring. Don't doubt that."

Slane nodded, satisfied. They rode in silence for a few moments, the hot sun beating down on their shoulders. "You used to work for Lord Sullivan, did you not?" He felt Jared's gaze turn to him.

"Aye," Jared replied. "A long time ago."

"Tell me of the girl," Slane ordered.

"The girl?"

"Taylor Sullivan," Slane clarified. "What did she look like?"

"That was a long time ago," Jared replied, keeping his eyes on the road. "I was surprised she ran away. Didn't think she had it in her."

Slane looked steadily at Jared, not saying anything. After a moment of silence, Jared added, "I suppose when your mother dies, you do impulsive things."

"So you haven't seen her since then?"

"No," Jared said. "Don't know if I'd recognize her anymore."

"What do you remember of her?"

"Why do you want to know?"

Slane watched Jared's knuckles tighten on the reins of his horse. He had no intention of telling him his reasons. Not with his unusual behavior. "Just curious."

Jared looked at him then, and Slane swore he saw hostility in his blue eyes. But then it was gone. "She was a fat, lazy thing, from what I remember," Jared said. "There was one pretty thing about her. She had the most brilliant blond hair that I've ever seen. Almost like gold."

"Golden hair," Slane murmured. "Indeed." He allowed his horse to fall behind. He studied Jared's back for a long moment. Slane's eyes narrowed slightly. Why would Jared lie? What was he hiding?

Taylor walked back and forth before Jared, who sat beneath a tall tree. With each step, her muscles stretched and she almost groaned in delight. After such a long ride, it felt good to be off the horse. She paused to glance over her shoulder at the stream, where the horses drank, to see Slane bent over near the water, splashing his face.

"What do you think he wants with the ring?" Taylor wondered.

Jared snorted. "Don't know," he said, lifting a flask of ale to his lips. He lowered the bag and wiped his mouth with his sleeve, then offered the flask to Taylor. "But that's not all he's interested in."

Taylor took the flask and lifted it to her lips. The refreshing ale slid down her dust-filled throat.

"He was asking about you," Jared whispered.

Taylor lowered the flask and shifted her startled gaze to Jared. He raised his eyebrows and nodded. She returned her gaze to Slane. He was standing now, stretching, reaching toward the sky with his arms.

"What did you tell him?" Taylor asked.

Jared chuckled. "That you were a fat, lazy girl with blond hair."

Taylor lifted an amused eyebrow. "And he believed you?"

"They don't know you like I do," Jared said, chortling deeply.

She squatted beside her friend and handed back the flask. "Do you think Father sent him?"

Jared's eyes narrowed as he looked at Slane. "I don't know," he said quietly. "All I know is I don't like him." His gaze turned to Taylor. "So stay away from him. You hear?"

"You know me, Jared," Taylor said, standing. "I don't court trouble."

Jared groaned and rubbed his hands over his face.

Taylor walked across the small clearing toward the horses. Slane was checking his animal's bridles and straps, and she watched his strong shoulders and golden head over the horse's back. How many stories she had heard about him! Lord Slane Donovan of Castle Donovan winning the tournament at Warwickshire. Then the tournament at Glavindale. Then another tournament. And there were the great battles, fighting at the King's side. She shrugged. It all seemed so unreal to her. She had just turned away when his soft voice reached her.

"Where was Jared when you got those bruises?"

Taylor turned slowly. "Jared is not my protector," she said. "I am a free woman and I do as I please."

He lifted his gaze to her, and she was suddenly startled at how blue his eyes were. Then those tawny brows slanted over his eyes, and he returned his concentration to his horse.

He had dismissed her without a word! Exasperation filled her. But in that exasperation was a sense of victory. For the woman he sought stood face-to-face with him and he didn't even know it!

CHAPTER THREE

They rode into Briarwood just as the sun was setting. Jared and Slane went ahead to the inn to secure rooms and order a hot meal for them, and Taylor led the horses to the stables. As she dismounted, she noticed dark clouds brewing in the distance, promising rain.

"It looks ta be a bad one," a boy's voice said.

Taylor turned to the young stable boy as lightning ripped through the churning clouds and thunder rumbled in the distance. He had sandy blond hair that hung into his eyes. She handed the reins to him, nodding. "That it does," she answered. She motioned to the horses. "See to these horses."

"I'll take good care of 'em," the boy promised, swiping the hair from his eyes. "I've done lots before. I've even done a warhorse once."

Taylor smiled at him. "I'll bet you're the best," she said. The boy beamed, nodding his head. Taylor turned to leave, but the boy added, "I never seen no lady carrying a sword like you do."

Taylor turned around, the old feeling of defensiveness surging within her. He studied her face for a moment. She straightened her back.

"Looks like you been in lotsa fights, too," he added.

After a quick moment, Taylor decided he meant no ill will and a smile split her swollen lips. "That I have," she answered. "Maybe I'll come back later and tell you about some."

The boy nodded enthusiastically. "That'd be grand!"

"Then you take care of these horses for me," she said.

He nodded and led the horses away. Taylor turned to leave, only to find Slane standing in the doorway of the stable, watching her. The sight of him so relaxed caught her off guard and she became flustered. "What?" she demanded.

"I've secured rooms for us," Slane told her. "Are you hungry?"

The thought of real food, hot from the pot, made her mouth water. Food like porridge was a luxury. Much of the time, she and Jared had to eat what the land offered them. Berries. A rabbit here and there. A handful of nuts. Roots. A fresh bowl of porridge sounded heavenly! "A little," she admitted grudgingly.

He swept his arm out before him, guiding her toward the inn.

But Taylor's feet wouldn't move. What was Slane doing out here? Why wasn't he in the inn waiting for her? Something was very suspicious. "I can make sure the horses are properly taken care of," she said guardedly. "I don't need help."

"I'm quite aware of that," Slane replied.

"Then what are you doing out here?" she wondered. "Checking up on me?"

Slane straightened slightly. "Making sure you're all right," he said.

Taylor eyed him skeptically. "I'm just fine," she said in a condescending tone. "I don't need an escort, thank you. I'll be there in a minute."

"As you wish," he said unflustered, then moved off toward the inn.

As Taylor watched Slane disappear into the inn across the road, an odd feeling came over her. She suddenly had the distinct impression that Slane had somehow been watching over her just now, making sure she was safe. *Don't be a fool,* she chastised herself. *He has no interest whatsoever in your well-being.*

But still, the thought lingered, leaving her feeling unsettled. She decided she would tell the boy one quick story. By then, she was sure that the feeling would be gone.

Jared lifted the mug of ale to his lips and took a deep drink. When he replaced the mug on the table, he noticed Slane standing in the doorway, searching the room. Jared waved him over.

"Where's Sully?"

"Seeing to her horse," Slane answered, taking the seat opposite him.

Jared signaled the innkeeper, and the short, rotund man started in their direction. They ordered three bowls of porridge and a duck. The innkeeper nodded in satisfaction and went off toward the kitchens.

"You know Sully well," Slane surmised.

"Well enough," Jared said.

"Where did you two meet?"

"You ask a lot of questions for a man who refuses to be questioned in turn."

Slane made no reply.

"We were hired by the same lord years ago. When that job ended, we just stuck together." Jared shrugged as if that was all that needed to be said. Slane opened his mouth as if to ask another question, but Jared cut him off. "After we eat, I'll talk to the innkeeper here and see if he's seen the ring or if anyone's tried to sell it."

Slane's eyes narrowed. "Sell it?" he asked. "Why would they try to sell it?"

"It's silver—must be worth a lot of coin. If it was stolen or—"

"Who said it was stolen?" Slane demanded.

"Well, I just assumed—"

"And how did you know the ring was made of silver? I never mentioned that."

Jared swallowed hard and looked away.

The door opened again, causing a gust of wind to sweep the room and the flames in the hearth to flicker. Taylor entered and shut the door behind her.

Jared felt relief course through his body as she approached. She stopped before the table, dusting her hands off on her leggings, eyeing the two men. "You two boys getting along?" Taylor inquired innocently.

Slane slapped his palm on the table. "Enough of this," he ordered. "I want answers."

Taylor ignored his outburst and casually took a seat at the table, grabbing the third ale. "Answers to what?" she asked after taking a deep drink of the brew.

"He wants to know why I thought the ring was stolen," Jared told her.

"And how he knew the ring was made of silver," Slane added quickly.

"He used to work for Lord Sullivan. Of course he knows what the ring looks like."

Slane's gaze shifted from Jared to pin Taylor to her seat. Jared tensed, but then quickly remembered that Taylor was not one to squirm. Not even under the piercing glare of an angry lord. "How did you know it was Sullivan's ring?" Slane asked.

The grin never slipped from her lips. "I know his crest. I worked for him once, too."

Jared smiled inwardly. She was a quick thinker and it made him proud.

Slane sat back in his chair, but the suspicion still shone in his eyes. He crossed his arms over his chest. "That still doesn't explain why he thinks it's stolen."

Taylor imitated him, leaning back in her chair, crossing her arms over her chest.

It took all Jared's will not to burst out laughing.

"Well," Taylor answered, "if Sullivan doesn't have it, then it must have been stolen."

Slane winced. He leaned toward her over the table. "How come you have all the answers?"

Taylor leaned toward him. "Jared and I have talked about it," she said simply.

A rumble of laughter sounded from Jared's throat. When two pairs of eyes shifted to him, he covered his amusement by clearing his throat and looking away from them toward the door.

His humor died quickly as he saw their prey enter the inn, flanked by four rather large men.

Taylor watched the mirth leave Jared's blue eyes as he gazed at something over her shoulder. A tingling raced across the back of her neck and she turned. When her gaze locked on Irwin, every muscle in her body tensed. She felt a sudden surge of anger rush through her, followed just as quickly by resolve.

Jared's hand covered her own. "Don't do something rash," he warned her.

"I never do anything without thinking it through," she replied coolly, forcing the words through tightly clenched teeth. She never took her gaze from Irwin.

"What's going on?" Slane wondered.

Taylor could feel her blood pounding through her veins. She attempted to rise, but Slane grabbed her arm.

"Where are you going?" he asked, turning his gaze back from the men entering the inn. "I'm not paying you to settle the score with an old lover."

"This one's on the house," she quipped with her usual sarcasm and attempted to pull her arm free. But when Slane didn't release her, she turned her enraged glare on him.

"It will do me no good if you're dead," he said.

"It's not me who's going to die," she replied.

"He has the ring you're searching for," Jared broke in.

Slane's gaze slid past Taylor's shoulder to again eye the men who were now moving into the inn. "A man?" he murmured.

"Stay out of it," Taylor warned. "This is my fight and I wouldn't want that pretty face of yours to get messed up." She smiled at him with her still swollen lips before pulling her arm free and turning to face Irwin.

As soon as Taylor stood, Irwin's eyes locked on her. Dread filled his pinched features, and his beady little eyes glanced nervously from side to side. For a moment, Taylor would've bet he was going to run. But apparently the four men behind him gave him courage because he suddenly straightened up and approached her.

Her eyes narrowed, and she licked her lips in anticipation of giving him a taste of what he had done to her.

"Well!" he smirked. "I see you enjoyed being taught a lesson. Back for more?"

Taylor had to take a deep breath before the customary calm washed over her. "Not as much as you'll enjoy the lesson I'm going to teach," she replied.

"Still so proud?" Irwin reached out to touch her face, but before his grubby fingers touched her, she seized his arm and twisted it. "I believe you took something," she stated calmly.

His body twisted with his arm as he cried out in pain.

"I offered to work this out before, Irwin. But now it's gone far beyond that."

"Please!" the innkeeper called. "I want no trouble here."

"Give us the ring and we'll go quietly," Jared said, leaning forward in his chair.

Taylor held Irwin's hand tightly. He squirmed in her hold. She wanted nothing better than to beat this little rodent, to make him feel a portion of her own pain. But if Irwin gave her the ring, she would leave.

She hoped he wouldn't do it. She twisted his hand slightly and he stiffened, groaning.

The four men behind him moved forward, hesitantly. Their glowering faces locked on Taylor.

"I would give it to you, I swear! But—" Irwin yelped as she twisted his arm farther.

"All you have to do is give us the ring. I'm not even asking for the coin you stole from me."

"Take it outside!" the innkeeper hollered.

One of Irwin's companions smiled, revealing two rows of crooked brown teeth. "He lost it to me."

She bent to Irwin's ear. "I'm disappointed, Irwin. Very

disappointed." She shoved Irwin away from her and the little man tumbled to the ground.

Slane put his hand on her wrist. "There's no need for this. The ring isn't that important to me. I just want to find the woman who was supposed to be wearing it."

"It's important to me," she returned hotly. She jerked her hand free and drew her sword.

The sound of Jared freeing his weapon echoed Taylor's.

"Please, no swords!" the innkeeper shouted.

Taylor heard Slane's muttered curse as she pointed her weapon at the burly man's neck. "Just give me the ring and we'll be on our way."

He walked toward her slowly.

"Don't make me use this," she said.

"You won't use it," he said, laughing. "I have no weapon. It is against your code to hurt me."

Her eyebrows rose and with a slight jerk of her wrist, she slashed his arm with the tip of her blade, drawing blood. "You obviously have me mistaken for a knight," she said lightly. "Now give me the ring or I'll run you through."

The wound seemed to enrage him. He rushed at Taylor, and she had to step quickly aside to avoid his rampaging bulk.

Jared stuck out his leg and the burly man tripped over it, his momentum propelling him forward. As the big man flew past, Jared snatched the man's coin pouch from his belt. The burly man charged straight into a table. Mugs and trenchers went flying everywhere.

Taylor watched Jared glance into the coin pouch. Anxiety tensed her body. What if the ring wasn't there? But Jared looked up at her and nodded. She allowed a grin to form on her lips, but suddenly she was shoved from behind into Slane. As their bodies collided, she caught sight of

Irwin fleeing the tavern. She pushed herself away from Slane to dash out the door after Irwin.

"Sully, wait!" Slane called, but he had to duck the blow that was meant for his chin as the room erupted in fighting.

CHAPTER FOUR

"Someone must pay for all of this!" the innkeeper shouted, spreading his hands wide to indicate the broken tables and smashed mugs and spilled foods scattered over the floor. "Look at my inn! Who will return here to drink?"

Slane ignored him, rubbing his cut lip. He and Jared had made quick work of the rat-faced man's companions. Three of them had quickly fled; the burly man still lay unconscious on the floor. The one hit Slane had taken on his jaw was the first, last, and only blow that came anywhere near touching him. Now he lifted his head and cast a glance at Jared, who still stood guard at the door, waiting for Sully's return.

Jared paced the doorway like a father worried about his daughter. Slane could see the tense muscles along Jared's shoulder blades as he clenched and released his fists. Once he jerked forward as if to pursue Taylor, but then pulled back, resigned to let her deal with Irwin alone. Jared caught

Slane's gaze and shook his head. Slane was sure now of their relationship. If they had been lovers, Jared would have gone out after her.

"How am I to do business? Where are my customers to eat?" the innkeeper was going on.

Slane was tired of hearing the man complain. His head was pounding from the blow. "It will be taken care of," he snapped impatiently. The innkeeper withdrew at Slane's harsh tone. For some reason, Slane felt uneasy. He wasn't sure if it was because Sully hadn't returned yet or because they had found the ring but not the girl he sought. He groaned softly and raked his hands through his hair. *God's blood!* he thought. *Perhaps she isn't even alive anymore.*

Slane's thoughts turned to Sully. She should have been back by now. He looked at Jared, who was straining to see down the darkening street. Outside, thick sheets of rain cut off any visibility beyond a few feet. Slane could hear the heavy splashes on the roof and just outside the open door. Despite her battered face, she appeared to be able to take care of herself, he reminded himself. But she was rash and impulsive; what if something had happened to her?

Slane rose and stepped over a fallen man to place a comforting hand on Jared's shoulder. "She'll be back," Slane assured.

Jared sighed, keeping his gaze on the street. "I'll give her a few more minutes and then I'm going out after her."

"You'll never find her in this rain," Slane said, dropping his hand. Despite his pessimism, Slane knew he would help Jared find Sully. Even in this torrential downpour. Part of this was his fault, after all. He leaned against the wall and fingered the pouch Jared had taken, then turned it over to empty the contents into his palm. Four shillings and the ring fell into his hand. Slane snorted. What good was the ring if the Sullivan girl was not wearing it? He tossed the four shillings onto the body at his feet. They disappeared into the folds of the burly man's shirt.

Jared picked up a fallen chair from the floor and righted it. He sat down heavily, shaking his head.

A worried father, Slane thought.

Silence descended on the room like a cloak. Slane caught the innkeeper peering at him from around a corner, but the man quickly ducked back into hiding when he met Slane's gaze.

"I can't leave you two anywhere." Slane looked up at the cheery voice to see Sully sloshing in through the open front door, her clothing soaked through to her skin, her hair dripping with the heavy rain's wrath. "Look at the mess you made."

A strange feeling of relief engulfed Slane at the sight of her bruised and battered face. And he noticed with satisfaction that there were no new marks.

Jared shot out of his chair. "Are you all right?"

Sully nodded.

"And Irwin? Is he . . . ?"

"He won't bother us again," she promised gravely. Her gaze swung to Slane. "Well, did you get what you were after?"

Slane grasped the ring by two fingers, holding it up so she could see it.

Taylor strolled over to him and snatched the ring from his hand, inspecting it.

She shifted her gaze to Slane, and he saw the sparkle of triumph in the one green eye that was not swollen. Slane grabbed Taylor's wet forearm, leading her away from the prying ears of the innkeeper to a still standing table near the flaming hearth.

Taylor quickly pulled out of his grasp, moving away from

the fire. Slane glanced quizzically at her, then followed her to a table well away from the warmth of the flames. He took a seat opposite her. "First, a word of thanks for helping me find the ring."

Taylor shrugged slightly and opened her mouth as if to speak, but Slane hurried on. "How did you know who had it?" he asked.

"I know a lot of things," she said evasively.

Slane grunted. "He took it from you, didn't he?" He watched the unease spread across her face. Then she straightened, as if readying herself for something. But for what? To battle him? "I will let you keep it if you tell me one thing."

Her posture didn't relax; she remained as stiff as a board.

He leaned closer to her to whisper, "Who did you steal the ring from?"

Something flashed over her face. Slane couldn't tell if it was fear or anger.

"Where is she? Did you kill her?" he continued.

Her eyes narrowed to thin slits. "I'm wounded, Slane," she said in a clipped tone. "Really I am. I'm not in the habit of stealing." She shook her head, her long, wet locks waving about her shoulders. "Furthermore, I don't kill women. That is unless they deserve it." Drops of rain fell from her wet clothing as she rose before him, planting her hands on her slim hips. "You disappoint me, Slane." She took his hand and opened it, depositing the ring in his palm. "Give us our payment and we'll be gone."

Slane set the ring back down on the table, pointing to it. "How did you happen to be in possession of this when that Irwin took it from you?"

"I'm afraid the time for questions is over," she said. "And so is our employment. If you'll just hand over our payment . . ."

Slane frowned, cursing the irrationality of females. He searched her eyes as if trying to find the answers there, then snatched the ring and placed it in a leather pouch at his waist. With a muttered curse, he reached into his coin pouch to pay her.

Slane removed the pouches from his belt and tossed them onto the table beside the bed. He shook his head. He wasn't quite sure where to pick up the trail of the Sullivan woman. Jared and Sully had been his best chance.

He removed his sword and belt and was preparing to take off his tunic when a knock sounded on his door. Slane growled in frustration and impatience, then moved to the door.

The innkeeper stood there, wringing his hands. "There is a man downstairs asking to speak with you."

"Fine," Slane said and followed the stocky fellow down the stairs. When they came to the common room, Slane's eyes scanned the area, but no one seemed to be looking for him. He turned to the innkeeper.

"He must have left," the innkeeper said, shrugging.

"What did he look like?" Slane asked.

The innkeeper shrugged. "Tall, dark hair. Slim."

Didn't sound familiar. "Well, if he comes back, tell him to wait until morning," Slane said and stalked back up to his room.

He removed his tunic and fell onto the straw bed. He wondered briefly who would be looking for him here. Had John sent him word about Elizabeth? Or was there news from Castle Donovan? He shrugged the questions away and his weary mind immediately focused on Sully. There was something about her. . . . He couldn't quite put his finger on it. She was like no one he had ever met before.

Intelligent, brave, impulsive. But she was also defiant, head-strong, and impetuous.

He reached over to the table beside the bed and grabbed the pouch that held the ring. It crunched.

Scowling in confusion, Slane pulled the pouch open. It was empty save for a piece of parchment. The beginnings of outrage ate at the borders of his mind. His jaw clenched tight as he pulled the parchment out and unfolded it.

> Lord Slane,
>   *Thank you for helping me retrieve my mother's ring.*
>   *Sully*

Awash in amazement, Slane could only stare at the note. But then his hands began to tremble with anger as he slowly crumpled the note in a clenched fist.

CHAPTER FIVE

"You shouldn't have told him." Jared practically had to shout over the din of the falling rain.

"I couldn't resist knocking his arrogance down a notch. Can you believe he thought I killed myself?" Taylor hooted.

"He'll be looking for you now," Jared reminded her, as their horses struggled down the dark, muddy road. "Before, he had no idea who you were."

Taylor shrugged slightly. "It should be no problem keeping ahead of him. He doesn't know the towns and people like we do. Besides, he's no tracker. Why do you think he had to hire us?"

Jared grunted his disapproval, wiping the steady stream of rain from his eyes. "It's dangerous to ride at night like this, Sully," he said. "I don't like it."

"We've done it before," she said. "The only thing *I*

don't like is this rain." She glanced up at the black, black night, which hid the moon and stars, and she blinked away the raindrops that splashed in her eyes.

"It's the only reason I agreed to travel tonight. No one in his right mind would be out on a night like this," Jared said. He paused for a moment, thinking. "You know what this means. We sleep in shifts again. In the forest."

Taylor narrowed her eyes. "Not quite yet," she murmured.

Jared scowled at her. "What do you have in mind?"

"I plan to teach the arrogant lord a lesson," Taylor promised. "One he won't forget."

Jared groaned. *"Sully.* You're only going to make him more determined to find you."

Taylor pushed the wet hair out of her eyes. "After about a week, we'll disappear. He'll never find us," she said smugly.

"Don't you wonder what he wanted?" Jared asked.

"No," Taylor answered curtly. "If he couldn't tell us from the beginning, it couldn't be good." True enough, but part of her couldn't help but wonder. She just wished she could be there when he realized she'd gotten the better of him, to see the flash in his handsome blue eyes. . . . *What are you thinking?* she chastised herself. *Forget him. You'll never see him again.*

For a moment, she felt strangely sad.

"She had a bruised and swollen face, and she was traveling with an older man," Slane said.

The stable master nodded. "Yeah," he said. "They were here early yesterday." He dumped a bucket of feed into a horse's trough. "They didn't say much, but they stopped over by the inn. They were gone by midday."

They're traveling at night, Slane thought. *Just as I would if I were them.* He cursed his brother quietly as he walked away. If it wasn't for Richard, he wouldn't be in this mess. The little vixen was leading him a merry chase. He didn't have time for this. Elizabeth was waiting for him.

"Which way did they go?" he asked.

"West. Toward Woodland Hills," he replied.

"Thank you," Slane grumbled, leading his horse out of the stables. He looked west. A child was running along the roadside. A farmer led a horse, pulling a cartload of hay down the road. But Slane paid them no attention.

She was heading away from Castle Donovan. She was taking him away from Elizabeth. But he couldn't stop his pursuit of her. Now it went beyond his debt to Richard. It went beyond his allegiance to his family. She had insulted him. She had wounded his pride. And she was laughing at him. He would find her soon and show her that no one—*no one*—laughed at Slane Donovan.

Taylor threw back her head and laughed, her voice ringing out through the woods. The small campfire Jared had lit shone brightly on her face. "So Slane was in town just yesterday?"

Jared nodded, poking the fire with a stick.

"Well, I must say one thing for him. He certainly is persistent. Any other man would have given up," Taylor said, lying back on the bed of leaves she had made for herself. "It's been over a week now."

"That blacksmith also said that there was another man asking about the ring and the woman who wears it."

Taylor's smile faded.

"He said the fellow looked like a mercenary. He wore a sword and quilted armor. I don't like this. If it were one man . . ." He shook his head. "But now there's more than one. I don't like this at all. Something dangerous is going on here, Sully."

Suddenly, something shifted just at the corner of Taylor's vision, a quick flash of movement in the forest. She straightened up, reaching for her sword. "Jared," she whispered urgently.

Without hesitation, Jared snatched his sword from the ground and faced the dark woods before them.

Taylor, too, quickly got to her feet, putting her back to Jared's. She held her sword before her, ready for any enemy, her gaze scanning the dark trees, assessing the area with a practiced eye. They waited for something or someone to come out of the darkness.

But there was no movement from the forest. Only the wind rustling the leaves of the trees answered their silent challenge.

"What did you see?" Jared asked.

"Something moved," Taylor answered, straining to see into the shadows of the night. "Someone's out there." She cocked her head, listening. But silence answered her. No crickets chirped, no owls hooted. All the animals had become silent. Her grip tightened on the handle of her sword.

Jared turned and she moved with him. "Maybe it's just an animal."

Taylor continued to stare at the shadows. Maybe it was just an animal. A boar, maybe. Or a—

The forest erupted in a cacophony of movement! Figures leapt from the darkness, seeming to come alive from the very trees themselves, men brandishing swords and axes.

Taylor swung instinctively at a man charging straight for her! But the attacker parried, expertly nullifying her blow. She deflected his blow in return and had to spin quickly to block another strike from a second attacker. She feinted and lunged at the first attacker, catching him in the stomach. But her blow bounced harmlessly off metal. They were wearing armor beneath their black tunics!

The second attacker, not much more than a black shadow dancing in the light of the fire, lunged. Taylor knocked the second attacker's blow aside and lashed out with her booted foot, throwing the first man back as he tried to get near her.

She knew she had precious seconds to rid herself of the second attacker before the first one rejoined the fight. She drove forward, attacking the second man relentlessly, swinging, thrusting, lunging. But he blocked all her blows. She gritted her teeth and thrust. Again, the man parried her blow, pushing her blade up away from him. She snapped her wrist down sharply, tipping the blade toward his neck, and used every ounce of strength she had to thrust downward. She was rewarded with a wet gurgle and then the man went down.

They were good, she thought, quickly moving away from the fallen attacker. Too good for robbers or cutthroats. She quickly glanced at Jared and saw him busy fighting off two more attackers of his own. Another lay dead at his feet.

Footsteps came in fast behind her, and she whirled in time to sidestep a blow from the first attacker. She swung her blade again and again, driving him back. Suddenly he stood his ground and thrust, but Taylor stepped away from the blow, countering with a swing of her own, catching the man's outstretched hand. He howled in pain, dropping his sword. Taylor kicked the weapon out of his reach and waved her blade threateningly before him. He cast a quick glance at his fallen comrades and abruptly whirled away from her and ran, disappearing into the woods.

Taylor turned to help Jared battle the last man standing. He swung an ax at Jared, and Jared ducked at the last moment, letting the blade *whoosh* over his head. From his crouched position, Jared thrust with his sword. The blade bounced uselessly off of the man's armor.

Taylor swung at the man, catching him in his shoulder. He yelped and swung the ax sharply at her, but she side stepped the whistling blade and the ax buried itself into the ground. Taylor lashed out with her foot, kicking the man back.

Jared finished the man with a blow to his side. The blade pierced a gap in the attacker's armor, and the man froze for a second before plummeting to the earth like a fallen tree.

Taylor whirled toward the forest, looking for any other attackers. But no one emerged.

"Are you all right?" Jared asked breathlessly.

Taylor nodded, turning to him. Her gaze swept her friend for any wounds, but there were none. When her heart stopped racing and she allowed her battle lust to fade, she knelt down by the fallen man and pushed him over onto his back. His face was covered with a black cloth, giving him the unnerving appearance of an executioner. She checked his armor and the coal-black tunic that covered it. She looked up at Jared. "No crest," she announced.

"What the hell is going on?" Jared demanded.

With one swift movement, Taylor ripped the mask from the man's face. She had half expected to know him on sight. But she had never seen the face that was revealed. She ran her blade across the mask, wiping it clean of the blood. She turned to Jared, her eyes dark with determination. "That's what I'm going to find out," she vowed.

CHAPTER SIX

Slane was surprised at how easily he had been able to track Taylor. At first. For a week, Slane had dogged their steps, missing them by as much as half a day. But by the end of that first week, their trail had suddenly disappeared, as if they had vanished into thin air.

Slane realized with mounting fury that she had been toying with him. She had allowed him to follow her, leading him through dangerous forests and crowded towns. When the game grew tedious, she had simply ended it, leaving him stranded.

For another week, he had hunted for any trace of them, searched, questioned, and analyzed until he was left with no options. Frustrated, disgruntled, and angry beyond rationality, Slane took a room at the Traveler's Inn.

Now he sat alone in his room, pondering his misfortune within the confines of a large wooden tub. He shifted, moving his body lower in the steaming water. It was hopeless. He grabbed a ceramic pitcher from the floor next to the tub and poured its contents over his head, sighing heavily as the warm water splashed over his body, cleansing the dirt away. He would never find that deceitful wench. He banged the pitcher abruptly against the side of the tub before setting it back on the floor. His anger simmered hotly in his veins every time he thought of how easy it would have been to club her in the head, if only he had known she was the woman he was looking for. The clues had been there—her strange behavior, her quick knowledge of the ring—but he had been too blind to see them at the time. *Too blind and just too damn stupid,* he berated himself harshly.

Slane plunged his face into the water, trying to douse his growing rage, but the heat of the water only seemed to inflame his anger. *When I find that accursed woman, I will wring her neck. She'll learn the true meaning of respect.* Slane pulled his head out of the water, and as several streams of the warm liquid trailed down his face, he felt a slow grin form on his lips. He saw himself teaching her the proper way to treat a knight of the realm.

Suddenly, a dark shape shifted in the shadows across the room and Slane felt his body stiffen. Somebody was in his room! He glanced quickly to his right, at the sword still secured in its scabbard, leaning against a chair leg on the other side of the room. *Damn. Too far.*

"I would have given my payment back to see the look on your face when you got my note," a feminine voice said, its owner stepping out of the shadows to the side of the tub.

Even though she was clothed in a dark brown robe, a hood half concealing her face, Slane recognized her immediately. "You . . ." he muttered, his voice an unbelieving whisper. The Sullivan woman! His fingers dug into the edge of the basin; he could feel his nails sink into the wood. His eyes narrowed to thin slits as his mind transformed the wood into the soft flesh of her neck. What in God's blood was she doing here?

"Are you happy to see me?" she wondered, laughter in her voice. She grabbed a chair from the bed side and slid it over to the tub so its back was near his hand. She threw her leg over it, straddling it. "I heard you were looking for me."

Slane sat motionless. Here she was, the woman he had been searching for, sitting in a chair not more than a foot from him, and all he could do was stare dumbfounded at her. In the flickering candlelight, the bruised and battered face he remembered was gone, replaced by a cheek so smoothly rounded that he found himself entranced by its perfection. He caught the scent of lavender about her as a soft breeze brushed past the open shutters and circled the room, blanketing him in the delicate aroma. He felt a stirring beneath the water and shifted his body lower into the tub so his manhood would not break the water's surface. *It's just a woman's cheek, man,* Slane derided himself. *You've seen hundreds of them before.*

He watched her lips turn down in a slight pout before she threw back the hood. Her dark hair tumbled wildly over her shoulders as the material slipped away from her head. He immediately noticed the perfect fullness of her lips; the earlier swelling that had disfigured them was completely gone.

"Were you looking for me or have my sources been wrong?"

Slane felt the throbbing in his loins increase tenfold. He slunk lower into the tub, draping his arm casually between his thighs. She was an absolutely stunning creature. How could he have known that hiding behind those bruises was one of the most beautiful women he had ever seen? He forced himself to look away. She deserved his contempt for what she had done to him, not his lust. "You know damn well I've been looking for you," he retorted. "Have you come here to ridicule me for failing to find you?"

"Well . . ." she teased, laughter still in her voice, a smile on her face.

Blast her. Slane studied her reflection in the smooth water of the bath. "Why are you here?" he gritted, thinking again of his sword lying uselessly on the other side of the room.

"Cut to the point, eh, Slane? Well, all right." Her face lost all its humor. "Why were you looking for me?"

"Why ask me? Didn't your 'sources' tell you?" Slane drawled, his voice thick with acrimony.

"Slane Donovan," she mused and he was startled by the tenderness in her voice. "I used to hear about you all the time when I was young. You were a hero. Slane Donovan this, Slane Donovan that. You were the best gossip around."

Slane raised his eyes to meet hers. He was surprised by the warmth he saw in those bright green gems . . . and was that admiration? Then the wall slammed down and the glimpse of her soul was gone.

"Are you going to try to kill me?" she asked.

Slane bridled. He was a knight; he did not cut down women . . . even if they wielded a sword. "If you really thought I was hunting you down to kill you, you wouldn't be sitting a foot from me and flitting your hair about like some tavern wench looking for a fresh bed," Slane said. The comment was harsher than he had intended and he saw the anger ignite in her eyes. Again, he wondered why she had come back to reveal herself to him. She had to have some ulterior motive. *She must need me for something,* Slane realized. He knew she wouldn't risk exposing herself for any other reason. *Now why would this little scrapper of a woman need me?* Slane felt curiosity loom larger in his thoughts.

"Well, believe me, if I needed a bed to sleep in, it wouldn't be yours!" she snapped, jumping from the chair. "If you won't tell me what I want to know, I'll find someone who will." She moved to leave.

Slane rose out of the water like the ancient god Poseidon, the liquid sliding off his body in thick sheets. His expression was grim, his mouth tight, his teeth clenched. He seized Taylor's wrist in his strong fingers and squeezed tightly. "You ran away from me once," he growled. "You shall not do it again."

He watched her eyes slide over his body as easily as the water, but then hesitate at his waist. Quickly, they rose to meet his. Was that embarrassment in her eyes? he wondered. Or contempt?

"You are arrogant, aren't you?" she wondered softly. The smile slid easily across her lips. "Tell me why they're after me." It was half plea, half command.

They? Slane wondered. "Mercenaries," he said aloud. Had some of the others found her already? There seemed to be genuine concern in her voice, a vulnerability that touched him despite his anger. Slane loosened his grip on her arm.

She pulled free of him and stepped away. "These men were not mercenaries," she replied and turned her back to him.

Slane reached after her, then immediately pulled his arm back, staring at it as if it had taken on a life of its own. As he looked at his arm, he caught sight of his body below it and realized that he was naked. He grabbed his leggings off the floor and quickly slid into them. When he glanced up again, he found her staring at him with those cursed eyes—eyes that made him want to probe deeper to find the strange mysteries they promised to reveal one day. He reached out for his tunic and pulled it over his head, then quickly donned his boots.

Suddenly, there was a loud bang from outside the door, then the clang of swords.

Taylor whipped off the cloak, drawing her weapon from its sheath, and raced toward the door.

But before she had taken two steps, the door splintered open and Jared's body came flying through it!

CHAPTER SEVEN

Jared hit the floor before Taylor and lay still, his open, glassy eyes staring up at her. A large stain of blood spread across his abdomen, growing wider and redder with each passing moment. She heard noises all around her and knew she should look up, knew she should look away from her friend lying motionless on the hard floor, but for the moment, she couldn't seem to take her gaze from Jared's deathly still body. *This isn't happening,* she thought. *This isn't happening.*

"What the hell?" she heard Slane cry, his surprised shout finally pulling her from her stupor. She looked up to see four men dressed in black rush into the room, their swords ready. A dagger whizzed toward Slane's head and he dove to the floor, the sharp tip of the deadly blade sinking into the wall behind him. He rolled across the floor and grabbed his sheath, diving back behind the large washtub in the middle of the room.

Struggling to clear the haze of disbelief that numbed her, Taylor turned her eyes back to focus on Jared. What was he still doing on the floor? Why hadn't he gotten to his feet to meet the attackers? She thought she heard Slane shout her name, but her confused mind refused to concentrate on anything but Jared.

Out of the corner of her eye, she caught a quick flash of movement and turned to see one of the men in black lifting his sword to strike her. Suddenly, Slane was there, leaping up from behind the tub, smashing the attacker in the back and pushing him to the floor.

"Taylor!"

In the vague distance, Taylor heard Slane call her name again. But it wasn't until Slane grabbed her roughly and spun her around to face him that the urgency in his voice reached her.

These men had hurt Jared. The horror of that truth whispered at the edge of her thoughts, trying to force its way inside.

A sword flashed hotly just over Slane's shoulder and he whirled in time to engage the soldier.

A flash of pain seared through the muscles in her forearm. She glanced down, surprised to see the familiar sight of her sword clutched tightly in her clenched fist. Only when she forced her bunched fingers to relax did the pain in her arm vanish. When a second and third soldier came at her, Taylor defended herself, feinting right to duck a blow and parrying an incoming swing. She acted instinctively, without thinking, until finally the familiar feel of the weight of her weapon brought life back to her numb senses.

These men had hurt Jared. The thought grew stronger, kindling the rage that burned in her heart.

She lashed out strongly with her foot, kicking one of the men in the groin. He doubled over, and Taylor kicked him again in the side, sending him toppling to the ground. She caught the silver flash of another blade arcing toward her, but didn't have time to dodge the blow. The sword caught her hip, sending a blast of pain through her waist, but her leather armor absorbed the brunt of the blow, and the pain quickly subsided into a dull ache. She swung a backhanded fist toward the soldier, and her knuckles cracked into his cheekbone. He grunted sharply and staggered back. Taylor backed away, quickly assessing her surroundings.

She saw Slane down his attacker with a quick jab to the stomach; then she turned quickly back to see the other three men, now all on their feet, closing in on her, surrounding her.

Slane turned to help Taylor, attacking the man closest to her, arcing his sword high overhead and bringing it down. The man sidestepped his strike and lashed out with a swift kick, catching Slane in the ribs. He dropped to one knee, gasping. He barely raised his sword above his head in time to block what would have been a killing blow. He lashed out a fist and his knuckles crunched as they collided with his attacker's face. The man stumbled, then fell to his knees. Slane launched another punch, and the man's teeth gave way under the power of his blow.

These men had killed Jared. *No!* a voice cried out inside her in a desperate attempt to hold that terrifying possibility at bay. *He's not dead!*

Taylor swung, expertly catching one of the men in the throat. He dropped to the floor, falling into another of the attackers, knocking him off balance. Taylor's grim eyes returned to Jared. He still had not moved. His eyes remained wide and unblinking. His chest was still. *I have to get to him!* she thought and took another step toward him.

The soldier who had been knocked to the ground pushed his dead comrade off of him and rose to block Taylor's path. *"No!"* she cried out and attacked relentlessly, swinging her blade again and again and again, the metals colliding with a sharp *clang* on each blow. But this soldier was obviously a trained fighter; he dodged all of her anger-fueled swings with little effort.

Taylor finally lashed out with her booted foot and struck him in the gut, throwing him back. She whirled to move to Jared, only to find another man arcing a blade at her. She raised her weapon just in time to block the large sword. The force of the blow knocked her back a step.

Suddenly, the three remaining soldiers broke off the fight, pulling away from them.

Taylor frowned, her body tensing, expecting a sudden rush from their attackers. Then the unnerving sound of dozens of footsteps on the wooden floor in the hallway outside the room drew her gaze toward the door. Half-a-dozen men dressed in the same black attire rushed into the room, their weapons drawn!

Taylor cursed. They were vastly outnumbered.

Slane stepped protectively to her, standing slightly in front of her.

But strangely, the men did not attack. They stood silently, like dark, faceless statues. Then the dull thud of a single pair of footsteps filled the silence.

A tall man adorned in black swept into the room, an ebony cape swirling about him. He had a hard face—a face of sharp angles and sun-worn leathery skin. A thin mustache carved out a narrow black line atop his upper lip. Taylor's gaze stopped on his eyes, momentarily frozen by the sheer, uncompromising blackness she saw within his stern look. Taylor felt Slane stiffen at the sight of the man.

When the man's eyes came to rest on the scene before him, he snarled, "Weak fools." Then his black eyes fell on Slane and his lip curled with hatred. His dark eyes narrowed. "Kill him," he ordered. "And do it slowly. Bring me the woman. Make sure she is alive." He whirled, his black cape flowing behind him like a flag.

Taylor felt a wave of defeat surge inside her. She had barely held off the first attackers, and now their numbers had tripled. She knew she would be taken . . . and Slane killed. She cast a sidelong glance at Slane.

He was looking at her, his eyes filled with a grim determination. She glanced around the room once, looking for a way to escape. But there was only the window. And they were two stories up.

Suddenly, the attackers surged forward, a wall of black threatening to crush them under its weight.

Then Slane was moving, sweeping her into his embrace, pulling her tight against his chest. He charged forward, his momentum driving them toward the window on the side wall. Toward the window . . . and through it! Wood and glass splintered into tiny pieces all around them as their bodies crashed through the pane!

As they fell through the air, Taylor found herself staring up into a dazzling, star-filled sky as a rush of wind whistled through her ears. But then suddenly her vision blurred as she felt her body being sharply twisted in midair. And she knew in that instant that Slane had turned her body so that he would receive the brunt of the impact. The stars disappeared, quickly replaced by a solid wall of flesh as Slane pulled her head down to his chest.

She heard a loud crash and wood cracking, and then the air exploded out of her lungs as they struck something hard and the momentum of their fall was stopped cold. A flurry of objects whizzed past her vision as if she were suddenly thrust into the midst of a savage tornado.

Dazed, Taylor couldn't move for a long moment; her head rested against something firm and yet warm at the same moment. And then the hard warmth was moving and she was being pushed away from it. She struggled to catch a breath.

Slane held her firmly at arm's length, trying to look into her eyes. "Are you all right?" he asked.

Taylor shook her head, trying to clear the fog that threatened to overtake her. She tried to nod, but wasn't sure if she succeeded. Something tasted very salty on her lips and she quickly licked it away. Slane pulled her to her feet. She took in her surroundings, realizing that they had leapt into the back of a merchant's open wagon, a wagon that had been filled with linens and sacks of spices and grains. Most of the sacks were split open, their contents spilled everywhere, littering the ground with white smears of salt, black hills of pepper, and brown pools of wheat.

She looked up at Slane to see him bending to retrieve his fallen sword, his frowning stare fixed on something above them. She followed his gaze up to the window two stories above them. Two of the soldiers were staring down at them from the splintered windowframe above. One of the attackers stepped out onto the ledge. A sudden rush of adrenaline surged through her veins, overriding any pain. Overriding any feelings.

"Let's go," Slane whispered sharply, grabbing her wrist and pulling her after him. Taylor snatched her sword from the ground as Slane pulled her down an alley. Just as they rounded the corner, she saw the black-clad man leap from the window.

Slane led her down the alley past the backs of houses. He recrossed their path and headed up a different alley.

Again and again, he moved through the town, doubling back several times, until Taylor lost her way. Her head swam with the sudden turn of events. Disoriented and confused, she clung to his hand as if it were her lifeline.

Finally, Slane led her out of the village and into the forest. There, he moved quickly, not running, but not walking, forcing her on until her legs ached. Until she stumbled.

Slane stopped suddenly and turned to her, his searching eyes scanning the thick growth of trees. She saw his shoulders relax, the tension draining from them. He sheathed his sword and looked at her, his gaze dark and piercing. "Are you hurt?" he demanded.

With the exertion taking its toll on her body and her swirling feelings taking their toll on her mind, she began to shake. Taylor looked at the canopy of trees above them. She glanced at the forest around them. Finally, she turned back the way they had just come and took two steps toward the town. "I have to go back," she announced.

"Are you out of your mind?" Slane asked, coming up behind her like a storm cloud.

Taylor whirled on him. "I won't leave Jared like that!" she objected.

Slane stared at her for a long moment. His scowl diminished and the hard edge to his gaze softened. "Taylor, he's dead."

"You don't know that!"

"I've seen death many times," he said.

"As have I. And he wasn't dead!" He had known the risks of being her accomplice, she thought. "He's not dead!" Jared had known how dangerous it was to travel with her.

Slane looked at her with a sad calmness in his face, his blue eyes penetrating to her very soul.

"He's not dead," she repeated, even though she knew her words weren't true. She had seen death numerous times, had delivered it herself. But she had never thought it would happen to Jared. Taylor felt the anguish ripping at her heart, felt her eyes burn with tears. They had known her father would send men after her someday. She whirled away from Slane as the hot tears filled her eyes. *He's gone,* she thought. *Just like Mother.*

"Taylor," he called. Slane's voice was a gentle whisper, a caress.

With all her heart, she wanted to give in to her feelings; she wanted to be comforted. She almost turned to him . . . almost allowed herself to be touched.

But she didn't. She pushed the hurt aside as she had all those years ago and wiped a sleeve across her eyes, wiped away the self-pity. Jared was gone.

She was alone now.

And she had only herself to look out for her. No one to watch her back. She shrugged her shoulders slightly, trying to brush away Jared's death as easily, and looked away from Slane's piercing gaze. But she could not control the tears that threatened to overflow, no matter how hard she steeled herself. No matter how much she told herself it didn't matter. No matter how much she told herself that it was his fault for . . . for befriending her.

Her lower lip trembled; her entire body shook. A lone tear slid from her eye and traced a path down her cheek.

Then Slane's finger was at her chin, gently lifting it until her eyes locked with his. His deep blue gaze reached into her as if reading every thought, every agonizing memory. She couldn't hide the pain she was feeling. Not now, not yet. She couldn't manage to conjure up her infamous indifference.

"I'm sorry," he whispered.

And he meant it. She could tell by the sincerity in his voice, the shadow of hurt in his eyes. But all Taylor could do was stand there, stifling the sobs that threatened to consume her body.

He reached out and brushed a strand of hair from her cheek, tucking it neatly behind her ear.

She fought the loss of control that threatened, the dark abyss that had been waiting to swallow her up since her mother's death. Taylor leaned her head against his palm, and he automatically cupped her cheek. She closed her eyes tightly, and tears squeezed forth from her closed lids. She felt his cool hand against her hot cheek, and then he slid it to the nape of her neck, pulling her against his strong chest.

It was strong and warm and safe. She put her forehead against his chest and felt strong fingers rub her neck. Her hair cascaded over her face, shielding it from him. For the first time since her mother's death, she let her sorrow overwhelm her. She sobbed silently, her tears trickling from her eyes like a soft rain.

Jared had been more than just a friend. He had been her only family for eight years. He had been there as a teacher, a protector. He knew her better than she knew herself. He could comfort her and tell her what needed to be done. He had guided her away from many foolish actions, had given her invaluable counsel on numerous things. And she knew she could always talk to him. About anything.

And now he was gone.

Slowly, her sobs lessened. She wiped her eyes and her nose and looked up. Slane was there, watching her with gentle eyes, his golden hair waving slightly in a soft breeze. And Taylor realized suddenly that his arms were around her, holding her.

And she liked it.

Slane lowered his arms, letting them slide down hers. A strange tremor raced through Taylor's body, startling her. She stepped back, away from him.

A cold wind slid between them and Taylor lifted her hand to swipe at a lock of hair that had blown before her face.

Slane's gaze dropped to her wrist. "You're hurt," he said softly.

Taylor looked down to see the dark black and blue marks marring her skin, the large bump that had appeared. She realized she must have struck something in the wagon. The pain erupted from her wrist as she laid eyes on it, as if her body just realized that it had been wounded, but she shook her head. "It's nothing," she murmured. And then more aches started to surface, dull throbs that seemed to cover her entire body.

Slane took her hand, his blue eyes drawn to her wrist. Taylor followed his gaze. But it wasn't her bruised skin she was looking at. It was the tender way in which Slane held her. His large fingers engulfed her hand, shielding it, holding it carefully. Her fingers wrapped around his thumb. "Does it hurt?" he wondered.

A crooked smile formed on her lips. "Only when I move it," she said.

"You can move it?"

"Only if I want to feel some pain."

Slane put his hands on her shoulders to ease her to the ground. Taylor let him tend her. She let him move her wrist tentatively. She knew it wasn't broken. But she liked the way he touched her, the gentleness and concern he bestowed upon her.

For a moment, she wasn't the hunted woman. For a

moment, he wasn't the hunter. They were just a man and a woman.

"How long have you known him?" Slane wondered, not raising his eyes to hers.

"Eight years," she answered. He lifted his gaze to lock eyes with hers and Taylor read the surprise there. She smiled humorlessly. "We left the castle together."

He bent his head over her wrist again. "He taught you to fight?"

"Jared said there were two ways we could make a living. Fighting or prostitution." Taylor watched the distaste curl Slane's lips. "He said he couldn't bear to see me doing that. So he taught me to fight."

Slane turned her hand over to inspect her palm. He ran his forefinger over the calluses across her knuckles and near her thumb. "You shouldn't have had to do that."

"It was my choice."

"Why didn't you return to the castle?" Slane asked.

"After what Father did?" Taylor snorted. "I never want to see him again."

"He wants to see you."

Taylor froze. After all this time, he finally wondered what his daughter was up to! A sudden longing surged inside her breast. To return home to the friends she had left there, the lands she had loved. But then the image of her father danced mockingly over the serene scene. She had tried to prepare herself for this moment, but now that it stared her in the face, she felt nothing but bitterness. She yanked her hand from Slane's grasp. "So that's why you came after me." Why did she feel so betrayed?

"He's old. He wants to make amends," Slane defended.

"He wants to have an heir," she retorted and shot to her feet. "Well, you can forget it, because I am not going back."

"You won't see him? You won't speak to him?" Slane demanded, rising after her.

"I have nothing to say to him."

"He's your father, for the love of God! If he wants to see you again you have a duty, an obligation—"

"This is good advice from a man who didn't listen to his father," Taylor retorted.

Surprise rocked Slane and he straightened.

"Oh, I know, all right. I know all about how your father wanted you to become a priest. But you ran away to your . . . Was it your uncle's castle?"

Slane crossed his arms, staring at her through chilly blue eyes.

An icy smile slid over Taylor's lips. "And instead you trained to become a knight. Against your father's wishes. You're a fine one to tell me to listen to my father."

"This is different," Slane said stubbornly.

"How so?"

"I had a calling. And it wasn't to be a priest."

"I have a calling, too." She turned her back on him. "And it's not to see my father again."

Slane grabbed her arm, halting her movement. "Where will you go? What do you think you will do? A lone woman in this world? You'll be killed at the first inn you stop at. Or maybe on the road to the inn."

Taylor pulled her arm away from him. "I survived this long."

"You had Jared," Slane snapped.

His barb stung her. She stood absolutely still, warring with her anger and her loss for a long moment, staring up into his hard blue eyes.

"You have nowhere to go," Slane replied in a softer tone. "Come with me."

She knew he was right. She had to decide on a course

of action, figure out where she was going. But her mind refused to focus. It refused to think of anyone except for Jared. And large blue, comforting eyes.

"You can travel with me safely until you decide what you want to do."

Taylor turned her head to the empty shadows of the woods. "You'll be heading for Sullivan lands." Her words were half statement, half question.

"Yes," Slane said.

Taylor felt a growing sense of anxiety in the pit of her stomach. She didn't know what to do. If Jared had been there, they could have talked about it. But he wasn't there. And he never would be again.

And it was all her fault. Tears threatened at the corners of her eyes again, but she quickly fought them back.

"I'll pay your way," Slane coaxed.

The statement jarred her. Pay? Laughter bubbled in her closing throat. "With what?" she asked. "Your gold is in your room at the inn."

Slane frowned, turning to look back in the direction they had just come from.

Taylor could almost see the silent curse on his lips. Humor and tears battled for control of her body.

Slane turned a questioning stare to her.

She removed a heavy pouch of coins from her waistband. When Slane's eyes widened incredulously, she broke out in laughter even as tears ran over her cheeks.

"That's mine!" Slane exclaimed.

"I lifted it from your room," she admitted. And then the laughter was gone and sorrow engulfed her like the hand of a giant crushing her in its palm. It was her fault. Jared had known. He had the foresight to know not to return. But she had insisted they find Slane. And now her stubbornness had killed the only man she had ever called friend. She had thought to ease Jared's worry with a fat pouch of coin. Instead, she held the pouch in a shaking hand, with no one to present it to except its rightful owner.

Slane stepped forward and Taylor thought that he would take her memorial from her. He reached out, but it wasn't the pouch he took. He wrapped his arms around her, pulling her into his embrace.

She stiffened for a moment, resisting his comfort. But she couldn't withstand her agony, her loss. It encompassed her body, sending her into fits of grief. She slumped against him and followed him to a nearby outcropping of rocks.

Exhausted, Taylor let Slane pull her down to the ground between a sheltering pine and a large rock.

The bag of coin lay on the ground near their feet, forgotten.

CHAPTER EIGHT

Slane stared down at Taylor as she slept cushioned against his body, his arm around her. He didn't think that a herd of thundering horses could awaken her now. He stroked her hairline again, running his fingertips over her smooth skin, marveling that the bruises had so completely disappeared and left such smooth, untainted skin in their wake. Her lips were not swollen and distorted any longer, but rather perfect in their symmetry, full, and sensual. He had a sudden desire to touch them.

Horrified at the direction his thoughts were heading, Slane quickly eased her to the ground and stood away from her. She groaned softly and curled into the warmth his body had left on the ground. *God's blood!* he thought. *What am I thinking? I have to think about Elizabeth. Waiting for me. Yes, Elizabeth.* He ran a hand over his eyes, trying to wipe the fatigue from them. *I must be tired and confused.*

But he found his gaze returning to Taylor. *If it weren't*

for me, she wouldn't be in this mess, he thought. *I found her. I brought her into this hell of running from Corydon's men, of losing her friend.*

Slane paced, raking his hand through his golden hair. If he hadn't found her, then it would have clearly been someone else. And she was better off with him than with a mercenary seeking the reward his brother had put out for her! Slane was sure that every mercenary this side of France was looking for her.

The sun rose steadily over the horizon, the sky lightening with the coming dawn. Slane knew they would have to move on soon. They couldn't put enough distance between themselves and Corydon. A hundred miles was too little. Still, he was reluctant to wake her.

His gaze shifted back to her as she lay hidden between the rock and the pine tree. He could see one of her boots sticking out of the shelter. He couldn't wake her. She needed all her strength to deal with the future. He would let her sleep, let her have a moment's peace.

He shifted his royal blue eyes to the path that stretched before them. To Castle Donovan.

Taylor had barely opened her eyes when everything came back to her in a rush of images. Jared's body splintering the door. Black-clad men swinging deadly blades at her. Slane diving at her, taking them both through the window. Slane holding her in his arms, comforting her. She sat up quickly, scanning the area, but Slane was nowhere to be seen.

She eased herself from the cover of the pine tree and the rock, stepping into the sunlight, squinting at the brightness. The sun was almost directly over her head. She lifted her eyes to regard the blazing orb with astonishment. She never slept this long! Her gaze swept the clearing, finally coming upon Slane, who was strolling back to her, his hands cupped before him.

For a moment, she was taken aback. He looked like some ancient god, his blond hair waving over his shoulders, his bronzed face kissed by the sun, his blue eyes sparkling like the most treasured gems. But it wasn't their sparkling brilliance that caught her attention; it was the way he was looking at her, with a guarded reserve.

Taylor climbed to her feet. She eyed the berries he was holding in his cupped hands; then she glanced back up at him.

He popped a berry into his mouth. "Are you rested? Because I think we should be moving on." He held out a handful of berries.

Taylor plucked a berry from the top of the pile. She studied it absently, not really seeing it. Moving on. To Sullivan Castle. She didn't want to see her father again. Seeing him wasn't going to change the past. Seeing him wasn't going to bring her mother back. "Slane, I think you should know that I have no intention of returning to Sullivan Castle."

She lifted her eyes in time to see disapproval cross his face. "That decision is yours to make. But I'm sure there are other mercenaries—"

She held up her free hand. "I know. You've told me. But what you haven't told me is who those black knights were."

Slane took a deep breath and lowered his hands. "They're Corydon's men. Your father and my brother, Richard, have banded together to fight Corydon. He's been threatening to take over their lands."

"Corydon?"

"Five years ago, he took over the lands west of Sullivan.

Corydon thinks that with your father growing old he poses no great threat. He is just biding his time."

"And how is my return supposed to help?"

"The knights at Sullivan Castle have been growing restless. They think that with no heir to rally behind, if your father dies, Sullivan Castle will fall easily to Corydon. Many of them have left already. Your father needs an heir."

She popped the berry into her mouth, chewing thoughtfully. "And what's your brother's story?"

"Richard has squandered the treasury, depleting his funds. Castle Donovan is precariously defended. He doesn't have long. He'll be out of gold to pay his knights in two months' time."

"So my father has the gold, and Richard has the knights."

"Your father asked Richard's help to locate you."

"And in exchange, Richard gets the gold," Taylor added knowingly. "So that's where you come in."

Slane nodded. "Richard asked me to find you. And he sought the help of a score of mercenaries. He's quite insistent on the matter."

Taylor sighed and stared up at the sky for a long moment.

"Taylor, there is much more at stake here than you realize," Slane said gently. "The lives and well-being of two kingdoms, of hundreds of families, depend on your returning to Sullivan Castle."

"Really?" she gasped, mockingly. His eyes were so blue, so damned . . . pure. "So what?"

She saw shock in his widening eyes, in his open mouth. She felt a surge of satisfaction. Then his lips closed with disbelief. "Maybe you didn't hear me correctly," Slane said.

"I heard," she said. "I just don't care. Where were they when my mother was burning eight years ago? Where were they when Jared was being killed?" She shook her head. "I just don't care."

"But—"

"No buts. I don't give a rat's ass about the poor peasants who have worked hard all their life. Haven't we all?"

Slane studied her for a moment. "Why don't you come with me to Castle Donovan? You'll be safe from Corydon, and it will give you time to decide what you want to do."

Taylor already knew what her decision was. She would never go back to her father. Never. But the lure of a warm bed and hot meals was too much for a starving mercenary to pass up. Besides, it would give her time to think about her own plans for the future. "We'll see," she mused.

Slane nodded and started walking north.

Taylor joined him. "Are we going to walk the whole way there?"

"Until I can secure us some horses," Slane replied. He held out his handful of berries to her.

This time, Taylor scooped up a handful of her own.

After moving briskly for more than half a day without rest, they came to a clearing lined by a thick wall of trees on one side and a river on the other. "We'll stop here," Slane announced, glancing at the setting sun.

Taylor shrugged slightly and moved to the river to clean off the day's grime and sweat.

Slane watched her for a long moment. She hadn't braided her hair today, instead choosing to let it hang down in long waves. He had caught her running her hands through the luxurious locks several times throughout the day and had to smile to himself. He was glad she had not braided it. He liked the way the sunlight reflected off the blue-black highlights in her hair. Once, he even imagined what it might feel like. He had never paid such attention to Elizabeth's brown hair. Of course, he rarely even saw her hair. She always kept it up, hidden beneath one of those horrible coifs or ridiculous headdresses.

He strolled to the middle of the clearing and removed his tunic. *A good hour of practice is what I need,* he thought to himself. *Just me and my blade.* He liked to work shirtless, with the warm sun bathing his skin. He always felt strong in the bright sunlight, strong and energized. He removed his sword from its sheath and stared for a moment at his reflection in the polished metal.

A splash caught his attention and he raised his eyes. Taylor was on her knees by the river's edge, her small, shapely bottom pointing directly at him.

A flush of desire exploded through him. It was so startling and so unexpected that he had to turn his back lest she see how she affected him. He turned the sword over in his hand. Where had that come from? he wondered, fighting down the surge of passion that simmered in his blood. He took a deep breath, but it was still a long moment before his desire faded to a more controllable impulse.

He swung the heavy sword with two hands, the muscles in his shoulders and forearms straining during the practiced motion. He moved his arms in a large circle, slowly drawing the blade over his head. He stood that way for a long moment, the sword raised above his head, the fading sunlight glinting like fire from his blade. His golden hair cascaded over his shoulders to touch the midpoint of his back.

He concentrated on stretching his muscles, training them to be ready for action at a moment's notice, to keep them honed for battle. And they were. He was a warrior, a knight. He had faced and defeated every foe he had stood against.

He lowered the weapon slowly across the other side of his body until the blade was pointing toward the river. And then he froze.

A pair of hunter green eyes stared at him.

Taylor sat with one knee drawn up to her chest, watching him. But there was no sarcastic gaze chiseled across her face. No, it was not the disrespectful, mocking stare he was used to. She turned away then, a long, dark strand of her hair falling across her breast.

For just a moment, he could have sworn she had just been gazing at him admiringly, like all the ladies at court did. There had been surprise in those eyes. But he must have imagined it. Because Taylor was unlike any woman he had encountered before. She was different.

He took a step toward her. "Don't you practice?" he asked.

She shifted her stare to him and the sarcasm was back in those lidded eyes, as if it had never left. "I'm sure there will be plenty of opportunities to practice. Right now, I'm tired."

He watched her settle down beneath the branches of a large oak tree, cushioning her head on her arm, before he turned back to concentrate on his work.

Taylor watched Slane practice from slitted eyes. She was anything but tired. She was restless. And the strange restlessness churned within her the more she watched Slane.

CHAPTER NINE

"Hey, Slane," Taylor whispered, tapping her new traveling companion on the shoulder. "Can we stop at the alehouse after we finish sneaking through the streets?"

Slane turned to her, the scowl etched deep into his brow, the irritation clearly visible in his eyes. "We are not sneaking," he told her.

Taylor blew a scoffing blast of air from between her lips. "You've been hugging the shadows ever since we reached Sudbury this afternoon. I'd call that sneaking."

"And why are you whispering?" he asked.

"Isn't that what you do when you sneak around?"

A merchant rode past, his overloaded carriage jostling and jangling loudly as it moved along the pockmarked dirt road that ran through the center of Sudbury.

Slane grabbed Taylor's arm and pulled her into a pool of dark shadows. "We're not sneaking around," Slane insisted.

Taylor held up her hands in surrender. "All right. All right. Can we stop at the alehouse?"

Slane nodded. "We need flasks and drink."

"I can try to purchase us horses—" Taylor began, spying a small stable situated next to a blacksmith's shop nearby.

"No," Slane erupted. "We stick together."

Taylor stared into his determined blue eyes for a moment longer, then nodded her agreement. All she wanted right now was a good ale to quench her thirst. She didn't feel like arguing with this stubborn noble. She didn't feel like disagreeing about such petty things. She was just tired of walking. Her legs hurt and her feet were throbbing.

They moved down the road, passing the tightly packed houses. Some of the merchants had additional stands set up on the streets to sell their wares, but most used their homes as a front for their shops, their brightly colored awnings and hand-carved wooden signs indicating what goods they sold. Peasants filled the streets, gathering around the merchants' shops and stands, haggling over price. Market day was in full swing.

Slane paused at one of the carts to negotiate with a leather maker. No doubt trying to purchase a few decently made flasks or wine pouches, Taylor mused as she moved on.

She meandered down the rows of storefronts, inspecting some loaves of still steaming bread on a ledge outside a baker's shop, sampling a shred of some salted venison at another merchant's stall. Then she reached the stall of a spice vendor. Bowls of chopped herbs, peppers, and salt filled his long wooden table. Taylor caught herself staring at a large oak bowl filled with freshly chopped garlic. A tremendous tide of sadness welled up inside her. Jared had always loved to visit the spice merchants. Garlic had been his favorite. She always told him he stunk for days after eating it, but he only laughed at her and told her he'd rather stink of garlic than of the horrible perfumes the nobles soaked their skins with. He would stay and talk to the merchants for hours, discussing the best ways to use aniseed or ginger or pepper to enhance the flavor of food. He never seemed happier than when arguing over the best way to spice a rabbit or duck.

"Ah, you like my onion?" Taylor heard someone say. She glanced up to see the merchant, a surprisingly thin man with a freckled face and a mere growth of red stubble on his chin.

"What?" Taylor asked, not certain if he had been talking to her.

"My onions. You find them to your liking, I see."

Taylor squinted at the man, confused.

The freckled merchant pointed to her eyes. "Only a good onion can do that, no?"

Taylor reached up to her eyes to find the edges were moist. "Yes, you have good onions," she said, her voice barely above a whisper. "Very good onions."

She moved on, still careful to remain within sight of Slane. She wiped her eyes dry, hoping Slane hadn't noticed her moment of weakness, and swatted aside a strand of hair that had come loose from the braid she had wound tightly in her hair that morning. She glanced into the street, at the peasants scurrying by in their hurry to reach their destinations.

When she looked away again, a reflection of light in the middle of the road caught her eye. She spotted something half buried in dirt, but Taylor could see the silver sparkle in the sun. She bent down and came back up with a muddied metal band.

Just then, from the stand nearest her, a loud voice called, "Thief!"

Taylor's knees bent slightly and her hand flew to the hilt of her sword. The short merchant bedecked with gold jewelry, however, was not pointing an angry, quivering finger at her, but at a man dressed in ripped leggings and a soiled tunic who was standing near the merchant's stall. The man had a thick beard, its sandy brown hairs littered with the crumbs of what probably had been his last meal. He certainly didn't look like a thief, nor did he act like one. Most thieves would have raced into the crowd to disappear amidst the throng of people, but this man just stood there with a bewildered, almost frightened look on his face.

"Thief!" the merchant screamed again as he lunged forward and grabbed the man's arm, pulling him roughly against the stall's display counter. "Give me back that ring!"

The bearded man's eyes went wide with surprise. "I . . . I didn't take anything," he protested meekly.

Taylor glanced down at the ring in her palm, scowling slightly.

"That's an interesting piece of jewelry," a familiar voice mused, jarring Taylor. She looked up to see Slane studying the ring she held in her hand. He raised his eyes to meet hers. "Did you purchase it with that overstuffed bag of coin you carry around with you?"

Taylor's brows furrowed. "I found it in the road," she answered.

At the stall next to them, the merchant had a tight grip around the man's wrist and was holding the struggling man's hand flat against the counter. The merchant turned and reached for a large, menacing blade hanging on the wall behind him.

"I think it belongs to that merchant, don't you?" Slane asked.

Taylor opened her mouth to reply as the merchant growled angrily at the man, "Do you know what I do to thieves?"

But Slane interrupted her before she could explain. "You'd let him chop off that man's hand just so you could wear a new trinket?" He did nothing to hide the anger in his tone.

Her eyes narrowed at his painful accusation. He thought so low of her! Well, she'd let him think what he would. She turned away.

Slane darted his hand forward and grabbed Taylor's wrist, squeezing it painfully, forcing her fingers open. He snatched the ring from her. Slane turned to the merchant just as he was about to bring his blade down on the bearded man's immobile wrist. "Hold!" he commanded. "I have your ring!"

The merchant looked up at Slane and slowly lowered the blade. But he still kept the peasant in his grip. "So where is it?" the merchant asked sharply.

Slane held out his hand and dropped the ring on to the merchant's counter. "Now let that man go."

The merchant eyed Slane suspiciously. "And where did you get it?" he wondered hotly.

"It had fallen into the street." Slane stepped forward toward the merchant, fingering the hilt of his sword. "Now let that man go."

The merchant obeyed and released his grip. The bearded man wasted no time in running as fast as he could into the crowd, disappearing into the swarming mass. Slane stepped even closer to the merchant. "Maybe next time you won't be so quick to judge a man before your anger blinds you."

Taylor rubbed her sore wrists absently. So damned noble. What if the ring she'd found hadn't been the same ring the merchant was looking for? Or what if the man had stolen it from the merchant and dropped it in the middle of the road for his accomplice to pick up? The ring had gotten into the middle of the street somehow; it hadn't just walked there on its own. Perhaps the man was not as innocent as Slane believed him. She shook her head. She and Slane were very different. They would never see things the same way. Besides, she would have returned the ring . . . if Slane had given her the chance.

Taylor turned to move off down the road.

Slane quickened his pace to catch up with her. He reached her side in a matter of moments and slowed his walk to match hers. "Why didn't you just give the ring back to the merchant? Didn't you care if that man had gotten his hand chopped off?"

Taylor stopped for a moment, looking up into the sky. Her eyes held the faintest hint of sadness. "You must think very little of me."

Slane stopped beside her. "Maybe I just don't understand your way of thinking. I have been raised to adhere to a strict code of behavior. One, it appears, you do not follow."

"The only code I follow is the one that's going to keep me alive," she said. "For eight years now, I've been constantly looking over my shoulder. You get suspicious of everything . . . and everyone." She looked at him for a long moment, not even understanding herself why she trusted him when everything she had learned told her to walk away from him and never ever look back.

"You don't have to be suspicious of me," Slane told her quietly. "I'm here to help you."

Taylor looked deep into his eyes, trying to see past the blatant honesty that shone through his features. But she couldn't. "That's what I don't trust," she replied and continued down the street.

The common room of the Sudbury Inn was quiet, most of the tables empty. Slane studied Taylor across their table. Despite the chill in the air, she insisted on sitting at the table farthest from the burning hearth. She leaned back in her chair, a foot resting casually on the edge of her seat. She purposely put her back to the fire, her gaze locked on her ale, as if pondering something. Her meal of duck was untouched.

Slane watched the distant firelight dance over her black hair like little imps. She was a very vibrant woman, one full of life, yet full of mysterious emotions he could never hope to understand. Perhaps he was reading too much into her. She was just a woman after all. He turned to his own meal and lifted a leg of lamb to his lips, ripping a large bite from its flank. "What are you thinking?" he wondered around a mouthful of meat.

She tore her gaze from the ale to face him. "Doesn't your code say anything about talking with your mouth full?" she quipped.

Slane felt a flush of embarrassment rise to his cheeks and didn't like it one bit. He had never felt embarrassed in his life. He covered his mouth with his hand and looked away from her, finishing his bite of food. *Damn her for making me feel like a fool. And damn me for caring what she thinks.*

"I'm thinking about my options," she finally offered after a long moment of silence.

Slane glanced up at her, lowering the leg of lamb to his plate in surprise. "I thought that was settled. I thought you were coming with me to Castle Donovan."

"I said I'd see."

Slane thought of letting her go and traveling back to Castle Donovan alone. Her mere presence was becoming unsettling. But he thought of another vow he had made. One to his brother. A vow that his honor would not let him break. "There are other people looking for you. Even if you left me, you might still end up at the castle."

"And I might not."

"Are you prepared to live your life like that? Constantly looking over your shoulder?"

"I have for eight years."

"It should be time you didn't have to," Slane said. "Face your past and put an end to it."

"That's easy for you to say, Slane," she retorted. "You don't have to do it."

Slane snorted. "I did," he murmured. "Once." He felt her eyes on him, felt a curiosity in her gaze.

"When you defied your father? When you became a knight?"

She was looking down into her mug of ale and it gave Slane an unwanted, but irresistible, chance to study her features. Her long, long lashes brushed her soft cheek as she glanced at her drink. Her full, captivating lips were wet with the shining residue of ale. God's blood! There was no denying the beauty in her features. Had she been dressed in a gown of rich velvet and cradled roses in her arms instead of donning leather armor and strapping a sword to her waist, every man in England would be vying for her attention, for her hand in marriage. His gaze roamed to her lovely hair, hair as dark as a midnight sky; to the soft, smooth sleekness of her neck, her sun-kissed skin so creamy, so flawless. He looked away suddenly, realizing with an uncomfortable start that he could watch her do nothing all day and still be mesmerized. What had they been talking about? Oh, yes. His father. "Yes, it was quite a scandal then," Slane said. "Father wanted me to be a priest, a servant of the church. He already had a knight in my brother Richard." He laughed somewhat bitterly, shifting his legs. "Can you see me as a priest?"

"No," Taylor answered honestly.

Slane was struck by what might very well be the first honest answer she had given him. "Neither could I," he admitted. "So I sneaked off to my uncle's castle. He secretly trained me and sponsored me."

"Your father must have been furious."

"Oh, he was more than furious. Not only did he refuse to speak to my uncle again, but he banned me from my home and threatened to disown me."

"You would have been scorned by every knight in the realm, just a wandering warrior without a home," Taylor said tonelessly.

"With no honor." Slane's eyes narrowed slightly. "But Richard convinced Father to change his mind. He told Father he would leave the castle if I wasn't allowed to return home with my honor intact. Father needed an heir, someone responsible, like Richard. So he agreed." He chuckled darkly as a bitterness crept into his voice. "But I didn't return then. I stayed away from Castle Donovan for years, attending tournaments, fighting wars."

"Why didn't you go home?" Taylor wondered.

It was Slane's turn to look into his mug of ale. "I did," he replied. He swirled the liquid around and finally took a long drink. "Just over a year ago. I was ready to make amends, to face my future with a clean start. But Father died shortly before I returned."

"I'm sorry," Taylor whispered.

Slane shrugged slightly, but he could feel the tension lining his shoulders. "Richard was lord of Castle Donovan." Slane's eyes narrowed. It was true Richard had saved his honor—and had held it over his head ever since he had returned.

Taylor smiled, shaking her head. "That's not the story I heard."

Slane's wide-eyed gaze swung to her. "It's not?" He saw a strange satisfaction in her eyes, a glow of mischief that gleamed from them tauntingly.

"I heard you left the castle to seek your own destiny. You traveled through many towns looking for a way to prove your valor. Finally, you came upon a town besieged by a dragon. You slew him quite completely and became a hero to that town. And in subsequent towns you wrestled a giant, slew an evil wizard, rescued a maiden—perhaps a princess—from being kidnapped. One story even had you finding the Holy Grail."

He felt the laughter churning in his throat.

"Very impressive work for someone who just attended tournaments and fought in some little wars, don't you think?"

"And what about you?" Slane taunted. "Slain any dragons yourself?"

She shook her head, her lips curling up in amusement. "Only the human kind," she answered. "You know very well that I don't do heroic things."

"Then tell me what you did after you left the castle. Where did you go? What did you do?"

Slane watched her look change from one of mild mirth to painful reminiscing. "Jared . . ." she said, then immediately stopped. The mere mention of his name seemed to bring a tightness to her throat. She closed her eyes for a moment, and Slane could see her fighting back the sadness threatening to reach all the way to those eyes. She looked at Slane and continued. "Jared didn't know what to do with me. I'm not really sure why he stayed with me at all, but I'm glad he did. I was horrible at first. Headstrong, willful, defiant. I had no respect for authority."

Slane chuckled. "And what's changed?"

Taylor cast him a startled look, then grinned. She continued as if he hadn't interrupted. "Finally, we ran into an old friend of Jared's. He lived out of an old gypsy wagon in Grey's Woods. That was home for a while. Jared taught me there. And Alexander . . . Well, let's just say that I was young then. And very impressionable. I became totally enamored of Alexander."

Slane felt a stiffness creeping across his shoulders. His hand tightened convulsively around his mug. "And this Alexander—did he return your affection?"

The moment of silence stretched and Slane finally lifted his gaze to Taylor's. She was staring at him with a strange look on her face. "I don't see where that's any of your concern."

Slane relented with a nod. He didn't like the feeling of anxiety that raced through his body. He chose to end the conversation about her past then. There were things he shouldn't know about. There were things he shouldn't even want to know about.

"If you'll excuse me," Taylor said as she rose to her feet. "I'm tired. I'm very tired."

Slane stood and nodded to her, bidding her good night. He watched her move up the stairs toward her room; then he lifted his mug to his lips, drinking deeply. It seemed she was affecting him far more than he cared to think about. That would have to change.

Taylor lay awake on her bed of straw, thinking about what Slane had said to her earlier that evening. "Face your past and put an end to it," he had said. "Are you prepared to live your life like that? Constantly looking over your shoulder?" Yes, she had done it for eight years, but Jared had been with her those eight years. Watching out for her, caring for her. Could she do it alone?

Maybe it was the fatigue of eight years of traveling finally catching up to her, the scrounging for work, the struggle for every meal. Maybe it was the fact that she was finally accepting the reality of Jared's death—the horrible reality that Jared would never fight at her side again, would never share another secret smile or tender embrace. She missed him terribly. Maybe she was simply tired and not thinking straight. All she knew for certain was that she felt a new resolve burning in her blood on this night. And she knew the burning could only be extinguished by one thing.

Taylor descended the stairs of the inn late that night. She moved quietly to the innkeeper and held out a small, rolled piece of parchment. He grasped it and looked at it for a long moment before shifting his gaze back to Taylor.

"Give it to Corydon," she instructed. "Tell him it's from Taylor Sullivan."

CHAPTER TEN

After a fitful night filled with dark dreams of Jared and black-robed men glaring at her from the shadows of her mind, Taylor woke to a pleasantly sunny day. Though they did not wipe her dreams away entirely, the warm rays of the sun did help to diminish the unpleasant lingerings of her night's unrest.

After quickly dressing, Taylor descended the stairs with Slane to break their fast. As she stepped into the large main room of the inn, she instinctively scanned the area. About half of the tables were occupied by farmers or warriors. None of the warriors bore crests. Taylor saw Slane's shoulders relax as he turned to a man carrying a tray filled with mugs of ale.

Taylor stepped deeper into the room, taking a table near the rear of the inn. As she slid into the seat, her gaze again swept the room, taking further stock of the occupants. A tired, overworked farmer lifted a mug of ale to his lips, the dark circles under his eyes clearly telling the tale of a man who hadn't seen much sleep lately. Taylor wondered if her eyes looked as dark and weary. Her stare moved past the farmer to a table where several warriors sat, all of them engaged in earnest conversation. One of the men glanced up at Taylor, but his gaze lingered no more than a second before he turned his attention back to his fellows. Her gaze moved on, stopping on Slane, where he stood talking with the innkeeper. She started to look away, but there was something about Slane that drew her gaze back to him. He was quite an imposing figure, taller than the innkeeper by two handbreadths. His strong hands rested on his hips as he spoke, the hard edges of his muscles plainly visible beneath the sheer fabric of his tunic. His blond mane coursed past his shoulders in a shimmering yellow-gold waterfall of hair. As if feeling her gaze on him, Slane turned to her and smiled a soft, pleasant smile. She smiled in return and kept smiling even after he'd turned away.

A morning yawn broke her reverie. *I must be more tired than I realize,* Taylor mused to herself. That was the only reason she could think of to explain the warmth that flushed into her belly at Slane's smile. *Jared would be ashamed of me,* she thought. He had taught her to stay alert, to keep her senses sharp no matter how tired her body felt. It was the only way to survive, to avoid any men her father had sent out after her, and Jared insisted it become as natural to her as taking a breath: Be wary of everyone; trust no one. Now it was second nature to her. Or so she had believed. Yet here she was, feeling muddled by a simple smile from a man she knew very little about. Why was she blindly following Slane to his brother's castle? Because she had nowhere else to go?

Or was it because Jared was gone, because she needed

someone on her side when the world seemed so against her? And Slane was the only one who was around. But she knew there was more to it than just that. She liked provoking him. She liked sparring with him. She liked Slane. He was everything she was not. He had everything she did not. And even though he so obviously disapproved of the way she lived her life, every once in a while she would catch him watching her. And there was an amiable look in his eyes, a fond look, a look that made her want to be in his arms.

No. She never wanted to feel that way.

She quickly continued her scan of the inn, turning her thoughts away from Slane. Two men—merchants by the looks of their bejeweled fingers and foppish hats—were watching her from a table near the hearth. Her perusal was interrupted by a large man rising noisily from another table. He pushed his chair back quickly, almost violently, never taking his gaze from Taylor as he left his two companions and approached her.

For a moment, she met his gaze evenly, but there was something disturbingly familiar about this fat man glowering down at her. Slowly, recognition dawned on her face and her body tensed. Taylor looked back at his table to see his two friends watching her with crooked smiles on their lips.

The fat man slammed his hands down onto the table before her. "Sully?" His chortle reverberated through the room. "I knew we'd meet up again someday." His voice was nasal, marked with an unpleasant wheezing that instantly grated on her nerves. She remembered him all right.

"Hello, Hugh," she greeted coldly. "It's been a long time."

Hugh turned, his gaze sweeping the room. "Where's Jared?"

"He's not here," she told him.

Hugh returned his stare to her, his brows furrowing. "What do you mean he's not here? You two are inseparable."

"He's not here," she repeated.

Hugh pulled out a chair and seated his bulk in it, grunting as he sat. The chair legs bowed beneath the weight. "That's a damn shame," Hugh said softly. "A damn shame." His breath whistled in and out of his squat nose.

"You still working in flesh, Hugh?" Taylor wondered.

Hugh smiled a grotesque grin, full of missing and decaying teeth. "I prefer to call it pleasure."

His laugh sent a waft of rotted meat her way and Taylor couldn't help but grimace.

"You and Jared owe me a lot of coin," Hugh said. "That girl could have brought in a lot for me."

"She was a child," Taylor almost snarled.

"Many lords like 'em young," Hugh retorted.

Taylor felt her teeth clench.

"Innocent," Hugh added, reaching across the table to rub his greasy hand up and down her arm. The trilling whistle of his breath set her teeth on edge. "The way I figure it, if you come work for me, I can make up the coin in no time. I bet you're a wild ride."

Taylor's eyes narrowed slightly. "It's like this, Hugh," she said calmly. "The world would be a better place if you weren't in it. And if you don't take your hand from me this instant, I'm going to have to make the world a better place."

Hugh stopped stroking her arm, and Taylor was pleased to see the anger in his eyes. He withdrew his hand. "I'm sorry you see it like that. Then I have two choices left. Give me the coin you owe me."

"I owe you nothing."

"You killed two of my men that night," Hugh snarled.

"And I'd kill ten more to keep a child out of your repulsive grip. Get out of here now before I have to slit your throat. You make me sick."

Hugh shot upward, overturning the table in his angered rush to get to his feet. His hand went to the dagger stuck into the sash at his waist, but Taylor was ready for him. Her sword was already freed and pointed at Hugh's rotund belly.

"What seems to be the problem?"

Taylor recognized the familiar voice and swiveled her eyes to see Slane standing at her side.

"This doesn't concern you," Hugh spat. "So back off." His shrill breathing seemed to grow louder with each passing moment.

Slane cast Taylor a cursory glance. "It does concern me. You see, the lady is with me."

"Lady?" Hugh glanced at his men. "You fellows see a *lady* anywhere near here?"

His men laughed snidely.

Taylor didn't respond to his goading, keeping the tip of her sword a mere inch from his jutting belly, the distaste for the huge man towering over her clearly etched into every line of her face.

Hugh turned his attention to Slane. "She stole something that was mine. She owes me quite a bit of coin."

Slane dipped his hand into the pouch at his waist.

Taylor pushed herself to her feet instantly, pressing her hand over Slane's to still his movement. "He gets no coin," she said quietly.

"Then you die," Hugh replied.

"That remains to be seen," Taylor snapped back.

"This can all be negotiated," Slane said. "There's no need for fighting."

Hugh glared at Taylor, his eyes red and burning with rage and wronged pride. Finally, he looked at Slane, his gaze sweeping his body as if summing him up. "Yes," he said after a long moment. "I believe we men can work this all out." His breath wheezed in and out.

Hugh swung an arm up around Slane's shoulders as if they had been friends all their lives. Taylor felt her teeth clench. She felt bile rise in her throat. She wanted to slap Hugh's arm off of Slane's shoulder.

Just as she began to lower her sword, she saw Hugh's hand dip to his sash. The dull edge of his dagger gleamed from his waist as his hand slithered down to it. Taylor rushed forward, instinctively tightening her hold on her weapon.

Hugh's hand closed over the dagger's handle and he pulled it from his sash. But he never had a chance to raise it before Taylor's weapon cut deep into his wrist. Hugh dropped the weapon, howling in pain, clutching his bleeding wrist.

Slane turned furious, shocked eyes to Taylor. She stood at the ready, half expecting Hugh's friends to join the battle, but they remained seated at the table, watching the events play out without making a move.

"The witch cut me!" Hugh protested, his voice thick with pain.

"You did that for revenge!" Slane accused Taylor. "And when his back was turned."

Amazed at Slane's verbal attack, Taylor opened her mouth to defend herself. But slowly, she closed it. She didn't need to explain her actions to anyone. Jared would certainly never have questioned her judgment. But Slane was not Jared. Taylor thrust her blade back into its sheath. Her hands were clenched so tight that they ached. The thickheaded fool! She couldn't believe he took Hugh's side over hers!

Taylor lifted her chin, refusing to acknowledge the ache in her soul. *That's how he sees me,* she thought. *As no better than Hugh. And why the hell should I set him straight? Why should I . . . ?*

"Why did you do it?" Slane asked.

She whirled to face him, her angry eyes lashing him with a thousand rebukes. She faced him furiously for the beat of a heart. At just that moment, the sun shone in through one of the inn's windows, capturing his sapphire eyes in its glow. She was furious with him, yes. Furious with him for being so damned self-righteous. Furious with him for being so damned noble. Furious with him for being the most handsome man she had ever seen. But she was more furious with herself for caring what he thought of her, for letting him get close enough to make her this angry.

She brought her steaming anger under control and faced him with a cold calm. "I guess I did it for revenge," she snapped before whirling away from him and storming outside.

Slane watched her move away. Then he looked down at the floor, where Hugh's dagger blinked up at him in the glowing light of the sun.

They traveled the entire day, pausing only twice to rest the horses Slane had purchased in Sudbury. As the sun set, they came upon an inn. Buried in the middle of the forest, the building was more like a two-story cottage than an inn. They tethered the horses in the pen, where a stable boy promised to care for them.

Slane stepped through the dimly lit doorway. Taylor followed and immediately ordered an ale. The tall, lanky innkeeper's gaze swept her; then he snorted in disapproval before turning away from her, only to reappear seconds later with an ale.

Slane spoke with the innkeeper and Taylor moved by them to wait for Slane near the stairs. The inn was totally empty. *Slane should be thankful for that,* Taylor thought. *At least he won't have to worry about me stabbing some undeserving fellow.*

Slane approached her with a weary look in his eyes. The day of traveling was getting to him, too. With a jerk of his head, he signaled her to move up the stairs toward her room.

It was late that night when Taylor descended the stairs of the inn. She found the innkeeper in a back room, mixing water and ale. A grin curved her lips as he tried to hide the bottle from her.

She held out a rolled parchment. With a trembling hand, he took the scroll, surveying it.

"Give it to Corydon," she instructed. "Tell him it's from Taylor Sullivan."

Slane stared at the ceiling, his hands clasped behind his head. It was late, but he had been unable to fall asleep. The straw was too stiff, the inn too quiet, the night too chilly. He wondered if Taylor was cold. They had traveled most of the day in silence. Now he stared at the door separating their adjoining rooms. Was she asleep? Was her hair fanning her pillow in luxurious waves of spun silk? Were her lips parted as she took in sweet breath after sweet breath? Was she naked beneath the blankets? Cursing silently, he turned onto his side, away from the door. What right did he have envisioning such things?

He forced his thoughts in another direction. Why hadn't she told him about the dagger Hugh had pulled? He had tried to talk to her while they rode, but she refused to listen, raising her defiant little chin and blatantly avoiding his efforts to apologize.

He had wrongly accused her when all she had done was defend him. *Defend me?* Slane thought. *She very possibly saved my life!* He shook his head and turned on his back again. But she had taken none of the credit she was due. She had let him believe she cut the giant for selfish reasons. And what had she done that made Hugh believe she owed him coin? He wanted to ask her, but he knew he had already done her a great disservice by assuming her guilt, so he kept his prying questions to himself.

He looked back at the door, remembering the fury in her bright eyes. She was a creature of uninhibited emotions. She was stunning, defiant, bold, and brave. Things that did not describe Elizabeth.

Elizabeth. He thought of her frail figure, her kind eyes. Her lips. But it was not Elizabeth's lips his imagination summoned. These lips had a sarcastic curve to their fullness.

Suddenly, a short cry came to his ears. A cry that had somehow been cut off. A cry coming from a very familiar voice. Taylor's! In the next instant, Slane was out of bed, sword in hand, throwing open the door that separated them.

CHAPTER ELEVEN

The sight that greeted Slane tensed every muscle into fury. One man with a cleft lip was at the bottom of Taylor's bed, holding her legs apart. Another man with a ragged scar under his left eye had a hand over her mouth and a fist knotted in the thick strands of her hair.

But that wasn't the sight that caused waves of anger to crash over Slane. That wasn't the sight that caused him to grip the handle of his blade so hard that his knuckles crackled with rage. That wasn't the sight that brought up a snarl of outrage the likes of which he had never heard in his life. It was the sight of Hugh straddling Taylor, pinning her arms to her side with his legs.

The fat man's lascivious eyes were wide, feasting on Taylor's exposed breasts. "You'll bring me more than my share," he snarled happily, his breath wheezing out in a shrill threat. "Bruised or not."

"No!" Slane roared, launching himself at the nearest

man, swinging his sword in a blind rage. The scarred man dove away from Slane's wild strike, falling over Hugh and Taylor, crushing them beneath him.

The cleft-lipped man at the foot of the bed quickly released Taylor's feet and drew his sword. Slane engaged him, crossing weapons, but his rage so consumed him that his blows were ineffective, the man cleanly deflecting them into harmless swings.

"Get off of me, you fat pig!" Taylor yelled, kicking and thrashing, trying to get free.

Hugh grabbed hold of the scarred man and pulled him off of Taylor; then he moved his bulk down her legs, effectively trapping them beneath his weight. He tried to grab her flailing arms, but one of her clenched fists smacked his chin. He immediately lashed out at her, catching Taylor in the side of the head. She went limp for a moment, and Hugh took advantage of her dazed state, shoving her hands beneath his legs. "Kill him," he ordered the men. "Then we'll break her in."

The cleft-lipped man joined the first in confronting Slane with a dagger, blocking Slane's view of Taylor. A savage fury ignited Slane and he shoved the scarred man away from him, following with a whirlwind of vicious blows. The man tried to parry again, but the rage boiling inside Slane was too great for him to deter. Slane cut through the man's defenses and shoved his blade into the man's gut. The scarred man gurgled and went down, dropping like a stone. Slane turned wild, feral eyes to the cleft-lipped man.

Fear flashed across the man's eyes. He glanced at the dagger in his hand, then at the blood-stained sword in Slane's. He let the dagger fall to the ground.

Behind the man, Slane saw Hugh pull the blanket down

from Taylor's torso over her flat stomach. "Get out of my way," Slane snarled.

The man took a hesitant step toward the door.

"Now!" Slane demanded.

The man turned and ran, fleeing the room.

"Wonderful job."

Slane looked up to face Hugh, and dread shot through him. Hugh's wounded hand held Taylor tight against him, while his good hand pressed a dagger to her white throat. The blanket was now wrapped around her body, cocooning it from Slane's view. The brown blanket dipped provocatively across her breasts, and Slane couldn't look away from her bared skin.

"We can share her, you know," Hugh suggested, following his gaze.

Sickened at the thought, Slane lifted his sword.

"No, no," Hugh warned. "You will let us pass or she will die."

Taylor seemed dazed and weak somehow. Limp in Hugh's arms. "I can't believe you let his friend go," she whispered.

Slane gritted his teeth. She was right. He should have killed the man. He should kill them all. His fist tightened around the handle of his sword.

"Let us pass," Hugh warned again in his raspy voice. He pushed the blade tighter against Taylor's flesh.

"If you hurt her, your death will be a most unpleasant one," Slane replied evenly.

"Your brave words don't fool me," Hugh snorted. "I know of your kind. Your code. You're supposed to protect her. If I kill her, you've failed—a dishonor that my death could never repair. Now step back or she dies!"

After a long, troubled moment, Slane slowly lowered his weapon. He couldn't risk Taylor's life. He knew it and

Hugh knew it. *Damn the fat man and the ugly truth of his words.* He took a step away from the door.

"I'm disappointed, Slane," Taylor said as Hugh pulled her toward the door. Her familiar mocking smile stretched across her lips. "At least spit on him or something."

Hugh moved closer and Taylor was now within a foot of Slane, held before the fat man like a shield. Taylor and Slane locked gazes for a quick second. Something flashed through her eyes. Something that was not the least bit dazed nor limp. Slane tensed, sensing something was about to happen.

Suddenly, Taylor dug her finger into the wound in Hugh's hand and pushed the dagger away from her neck with her other hand.

Hugh tossed her away with a yowl of pain, but Slane's thrust cut his cry short. Hugh glanced at his bloodied hands; then he lifted his stare to Slane. Slane pulled his sword from Hugh's stomach. Hugh grimaced, revealing yellowed teeth; then he lurched forward.

Slane easily sidestepped his rush and the giant fell heavily to the floor. He wheezed once more and then was silent.

In the instant quietness, Slane could hear his heart hammering in his chest, could feel it beating in his throat. He whirled toward Taylor. She was sitting very still on the bed, her legs tucked beneath her body. Anxiety swirled through him. Had she been hurt? He could see no blood.

The blanket swept about her body like a casual cloak. Slane could see her tiny foot peeking from beneath the blanket. His eyes moved upward, inspecting her for a wound. They moved up to her chest and the bared skin just above her breasts. In the soft light of the moon, which shone in through an open window, her skin looked as soft as a rose petal and just as delicate. His eyes moved up to her neck, but it was untouched by Hugh's dagger save for a small red welt that was quickly disappearing. Relief surged through his body. He swallowed in a parched throat. "Are you all right?" he asked.

Taylor nodded and a lock of her black hair fell forward across her shoulder.

Slane stepped closer and extended his hand toward her. She turned her gaze from Hugh's body to Slane. She lifted her hand and grasped his outstretched fingers.

The touch seared him through to his bones. He tore his gaze from hers and stared at her hand, marveling at the smallness of it before enfolding it in his. He pulled her to her feet. She rose as regally as a goddess to stand just before him, her dark hair cascading about her shoulders like a waterfall. The blanket slid a fraction lower.

Slane had a sudden desire to ease the blanket over her breasts, to gaze on their luscious, perfect peaks.

"It took you long enough," she whispered.

Suddenly, his throat felt even drier. "Did they . . . hurt you?"

"Just my pride."

Slane felt something move in his hand, and he glanced down to see that he still held her hand in his. He knew he should let go of her now, but something in his stubborn fingers refused the command his mind had given them.

The green of her eyes shone through the tendrils that coiled around her face, blazing like hot emeralds sparkling in bright sunlight. How could she stand there looking so beautiful after being viciously attacked? he wondered. God's blood! She was almost glowing. Didn't she know what she was doing to him? She knew. Slane was sure of it. The little vixen was trying to seduce him, to draw him away from his code, his oaths.

And it was working. He quickly let go of her hand and took a step back, almost tripping over his own feet in his hurry. "Yes, well . . ." He cleared his throat as he shifted his gaze to Hugh. "I'll have the innkeeper remove these bodies and—"

She straightened up, and he could have sworn he saw something akin to fear cross her face before the familiar look of nonchalance entered her eyes.

Slane faltered. Who knew what other men were looking for her? He already knew Corydon was hunting her, and if this buffoon Hugh could enter her room so easily . . . How could he just leave her on her own after all this?

How could he not?

"How did they get in?" Slane wondered.

Taylor shrugged and pulled the blanket up slightly. "They were here when I woke up."

Slane felt a twinge of disappointment as she turned her back on him. He wanted to keep looking at her beautiful face forever.

Gripping the blanket close to her chest, she looked imperious as she stepped over Hugh. When she sat on the bed, it was as if a queen was taking her royal throne.

"Did you lock the door?" he asked her.

"Do I look like a fool?"

No, he thought. He knew she had locked the door. He had reminded her to do so at least twice. Then there was only one other answer, only one person who could have opened the door. Or allowed it to be opened. The innkeeper. Slane turned to the door.

"Slane?"

He slowed his steps at the softness in her voice, not quite sure he had ever heard such hesitant uncertainty in her words before.

"Maybe you could . . . stay for a little while," she suggested.

Slane faltered. "Stay?" he repeated. Lord, how he

wanted to. But Elizabeth. No. Taylor was dangerous. He couldn't stay. Not another moment. "I can't." A long silence stretched between them. "You'll be all right if you lock the door," he urged, trying to reassure himself more than her. When she didn't reply, he looked over his shoulder at her . . . and knew he shouldn't have.

She sat with her back as straight as a board, her toes just barely touching the floor. She held the blanket in a balled fist at her chest. Her hair hung in dark waves around her shoulders, down her arms to her waist. She was a damned goddess.

"Yes," she whispered. "I suppose you're right."

Slane took a deep breath. He was glad she was being rational. He was glad she could see his side of the dilemma. He reached for the handle of the door, a great weight lifted from his shoulders.

"After all, we wouldn't want to compromise your reputation. It would be most dishonorable for you to spend more than five minutes in a room with the likes of me. Why, what would those toothless farmers think of you?"

Slane's shoulders slumped as her words stung him. Because they were the truth or because they made a mockery of who he was? Or was it both? he wondered. Slane hesitated for a moment, his sense of duty warring with his sense of right and wrong. Then he left the room, closing the door quietly behind him.

Slane cleaned his sword in his room with a rag, sheathed it, and then headed down the stairs. His eyes took in everything: the empty room, the dying fire, the long shadows on the wall. He was certain the man he had let live had long since fled the vicinity. Finally, he spotted the innkeeper seated at a table near the back of the common room, his head slumped forward, resting on his chest. As Slane moved over to him, he could see that the innkeeper's eyes were closed.

So that's how they managed to sneak by, Slane thought as he stopped before the man. *He was sleeping and they lifted the keys from him.* His outrage grew, simmering in his blood, ready to explode like an angry volcano. When he thought about what could have happened to Taylor because of this fool . . .

"Sir, I am displeased with the service here," Slane snarled in a clipped tone.

The innkeeper did not move.

Slane reached across the table and placed a firm hand on the innkeeper's shoulder. "Listen, you bloody fool—" he began, but stopped short as the man slumped forward, his face hitting the table.

Slane pulled back at the sight of the dagger that protruded from the innkeeper's back. His gaze shifted up the stairs toward Taylor's room. What had he gotten himself into? he wondered.

CHAPTER TWELVE

Slane spent the entire morning explaining to the Sheriff what had happened at the inn. Taylor would have left their corpses to rot without saying a word to anyone. But not Slane. She doubted he could even conceive of such a thought.

As it was, Slane did all the talking. The Sheriff never even bothered to ask her any questions. Not one. For that alone, she was grateful to Slane. Then, finally, the Sheriff let them go on their way. She and Slane set out for Edinbrook.

Now, after riding for hours, Taylor could see the town in the distance. Nestled in the small valley that spread out below them, small thatched buildings budded from the landscape like tiny flowers, all of them encompassed by a stone wall. Like a brooding overlord, the towering castle of Edinbrook loomed over the town from the east—a stone-faced, stern parent looking down upon its innocent children.

She looked away from the castle, back to the town, and sighed quietly. Another bed. She could get used to traveling this way. A smile curved her lips.

"You find the landscape pleasing?"

Taylor turned her gaze to Slane. He rode beside her, his body gently rolling back and forth with the horse's steps. She shifted her gaze back to the hills. A soft breeze floated to her and she inhaled the scent of the valley's flowers. "Not particularly."

Slane scowled slightly. "What did you take from Hugh to make him so angry?" he finally said.

Taylor's gaze swept his face, his furrowed eyebrows, the set of his jaw. He was used to having his questions answered—that much was obvious from the expectant look in his eyes. But it wasn't just those clear blue eyes she saw. It wasn't just the anticipation of her response that lingered there. It was his disapproval. His judgment. The way he had turned on her when she had cut Hugh. She looked away from him. "You wouldn't believe me," she answered.

"I always believe the truth," he told her.

Taylor pursed her lips in thought. She knew she could lie to him to save her own dishonorable reputation. The last thing she wanted was for Slane to see her as some mercenary with a heart of gold. Because she wasn't that. In fact, she was just the opposite. But Slane wanted the truth.

"Hugh was a worthless bag of human filth. He was probably out here looking for new flesh for his business."

Slane nodded. "A brothel."

"No," Taylor answered. "Servitude. Of course, if he couldn't get his price from a lord or a knight or even a freeman, he'd turn to pimping. He'd wear out the body and leave the woman on the street for the vultures." She'd seen him do it. She'd seen him abandon a woman so used and hurt that she couldn't defend herself against the ravages of the street. It sickened Taylor.

"Are you saying . . . that you . . ." Slane seemed shocked.

She turned her gaze to him in disbelief. She had never whored a day in her life! She sighed and shook her head. "I told you you wouldn't believe me," she murmured and spurred her horse on to a canter. He would never understand her. He could never see past the tough outer skin. And she didn't want him to.

Slane overrode her, catching her horse's reins in his hand and bringing her mount to a halt. "So you escaped?"

Taylor remembered the fighting and the screaming. "Yes," she said placatingly. "We escaped." She didn't have to mention the small girl Hugh had taken from her parents.

"With Jared's help."

"I couldn't have done it without him." Jared had fought beside her, protecting both the girl and Taylor's back.

"And Hugh wanted you back?"

"Look, it was a long time ago. Why don't we just forget it." She smiled at him, but there was such pity in his large blue eyes that it made her angry. "You fool," she growled. "It wasn't me. Hugh had stolen a gypsy girl from her mother. Jared and I—"

"You *rescued* the girl?"

His incredulous tone made her even angrier. "We were well paid," she said.

A look of comprehension cleared his face of doubt. He released the reins of her horse, nodding as if he had finally figured her out.

Taylor waited until he moved past her, spurring his horse down the road. *Yes*, she thought. *We were paid well. With a palm reading, the only payment the poor gypsy woman could afford*. And that had been just fine. It was enough just to get a child out of Hugh's horrendous clutches. But Slane didn't need to know that.

Slane dismounted, handing the reins of his horse to a stable boy. The boy beamed him a smile and led the horses away. Slane turned his gaze to Taylor, who stood in the doorway of the stables, her gaze pinned on something across the street. She had refused to even look at him after galloping into town ahead of him. But he hadn't refused to look at her. No, far from it.

She stood straight and proud, her long black hair hanging in a thick braid down her back. He had watched her that morning when they were still at the inn, trailing her fingers through it, twisting it and entwining it with the same easy grace of the ladies of the castle plaiting their hair.

He shook his head and tore his gaze from her. He would never understand how she could be a mercenary. To take money for saving a little girl from the likes of Hugh! He felt a twinge of disappointment and wasn't exactly sure why. He had no reason to expect anything more from her.

Slane moved out of the stables to stand at her side. For a moment, just a moment, he felt a strange quickening of his pulse as his gaze trailed over her smooth cheekbone to the curve of her full lips. Then she turned to look at him.

Everything stopped in that instant. Those green eyes peered into his soul, searching the very depths of his being. They reached deep and pulled forth something warm and tender that he didn't know dwelled within him. The feeling surrounded him like the heat from a gently flaming hearth.

He quickly shifted his gaze away. He hadn't realized he

had been holding his breath until he let it all out in a quiet rush. He blinked for a moment, unsure of what had just happened. Uneasy, he handed her the robe he had bought from a merchant in Sudbury. "Put this on," he instructed and headed toward the heart of town.

In a moment, she was at his side, and when he glanced down, he was happy to see that the hem of the brown robe swished around her booted feet. It was a little too big on her, but it would do for now as a disguise. Corydon knew who she was. With her face hidden by the robe, she would at least have a chance to escape.

She hadn't even questioned him, Slane realized with a smile. Was there an understanding forming between them? He felt a moment of jubilation ... until he saw a large garrison of soldiers heading in their direction. Slane recognized them immediately and faltered. Their black tunics announced their allegiance: Corydon.

He took a step backward and turned, only to see another, smaller group of black-clad knights heading down the street.

Taylor jerked forward, but Slane caught her wrist and pulled her into the shadows of a nearby doorway.

Slane glanced furtively up and down the street and was dismayed to see that the street was suddenly devoid of the usual assortment of peasants and other marketplace patrons. If they stepped out into the street now, they would surely be seen.

He heard the handle of the door behind them rattle and glanced down to see Taylor's hand on it. But it wouldn't budge even under her insistent shaking.

Slane glanced down the street. The soldiers were coming closer. There were so many of them. If they fought now, it would only mean Slane's death and Taylor's capture.

"Stand here," Taylor instructed, pulling him in front of her like a shield.

At least that would protect her, Slane thought.

But suddenly, she threw herself at him, wrapping her arms around his neck. Slane would have tumbled backward, had he not braced himself by splaying his hands on the sides of the doorway. He opened his mouth to reprimand her, but she quickly pressed her lips and her body against his.

Stunned into immobility, Slane gaped as she slid her lips across his, pressed her tiny body to his quickly hardening one. He jerked and tried to pull away, but her embrace held him tightly to her chest.

Slane managed to slide his lips off of hers and exclaim, "What in God's blood are you doing, woman? Have you lost your senses?"

"Unless you want to lose more than your senses, you'll return my affection and make it good," she warned in a whisper, nibbling his ear.

Jolts of pleasure shot through Slane's body. His mind told him to resist her, but his body was already succumbing to her seduction. Then his quickly fogging mind focused enough to realize what she was doing. A desperate disguise: a harlot and her customer.

She slid her lips across his jaw and pressed her lips against his again, running her hands through his hair, clinging to him as if his lips were the only thing that could save her. Slane wrapped his arms around her tiny waist, wanting to reassure her. He knew it had to look convincing or they were done for.

He ran his tongue lightly across her lips, coaxing her to open to him. He felt her quiver beneath him as she parted her lips. She was either a very talented actress or . . .

Distantly, Slane heard footsteps march closer in the

street, and he pulled her tighter against him. He thrust his tongue deep into her mouth. A soft groan escaped her parted lips. A groan that sent his world tumbling end over end.

The curves of her body fit snugly against the ridges in his; her full breasts pressed heavily against the battle-hewn muscles in his chest. Tingles followed the trail her fingers left along his skin; prickles of heat inflamed his soul. The essence of her seemed to take on solid form, enclosing him in a swirl of passion. He no longer heard the footsteps in the streets, no longer cared if they were caught; he only wanted this moment to go on forever.

Then a man cleared his throat behind Slane. Even as Taylor's kiss warmed his body, the threat of danger pierced the moment like a dagger. He almost reached for his sword.

Taylor's hands moved over his waist and down to his buttocks. He battled with control as she gently squeezed, running her hands over the firm rounded portion.

He pulled back slightly to gaze deeply into the green pools of her eyes. What did she want of him? Did she truly do this for disguise? Or did she dare to challenge him so blatantly? He ran his fingers through the long locks of her glorious hair, loosening it from that accursed braid. He almost growled with the passion she had aroused within him. Then he claimed her lips again with a fierce painful lashing. If she was toying with him, he would teach her what it was like to enrage his lust so powerfully.

She matched his kiss, his intense need with a longing of her own. He felt her tremble beneath the onslaught of his kiss. He wanted her as he had never wanted anything in his life. He wanted to see what her body looked like beneath the leather armor she wore. He wanted to kiss her breasts and her stomach and . . .

Suddenly, she tore away from him. Slane stared at her

for a long moment, trying desperately to regain control of his heated body. She stood before him like a vanquishing hero, her chin raised, her eyes glittering with—

With what? Was that passion in her eyes? Or was it mockery?

Slane felt a chill seep through his clothes to his heated skin as the cold reality of what had just happened set in. What had he been doing? What had he been thinking?

"You made it good," she said. "Damn good. Very convincing. Even to me. But the soldiers are gone."

And indeed, they were gone. Long gone. The streets were empty.

He stood stoically for a long moment. Could she really have been acting? Could that kiss have meant nothing to her when it had enflamed him so? "Yes, they are," he said awkwardly. He stepped away from her out into the street. He had been wrong to kiss her so passionately, to want her like that. He was betrothed, for the love of God!

"Don't worry, Slane," Taylor said, patting his back. "I won't tell anyone you liked it."

Slane whirled on her, a fierce rage consuming him. "We will not speak of this again!" he shouted. "I did what I had to do, but that's all there was to it."

For a moment, Taylor stood with her mouth open, her eyes wide. Then she brushed past him, but tripped over the long hem of her robe. Angrily, she bent, grabbed the hem, and slid the robe over her head. She carefully folded it and held it out to him. When he reached for it, she dropped it in the dirt and dust of the street.

Taylor turned her back on him and walked quickly down the road.

Slowly, Slane bent down and picked up the robe. The lavender smell of her seemed to permeate the fabric. He brought the robe to his face and filled his lungs with the essence of Taylor Sullivan.

Taylor couldn't even look at Slane. Her anger and hurt were too fresh. She couldn't bury them that easily.

Because of Corydon's soldiers in Edinbrook, Slane had decided it would be safer if they slept in the woods. She had slept restlessly on the hard, cold ground of the forest.

But it wasn't because of the natural elements, the rocks jabbing at her back, the shrill wind, the unsettling cries of strange animals, and Taylor knew it. His fierce reaction to her feeble attempt at communication after the kiss had wounded her deeply. She hadn't expected the passion that had ignited her body at his touch, his kiss. And before she even had a chance to understand it, he had rejected her, humiliating her.

She still burned to tell him about the so-called payment she and Jared had received for helping the gypsy girl, but she refused to give Slane what he claimed to want. The truth. *Let him think of me as he will,* she thought. There was something morbidly satisfying about keeping the truth to herself. She'd be damned if she'd seek his approval.

She had looked with distaste at the berries he had offered her to break her fast and turned her back to him. Now she saddled her horse, readying the animal to continue the trip to Castle Donovan. Why was she even going there?

She should end this farce and bid Slane farewell. But what would she do then? Look for another job? Perhaps she could find work at Castle Donovan. It was as good a chance as any.

Taylor put her hand on the saddle, preparing to ease herself up. That was when she heard the silence of the forest around her. The eerie quiet where there should have been dozens of different sounds filling the air. She froze, remembering the attack by the black-clad knights when Jared was with her.

Taylor eased her sword from its sheath, her eyes scanning the surrounding woods carefully, looking for any signs of attackers. The wind blew softly through the trees, rustling the leaves and branches.

As she turned, she saw Slane bent over, pulling a belt tight on his horse. He stood to inspect the bridle and caught her gaze. She saw the tension coil around his body as his hand flew to his sword, his eyes wide with alarm.

Taylor heard her horse nicker behind her . . . and knew it was too late. She whirled—only to find the tip of a sword pressed against her throat.

CHAPTER THIRTEEN

Slane's body exploded with motion as he bolted forward, moving to Taylor's aid. The sharp edge of the attacker's blade pushed dangerously close to the soft hollow of her throat. He was going to be too late. She was going to die. The thoughts came unbidden, igniting a powerful fear in his body.

But suddenly, surprisingly, Taylor launched herself forward into her attacker's arms, flinging her hands around his body, laughing with true delight.

Slane stumbled and almost fell as the man swept his arms around Taylor in a cloak of joy. Slane immediately straightened up, holding his body as rigid and tense as a board. A fierce wave of resentment shot through him, and he wanted to run the man through.

Why didn't she smile at *him* the same way? But the thought was preposterous! Why should she? And why should he even want her to?

"I can't believe it!" Taylor was exclaiming. "What are you doing here?"

Slane's gaze slid to the man. His deep blue eyes gazed at Taylor with such delight that Slane wanted to hit that square jaw of his and knock the smile from his lips. He hated the man instantly. He hated the man for being able to make Taylor so happy. Slane's jaw clenched, his eyes narrowed.

"I heard about Jared," the man answered.

Sadness crept into Taylor's eyes as her brows met in a scowl of pain. And suddenly, Slane felt guilt enfolding him in a shroud of shame. What was he thinking? Why was he being so selfish?

"Yes," she said softly, disengaging herself from the man.

"I wanted to know you were all right," the man said.

Slane stepped forward. "She's all right," he snapped. Taylor turned her gaze to him, and Slane felt the look of pain spear him like an arrow.

The man shifted his gaze to Slane. "Who are you?" he said evenly.

"I was going to inquire the same of you," Slane replied.

"This is Slane Donovan," Taylor said. "Slane, this is Alexander Hawksmoor."

Alexander! The word sent tremors of trepidation through Slane's body. Was this the same Alexander of whom she had been so enamored years ago?

"You can put your sword away," Taylor advised.

Slane looked down as if shocked that he still held the weapon tightly in his fist. He sheathed his blade as she returned her gaze to her friend.

"I'm fine," Taylor told Alexander.

"Are you sure?"

"Why wouldn't she be?" Slane demanded. "She is in my care."

Again, Alexander's and Taylor's gazes swiveled to him. Slane suddenly felt like an outsider listening in on a private conversation. His fists clenched tight and his teeth ground together hard.

Alexander ignored him. "Sully, you're all right?" His voice lowered and he went on. "He's not forcing you to travel with him?"

Every muscle in Slane's body stiffened.

"No," she said.

Alexander cocked his head and gave her a suspicious look.

She smiled. "He's paying for food and lodging."

Alexander looked around at the forest. "Pretty cheap lodging."

"Last night was better," Taylor said. "Unfortunately, you know how I attract trouble at inns."

Alexander nodded. "That's how I tracked you. And I saw you leaving town last night." He motioned to the woods. "I followed you here."

"That easy, eh?" Slane asked.

Taylor turned to him with her hands on her hips. "Alexander is an even better tracker than Jared is." Taylor paused, then softly added, "Was."

Alexander locked gazes with Slane. "It wasn't difficult."

Unable to stand another moment in this man's presence, Slane turned away from them and moved to his horse. Their voices floated to him on a breeze.

"You can't keep still," Alexander said. "Not for a moment. There are too many people looking for you."

Slane grabbed the reins of his horse a little too roughly and the steed whinnied and took a step back. Leading his horse, he returned to Taylor's side. "Are you ready?"

Taylor looked at Alexander with something akin to longing in her eyes.

Slane's hand tightened around the reins.

"Will you travel with us?" she asked.

Slane opened his mouth to object, but slammed it shut into a tight-lipped sneer.

Alexander cast a glance at Slane. "I'd love to. For a while."

Slane knew he should be grateful for another sword to help protect Taylor. But he wasn't. Tension, distrust, and dislike coiled his body as tight as a spring. He didn't want this Alexander with him . . . or rather, with Taylor. He swung himself up onto the horse.

What was wrong with him? It would do Taylor good to have an old friend with her. Especially after Jared's recent death. But why did it have to be Alexander?

Alexander dismounted, tethering his horse to a tree near the stream. He turned in time to see Taylor glance at a brooding Slane. Donovan had ridden a good two horse paces in front of them the entire trip, his back ramrod straight, his hands clutching the reins of the horse so tightly that they turned white.

Taylor was pensive the entire ride. She had glanced repeatedly at Slane with that troubled furrow etched in her brow and the thoughtful look in her eyes. Something had happened between them, Alexander was sure.

Taylor swung herself from her horse and bent at the stream, rinsing her face with a handful of water. She stood and faced him.

There had been a time when he had seen infatuation shining from those eyes. Now there was only friendship. And it was as it should be.

"What do you think you're doing?" he asked softly.

"What do you mean?"

"Don't play that game with me," Alexander warned. "I know all about those wide-eyed looks of yours." Taylor laughed softly, but Alexander continued. "This Corydon is no fool." He watched the laughter drain from her face and caught just a glimpse of the anger that narrowed her eyes before she turned away. "He's not far behind you."

Sully moved to her horse and opened her pack, busying herself with fumbling through the items inside.

Alexander stepped up behind her. "He means to capture you or kill you. Either way it's crazy to leave such an obvious trail for him."

"I don't know what you mean," she snapped.

Alexander grabbed her arm and spun her around to face him. "I know what you've been doing."

"You don't know anything. We weren't important enough for you six years ago, so don't pretend I am now."

"I have a job," Alexander said, his spine straightening.

"You did then, too," she said quietly and turned back to her horse. "You left us when we could have used your help."

Alexander stared at her back. "Jared had his way of doing things. I had mine. There was no way to reconcile them." After a long moment, he asked, "Why are you going to Castle Donovan?"

She shrugged. "Maybe Slane's brother will be looking to hire mercenaries."

Alexander scowled at her. "You're impetuous. You're reckless. You can't work under a noble without Jared here to smooth things over."

"Then why don't you take Jared's place?" she said sarcastically.

Alexander sighed. "I still have gypsies to hunt."

Taylor shook her head. "Still on that campaign, huh?" Ridding the land of the gypsy scourge was a quest he had begun long ago. He was not going to give it up to be her companion. Still, he couldn't help but feel the old guilt raise its head. She had no one now. She was as alone as he felt. Alexander placed a hand on her shoulder and squeezed gently. Taylor shrugged his hand off her shoulder, turning away from him. Alexander stood for a long moment, staring at her tense back. They had been the best of friends long ago. And he knew she was hurting. He reached around her and pulled her against his chest, wrapping his arms around her stiff body.

She resisted at first, fighting the gesture of friendship. But then she sighed and leaned into him heavily.

"I wish you luck with this crazy scheme of yours. Whatever it is that you're planning, I hope it turns out as you wish," Alexander whispered. But he knew it wouldn't. And he knew there was only one way to protect her. His gaze shifted to Slane Donovan.

Slane pulled a loaf of bread from his saddlebags. He had bought the loaf back in Sudbury, and the crust was now hard and flaky. He broke off a small piece and raised it to his lips, turning to look for Taylor. But the small chunk of bread never reached his mouth as he froze at the sight that greeted him. Fury flamed through his body with every stroke of Alexander's hand on Taylor's back.

A nagging pain flared in Slane's jaw, and he realized he was clenching it so tightly that his muscles ached. Taylor rested her head against Alexander's shoulder with all the familiarity of lovers. With the ease she displayed around this man, he half expected her to be rolling in the grass with him by nightfall.

He whirled away from the troubling scene, and more, his sudden impulse to bash this man's face in. He looked down to find his hands were clenched into fists, the bread smashed between them.

Disgusted with himself, he tossed the loaf away. He should be thinking of Elizabeth, alone, waiting for him, instead of dwelling on another man touching Taylor.

He forced himself to walk calmly to the stream. It wasn't his concern what Taylor did with her life. He had his own life to live. Elizabeth. He forced an image of her to the front of his mind, struggling to find it in his memory, shocked at how long it took to remember that she had large brown eyes. Large brown eyes that would look at him with complete trust. Over the course of the year, the unease between Elizabeth and himself had diminished. Now they could sit in companionable company and even laugh together. He remembered her soft little chuckles, the way her hand covered her mouth as she laughed, almost as if it had been unladylike to show any sign of amusement. He missed her. Yes, as one would miss a sister.

He glanced over his shoulder at Taylor and Alexander, catching a glimpse of them between the horses. They had separated but still stood close. Close enough for Alexander to reach out and caress her cheek.

Slane scowled. What was Taylor doing to him? It was the kiss, he told himself. The lingering, ghostly taste of her lips. He had to remember his duty. He had to see her back to Castle Donovan. Beyond that, she wasn't his concern.

"Donovan?"

Slane turned to find Alexander standing beside him. His jaw started to throb.

"This is as far as I ride," Alexander told him.

Relief coursed through Slane so completely and intensely that he suddenly felt light-headed. His hands opened; his jaw relaxed. The muscles in his shoulders loosened. All he could do was nod in response.

Alexander chuckled softly. He cast a glance back at Taylor, and Slane followed his gaze. She stood beneath a large maple tree, looking small and very vulnerable. When Alexander returned his eyes to Slane, there was a hardness there. "Sully's been leaving scrolls behind for Corydon, inviting him to find her."

"No!"

"It was one of the ways I found you so easily. And rest assured that Corydon's men are very close behind."

"She wouldn't do that," Slane said, casting a glance at Taylor. She had seated herself beneath the tree, her knees drawn up to her chest.

Alexander shrugged. "I found a letter in Sudbury and another at an inn between Sudbury and Edinbrook."

"You're lying," Slane snarled.

Alexander's eyes narrowed slightly. "If I were a lesser man, I'd have to challenge you for besmirching my good name. Just keep an eye on her." He turned away from Slane, heading for his horse.

Why? Slane asked himself. *Why in heaven's name would she do something like that?* It made no sense. But what about Taylor Sullivan ever made sense?

CHAPTER FOURTEEN

Taylor studied the thatched ceiling of the Village Inn in Trenton. The candle burning beside her bed threw shadows up onto the ceiling. Deep shadows. Dark shadows. Black shadows. Black shadows that looked like men dressed in black robes. The flames flickered, taunting her with shadows that stalked along the thatch, wielding their shadowy weapons as they hunted their prey.

Her anger had kept her awake well into the night, her determination fueling her mission. Seeing Alexander, talking of Jared, had only served to reignite her rage. Jared would be avenged. She would see to that. No matter what the cost to herself. Or even to Slane if he stood in the way.

Slane. Why did he leave her senses so muddled and confused? Everything else seemed simple and clear. Simple because there was only *one* thing: Avenge Jared. That was all that mattered. *If I concentrate on that, then nothing else can interfere.*

Finally, she rose from her bed, took a piece of parchment and a small container from her sack and settled down on the floor beside the bed. She lifted her right hand and stared for a moment at the ring that encircled her finger. Two crossed swords over an S. The Sullivan crest. Her mother's ring.

Taylor plugged the small container with one finger and turned it upside down. She carefully replaced it on the floor. A large black circle now covered the tip of her index finger. She carefully smeared the ink over the crest on the ring and then pressed the crest to the paper, giving it an official seal. She wiped her finger and the ring on the blanket.

Then she rolled the parchment and stood, moving to the door. She paused, listening for any sounds, but there was no noise. Carefully, she opened the door and glanced down the hallway. Slane's door was closed, the hallway empty.

Taylor headed out of her room, quietly closing the door. She moved out into the common room, searching for the innkeeper. She found the man fixing a broken chair leg. His head was bent over his work, his bald head reflecting the dying firelight from the hearth. He glanced up at her as she approached.

She held out the rolled parchment to him. "If a lord named Corydon comes here, give this to him," she instructed. "Tell him it's from Taylor Sullivan."

The innkeeper lifted his gaze to lock with hers, then shifted it to the parchment. He reached out to take the offered paper, but suddenly another, larger hand darted in and snatched it from Taylor's fingers.

"I'll take that."

Taylor jumped slightly and spun to find Slane standing behind her, the parchment firmly in his grip. Her heart lurched in her chest. She reached out to seize the scroll from his hand, but he deftly moved it out of her reach.

He unrolled the parchment and his blue eyes studied the paper for a long moment before rising to gleam at her.

She swallowed hard, every instinct in her body telling her to run, to escape the fury she could see burning in his gaze. Instead, she lifted her head and boldly stared back at him.

His eyes never left hers as he told the innkeeper, "If you'll excuse us."

Taylor could hear the barely restrained anger in his voice. Shivers of dread shot up her body.

With an understanding nod, the innkeeper set the chair aside and moved off down the hall.

Slane's heated gaze bored into her. He lowered his hand and she saw it clench around the parchment. For one, wild moment, she thought he would strike her. And he did, with his words.

"Are you mad?" he demanded in a hushed whisper. "Do demons possess you?"

Oh, yes, demons possessed her. But not the kind he meant. Her chin rose a notch.

He lifted his clenched fist to hold the wadded parchment before her eyes. "What is this all about?"

She opened her mouth to explain, but then stopped. How could she tell him of her fierce determination to avenge Jared's death? Of her agony over losing him? She had no intention of exposing herself to his ridicule. She closed her mouth and moved to turn away.

Slane grabbed her arm in a brutal grip and dragged her deeper into the common room, closer to the hearth. Her eyes shifted anxiously to the flames before she ripped free of Slane's grip and moved away from the hearth toward the stairs. Slane quickly followed, grabbing her arm to halt her. "You will tell me what you intended with these letters. Did you intend to betray me?"

Confusion flashed in her eyes. Then she shook her head. "I intended for Corydon to find me," she admitted.

Slane's eyes narrowed to mere glints of hot blue. "He killed your friend. Have you a wish to join Jared?"

Taylor's gaze narrowed to match Slane's.

He shook her arm. "We were lucky last time to escape unscathed. Jared was not so lucky. He died protecting you!"

Her own guilt spoken on Slane's lips drove a dagger into her heart. Her vision suddenly blurred.

"He sacrificed his life for your freedom. Well, I'm not going to give my life for you." He tossed the parchment to the floor and moved to step past her. "You can play that game alone."

"He knew the risks of traveling with me," she snarled. "He knew his life was in danger every day he spent with me."

Slane whirled on her, his teeth ground tight. "He was your friend! And now you court his killer like some lover! If Corydon knows where we're headed, don't you think he'll do everything in his power to stop us?"

Taylor faced Slane with clenched fists. Her entire body trembled with her whirling emotions—grief, anger, disappointment. "That's what I'm counting on."

Slane took a step forward. "You *are* mad," he hissed with conviction. He grabbed her shoulders suddenly and Taylor could see the anguish in his blue eyes. "Do you know what he'll do to you?"

"Do you know what I'll do to him?" Taylor gritted.

Slane stared at her for a long moment as if reading her

deepest thoughts. The anger faded as understanding slowly lit his eyes. Something washed over Slane's face and his grip eased on her shoulders. "That's very honorable of you, Taylor, but—"

"Honor has nothing to do with it," she retorted vehemently, jerking free of his hold. "Jared was not just my friend—he was my family. I would be dead if it wasn't for him. I owe him that much."

Slane stood motionless, apparently unmoved by her confession.

Shaken by the fierce emotions raging in her body, she turned her back on him, facing the flickering shadows thrown by the dancing flames of the hearth. She crossed her arms before her heated body.

"You think you stand a chance against Corydon?"

She raised her chin in defiance. She didn't care. All she knew was she had to try.

"He'll kill you, and then your death and Jared's will be for naught." Slane took a step closer. She could feel his gaze on her, the nearness of his body. "You don't want his death to be unavenged, do you?"

"No," she said after a moment.

"Then join forces with my brother," Slane suggested.

"I don't need anyone's help," Taylor insisted.

"Corydon has men to protect him, guards with him all the time. He is not a foolish man, or I would have killed him myself a long time ago for daring to lay his sights on Donovan lands." He stepped around her to look at her face. "With Richard's men and resources, you can avenge Jared's death. I think deep down you know that."

Taylor stared at the wavering shadows on the wall. A log popped and sparks flew into the air behind her. She knew he was right. But the fact remained that she didn't trust nobles. To trust this Richard, to ally herself with him? She didn't know if she could do that.

She turned to tell Slane that, but the tender way he was staring at her caught her off guard; she could have sworn she saw admiration in his eyes. She shut her mouth and took a deep breath. "I suppose you're right," she found herself saying.

Slane captured her hand in his and a smile lit his face. Taylor suddenly found it hard to breathe. He lifted her knuckles to his lips. When they touched her skin, a powerful shock seared through her body. She eased her hand free of his hold.

His smile wouldn't fade. "Then we ride to Castle Donovan," he proclaimed. "We should be there within the week, if the weather holds."

But she wasn't listening to his words; she was massaging her knuckles. A strange prickling sensation remained where his lips had caressed her skin. She knew that joining forces with Richard was the only way to defeat Corydon and avenge Jared's death, but she couldn't stop the nagging feeling that this was too easy. Why would Richard join forces with her?

As she turned away to return to her room, Slane halted her by gently grabbing her elbow. "No more letters?" Slane asked softly.

Taylor shook her head in agreement. "No more letters."

He ran a finger along the length of her jawline, bestowing on her another smile. It warmed her insides, blanketing her in a rush of delight. She couldn't help but grin back. Then he turned away from her, and she found that her moment in the sun was gone. Slapped back to reality, her grin faded and apprehension replaced it.

* * *

Just as they reached Sherville, a misty rain began to saturate the air. They ducked inside an inn just in time to miss the downpour.

Slane had never seen so many people crammed into an inn at one time before. Some of the people seemed sick beyond anything he had ever experienced himself. Their faces were pale, their skin hanging in loose folds on their bones.

Slane shouldered his way through the peasants to the innkeeper to secure their lodging. When he turned back to the inn's common room, he was frowning. Near the back of the room, a man coughed harshly and bent over, clutching at his chest as if it were on fire.

"This damn scourge is everywhere," Slane heard one man mutter.

"Everyone who can still stand is fleeing the city," another voice added.

Slane made his way to the table, where Taylor waited for him among a dozen other men and women; every table in the place was just as overcrowded. Slane sat on the end of the bench, opposite her, and reached for one of the ales the bar wench had just set down in front of him. He took a long drink and set the mug back down. "I got us a room here for the night," he said.

She nodded slightly to indicate she had heard him, but she said nothing. She brushed a lock of hair from her face, her eyes on the man beside her. His arm shoved into her ribs as he ate. She moved over farther, but Slane could see the irritation etched in the tight lines around her mouth.

She glanced at him, scowling fiercely and stood, swiping

one of the ales from the table. "I think I'll go up to my room now."

Slane deliberately cleared his throat, drawing her gaze. "*Our* room," he corrected her.

She stopped cold. "What?"

"The innkeeper only had one room left. It was probably the last room left in this whole town." Slane saw a troubled look sweep over her features.

"Aren't you worried about your reputation?" she wondered.

"I have little choice."

Taylor whirled away from the table, her mug held tightly in her shaking hand. As she pushed her way through the throng of people, she was shoved from behind. She jerked forward, her mug flying free of her hold. It landed on the floor and rolled, leaving a trail of lukewarm ale behind it. Taylor righted herself, whirling on the hapless man who jostled her.

Slane felt his spine stiffen. Was she going to run the poor farmer through?

The man was apologetic, sincerely begging her forgiveness. Taylor grumbled something that made the poor farmer's face turn pale; then she stormed for the door.

Slane shook his head and rose, clutching his mug of ale, and followed her. Once outside, he saw her sitting beneath the cover of a large tree with her head buried in her arms. Rain fell lightly around her. He remembered that, when he had first hired her and Jared, she had seemed so cocky, so confident—confident enough to lie through her teeth about her true identity and get away with it. But the last few weeks had been too much. She had lost her closest friend. She had learned that her father—a man who had not given a damn about her in eight years—wanted to see her. She seemed overwhelmed by it all.

The shadows thrown by the gently swaying tree cast her in darkness, allowing only a teasing glimpse of her when the moonlight happened to shine through the thin clouds.

Slane knew he should leave her alone, knew she needed time to sort everything out, but somehow he couldn't stay away from her. He hunched his shoulders and dashed across the road through the rain. He sat down in the grass beside her, casting furtive glances in her direction.

"I don't want your pity," she told him.

"I'm not giving it," Slane said. "I just want you to know that you're not alone."

She snorted softly in disbelief.

He handed his mug to her and she cast him a speculative glance before accepting it.

Slane knew now that she wasn't what she appeared to be. She pretended to be someone who was strong and unfeeling, someone who didn't care what was right. And yet she felt things very strongly. She had a strong sense of honor. And she had saved his life from Hugh's dagger, never once taking credit for it. He chanced a glance at her.

In a stray ray of moonlight, her hair shone like black onyx. Slane wanted to touch the dark silkiness, to see if it truly was as soft as it looked. He knew he shouldn't, but in the next instant, his hand was rising to touch her hair. It was softer than he had even imagined. His eyes shifted to hers. They were so bright, so expectant. And there was pain in there—pain that Slane wanted desperately to relieve.

He cupped her cheek in his palm, rubbing it with his thumb. Against her moonlight-white skin his shadowed hand looked black.

His gaze returned to her eyes. The brightest, most precious emerald gems he had ever seen stared back at him, brilliant, sparkling. "Taylor," he whispered.

"Slane, don't," she murmured.

He wasn't sure he understood.

"I don't think I could stand—" She pulled her face free from his touch and stood. "Maybe we should go inside."

Slane rose before her to tower over her. "What, Taylor?" But she would not turn back to him.

"Have I hurt you somehow?" he asked.

"I'm just protecting your reputation," she answered quietly. "I don't want you to be found out here alone with the likes of me."

"Do you think you endanger my reputation so much?"

"I think you're afraid of me," she answered.

"Afraid of you?" Slane laughed.

But Taylor was not laughing. She turned to him and her incredible innocent beauty did indeed make him fearful. He suddenly knew he would do anything for this creature, this woman who was driving him crazy with need. His laughter stopped instantly, catching in his throat. He knew he should look away before she saw the truth in his eyes, but when he saw her sarcastic grin he knew he was too late.

She began to move past him.

Slane recognized the indifference in her face, the shield she used so effectively to hide her feelings. He hated that sarcastic side to her. He grabbed her arms, halting her movement. "Don't. Don't raise that wall to me, Taylor. I've seen the person you can be. I've seen the person who hides behind that wall. Don't shut me out. I care for you." He saw the determination reinforce the wall in the way she angled her chin, in that stubborn glare in her eyes. Slane shook her slightly. "Do you hear me?"

"I heard," she whispered. "I just can't."

"Why?" he asked in agony, refusing to release her, afraid she would slip back behind the wall.

Taylor's eyes darted from one of his to the other, as if desperately searching for something.

"Why?" he demanded, shaking her hard, desperately. He had to know. She had to tell him. Why wouldn't she let him comfort her?

"I'd destroy you," she whispered.

Shocked, Slane released her, and she raced into the misty rain, disappearing in the shadows beyond the inn.

CHAPTER FIFTEEN

Taylor spent the night walking in circles around the inn, trying to find something to occupy her mind, trying to think of anything but Slane. Anything but the way he made her feel.

The rain had stopped, and the moon was taking its downward descent as she returned to the inn. She pushed the door open and found that the common room was now virtually empty. One small boy sat in a corner, his head nodding into his shoulder. He came to his feet at once when she entered.

Taylor smiled at him and waved him back into his seat, shaking her head. The boy slowly, dubiously, eased himself back into his corner. He couldn't have been more than eight. He should have been in bed long ago.

Taylor's gaze shifted to the stairs. She didn't even know which room was hers. Theirs. She sighed. *Looks like I'll share the corner with the boy,* she thought.

"You ready?"

She jumped at the deep rumble and swung around, her hand going to her sword handle. Deep blue eyes watched her movements with an intensity that saw through to her soul. She relaxed her grip, easing her hand from the weapon, even though she felt no lessening of the tension in her shoulders. Her eyes assessed him with a quick glance. "You waited for me?" she asked suspiciously.

"Of course," Slane responded, turning toward the stairs.

She watched his tunic stretch across his strong shoulder muscles as he reached for the banister. "Oh," she said, following him. "Had to make sure I didn't change my mind about those notes."

Slane halted and Taylor almost slammed into his back. He turned and gazed down at her. "No," he said plainly. "I had to make sure you knew which room was ours."

Ours. The word sent shivers through her body.

He turned his back to her and continued up the stairs. Unnerved, Taylor glanced around the common room. She spotted the boy, again asleep in the corner, his chin on his chest. A sense of envy filled her at the peaceful look on his face, and she found herself shaking her head as she followed Slane to their room.

She had hoped to be so exhausted that she would fall asleep the instant she got into bed. But as she followed Slane into the room, she knew this was not to be. There was barely enough room for the bed, let alone two people. Taylor felt uneasy and out of place. She glanced down the hallway as if an escape route would suddenly open.

"Are you going to leave the door open all night?" he wondered.

Her sarcasm returned with whiplash severity. "I thought it might help to protect your reputation." She stepped into the room.

He turned to her then, and they were almost chest to chest. She could see the weariness in the black lines beneath his eyes. "Maybe you should be more concerned with your own reputation."

"My reputation?" she echoed, her voice rising a notch. "I don't think it could get worse."

Slane took a step toward her and her breath caught in her throat. His chest just barely touched hers. "I think it could get worse," he said in a throaty whisper. "Don't you?"

Taylor opened her mouth to reply, but nothing came out. Her throat was suddenly as dry as parchment paper.

Slane stared down at her with those infinitely blue eyes that reminded her of a cloudless sky. He lifted his arm and it brushed her shoulder. *He's going to kiss me,* she thought. Her gaze dropped to his lips, anticipating the feel of their brush against hers.

Something banged shut behind her, and it took a moment for her to realize that it was the door closing. *I'm alone in a room with Slane,* she thought. *A small room. A very small room with only one bed.* Heat flared through her veins.

"Taylor," he whispered in something close to a sigh.

Her body trembled and she realized that it was from desire—the desire to be kissed by Slane. Of his own free will.

"I'm tired. We've got a long day tomorrow," he said.

Tired. So her plan had worked. Too bad it hadn't worked on her. Disappointment flooded through her as Slane stepped away from her and cold reality slapped her in the face. There would be no kiss.

"You should get some sleep, too," he said, bending down next to the bed to settle onto the floor.

"You're sleeping on the floor?"

"Where else would you have me sleep? Out in the hallway?"

Taylor lifted the ripped fabric that covered the bed. "There's only one blanket."

Slane waited expectantly for her to continue.

"It's not big enough to cover both of us."

"Then it shall cover you," he stated simply and lay down on the floor, turning his back to her.

Taylor stared at the blanket in her hand for a moment, then dropped it back onto the bed, plopping down after it. She unstrapped her sword and laid it on the bed beside her. Then she pulled her boots off, tossing them unceremoniously to the floor, and pulled the blanket up over her body.

She snorted slightly. Who said she wanted him to kiss her anyway?

Her eyes drifted closed.

Taylor awoke with a start. She was soaked with perspiration, her tunic clinging to her wet skin. She remembered dreaming of flames and Jared and black-clad men with glowing red eyes. She reached out in the darkness to find her sword and relaxed slightly.

In the moonlight that shone through the window, she saw Slane sleeping on the floor beside the bed. She reached out a hand to wake him, but stopped cold. What could she tell him? That she was frightened like a child?

Taylor swung her legs from the bed, but as the straw rustled, she froze. Her eyes moved to Slane, but he hadn't stirred. Quietly grabbing her sword, she stood up. She cast another cautious glance at Slane. Then she picked up her boots and headed for the door.

She reached for the handle.

"Where are you going?"

She jumped. Slane was still lying on the floor, but his eyes were open.

"To get an ale," she explained in a whisper as if still trying not to wake him.

"I don't think it's wise to go down to the common room by yourself."

"Would you like to hold my hand while I go to the privy?" she quipped. "Or maybe you can spoon-feed me my meals since I'm clearly not capable of doing anything by myself."

After a long moment, Slane answered, "At least put on the cloak I bought."

She grabbed the cloak he tossed to her, then headed out of the room. She paused in the hallway to pull on her boots and don the cloak before descending to the common room. She ordered an ale from the weary innkeeper and took a seat in the back of the room, in the shadows.

Staring into her ale, Taylor pondered the feelings that had coursed through her when Slane had touched her. She had felt warm and . . . loved. Love? Ha, she scoffed at herself. She knew there was no such thing as love. What she and Slane could share would only be lust. She wondered if what she was feeling was the same feeling that had gotten her mother killed.

Her mother. Even now, eight years later, the memory was still very painful. Taylor swiped at the tears in her eyes and raised the mug to her lips. Maybe it was so painful for her because she never understood how her father could have killed her mother. Or what kind of love would cause her mother to have so much faith in a man who never showed up to rescue her. It couldn't have been love. Her father couldn't have loved her mother. You didn't burn someone you loved.

There was no such thing as true love. Her father had told her that, and now she believed it with all her heart. Love was an illusion—something people whispered into their partner's ear but never truly felt. What she felt for Slane was only lust.

Suddenly, the door burst open and she glanced up to see six black-clad men entering the inn! Her heart froze. One of the men pointed to the rear of the inn and then to the stairway. Three men moved to the rear of the inn and two hurried to the stairs.

Taylor eased the edge of the hood forward, concealing her face deeper within the shadows of the cloak. She waited until the men passed her; then she stood and moved for the stairs. She walked slowly, carefully measuring each step, hoping the leader wouldn't see her, holding her breath in anticipation of discovery. Above her, she heard the soldiers methodically kicking in each door, searching.

She pulled the cowl closer around her face as she began her slow climb up the stairs. One of the guards appeared at the top of the stairs and raced down them toward her. Taylor hesitated as he approached, but continued her ascent. He sped past her, knocking against her shoulder. She stopped, gritting her teeth as he continued by her. She made it to the second floor and saw two soldiers kicking open a door three doors down from her room. She hurried to her own door and pushed it open, entering unseen. She had no sooner shut the door when a hand wrapped around her waist, dragging her against a rock-hard chest, and another hand pressed a dagger to her throat.

She held her breath for a long moment before she heard an exasperated exhalation. "Taylor?" the harsh whisper said in her ear.

"We can't stay here, Slane," she murmured. "Corydon's men are searching the inn."

Slane released her. "How many?"

"Six. Probably more." The sound of wood splintering nearby made her jump. Her heart beat frantically in her chest.

Slane grabbed her hand, paused to seize a sack on the table, and moved to the window. He shoved open the shutters and urged her out with a nod of his head.

Taylor climbed onto the windowsill and looked down. The ground was only about fifteen feet below. Slane grabbed her arm and eased her out, dangling her down the wall. When she was down as far as he could reach, Slane released her. Taylor landed in a crouch and quickly rose to her feet, moving to press her back against the wall of the inn. On the far horizon, the sun was barely beginning to appear; the world was still cloaked with night's darkness. She hid in the gloom, searching the murky street for any sign of Corydon's men.

Slane dropped silently to the ground beside her, making as much noise as a ghost would have.

They exchanged a glance and Slane started to move toward the road that led away from the town.

"What about our horses?" Taylor asked in a hushed whisper.

"They're in the stables around the front of the inn. We can't risk it."

Just then, a whinny reached Taylor's ears, and she glanced over her shoulder to see several horses tied to some trees. She slowed her pace for a moment, straining to see any guards. Slane joined her, whispering, "What is it?"

"I've got a better idea," she replied and led the way toward the horses.

The horses skittered nervously as she approached them, but she quieted them with soft words. She glanced over her shoulder at Slane, who was standing guard nearby. He signaled her to hurry with a quick flick of his wrist.

Taylor grabbed the bridle of the closest horse and the one beside it. She led them toward the gate with a triumphant look.

"You do this often?" Slane wondered as he took one of the horses and mounted.

Taylor pulled herself onto the other horse and cast an ingratiating smile at him. "Only from people I don't like." She jerked her head at the brand on the horses' flanks. Corydon's mark. Then she kicked her horse, urging it down the road.

With a satisfied grin, Slane kicked his own steed, following the impulsive little imp.

The incessant, persistent misting of drizzle covered Slane with a fine layer of moisture. The rain had started just as they had sighted the small city of Bristol.

Slane hunched his shoulders, his clothing and hair already soaked. He cast a glance at Taylor. She looked like a drowned rat, but somehow she was still lovely. She even managed a crooked smile. Slane couldn't help but return it. Neither of them had mentioned the kiss once since it happened. Slane refused to even think about it . . . except in the darkness of every night before he fell asleep.

And now Slane found that he couldn't take his gaze from Taylor. She was proud and courageous and . . . God's blood, she was the most beautiful woman he had ever seen. Slane tore his eyes from her.

She was also out of reach. And she always would be.

As they approached Bristol, a man dressed in a dark tunic and brown breeches blocked the road, waving his arms at them. Slane's eyes darted around the road for any sign of Corydon's men. But the flat lands held no hiding places. Frowning, Slane brought his horse to a halt.

"No sick people allowed in the city," the man announced, moving up beside Taylor's horse. He walked around both of them, studying them intently, taking particular notice of any exposed skin. "Are you ill?" he questioned.

Slane shook his head and exchanged a befuddled glance with Taylor.

"Then God be with you if you enter this town," the man murmured, stepping aside to allow them to continue their journey.

A feeling of dread snaked up Slane's spine.

Taylor's horse danced nervously in a circle before she finally brought it up next to Slane's mount. "Let's not go," she said. "We can go around."

"It will take days to go around," Slane replied. "There's a river blocking the route to the west and a thick forest to the east. Let's see what's causing all the commotion first. If it looks bad, we can go around."

As they neared the buildings on the outskirts of the town, a foul smell rose to assault their senses. It was a rotted smell. Pungent and noxious.

The smell of death.

CHAPTER SIXTEEN

As they entered Bristol, a terrible silence greeted them—
an odd silence that made Slane cock his head this way and
that as he rode through the heart of town, listening intently
for any familiar sound, any sound at all. His gaze searched
the storefronts, the narrow alleys, the small homes built
tightly together. But the town was empty and still, except
for their horses' hoofbeats echoing in the road.

Then, in the street ahead of them, Slane spotted a man
sprawled facedown. A rat scurried past, stopping to sniff
at the prone figure; then it moved on.

Taylor dismounted. For a long moment, she simply
stared down at the corpse.

Slane positioned his horse close by, hovering over her
in case this was some sort of trap.

With the tip of her boot, Taylor kicked the man over.
His eyes were wide open, staring lifelessly into the sky.

Suddenly, Taylor lurched away, almost leaping in her haste to distance herself from the body.

"What is it?" Slane demanded.

"His neck. Look at his neck."

Slane's gaze shifted to the dead man's neck. The glands in his neck were horribly swollen, the skin black and discolored.

"The plague," Taylor hissed, wiping her hands on her tunic, digging the tip of her boot into the dirt to clean it. She looked at Slane, and he could see that there was something close to panic in her eyes.

Suddenly, two dozen men, naked from the waist up, came marching down the street, shouting loudly at the sky above, chanting prayers to God. Each of the men held a cord or a rope of some sort. And they were whipping themselves with the frayed ends, drawing blood from the welts that already covered most of their exposed flesh. Slane slid his hand slowly over the hilt of his sword but left the weapon sheathed; he had never seen anything like this before and he didn't know what these men would do if he drew it.

Taylor mounted her horse. "Let's go back, Slane," she pleaded. "I don't want to stay here anymore."

Slane didn't answer. What were these men trying to accomplish? Would they attack the castle trying to find some sanctuary from all this madness? Slane stiffened, his eyes swiveling to the castle that loomed in the distance. Suddenly, he drove his boots into the horse's side, spurring the beast on at a frantic gallop, racing straight into the heart of town.

"Slane!" Taylor shouted. She followed him, madly dashing through the town.

Slane tried to ignore the growing number of dead bodies at the sides of the road as he drew closer and closer to the castle. He heard Taylor call, but he paid her no heed. He spurred the horse on, snapping the reins to get the beast to move even faster. Faster. He had to reach the castle!

Suddenly, a woman stumbled into the road, her clothing torn, some of the exposed flesh on her body covered with black patches, her armpits swollen to the size of overripe melons. Slane's horse whinnied sharply and reared back. He felt himself falling out of the saddle. He grabbed for something to cling to, anything, but there was nothing there. He floated in the air for a terrifying moment; then his back slammed into the dirt road, knocking the breath from his lungs.

"Slane!" Taylor was off her horse and at his side in an instant. "Are you all right?" she asked. She grabbed his arm, helping him to his feet.

"I have to get to the castle," he panted.

"Are you mad? Let's get out of here!"

"No," Slane gasped.

"Why?" Taylor asked.

Slane watched the dying woman stumble across the road and disappear into the shadows of a nearby shop. "I have to see Elizabeth," Slane replied.

"Elizabeth?" Taylor echoed, stunned.

Slane climbed back into the saddle and slid his boots into the stirrups. He spurred the horse on toward the castle, leaving Taylor standing forlornly in the middle of the road.

* * *

Taylor chased after Slane all the way to the castle. She expected him to stop there, but he didn't. The drawbridge lowered at Slane's approach and the guards called out a muffled greeting. Taylor glanced up at the guard towers as she passed them, and a strange feeling of doom settled in the pit of her stomach as she entered the outer ward. The guards seemed to know Slane on sight. What was this place? And who was this Elizabeth who elicited such foolhardiness in Slane?

She caught sight of Slane dashing in through the open inner ward gates and raced after him. She entered the inner ward just in time to see him run into the keep. Prickling goosebumps peppered her arms. She felt like an intruder in this strange, quiet castle, but she continued to follow Slane inside. He ran down a corridor and then up a set of spiraling stairs.

Taylor took the stairs two at a time as they rose into the unknown, trying to keep up with Slane.

He was far ahead of her, but as she reached the top of the stairs she saw him enter one of the rooms down the hallway. She raced to the room in pursuit, only to come to an abrupt halt at what she saw inside. Slane was embracing the woman who lay in the bed, rocking her slightly, kissing her lips gently, murmuring her name over and over. "Elizabeth. Elizabeth. Elizabeth."

Taylor's throat closed tightly and she had to choke down a swallow. Her eyes darkened with pain before she turned and left the room.

Taylor walked down the hall, keeping her back straight even though she felt like collapsing into sobs. She was not a weak person. She would never give in to those feelings.

Maybe Elizabeth was a sister, a cousin, some sort of relative. But Taylor knew she wasn't.

She moved through the unfamiliar castle like a specter. The image of Slane holding that woman, that Elizabeth, haunted her every step. She felt lost, abandoned.

Finally, she wandered into the Great Hall. It was empty and its vastness only seemed to enhance the loneliness she felt. She moved as far away from the doors as possible, searching for a place that would move her away from him, a place that would take her away from the confused and hurt feelings that were swirling through her. She turned to look at the large double doors she had just entered, somehow thinking Slane would materialize there and explain what was happening. But the doorway remained empty.

Taylor bumped into the wall and she came to an abrupt halt. What was she doing? She had never needed anyone. And she didn't need Slane. But what was she to do now? She had no coin. She had no food. She realized with a start that she had put her complete trust in Slane.

Desolation swept through her, and she slid down the cold stone wall and buried her head between her arms. She had never felt so lost.

Then she heard footsteps. She lifted her head slightly so that she could peer over her arms, half expecting to see Slane moving toward her. Disappointment stung her heart as she watched from beneath a wooden table as a peasant's woolen skirt swished toward her from a rear door. The table hid the rest of the woman from her view.

Behind the first woman trailed another woman, her green woolen skirt a bit shorter than the other's. "When did he return? Lord Slane was supposed ta be out lookin' for that girl," one of the women said.

Taylor stiffened slightly, holding her breath.

"Just minutes ago," an older voice answered. "And thank the Lord, he come none too soon."

"Lady Elizabeth was cryin' out for him just last night. I'm prayin' she lives."

Taylor's heart jumped. Did the woman just say Elizabeth was crying out for Slane?

"She'll be fine now that Lord Slane is here," the older voice reassured. "He'll take care of her—you'll see. Put this cup there."

"But if it's the plague—"

"Hold your tongue, girl," the older woman snapped. "I'll not have any talk like that. Lady Elizabeth don't have the plague. Besides, things will be better now, I'm sure. Lord Slane will want to be getting on with their plans."

"But no one will come near this cursed town."

"I don't think they'll be worrying about wedding guests. After all, they've waited a year now!"

Wedding? Taylor's mind refused to acknowledge the word, refused to acknowledge what the voices were saying.

"I guess you're right. If lady Elizabeth survives . . ."

"Of course she will. How many times do I have to tell you . . ."

Taylor watched the women move out of the Great Hall. She fought back the urge to race after them and shake them and demand an explanation. Instead, she sat stock-still for a long moment, unable to move, not wanting to think. But the thoughts came anyway.

Wedding. There was to be a wedding.

Taylor rose onto shaking legs. If she concentrated on taking one step at a time, the realization wouldn't come. She wouldn't have to think about it. About how Slane had kept the truth from her.

That Elizabeth was his betrothed!

CHAPTER SEVENTEEN

Taylor walked the castle, desperately trying to clear her mind. But the image that kept resurfacing was Slane embracing and kissing his betrothed. She felt a wretchedness of mind she'd never known before. Even the thought of downing a few quick ales left a sour taste in her mouth. *It's my own fault,* she thought over and over. *I let him get close to me.* And now she was stuck in a town ravaged by this dread disease with no coin, no food, and no friends.

She fought back the sudden tears that came to her eyes, angry with herself for letting a noble come very close to destroying her. She had to get away from him before he tricked her again with his damned charm, his warm words and gentle looks.

Just like the faceless, formless knight of her nightmares had destroyed her mother.

She quickly pushed the thought away from her and concentrated on trying to figure out a way to leave. She turned a corner of the hallway and came upon a group of four men drinking ale and playing dice.

A grin lit her face as she watched the dice tumble end over end on the stone floor.

An hour quickly passed, then another. Soon Taylor had a good pile of coin before her and an ale in her hand that didn't taste sour at all. She snatched up the dice and shook the small cubes vigorously in her hand, then flung them to the ground.

There was a moment of silence as the dice spun; then came a roar of disbelief that brought a warm smile to Taylor's face. She bent to collect the coin from the floor and add it to her pile.

"You're luckier than a wart on the king's hand!" one of the men across from her hollered.

"Let 'em fly again, boys," Taylor encouraged with a disarming smile. "My luck has to run out sometime."

The man sitting beside her laughed and flipped his long dark hair over his shoulder, then rubbed his hand along the length of her back.

"Unhand her, you filthy wretch!" a voice growled.

Taylor looked up to see a dark shadow moving toward her. She started to rise, but stopped when the form entered the circle of light cast by the flickering torch on the wall. Slane appeared, a snarl twisting his lips. He stepped up to Taylor's companion and planted a kick straight into his chest, knocking the man soundly to the ground.

Taylor gave Slane a look of disbelief, then scrambled over to her companion. "Are you all right?" she asked.

The man nodded and boosted himself up onto his

elbows. "Lord Slane! A thousand pardons . . ." He glanced from Slane's dark visage to Taylor. "I didn't know."

The other three men had risen to their feet upon recognizing Slane. Now they appeared nervous, shifting their weight as if to flee.

"If you men will excuse us, the lady and I have business to discuss," Slane said, his tone heavy and threatening. "Gather up your coin and dice and go."

The men quickly obeyed, casting curious glances at Taylor as they departed.

The man with the black hair hesitated long enough to ask Taylor, "Should I still wait?"

She nodded and he disappeared around a corner. She turned away from Slane and began scooping up her winnings, which were quite impressive.

"I see you've made yourself quite comfortable here already," Slane commented, the displeasure dripping thickly from his voice.

"I need the coin for food and the man for escort. You see, even though I am a mercenary, the roads are still dangerous for a woman. Especially at night," she said, sitting back on her heels to tie the sack of coins closed.

Slane slapped the sack with the back of his hand, sending it flying to the stone floor, its contents spilling out and rolling in all directions. "You have no need of coin," Slane told her firmly. He grabbed her hand and pulled her gently to her feet, but his voice was not so gentle as he added, "And you certainly have no need of an escort. If that man touches you again, I will break his fingers."

"You don't own me, you don't know me, and you can't command me." She forced herself to be calm. "You're betrothed, Donovan. And it's not to me. I'd be more worried about myself if I were you."

"Can you jump into bed with a stranger so easily?" Slane demanded.

She turned and bent to pick up her coins and put them into the pouch. "What do you care? I do what I have to to survive."

Slane tightened his hand into a fist. "If I didn't care, would I be standing here now?"

She sat on her buttocks and looked up at him. A portion of her hair fell before her eyes. "I don't know what you want." She chuckled quietly, sadly. "I must say you had me fooled. I thought I understood you. And then"—she jerked her quivering chin at the ceiling— *"her."* She quickly looked away, down at the bag in her lap. With shaking hands, she tried to tie the string, but couldn't quite manage it. Finally, she stopped and clenched her fists in her lap, trying to bring their trembling under control.

"Elizabeth is not the problem here," Slane commented flatly. "I gave my word I would return you."

She looked at him as if he had struck her. "You bastard," she whispered, the years of control Jared had taught her crumbling into nothingness before his cold manipulations. She rose to her feet, anger, fear, agony all warring inside of her. "Then that's one word you'll have to break!" She whirled to flee, her throat closing rapidly with the onset of unwanted tears. She would not show him how much he had hurt her. She would never let him see her tears!

Slane grabbed her arm and spun her back around to face him. "My word is my sacred bond. The oath I made to my brother will not be broken. I swear on my grave it will not. If I have to post four guards to watch your every move twenty-four hours a day, then so be it. It will be done, Taylor. It will be done."

"Your cursed oath . . . To your brother, it is fine. To a noble from a noble. But to a mercenary, to an outcast, your oath doesn't mean a thing, right? You lied to me! You manipulated me to get me to come with you. Is that part of your oath? Is it?! You lied. It was all a lie to get me to come all this way! When you said you cared, pleaded with me not to shut you out. Just pretending! Well, I was pretending, too. You mean nothing to me! You're just another noble who lies and makes a woman think you—'' She stopped herself short, her chest shaking. "You're no better than my father," she gasped, as a tear trickled from the corner of her eye. "I despise you, Slane Donovan. And I spit in your face." She tried to call forth some bile, but her mouth had suddenly gone dry. She turned away from him, wiping her face on her tunic sleeve.

Slane's brow furrowed as his eyes thinned to mere slits. "I have never lied to you, Taylor," Slane said softly. "I do not lie. It is against the code to which I have sworn my life and my allegiance. You may hate me, but a liar is one thing I am not."

"Your precious code is a joke!" she screamed, her eyes ringed with wetness. "Do not speak kindly to me. I will not be fooled again by your soft words, so save them for your betrothed." She tried to pull her arm away.

Slane kept a firm grip on her arm, even pulling her closer to him. "To think that I have used kind words to trick you is simply wrong."

"Let go of me, you lying bastard!" Taylor commanded.

Slane held her tightly for a long moment, looking deep into her eyes, trying to see the reason for her irrational behavior. But there was no explanation to be found. He suddenly released her arm. "Go now. Run off to your dirty friend if you want. Your insults have done me great dishonor."

Taylor's throat worked as she stared at him for a long moment, her tears sparkling like blood in the setting sun.

Finally, she turned and ran down the hallway, clutching the pouch to her bosom.

Taylor retreated to the quiet of one of the gardens. It was obvious these gardens had once been beautiful, but they had fallen into disrepair. Wild weeds sprung up around the rosebushes, as if trying to choke out their splendor. Taylor sat on one of the garden benches, with the pouch in her lap, and she dropped her head. Tears spilled onto the pouch, now golden droplets in the sun's dying rays. She couldn't stop them, it seemed, and she didn't want to.

She had thought he cared. And he had. But not about her. He cared about his brother's alliance with her father. About Elizabeth. But not about her. She had trusted him. She had trusted him with her feelings. And now they lay shattered into a million fragments.

These past eight years she had only one friend . . . one real friend. And he was gone. Then Slane had been there. And she had needed someone. To trust . . . to be a friend. She never expected to want him to care about her. And now that she knew . . .

Taylor rose to her feet. She paced the grass, trying to bring her torment under control. Frantically, she wiped at the tears that still dripped from her eyes.

What had she expected from a noble? More than he was capable of giving, that much was obvious. Still . . . his kiss. How could she have read more into it than there was? He had been so kind to her when everyone else looked at her as an outcast. *Curse him,* she thought. He had manipulated her. Had known what to say to her. She had been no better than a child to fall for his charade. Yet she had liked how he made her feel. Like an equal.

She headed for the inner ward. That was why she had to leave. He made her realize what it was like for a man to look at her . . . as a woman.

Her steps took her toward the stables. She tied the pouch to her belt and entered the gloomy building, moving quickly to her horse's stall. She was untying it when she heard the man's voice.

"I'm glad you came."

"Me, too, Forrest," she replied, recognizing the voice of the man from the dice game who had volunteered his services. "Mount and let's be out of here," she added. But as he emerged from the darkness, her heart froze.

Blood was trickling from his mouth.

Taylor stepped back, almost tripping over a bucket by the side of the wall.

Forrest wiped at his lips and stared at the blood on his fingertips. "It's been like this ever since the game," he said. "I can't understand it."

Taylor drew her sword. "Stay back," she commanded. The men she had played dice with had all talked about the signs of this Black Death. Bloody spit was one of the first signs. Then a large growth under one's arms, near the neck, or at other places on the body. The growth eventually turned to large black spots. "Don't come any closer."

He stepped toward her and she retreated. "Come on, love. Just a little kiss before we're off."

"I think I'll find another escort," she said. "Your services won't be needed."

"But yours will," he answered, reaching for her.

She knocked his arm away with the flat side of her sword. "Next time I'll use the blade. Now back off."

"I've wanted you since I first saw you. Your fire." He

stepped toward her. "And now it seems my time has run out. You won't kill me. And if you do . . ." He shrugged.

He reached for her again, grabbing for her arm.

Taylor screamed and thrust her blade with all her might. It pierced his stomach. He staggered back, then fell to the ground, clutching the deadly wound.

Breathing hard, Taylor staggered to the doors. This Black Death was everywhere. She looked at the fallen man and shuddered. He might have infected her just by touching her. Her entire body trembled as she turned and wiped the blade off on a horse's blanket that was draped over the edge of the stall. Then she sheathed the weapon and quickly mounted her horse, racing from the stables out into the night.

CHAPTER EIGHTEEN

Slane stood at the window, staring out into the light of the rising sun. *I shouldn't have let her go,* he thought for the thousandth time. *I should have stopped her. I have compromised the fulfillment of my oath. And for what? Because of my irrational anger. Because of my feelings.* He had never let his feelings get the best of him. He had always been able to control them. But not with Taylor. Her accusing words had bitten deep into his heart; and they had been so full of hate! *And truth?* a voice questioned. No. Not truth. He was no liar.

He dropped his gaze to the windowsill. He had tried telling himself to let her go. That it didn't matter. And it hadn't. At least not until his anger faded. Then he had searched the castle, every room, every damned nook and cranny. But the only thing he had found was her dead escort. The plague-infested man only made his concern for Taylor grow stronger. Not only did she face the threat of Corydon's men and Richard's mercenaries, but now she had to contend with the plague, too.

He had to fight the urge every second of every moment to forget everything else that mattered and chase after her. The need to protect her and to see her safe was so strong that it was tearing him apart. It was at odds with his code. How could he leave Elizabeth when she was so ill? He had to get her out of this plague-filled town or she would never survive.

He tried telling himself that Taylor was so strong, so worldly, she would be all right until he could see Elizabeth safely to Castle Donovan. Then he would return and find Taylor and bring her to his brother. But he knew deep down inside that Taylor was in danger—mortal danger. Every moment he spent at Elizabeth's side was one more moment that Taylor might be hurt. Or killed. He clenched his fist. Yes, she was strong and worldly, but she was also a woman—and now she was alone.

If only there was someone he could get to watch Elizabeth, to see her safely to Castle Donovan! But she was his responsibility. Responsibility. That was a strange way to think of his betrothed, he thought. But strange or no, he knew it was the truth.

"Slane?"

Slane whirled at the sound of Elizabeth's voice. Her eyes were open now, glassy with fever. He stepped up to her, seeing the sheen of perspiration covering her forehead. She had shown none of the signs of the Black Death and for that he was grateful. He knelt at her side, gently taking her hand into his own. Her skin felt hot against his.

"You've come," she sighed.

"Of course," he replied, staring into her glazed brown eyes.

"Oh, darling," she whispered. "I'm so happy you're here."

Slane nodded. "Everything will be fine now. Just rest," he whispered, brushing a strand of her dark hair from her moist cheek.

"But that horrible plague. Slane, we must leave."

With every fiber of his body, Slane wanted to scoop her up and leave this place. To go after Taylor. He hoped Taylor was moving toward Castle Donovan. But he knew she wasn't.

Elizabeth gently squeezed his hand and his mind focused on his betrothed again. Repentently, he pressed his lips to Elizabeth's knuckles. "When you're well again, we will leave," he replied.

A smile barely reached the corner of her lips, and her eyelids drooped closed again.

Slane returned to his vigil at the window, as if he might spot Taylor roaming the city, even though he knew she wouldn't be there.

Suddenly, the door creaked open. Slane turned to see his close friend, John Flynn, enter the room. Slane rushed forward to greet John, grasping his arm in the customary greeting. He'd wondered where John had gotten to; he was afraid this horrible plague had killed his friend. But now, seeing John standing in the doorway, Slane knew he could leave to find Taylor and Elizabeth would be well cared for.

"Slane!" John greeted, a grim grin spreading across his features. "I'm so glad you've finally arrived."

His hazel eyes showed none of the easy happiness that Slane remembered. He wore a sword strapped to his waist, which was unusual, especially inside the safety of the castle walls. His dark brown hair had been cut into a bowl shape, no doubt at Elizabeth's urging. She had been trying to get

Slane to cut his hair into the latest fashion for the last six months.

"Elizabeth's been calling for you," John continued. Warm hazel eyes stared hard at him. "You did come back for Elizabeth, didn't you?"

Slane looked away, unable to meet John's eyes. "I was escorting Taylor to Castle Donovan when—"

"You found Taylor Sullivan?" John asked, excitement in his voice.

Slane nodded. "I also lost her."

"What do you mean?"

"We had an argument and she left," Slane admitted.

"Left?" John wondered. "You didn't bind her?"

"I'm not a barbarian," Slane snapped.

"Maybe you should have," John suggested.

"She is not a possession. She is a woman."

Elizabeth tossed her head, shifting in the bed, and Slane raised his eyes to his betrothed. When she settled again, he lowered his voice. "Richard is wrong to do this to her."

John shrugged. "It's not your choice to make."

Slane grunted and turned away from John. "Regardless, I have to go after her."

"You can't leave Elizabeth like this!" John said sternly. "I don't think she has the Black Death on her, but she's quite ill nonetheless."

Slane's eyes shifted to Elizabeth. She was so pale and helpless. He groaned inwardly. He knew he couldn't leave Elizabeth's side. His responsibility was here. With her.

"Someone else will find the Sullivan woman," John soothed. "Richard will have his betrothed."

Slane's eyes snapped back to John. He seized his friend's arm in a painful grip. "You have to find her," he told him urgently. "You have to find her before someone else does."

Confused, but reading the obvious desperation and insistence in his friend's plea, John nodded his head. "I'll try."

The next day, Slane sat in the Great Hall, staring into a mug of ale. The large room was strangely empty, only the most loyal servants remaining behind to see to their lady. And they weren't numerous. Slane could count them on one hand. He cursed the deserters silently. Elizabeth hadn't needed them anyway. The fever had finally broken the previous night, and now she was resting comfortably. Slane knew she would make it.

He also knew that Taylor might not be so lucky. She was out there among the sick, fighting for her life. Alone. He shot to his feet and began to pace, cursing his brother for this mission.

And what had happened to John? He had sent him out a day ago and still had heard no word. Had he sent his friend to his death?

No sooner had the thought crossed his mind than he heard footfalls and lifted his gaze to the double doors at the opposite end of the room. John headed toward him.

Slane moved quickly toward his friend. "Well?" he asked. "Is she here? Did you find her?"

John scowled and shook his head. "I can find no trace of her. No one's seen her. It's as if she's vanished."

Slane sighed. He knew well about her vanishing. Too well. What could she be thinking? Where could she be headed?

"How is Lady Elizabeth?" John asked.

Slane nodded. "Much better. The fever's broken. She'll be fine."

"Thank the Lord," John sighed.

Slane knew he should feel lucky, but he didn't. He felt

miserable and concerned. "Have some ale," he instructed. "There's a pot of porridge in the kitchen. Help yourself." He continued past John toward the doors.

"Where are you going?" John demanded.

Slane hesitated for a moment. With all his being, he wanted to pursue Taylor. But he knew that was impossible. "To see Elizabeth," he said with a heavy heart.

Elizabeth opened her eyes. The sunlight streamed into her room through the open shutters. But something dark was blocking the sun from her eyes. For a moment, she thought it was John, but then her eyes adjusted to golden hair that hung in shimmering waves to thick shoulders and knew it was her beloved. Her spirits soared and she felt almost like her old self once again. She pushed herself up into a sitting position.

Slane turned from the window at her movement. There was worry and a slight scowl to his brow, which seemed to vanish when he saw her sitting up in the bed. He moved to her side and Elizabeth reached out a hand for him.

His large hand engulfed hers, sheltering it in warmth. "How do you feel?" he asked.

"Better," Elizabeth smiled. "Now that you're here."

A troubled look clouded his blue eyes for a moment, but it was gone as soon as it had appeared. He smiled at her, but Elizabeth could see the tension around the corners of his lips. "Is something wrong?" she wondered.

"No," he said. "Everything will be fine now that you're getting better." He patted her hand.

Elizabeth's gaze dropped down to his hand. He was patting her hand absently, as if his mind were on something else. "Your search for that girl isn't over yet, is it?"

Slane withdrew his hand and stood. "No," he admitted.

Elizabeth felt a twinge of disappointment in her breast. He was going to leave her again. That was why he was acting so distracted. She wished he didn't have to spend all of his time in search of another woman, but she knew that was what his honor demanded. And she would have him no other way. "It's all right, darling," she tried to soothe him. "Truly."

He studied her for a moment. Then he suddenly came forward and knelt at her bedside. He took her hand into his and pressed his forehead against her wrists. "Oh, Elizabeth," he groaned, "I'm so sorry."

She stroked his golden hair. "You don't have to be, Slane," she murmured.

But Slane remained in his reverent position for a long time. When he finally rose, his shoulders were squared, and there was determination in his voice. "We leave for Castle Donovan in two days."

CHAPTER NINETEEN

Slane reined his horse in outside the Queen's Inn and quickly dismounted. For three days, he had tried not to show his desperation and anxiety. John had gone out one more time to search for Taylor. But Slane knew that by then she would be long gone.

Now he turned to John and said, "Stay here with Lady Elizabeth. I will see if they have any rooms available."

John nodded and Slane stepped into the inn.

The inn was a tide of bodies. There would be no rooms tonight—that much was obvious. Slane doubted if there would even be any floor space come nightfall. Even so, something made him stand in the doorway and sweep the inn's large common room with his gaze. *She will not be here,* Slane reminded himself. *But I will find her again. This I vow.*

Eyes full of fear caught his stare; eyes full of hopelessness turned away. Men, women, children—all running from an invisible enemy, not knowing where or when or whom it

would strike. *I'm wasting my time here,* Slane realized and
started to turn back to the door. That was when he caught
a glimpse of something familiar. A woman's tunic. A familiar set of leggings. He turned back to the room. She was
sitting in the back, her unkempt hair shielding her face.
He moved forward and the crowd seemed to part for him.
She sat motionless, her hands folded on the wooden table,
her hair hanging wild as if it hadn't been combed for days.
Her tunic was ripped near her shoulder, and there was
dried blood around it. Her head and shoulders were
slumped as if she was sleeping. He could hardly believe
his eyes, his luck! "Taylor?" he wondered aloud.

"Hello," she muttered.

The relief that had begun to course through him at
finding her was instantly replaced by a growing concern.
She had been hurt recently, and badly. There were rips
in her clothing, sword cuts—he was sure of it. And from the
looks of the wounds, they hadn't been cleaned properly.
"Taylor?" Slane repeated when she didn't look up. "You
don't look so good." A fierce protectiveness flared within
him. "Come on," he said. "I'm taking you with me."

She moved her hands forward so that her tunic sleeves
slid back. Ropes bound her wrists tightly together, chafing
her skin. "Someone else had the same idea," she said.

"What kind of sick joke is this?" Slane asked hotly. "Who
did this to you?" He grabbed the ropes and shook them,
as if that simple movement would set her free.

She stiffened, her face twisting in agony. "I'd appreciate
it if you wouldn't do that," she managed to gasp between
her clenched teeth.

Mortified, Slane let go of the rope. "I'm sorry," he said.
He quickly slid onto the bench opposite her and leaned
close to her across the table. He reached out a hand and
carefully wiped strands of hair from her cheek, trying to

see her eyes. "Who has taken you prisoner? Where are they?"

She looked up at him through the strands of hair that fell back over her face. Behind the limp locks, her eyes were tired and glassy. "A mercenary named Magnus Gale."

Slane's eyes narrowed at the man's name. He had worked with the man before. Magnus was obviously intent on collecting Richard's reward money.

"He cornered me and we fought. He's a very good fighter, you know. Or else I wouldn't be sitting here."

He was horrified to see a dark bruise on her cheek, her cut lip. Anger simmered and boiled his blood. "Magnus. I partnered with him once. But he was such a brutal bastard I couldn't work with him anymore." Slane frowned, scanning the common room again. "Where is that vermin?" *And why are you just sitting here?* he wondered, but didn't ask aloud. *Could Magnus have already put that fire of yours out?*

"He went to get food," she said. "He'll be back. If he's not watching now. Slane . . ." she whispered imploringly, but stopped.

Slane turned his eyes back to her. He saw the desperation in her eyes and stood. "To the devil with him. Come with me now." He moved to her side of the table. "Wouldn't you rather be in my care? Even though you want to spit in my face?" he asked, his voice sincere. "At least I won't bind you like some slave."

She looked at him, gratefully. "Only if you'll buy me an ale when we are very far from here," she said, holding her hands out to him.

"I'll buy you two," he said with a smile. He reached into his boot and, after retrieving a throwing dagger, quickly cut her hands free of the rope.

She rubbed her chafed wrists, but suddenly froze as if

that simple movement had caused her pain. "Slane," she gritted. "I don't know if I can walk. The wound in my side hurts like the devil. It's still bleeding."

Slane felt his teeth clench. *That bastard will pay for this,* he vowed silently. He would have to carry her, but there was no way he could make it through this mass of bodies without aggravating her wounds even further. Then a sudden thought dawned on him. It wasn't pleasant, but there was no other choice. He ran the dagger across his forefinger and then replaced the dagger in his boot.

"What are you doing?" Taylor asked.

"Getting you out of here," Slane replied. He scanned the area around them until he spotted a drunk lying on the floor in a stupor. He bent down and wiped his finger near the corner of the man's mouth, smearing blood across his skin. Then he stood and backed up until he bumped into a farmer. The farmer turned and, upon seeing Slane's horrified look, followed Slane's gaze to the drunken man.

The farmer gasped and pointed a shaking finger. "Look!"

"My God, he has the plague!" someone shouted from behind Slane.

"The plague is here!" another woman cried out as she saw the blood near the drunken man's lips. "The Black Death has come to the inn."

Everyone who could stand bolted for the front door, pushing and shoving frantically to get out. A satisfied grin stretched across Slane's lips as he watched the mad dash for the door. But then, a little boy stumbled and fell to his hands and knees, and Slane's grin vanished. Feet pounded around the boy as people stampeded away from the Black Death. Slane leapt a fallen table to race to the boy, but he knew he was going to be too late.

Then Taylor was there, pulling the boy into her shielding

Take advantage of this offer to enjoy Zebra's newest line of historical romance novels....Splendor Romances (formerly Lovegrams Historical Romances)- Take our introductory shipment of 4 romance novels -Absolutely Free! (a $19.96 value)

Now you'll be able to savor today's best romance novels without even leaving your home with our convenient and inexpensive home subscription service. Here's what you get for joining:

- 4 BRAND NEW bestselling Splendor Romances delivered to your doorstep every month
- 20% off every title (or almost $4.00 off) with your home subscription
- A **FREE** monthly newsletter, *Zebra/Pinnacle Romance News* filled with author interviews, member benefits, book previews and more!
- No risks or obligations…you're free to cancel whenever you wish…no questions asked

To get started with your own home subscription, simply complete and return the card provided. You'll receive your FREE introductory shipment of 4 Splendor Romances and then you'll begin to receive monthly shipments of new Zebra Splendor titles. Each shipment will be yours to examine for 10 days and then if you decide to keep the books, you'll pay the preferred home subscriber's price of just $4.00 per title plus $1.50 shipping and handling. That's $16 for all 4 books plus $1.50 for home delivery! And if you want us to stop sending books, just say the word…it's that simple.

4 FREE books are waiting for you!
Just mail in the certificate below!

If the certificate is missing below, write to:
Splendor Romances, Zebra Home Subscription Service, Inc.,
P.O. Box 5214, Clifton, New Jersey 07015-5214
or call TOLL-FREE 1-888-345-BOOK

FREE BOOK CERTIFICATE

Yes! Please send me 4 Splendor Romances (formerly Zebra Lovegram Historical Romances), ABSOLUTELY FREE! After my introductory shipment, I will be able to preview 4 new Splendor Romances each month FREE for 10 days. Then if I decide to keep them, I will pay the money-saving preferred publisher's price of just $4.00 each... a total of $16.00 plus $1.50 shipping and handling. That's 20% off the regular publisher's price plus $1.50 for shipping and handling. I may return any shipment within 10 days and owe nothing, and I may cancel my subscription at any time. The 4 FREE books will be mine to keep in any case.

Name _____

Address _____ Apt. _____

City _____ State _____ Zip _____

Telephone ( ) _____

Signature _____
(If under 18, parent or guardian must sign.)

Terms and prices subject to change. Orders subject to acceptance by Zebra Home Subscription Service, Inc. .
Zebra Home Subscription Service, Inc. reserves the right to reject or cancel any subscription.

SP09A9

A $19.96 value.

FREE!

No obligation
to buy
anything,
ever.

embrace, hugging him close to her chest. Slane saw a man stumble over her, knocking her to the floor. He rushed toward her instantly. But even as he moved, Taylor scrambled to her feet, and slammed into the wall, cradling the child against her protectively as the crowd swarmed past.

Slane reached them, pressing his own body against them to protect Taylor from the pushes and jabs of the mad crowd. With the child squirming between them, Slane dipped his head to meet Taylor's eyes, a swelling of pride in his chest. But when she lifted her exquisite eyes to his, Slane saw the brightness of pain reflected in them. She began to slide down the wall, but Slane caught her around the shoulders with one hand and removed the child from her arms with the other. In the next moment, a woman appeared at his side and took the boy from him. Slane barely saw her embrace the child and rush him away into the night.

Slane scooped Taylor up in his arms, refusing to acknowledge the dread racing up his spine, encircling his stomach, and squeezing until he could hardly breathe. He gently moved her to a nearby table and eased her onto the bench.

"That was downright deceitful, Slane Donovan," Taylor muttered, but stopped as she closed her eyes, swaying. When she steadied herself, she lifted her left arm and glanced down at her tunic.

Slane followed her gaze. Her tunic was soaked with fresh blood. Worry sliced through him like a blade.

"Get away from her, Donovan."

Slane whirled to see Magnus Gale, a trencher of food in one hand, the hilt of his sword in the other. He was a muscular man, encased by a protective shell of chain mail armor.

"She's mine," Magnus added, his teeth clenched. "And so is the reward that goes with her."

"There will be no reward, Magnus," Slane corrected him, rising to face the man. "I am bringing her to my brother's castle." Slane turned back to Taylor. "We need to get you to a doctor," he said. He searched the room with his eyes, finally lifting his own tunic over his head and pressing it tightly to her wound. He took her hand and noticed how cold it was. Outrage engulfed him. He pressed a kiss to her knuckles before pressing her hand firmly against the wound. "Keep pressure on it or you'll bleed to death."

Magnus slapped his hand against Slane's bare shoulder. "She's not going anywhere with you. I'm taking her to Castle Donovan."

Slane whirled and struck with the speed of a cobra, wrapping his hand around Magnus's throat. The trencher fell to the ground, spilling the food across the floor.

Slane drove his body forward, forcing Magnus to stumble backward, picking up speed as he pushed the other man along, finally slamming him hard into the wall with such force that the entire building seemed to shake. Slane ripped the sword from Magnus's sheath and tossed it across the room. Then he tightened his hold on Magnus's throat.

"Maybe you didn't hear me the first time, you filthy scum," Slane said through gritted teeth. "The lady travels with me."

Magnus struggled for a moment. Then he went absolutely still.

"My lord," the barkeep called. "I want no trouble here. Please. Take your argument outside."

"That's a fine idea," Slane called out to the barkeep. He held Magnus still and turned to glance at Taylor over his shoulder. "Can you make it outside?" he asked.

"I—I don't know," she answered quietly.

Suddenly, Magnus lashed out his foot, swiping Slane's

feet from beneath him. Slane landed hard on his back. Immediately, the mercenary retrieved a dagger from his belt.

"Now you die, Donovan," Magnus sneered, bringing his blade crashing down.

Slane grabbed Magnus's wrist, stopping the strike, the deadly tip of the blade hovering only inches from his chest. Slane jerked his feet up, flipping Magnus over his head.

Both men quickly shot to their feet, eyeing the other warily. "What is she to you, Donovan, that you risk your life for her?" Magnus snarled, backing toward Taylor.

"If she dies because of your foolishness, then you will die."

Magnus chuckled, still inching back. Slane jerked forward, but Magnus slashed the blade at him, halting his movement. Then Magnus moved suddenly, racing toward Taylor.

A small scream escaped her throat as she instinctively swung her hands at him. But her reflexes were slow and Magnus easily ducked her arms, encircling her waist with his large hands. His brutal touch, so close to her wound, made her cry out as he lifted her off her feet.

Slane dove to his left, twisting his body in midair, rolling off the nearby table top to come to his feet right in front of Magnus. His fist wasted no time in connecting with Magnus's nose. He smiled with grim satisfaction as he heard bone crunch with the blow.

Magnus took the punch, his head rocking back, his hold on Taylor tightening. When the blood started to flow from his shattered appendage, he smiled. Then his booted foot lashed out, hitting Slane in the stomach. "She's mine," Magnus shouted. "You can have her after I get the reward."

"She's worth nothing dead, you fool," Slane snarled, fighting back the pain in his stomach. Slane reached for the hilt of his sword, and when he saw Magnus's eyes shift to follow the movement, he grabbed a nearby mug of ale with his other hand and hurled the liquid at Magnus's face.

After the ale splashed into his eyes, Magnus blinked rapidly, desperately trying to clear his vision.

Slane seized Magnus's wrist, then grabbed Taylor's arm, yanking her from the other man's hold. Slane pulled back and delivered a stunning blow to Magnus's already bleeding nose, then followed with another lightning-fast strike to his chin.

Magnus fell heavily to the ground, his dagger clattering across the floor.

Rage burned through Slane's body and he charged forward.

Magnus kicked Slane back and rose, speeding toward him, catching him around the midsection and falling on top of him.

Slane lashed out, landing a heavy blow to Magnus's throat. He heard a sickening crunch. Then, suddenly, Magnus fell heavily on top of him, his full weight crushing down on Slane mercilessly. Slane struggled to get free, finally managing to wedge a knee between himself and Magnus. He pushed with his leg, moving Magnus enough to be able to slide out from under him. He quickly moved to his feet and towered over the prone mercenary, waiting for him to rise.

But he never did.

Slane waited a long moment before finally bending down to grab Magnus's shoulder and turn him over. The mercenary's eyes were wide and glassy. Lifeless.

"My bar," the barkeep groaned, appearing from behind an overturned table. "Who's going to pay for all the damages? And the loss of my revenue?"

Slane's gaze slid to Taylor. She hadn't moved from the spot where she had fallen. She was facedown, her hair fanned out over her face, drops of blood beginning to drip from her side through her tunic.

"Fetch me a doctor," Slane said heatedly, "before I destroy the rest of your inn."

Slane moved to Taylor, kneeling at her side. His own thoughts mocked him. *She's so strong, so brave. She'll be all right.* His throat closed. She wasn't moving. He was afraid to touch her, afraid that he would never see her eyes open again. "Taylor?" he whispered in a husky voice. He reached out a hand, only to discover that it was trembling. He gently touched her neck and prayed, holding his breath. With a relief so intense that it drained him, he felt her blood pulsating beneath her hot skin. "Oh, God," he whispered in gratitude. He quickly grabbed his fallen tunic and pressed it tightly to her wound. He smoothed her hair from her brow and leaned over to see her face. "Taylor? Taylor, can you hear me?"

Her eyes opened halfway, as if she would fall asleep at any moment. "Oh," she groaned, and tried to push herself over. Pain stiffened every joint as it coursed through her veins. She curled her knees to her stomach and lifted her hand to grab her wound. Her hand brushed Slane's and her eyes opened to meet his stare.

The agony in her gaze tore at his soul.

"It hurts so bad, Slane."

He brushed the loose hair from her eyes, cursing himself for being too slow. "The innkeeper went to fetch a doctor. You'll be fine," he tried to assure her, attempting to hide the doubt in his voice.

"I could really use . . ." She stared up into his eyes for a long moment before agony tore across her face. "Slane," she gasped, tears coming to her eyes.

He pulled her body closer to his, pressing his face into her hair, kissing her temple. "I'm here, Taylor," he whispered. "I won't leave you."

"Slane?" A man's voice called from the doorway. "What's going on?"

Slane glanced up to see Elizabeth and John standing just inside the inn.

CHAPTER TWENTY

Slane's first impulse was to let go of Taylor and ease her back down to the floor. But his body refused to obey. His second impulse was to explain everything all at once in a torrent of words. But his lips refused to obey. His third impulse was to pull Taylor even tighter to his body as if she needed protection from the slender woman standing in the doorway with sharp, questioning eyes. His arms obeyed that one.

Elizabeth's brow furrowed slightly; then her gaze swept the room, taking in the broken tables, the dead man on the floor. When her eyes returned to Slane, they were scowling in confusion. "Darling, what happened? Are you all right?"

As she approached, Slane noticed the haughtiness and the slight tilting of her chin as she gazed at Taylor. He felt the stirrings of resentfulness somewhere deep inside him. But hadn't he been the same way when he had first met

Taylor? "Yes, I'm all right," Slane answered. "But she's not. She has a bad cut on her left side that needs to be sewn shut. I sent the barkeep to fetch a doctor, but I don't know if he's going to find one in time to help her."

"Let me do it," Elizabeth said, kneeling beside him. "I'm quite capable. You know I am." She tried to nudge him aside, but Slane refused to release Taylor. "Darling, fetch me some clean towels and warm water. I have a bag on your saddle. Bring it to me."

Slane glanced down at Taylor. Trepidation made him tighten his grip. If he left, if he released her, she might just slip away. She might close her eyes and never open them. Something akin to panic flared to life in him. He noticed the blood on his fingers. Taylor's blood. But if he didn't release her and let Elizabeth tend her wounds, she would bleed to death.

He eased her to the floor and watched Elizabeth lift Taylor's tunic. Her wound was worse than he thought. Blood oozed out of her body. Spilling over her creamy flesh, the dark liquid looked like an ugly stain moving across her skin.

Worry ate at the borders of Slane's soul. He turned his head to find Taylor staring at him. In her eyes, he saw such panic that he impulsively picked up her hand. "It's okay," Slane assured her. "Elizabeth has sewn me up more than once."

"Darling," Elizabeth reminded him. "My bag."

Slane nodded and rushed to the door, passing the order along to John. He spoke briefly with a barmaid, giving her instructions for clean towels and warm water. Even as he spoke, his eyes remained on Taylor. He watched her every intake of breath, her every grimace of pain. And he knew the second she closed her eyes. He waited for her to open them again. But her lids remained down. *Open your eyes, Taylor,* he willed. Her eyes stayed closed. She looked so peaceful now, as though she were sleeping or . . .

Unable to bear his gnawing dread any longer, Slane raced to Taylor's side. "Elizabeth?"

"We need to move her to a room. I can't do it here. She's going to have to rest for a while. You know how easily these stitches come undone."

Slane nodded in agreement. "I'm sure there are plenty of rooms available here now." Slane glanced down at Taylor, at her once again bruised and battered face, but this time he knew of the beauty that lay beneath the awful travesties that marred her features. And it was a beauty that still shone through the bruises and the dried mud. A lock of hair had again fallen over her eyes, and he desperately wanted to brush it aside. Instead, he bent and picked her up in his arms, trying to ignore the limpness of her body, the way her head lolled backward. He tried to ignore the anxious feeling in the pit of his stomach.

Elizabeth followed him to the stairs. She shook her head, dusting off her dress. "I can't imagine where a woman received a sword wound. She must be very ill bred. Who is she, m'lord?"

Slane's teeth clenched. "She's my brother's future wife," he replied.

"Poor Richard! I fear he will be gravely disappointed."

"Slane?"

Slane started awake. It took a moment to remember that he had seen Elizabeth to a room and then had left her to come and sit by Taylor. But he couldn't help it.

He had been so angry, so furious, with Taylor when she had left. But now, faced with the thought that she might very well die, he found his anger gone and something else—something he had not known before—surging in his chest.

His eyes adjusted to the dim light cast by the candle. Taylor's beautiful green eyes were open and looking at him. He surged to his knees before the bed and captured her hand in his. His body shook with relief. He leaned forward, brushing his knuckles over her cheek; he was not surprised that her skin felt feverish to the touch. Hurriedly he dipped a rag into the bowl of water that was positioned on the floor next to the bed and ran the cool cloth across her forehead.

"Taylor, Taylor," he whispered to himself, "what am I going to do with you?"

"You could get me an ale," she whispered lightly.

Slane grinned softly as he continued to rub the cloth across her forehead, but his gaze shifted to her eyes. "How are you feeling?" he asked.

She groaned. "I feel like a horse trampled me," she finally answered. She lifted her hand to her side, gently touching her wound. A slight scowl darkened her features. When she again turned her gaze to Slane, her eyes were resolute. "Why didn't you tell me?" she wondered.

Slane looked away, returning the rag to the bowl by the bed. Why did he feel guilty? As if he had betrayed her somehow? The thought was ridiculous. He had no allegiance to this woman, only to his brother. "It wasn't important," he said defensively. "Our relationship—yours and mine—is nothing more than it seems."

He still couldn't lift his eyes to meet hers. He heard a sound and turned his head to see that cynical twist to Taylor's shapely lips.

"I guess I was mistaken," she whispered.

Slane saw the way her lips trembled, the way her throat worked. "I never intended to hurt you, Taylor," he said quietly.

"No, it just seems to work out like that."

Determinedly, he pushed the guilt away. "Tell me. What were you going to do? Where were you planning to go after you ran out on me?"

"It didn't really matter where," she answered. "Just as long as it was away from you."

This time he managed to hold his gaze steady. Her eyes were large and the deepest green he had ever seen. They made him think of a lush green forest. The candlelight shimmering around her head made her almost angelic.

Unbidden, his fingers picked up a lock of her hair, and it curled around his knuckles. "My God, you are beautiful."

"You'd better get away from me. Very far away from me," she advised. "I'll bring you nothing but trouble."

Slane nodded. He knew she was right, knew he should get as far away from her as he could. But she needed him. "Very far away," he echoed. But he lifted his hand to rub it along her jaw, over her bruised cheek. He ran his finger across her hairline, whispering, "I thought I had lost you." Then he found himself leaning his arm next to her head, his lips mere inches from hers. Her sweet breath fanned his face.

She looked up at him. So beautiful. He lowered his lips to hers. . . .

A pounding at the door caused him to bolt upright. "Sir!" a voice called from behind the closed door.

Slane stared at the door, practically frozen in place.

"Slane?" the voice called and Slane recognized it as John's. "I've seen several strange-looking men walking the streets nearby. They haven't come into the inn yet, but I think they might soon.''

Slane shot a knowing glance at Taylor. Corydon's men. He rose and took a step toward the door, but then he faltered. He shouldn't be here. He shouldn't be in her room. He turned his gaze helplessly to Taylor. For a long moment, their gazes locked and held. There was sympathy in her gaze, yet he saw humiliation in the grim set of her lips.

"He's not in here," she called to John.

"Sorry to disturb you, Lady Taylor," John answered after a moment. "But if you see him, please tell him he's needed downstairs."

For what seemed like an eternity, they stayed motionless, their gazes lingering. Finally, the footsteps receded and the spell was broken. Taylor turned her face away, and Slane felt her agony, her shame. *What in heaven's name am I doing?* he silently demanded. *I shouldn't be here in the middle of the night feeling like a criminal. I only came because she is wounded.* But deep down, he knew that was not the reason he had come. He had feelings for her, strong feelings. And they compromised everything he stood for. He was honor bound to Elizabeth, to his brother. But in the face of all that, there was something inside of him that just didn't give a damn. He wanted Taylor. He wanted her with every muscle in his body.

Slane stood stiffly. "Are you going to try to run away again?"

"Not in this condition," she answered just as formally.

At least there was no sarcasm in her voice. "Please stay and let me see to it that your wounds heal properly."

She nodded her head. Slane moved to the door and paused. How could he stay away from her? How could he keep his vow to Elizabeth and honor his brother when Taylor was so near?

Slane opened the door and left the room. How could he not?

CHAPTER TWENTY-ONE

"We can't move her," Slane told John. He faced his friend in the common room, the fire from the hearth crackling behind him. "Not until her stitches heal."

"It's not safe here," John murmured, leaning close to him. "Think of how dangerous it is for Elizabeth."

"What would you have me do?" Slane demanded, his angry gaze burning into John.

John straightened up slightly under his harsh demeanor, but said nothing.

"I can't move Taylor," Slane repeated. He crossed his arms, scowling at his friend. "I was hoping the plague would scare Corydon away."

"I can take Elizabeth," John offered. "I can escort her to Castle Donovan and you can meet us there when Taylor is ready to be moved."

Slane shook his head. "By yourself, you are no match

for Corydon. And I can't leave Taylor alone. If only there was someone else I could trust with Elizabeth's safety."

John grunted and sat heavily on a nearby bench.

"Have you confirmed that it was Corydon?" Slane asked.

"No," John admitted. "But we have to assume it is him. Even if it isn't, it won't be long before he comes."

Slane dropped his chin to his chest. He knew John was right. He knew there was no way for the two of them to protect two helpless women against Corydon's forces. But if they moved, Taylor's stitches might open and the heavy bleeding could start again or the wounds could become infected. He sighed. "We have no choice but to wait until Taylor recovers enough to ride a horse. We'll have to take our chances here."

Corydon's men!

Taylor sat up quickly, her panicked eyes searching the room. A hot flare of pain speared her side. She touched her wound, feeling the soft cloth of the bandage that wound around her torso. She grimaced and sat still for a long moment, waiting for the pain to fade to a dull throbbing. Slowly, the agony eased and she took the moment to scan the dark room. The hints of sunshine inching between the shutters showed her nothing but an empty room. She eased her legs from the bed, favoring her wounded side, and she moved to the window slowly, taking careful, measured steps. With one hand still clamped over her wound, she pulled the shutters open; the strong sunlight that flooded the room blinded her. She covered her eyes and turned her face away from the blazing rays. After a moment, she shaded her eyes with a hand pressed to her forehead and turned her stare to the street below.

It, too, was empty. She didn't see Corydon's men. She

didn't see any mercenaries. As a matter of fact, she saw no one at all. Not even Slane.

Suddenly, the door behind her opened. Taylor whirled, her right hand instinctively moving to her waist for her weapon. But it was not there. Another slashing burst of pain bit into her side.

A woman entered the room, a tray of food in her hands.

Taylor grimaced and grabbed her side again, softly cursing. She knew that face.

She hated that face.

The woman paused at seeing Taylor by the window. For a brief moment, their eyes met. Elizabeth was beautiful. Her chestnut-colored hair shimmered in the sunlight; her skin was flawless. Taylor lifted a hand self-consciously to her bruised cheek, trying to hide it from the woman's searching eyes. Something drained from her. How could she have hoped to compete with a woman who was everything a man could want?

Elizabeth set the tray down on the table near the bed and rushed forward. "You shouldn't be out of bed so soon," she said in a soft, sweet voice. "The stitches will break open." She reached for Taylor's arm.

Taylor yanked away so violently that she rammed her elbow into the shutters behind her. The pain in her side ignited again and it took all her will not to double over. "I can make it myself," she ground out between clenched teeth. But despite her claim, she stayed by the window, cradling her side.

Elizabeth folded her hands before her. "I brought you some food. The porridge is surprisingly good for that of an inn."

What a wonderful wife she would make. What a wonderful mother. A well of grief opened inside of Taylor, threatening to pull her down into it. She forced the lump in her throat down. Elizabeth was everything Taylor could have been.

Elizabeth moved to the bed and gestured at it. "Please. I'll have a look at the stitches now."

Taylor couldn't take her eyes from Elizabeth's hand. So slim. So soft. Graceful. Uncallused. Capable.

Taylor hated her. Staring Slane's fiancée in the face, she couldn't find one reason, not one, why Slane shouldn't marry her. Even her damned hand was perfect. Taylor set her jaw. "I'm perfectly capable of tending my own wounds."

Elizabeth clasped her perfect little hands before her. "I see," she said simply.

"No," Taylor said with an anger and bitterness she had never felt before. "I don't think you do. I don't think you can."

A frown crossed Elizabeth's unblemished brow. "Slane has asked me to see to your needs. With all your knowledge of wounds, you should know that moving around might cause your stitches to open. And we wouldn't want you to bleed to death, would we?"

Taylor's infamous grin stretched across her lips. "Well, at least one of us wouldn't."

Elizabeth's eyes narrowed slightly. "Since my beloved has asked that I tend you, I'll come to your room twice a day with your meals."

Beloved. Taylor felt her jaw tighten. Afraid of what she might say, she turned her back on Elizabeth to look out the window. The bright sun blinded her. But she stared into the light nonetheless.

It was a long moment before Taylor heard Elizabeth's soft footsteps pad across the floor and the gentle closing of the door.

Taylor slowly returned to the bed and gingerly sat down,

holding her left arm tightly against her throbbing side. Anguish filled her, warring with the anger, the confusion, but most of all the sense of defeat.

She lifted her eyes to the tray. There were clean cloths on it as well as bread and a bowl of porridge. She knew her wraps should be changed. She knew it and she didn't care. Anyway, the longer she was hurt, the longer she would have a reason to stay near Slane.

Slane entered the inn quietly and spotted John sitting at one of the tables near the hearth. "Nothing," he announced with relief and stretched out his hands toward the inviting warmth. He had been out most of the afternoon, searching the area for any sign of Corydon or his men. But the only men to be found were either plague-infested shadows pleading for help or decaying corpses lying at the side of the road. There had been no sign of Corydon.

Slane heard soft footsteps and turned to see Elizabeth approaching him with a mug of ale. He smiled his thanks and took the offered mug from her hands. He took a long drink, quenching his parched throat before asking, "All went well today?"

Elizabeth cast a glance at John.

Slane straightened his back in dread. "What is it?" he demanded. "What's wrong?"

Elizabeth returned her eyes to Slane. "I tried my best—truly I did. Please don't be disappointed."

Slane quickly set his mug on a nearby table and grasped Elizabeth's hands. "Is it Taylor?"

"She's such an obstinate girl. She wouldn't accept any of my offers of help, wouldn't allow her wrappings to be changed," Elizabeth said.

Slane lifted his eyes to the ceiling, dropping Elizabeth's hands.

"And she wouldn't eat. Not all day," Elizabeth added. "I thought she was going to hurl the tray of food at me when I was last in her room."

Slane's face was flushed as he headed for the stairs. How did Taylor expect to get her strength back if she didn't eat? And she knew that the wrappings needed to be changed! What was she thinking? *God's blood!* Slane thought. *It isn't enough that I come back to the inn exhausted from a day of searching, but must I return to this nonsense?* By the time he reached the second floor, his fists were clenched so tight that his knuckles ached.

He shoved Taylor's door open so hard that it smacked against the wall. "You didn't eat . . ." he proclaimed, but his voice trailed off. Taylor was sitting up in her bed, the glistening candlelight flickering over her wild hair, highlighting the delicate curve of her cheek. His anger, as well as his breath, rushed from Slane at the sight of her.

"I wasn't hungry," she said.

God's blood! he thought. *Why does she affect me like this?* He crossed the room in two strides. He saw the dark rings beneath her eyes before she turned her head away. "You didn't let Elizabeth change your wrappings."

A scowl crossed her face and she looked toward the window.

The candlelight flickered, brushing her skin in its golden glow like the loving stroke of a painter. Slane had expected an argument, had prepared himself for one. Perhaps she really was as tired as she looked. He sat on the side of the bed. Still, she would not turn her eyes to his.

A grimace flickered over her face for a brief moment and then it was gone.

"It will do you no good to starve yourself," he said more quietly, hoping to draw her into conversation.

It worked. She snapped her eyes to his, and he saw the rage shining almost as bright as the fire snapping on the wick of the candle. "Then don't send your damned beloved with my food," she retorted hotly. Suddenly, her brows knotted in agony and her eyes swept closed.

Slane felt her body stiffen in the bed beside his. "Taylor," he said in alarm and reached out a hand to her.

"Damn you," she whispered through clenched teeth. She caught his wrist in a tight grip before he could touch her. "Get out of here."

His outstretched fingers curled into a tight ball. Why had he been such a fool? He knew the constant throbbing, the burning, the pain that she was feeling. Gently he removed his wrist from her hand.

She opened her eyes in surprise.

Slane leaned forward, smoothing a few strands of hair from her forehead. "You don't have to hide from me, Taylor," he whispered, gazing down into her eyes. "I know how bad it hurts."

A strange look crossed her face. Uncertainty. Acceptance. She seemed to relax beneath him, and he felt as if he had been granted the world. He didn't want to move for a long moment. He didn't want to ever move. In her room, in the cover of darkness, he could put aside his oaths and codes and concentrate on her recovery.

But if that was all he was doing, then why should he have to put aside his oaths? The beginnings of guilt pulled at his conscience. He sat up, almost painfully tearing himself away from her. He had promises to keep. His fiancée waited for him just two doors down.

And yet, he couldn't leave. His hands followed his gaze to her side. He touched the hem of her tunic and hesitated for a moment, steeling his nerves. Steeling his emotions against seeing her flesh. Slowly, he moved the tunic up her body. Over her curvy hips, past her waist.

A white wrapping encircled her stomach, holding some other cloths in place over her wound. Slane gently untied the wrapping and pulled it away. Then he carefully peeled the bloodstained cloths from her wound.

Slane's brows furrowed as he studied the ugly red line that marred her skin, the black crosshatching of the stitches. No sword should ever have touched such skin. Gently, he reached out to examine the stitches. When his fingers touched her flesh, a shock seared through him. He felt her stiffen beneath his touch, and he quickly slanted his gaze to hers. But there was no pain in her eyes.

Slane once again lowered his eyes to her naked flesh. He couldn't help but notice the swell of her breast peeking from beneath her tunic.

Desire heated his blood instantly and he felt himself grow hard. He realized with a start that he was stroking her skin and his caress had moved upward from her wound. Close to the rounded part of her breasts, the part hidden beneath the fabric. Why, in another second . . .

He tore his eyes from her breasts, focusing on her wound. He cleared his throat softly, but it sounded like the boom of thunder in the quiet room. "It doesn't look infected," he said.

"No," she agreed, a strange huskiness to her voice.

He lifted his eyes to hers again. They were locked on him and Slane felt a wave of warmth wash over his body. Slane quickly dropped his gaze. He ran his fingertips over her skin, down to her waist, where his touch lingered a second too long. *I'm just seeing to her wound,* he told himself. *The wrappings have to be changed . . .*

His gaze again moved to her breasts. The slow rise and

fall of her chest seemed to match the pounding of blood in his ears. Then he looked up, but it wasn't her eyes that captured his attention. It was her lips. They were slightly parted and moist, as if she had just licked them. And full, so damned full. Begging to be kissed. Calling to him.

He cursed quietly and grabbed one of the clean cloths from the tray beside her bed and slapped it onto her wound. She stiffened slightly. He lifted repentant eyes to her, mumbling, "Sorry."

He retied the wrapping around her stomach, knotting it to hold the fresh cloth in place. He ran a hand along the wrapping, wondering what her skin would feel like pressed up against his. Wondering how she would look with her hair wild about her shoulders, lying beneath him, those beautiful eyes lidded and her mouth parted in a gasp . . . He pulled away from her so quickly that he knocked the soiled cloths from the table. His body was trembling so ferociously that he fled the room without another word.

Slane pushed open the door to Elizabeth's room. She was sitting on the bed, her thin brown locks freed from her headdress and flowing down her back. She turned, a comb in her hand, and greeted him with a glorious smile. "I was just thinking that we should probably ask Duke Roza to attend the ceremony. Perhaps he'd bring some of his famous apple cider."

Slane hadn't heard a word she said. He marched up to her, seized her by the arms, and pulled her against him. He lowered his lips to hers, crushing them beneath his. He tried with all his might to picture her in bed with him, her thin body curled lovingly in his arms. But no matter how hard he tried, his thoughts returned to Taylor's body. And that bare glimpse of her creamy flesh so close to the rounded part of her breast. He knew in that moment that he was lost. He knew he could never feel the same passion with Elizabeth that he did with Taylor. He growled fiercely and released Elizabeth, stepping back from her. He couldn't meet her confused gaze. "I'm sorry," he whispered.

He turned his back on her and left the room, quietly closing the door behind him. Marry Elizabeth, he would. Taylor was betrothed to his brother. She would save hundreds of innocent lives by marrying Richard. Slane had promised Richard that he would bring Taylor to him. He had given him his word. His word was his oath.

CHAPTER TWENTY-TWO

As Taylor's wounds healed, she could feel herself growing anxious to be out of her room, itching for some sort of exercise. She had sneaked out of bed more than once to stretch her legs, to get her muscles working again, and it was on one of these occasions that she pushed open the shutters to look out at the bright morning. She heard a woman's laughter and her head swiveled to the road. At first, she saw no one, but as she strained slightly, leaning out the window, she could make out two forms: Slane and Elizabeth coming around the corner. He pointed to something and Elizabeth tittered.

Taylor pulled back from the window. But it wasn't quick enough. She saw Slane lean over and press a kiss to Elizabeth's cheek. With a curse, she drew back into the darkness of her room, closing the shutters on the sight. That had been three days ago and she had not opened the shutters since.

But now, the feeling of restlessness and unease grew again inside her, becoming stronger with every passing moment. *I have to get out of this accursed room,* she thought. *Before the walls close in on me.* She rose from the bed and, despite her better judgment, sneaked from her room, pausing in the doorway to check the hallway. When she found it empty, she moved out of the room and down the stairs. As she reached the bottom stair, her eyes scanned the room, and she noticed with some relief that the inn was quiet and empty. A fire burned brightly in the hearth at the far end of the room. She could feel the faintest hint of warmth coming from the flames, and it helped wipe away some of the residual chill she had brought with her from her cold room. She thought for a moment of moving closer to the hearth, closer to the warmth . . . closer to the snapping, popping logs that hissed dark promises of searing heat and charred human flesh.

She turned away from the fire and took a seat at a table near the stairs, turning the chair around to straddle it, habitually favoring her wounded side.

Slane had not been to see her in days. The only one to visit her in all those lonely days, to help her change her bandages and bring her food, had been the innkeeper's wife. Taylor shook her head.

What had she expected? She certainly didn't want to see Elizabeth. And she knew that Slane was doing everything in his power to stay away from her.

"Can I get ya something?"

Taylor glanced up to see the innkeeper. Rollins was his name, she remembered. She gave him a small grin. "An ale," she said. She heard his footsteps disappear into the rear of the inn.

Taylor rested her chin against the back of the chair. She

didn't need anyone. She could survive by herself. Then why did she feel such loneliness inside her?

Something rubbed against her leg and she looked down. A calico cat turned to brush against her leg again.

A feeling of desolation swept through her and she reached down to stroke the cat's fur. *I don't need anyone,* she stubbornly told herself. *Stop feeling sorry for yourself. And stop thinking about* him.

"There she is," Taylor heard a woman's voice whisper. Her hand froze and the cat dashed away.

Two sets of footsteps moved toward her. Her jaw clenched and her eyelids drooped as the familiar disdain washed over her, shielding her heart.

"Slane was worried about you when he found your room empty," Elizabeth said to Taylor's back.

Taylor couldn't look at them together. The image of Slane kissing Elizabeth's cheek surged to the front of her memory, and no matter how hard she tried to push it aside, it stubbornly remained embedded in her mind's eye.

"You shouldn't be down here," Slane said. "Not this soon."

The timbre of his voice sent tremors through her body. Taylor tried to ignore them, but a part of her heart was crumbling.

After a long moment of awkward silence, Elizabeth asked, "How are you feeling?"

Taylor didn't answer. How could she respond when she would feel better dead?

"You are looking better," Elizabeth observed. "Now all we need to do is give your hair a proper washing and you'll be quite an attractive girl. Won't she, Slane?"

There was no response, but Taylor could feel Slane's gaze on her back.

"I'm certain Richard will find you most delightful," Elizabeth continued. Taylor swore she heard contempt in the other woman's voice.

What difference would it make what Richard thought of her? All she wanted was to join forces with him and kill Corydon. For Jared. Taylor stood and turned, sweeping her eyes over the couple. They were perfect. A knight in shining armor and his lady. Her stomach turned over. They belonged together. There was no room for an outcast mercenary.

Her eyes locked on Slane's, and she thought she saw a shimmer of sympathy there before he averted his gaze to Elizabeth.

For a moment, silence settled over them like a storm cloud moving in front of the sun. Unease speared the quiet like lightning.

Finally, Taylor brushed past Slane and hurried up the stairs, preferring her chilly room to any company. She knew she couldn't stay here. Every day she stayed, she destroyed more of herself. She had never cared about too much in her life; so why should it hurt so much to see Slane kissing Elizabeth? She shouldn't care two coins about him. She shouldn't give a damn what he thought or whom he kissed.

But somehow she did.

She moved into her room and sat on the bed. She would leave; she must. Even if it meant facing another Magnus Gale. But her wound was still not healed; it ached and throbbed even now. She couldn't travel yet. The jarring movements of a horse might very well rip the stitches wide open.

The door opened. "Taylor?"

Taylor looked up, and the vision of Slane standing in the doorway, outlined by the dancing light from the hall-way torch, made her unguarded heart stop beating. The torchlight swept over his blond hair and painted the tip of his sword gold. Then he shut the door behind him, sealing himself in the darkness. In her darkness.

She reached for the sack on the table beside her bed.

"Where do you think you're going?"

"You should be more concerned about your fiancée."

"You said you'd stay until your wounds are healed."

She raised her eyes to lock with his. "Some wounds won't heal."

"What's that supposed to mean?"

Taylor stood up, her eyes searching his face. But the darkness in her room hid his expression from her. She lit the candle on the table, careful to keep her fingers well away from the flame, and turned to look at him. "It means that, if I stay any longer, one of us will be hurt."

"Don't talk nonsense," he replied, whirling away from her.

"Slane," she shook her head. "I can't stay."

"Why?" he asked.

Taylor gave a snort of laughter. "Because I don't like Elizabeth," she answered. "And I don't think she likes me."

"Elizabeth?" Slane turned back to her, surprised. "She's gentle, kind, beautiful. What don't you like about her?"

Taylor leaned against the table with a sigh. "I don't like her because she's gentle, kind, and beautiful." She watched anger deepen the lines near his eyebrows.

"Don't mock me," he warned.

"I'm not," Taylor said gently.

"If you leave, you'll be hunted down like an animal. You know what Magnus did to you. I couldn't bear to see someone else hurt you."

Taylor stared hard at him. His blue eyes sparkled with sincerity. Didn't he realize how much he was hurting her?

"Taylor." He grabbed her wrist. "Do you want to be shackled and dragged to Castle Donovan by some heartless mercenary?"

She glanced at his hand about her wrist. "No," she murmured. "Nor by a heartless noble."

Slane dropped her arm as if she had burned him. "I'm not heartless."

"But you wish you were." He frowned and she continued. "You can't even look at me with Elizabeth standing beside you."

Slane looked away from her, his fists clenching. She studied his back with intense eyes, as if trying to memorize every detail about him. As if trying to . . . To what? There was no hope for them. There could be no future for them. And she didn't want one, she told herself firmly as a lump rose in her throat and tears burned in her eyes.

Taylor sat on the bed, the wound at her side beginning to flare again. She looked down at her entwined hands. Why couldn't he just let her go? Why couldn't he be rational? Why . . .

Slane knelt before her, grabbing her arm tightly, forcing her to look into his eyes. "I don't want to hurt you."

"Then let me go," she begged.

"I *can't*."

"Don't you realize what you're condemning us to?"

"I'm not condemning you. I'm saving you." His grip eased.

She stared into his confused blue eyes, wishing . . . wishing she had never met him. Wishing her father had never wanted to make amends. How could she live at Castle Donovan seeing Slane happy with a beautiful wife? She might as well be burned at the stake.

"I am your friend," Slane said decisively.

Friends? Is that all we are? she wondered silently. Then why did it feel as if he was ripping out her heart and dashing it to the floor, stabbing it with the sharp edge of his blade? Bitterness consumed her. How dared he make her feel this way? "No," she said and it came out as a growl. She ripped her wrist free of his grip. "You're not my friend. We'll never be friends. So just go back to your little wench. I don't need your protection. I don't need anything from you."

Slane rose up before her, towering above her like a statue. "I am bound by my oath. I pledged to bring you to Richard. And I will."

A sudden suspicion started to form in her thoughts. Why had he made a pledge to bring her to his brother? Why did Richard need to have her at Castle Donovan? *Maybe my father is there,* she thought, *waiting for me, knowing that I'll refuse to see him.*

But then the suspicion drifted away as Slane's deep blue gaze reached into her mind, clouding her thoughts.

Fool, she thought. *Fool. You used to be such a practical woman. With a few looks from those deep eyes you're nothing but mud in his hands.* She hugged her elbows, shaking her head, her body trembling.

Slane stared down at her for a long moment, unmoving.

Her back stiffened, but she didn't lift her eyes to him. She chuckled and it came out like a strangled laugh. "Don't worry, Slane," she said, her voice thick with sarcasm and tears. "I won't die."

There was a long moment before she heard his footsteps move away and the creak of the door before it closed.

Taylor stood for a moment, unmoving, letting the anguish of being such a fool wash over her. Then she pressed her face into the pillow and sobbed. . . .

* * *

Slane stood with his hand on the doorknob, listening to Taylor's sobs. It took every ounce of willpower he had not to throw open the door and take her in his arms and whisper soothing words to her.

"Slane?"

He raised his eyes to see Elizabeth, worry etched in her brow. For a long moment, he just stared at her. His fingers wouldn't release the handle of the door. "She wants to leave," he whispered, and he was surprised at how broken his voice sounded.

Elizabeth laid a soft hand on his arm. "Then by all means let her."

Slane shook his head, drawing himself up. "I gave my word to Richard to see her safely to him."

Elizabeth sighed, wrapping her arms around him. "Oh, Slane."

Where once Slane's body would have relaxed in his future wife's arms, it now only stiffened.

CHAPTER
TWENTY-THREE

Moments later, Slane bid Elizabeth good night and softly closed her door. He turned to his room across the hall, but his gaze was caught by another door. Taylor's door. He stared hard at the wooden barrier, wishing that the door would fade away so he could see her sleeping peacefully behind it. Finally, he turned to his room.

"Slane?"

The voice spun him around.

"Are you all right?" John asked.

Slane nodded, running a hand over his brow. "Just tired."

John nodded. "I suppose it has been rather a trying journey," he said. He stared thoughtfully at Taylor's door for a moment. "She's nothing like I expected."

Slane dropped his hand from his brow. "What do you mean?" He felt a surge of defensiveness rise inside him.

"I don't know," John continued. "I never expected to

find her a mercenary. Maybe an alewife or a seamstress, but not a mercenary. A woman who fights with a sword . . ."

Slane forced the protectiveness from him and nodded. "It was a shock to us all." He slapped John's shoulder. "At least I found her." He moved to take a step past his friend, but John's whisper stopped him.

"There's a man downstairs. He entered a few moments ago. I think he's a mercenary."

Instantly Slane moved past John and descended the stairs. Was it one of the mercenaries Richard had sent? Slane cursed the reward his brother had offered for the return of Taylor.

He saw the man as soon as he cleared the second floor. He was warming himself by the fire, his brown hair brushing his shoulders. His leather armor was worn and barely reflected the light of the flames. The man glanced over his shoulder and Slane recognized him immediately. Colm Duffy—one of the men Richard had hired to find Taylor.

Colm rose as Slane approached. "Lord Donovan," Colm greeted, holding his hand out to him.

Slane clasped his forearm. "Duffy," he said and studied Colm's face. But the pale blue eyes gave away nothing.

"What are you doing here, m'lord?" Colm wondered.

"You've tracked her here, haven't you?"

Colm dropped Slane's arm. "It's true then." He rubbed the back of his neck. "Damn. That reward money would have come in handy."

"She is under my protection now," Slane said firmly.

Colm spread his hands before him. "You'll get no argument from me, but how'd you find her? I've been tracking her for weeks now."

"She came to me," Slane said evasively.

"Is it true she's injured?" Colm asked.

Slane gave him a sharp look. Then he caught a movement out of the corner of his eye and shifted his gaze to see the innkeeper duck out of the room. *Damn fool,* he thought. *He's got a mouth bigger than an abyss.* Slane nodded in answer to Colm's question.

"You can't stay here," Colm whispered. "It's too dangerous."

"I can't move her," Slane replied, turning his back to Colm to stare into the flickering flames. "Not yet."

"Corydon's men are all over. And they have no interest in any reward. They just want her dead. You *can't* stay here."

Slane's jaw clenched tight. It could be a week before she was able to travel. And every day would lead Corydon closer and closer to them. "I have no choice, right now."

"I'm glad I don't have to make that decision," Colm murmured, turning back to the fire. "I'm not spending but the night and I'll be on my way."

"Where are you headed?" Slane wondered.

"Not sure yet. I suppose wherever there's pay to be made," Colm answered. He glanced up the stairs, then back at Slane. "Is it true your betrothed is here, too?"

Slane nodded.

"M'lord, if the Sullivan woman is hurt, she has no choice but to stay. But Lady Elizabeth should not be here."

As long as she was trapped at the inn with them, Elizabeth's life was in as much danger as Taylor's. The constant tension Slane felt in his shoulders suddenly renewed its intensity, tightening his muscles until they were as taut as a freshly strung bow.

"I'd be willing to see your lady safely to Castle Donovan for only a few gold pieces," Colm suggested.

Slane's body stiffened. He knew escorting Elizabeth was his responsibility. He should be the one to see his future wife safely to his brother's castle. But he couldn't. Not with

Taylor lying hurt. He couldn't do two things at once. And Taylor needed his protection more. She was the one Corydon was after. She was the one Corydon wanted to kill.

Elizabeth should not be where the danger was. Two men could offer Elizabeth the protection she needed to travel safely to Castle Donovan. John and Colm. He would send John with Elizabeth and pay Colm to accompany them. She would be safe that way. No harm would befall her. And he would see her again when he and Taylor reached Castle Donovan.

He nodded his head in acquiescence, not at all surprised at how easy the answer had come.

Slane leaned against the wall just outside Taylor's door. He knew she wouldn't leave through the window. She had to know that her wound would start bleeding if she tried to hang from a rope. *No,* he thought. *She's stubborn, but not stupid.*

The shadows of the hallway would keep him hidden long enough to see her face as she emerged from her room. She would come this way. He was sure of it.

He had waited all night and was beginning to wonder if she had played him for the fool when he heard the creak of a door. His head snapped up and he saw a shadowy figure emerge from her room.

He sighed and straightened, preparing himself for the confrontation. He waited until she started down the hallway before moving silently up behind her.

Suddenly, she whirled on him, halting his movement. Those fabulous green eyes were slitted, but he couldn't help but stare into them as if he were caught in a spell. Then something glinted in the torchlight and he dropped his gaze to see a dagger, the tip pointing at his stomach.

"You're up rather late tonight, eh, Slane?" Her voice was rich and soft.

"What are you planning to do with that?"

She turned the blade over in her palm. "No one makes me stay where I don't want to. And I got the distinct impression that you weren't going to let me leave."

"You think to run me through with that?" he demanded in disbelief.

"I don't need to run you through to disable you," she replied.

Slane thought he heard sadness in her voice, but he couldn't be sure. Anger surged within him. "You would have to do more than run me through to disable me," he retorted.

"Don't make this difficult," she said, taking a step backward.

"I can't let you leave," he said, his voice rising a little.

"I don't think you have much choice." She took a step down the stairs.

Slane surged forward, catching her wrist in his hand. They stood that way for a moment, glaring into each other's eyes. "It will get you nowhere to leave. Face your destiny."

"My destiny is not to see my father," Taylor said.

"At least talk to him," Slane urged.

"I don't think so." She attempted to yank her arm away.

Slane held it tightly. "It's the only way you'll be free of this. Do you think—"

She brought her foot down hard on his foot. Pain exploded up his leg, but he did not release her wrist. On the contrary, his grip tightened until he saw agony glitter in her eyes, and she opened her hand, dropping the dagger to the floor.

Her eyes danced with anger and determination. Slane knew she would try to flee again and again. And he couldn't watch her every moment. The more he held her, the more she fought to be free.

Slowly, he released her wrist.

Shock made her eyes round. She backed up one step, then another, never taking her eyes from him.

Slane watched her back away. What was he thinking? He couldn't let her go! But he couldn't hold her either. There had to be a way.

Another step.

He wanted to cry out to her. He wanted to beg her to stay. If she walked out that door, he was sure the next time he saw her she wouldn't be capable of drawing a breath.

Another step.

He felt despair burn in his chest. He remembered when he first laid eyes on her. Her face might have been bruised, yet her spirit was indomitable. It always had been.

Another step.

But Slane was sure she couldn't get through this. Not alone. Not with Corydon and the mercenaries after her. Thanks to him, they knew who she was now. They knew her face.

Another step.

And he would miss her. Terribly. Miss her smile, her bright eyes. Her quick wit. Her unique outlook on life. She wasn't as unfeeling as she wanted everyone to believe. He remembered the child she had saved from being trampled at this very inn.

He took one step down the stairs to stop her, but halted.

She had reached the bottom stair. She too stopped, her hand resting lightly on the railing.

His hand curled over the wooden banister as if in answer. As if it would convey all of his feelings to her—the things he couldn't say.

A sad smile touched her lips and Taylor removed her hand. She turned her back on him.

Slane watched her. She was such a little fighter. Such a risk-taker. But it angered him that she was gambling with her life. She would be so much safer . . . Gambling! That was it! "Taylor!" he called.

She stopped, then slowly glanced at him over her shoulder, her dark hair curling around her shoulders in thick waves.

"You're a gambler. Care to make a little wager?"

Taylor lifted her head, her eyes narrowing in curiosity. She turned to face him.

Slane moved down the stairs. "I'll wager your freedom and a month's pay against your staying with me until we reach Castle Donovan." He saw the glimmer of interest in her eye. *Bless her greedy little heart,* he thought as hope blossomed in his chest. "You're pretty good with that sword." He saw her glance down at the sheathed weapon at her waist. "But I'll bet I'm better."

She lifted her eyes to his. Her full lips curled slightly. "That's hardly a fair fight," she said softly. "I'm wounded."

"We'll fight in a week's time, if you're up to it." He saw the doubt in her eyes as she glanced at her wounded side. "And I'll fight left-handed."

Taylor lifted those glorious eyes to Slane, a smile lighting her face.

CHAPTER TWENTY-FOUR

After spending most of the morning resting in bed, Taylor sat at the back of the common room, well removed from the hearth. Her legs were stretched out before her, her head tilted back over the chair so that her long black hair spilled almost to the floor

She heard heavy footsteps descending the stairs. A man clad in boots. The footsteps halted at the bottom of the stairs and her body came to life, tingling with fire. Slane. She knew without a doubt that it was him. It was unnerving the way her body instantly reacted to him. And she was just thinking about him; she hadn't even seen him!

The footsteps drew closer and she heard the scrape of a chair on the floor.

"You shouldn't be down here alone."

A smile stretched across her face. It was Slane all right. "You're here," she couldn't help but goad.

And Slane fell right into her trap. "I wasn't a few

moments ago,'' he said, his stern voice faltering a little as she parroted the words right along with him.

Taylor chuckled softly, opening her eyes slightly to look at him. ''You're so predictable.''

Slane stared quietly at her for a long moment, and she waited for a tirade. Instead, Slane sighed and sat back in the chair.

''Do you know me so well?'' he wondered. ''How is it possible, when I know nothing of you?''

Taylor turned away from him. ''I have to know people to survive.''

''Am I so easy to know?''

''Usually,'' she admitted.

''And what of you?'' he asked. ''Why are you so difficult to know?''

The wall of sarcasm and wariness formed around her. ''To protect myself.'' She felt Slane's gaze shift to her.

''Has it been so painful for you?''

There was such sympathy in his voice that it angered her. ''Don't pity me,'' she flared—and flushed when he said the words at the same time.

''I guess you're not so hard to know after all,'' he chortled.

Heat suffused her cheeks and she had to grin and shake her head. Unwillingly, she felt her body sink lower into the chair, relaxing. The warmth of his smile encompassed her body, reaching her soul where the heat of the distant fire could not. ''Have you always been so deceptive?''

''I learn fast,'' he murmured.

Startled, she looked at him and chuckled. ''Then I must be a very bad influence on your honorable character.''

''I'm not so certain about my 'honorable character,' but, yes, you are a bad influence on me in other ways.'' Slane paused for a moment. As if with a will of its own, his gaze slowly traveled up and down her body. "Very bad indeed."

"I guess it's good for you nobles to mingle with the commoners," Taylor said, looking at him through lowered lashes. "It's not good to stand on that pedestal all the time."

Slane nodded. "Yes, occasionally I do feel the need to sit down with the peasantry. It's the only way to stay in touch with what is really happening in the country." Slane scratched his chin, waiting for a response. When he received none, he added, "So, peasant girl, tell me of the local gossip."

"Oh, yes, m'lord. As you wish," she proclaimed. "Shall I bow before you as I'm telling you the gossip or do you prefer your wenches upright?"

"I prefer all my wenches to prostrate themselves before me in adoration," Slane replied.

"Then you must not have had many willing wenches," Taylor quipped. Suddenly, the thought of Slane holding and kissing a woman with long chestnut hair erupted in her mind. She cleared her throat and pulled her knees up to her chest.

"Actually I prefer the ones who put up a fight," he said. "They're much more intriguing."

"I'll bet," she murmured.

They settled into silence, the crackle of the distant fire the only sound in the room. Taylor couldn't help but turn to look at Slane. And when she did, she found him gazing at her. She had to grin at the fond way he was studying her. And he answered her smile with a grin of his own. It transformed his face from the dark and troubled look she had grown accustomed to into one filled with warmth and promise. She felt her wariness melting under his glow. Then she realized something with such clarity that it burned her heart; she wasn't worthy of him, even if he would have her. She would touch his white, flawless soul, and it would become black and charred, like her heart.

Taylor looked across the room at the hot flames in the hearth.

"Why do you turn away from me?" he wondered softly. "Are you afraid of something?"

"Afraid?" she laughed. And then she turned to face him, bravely, foolishly. "I'm not afraid of anything."

"I think you are," he said softly. "I think you're afraid of many things and you hide behind that shield of indifference."

Startled that he had read her so well, Taylor again turned away from him but this time she avoided looking into the fire. Instead she watched the light cast by the dancing flames shimmer over the rear wall.

"Tell me what you see, Taylor." His voice was soft. "Tell me what keeps you from facing the world."

The light played on the wall before her, flickering around their two dark silhouettes like fire burning victims at the stake. Tears rose unbidden to her eyes.

"You won't find the answers there," he whispered.

Slane's voice sounded so close, as if he were leaning over to murmur in her ear. She swiveled her gaze to him, and his image wavered before her teary eyes. He was close, very close. His blue eyes shimmered like the hottest part of a flame. Startled, she blinked and looked closer, only to see the firelight reflected back at her.

The seductive, dancing flames captured her, tormented her, their flickering strands beckoning.

She suddenly realized she was trembling, shivering even, in the warmth of the room.

"Taylor?"

She barely heard. She could see the dark smoke rising

like fingers against the blue sky at Sullivan Castle. She remembered the horrible smell of burning flesh as if it were happening again.

"Taylor?"

She blinked and whirled away from the horror the visions inspired. The memory was gone. But the smell was not. She could never erase its acrid stench.

She saw Slane staring at her with concern. It was a moment before she realized that he was holding her hands tightly. "Are you all right?"

All she wanted to do was curl up in the warmth and protection he could offer her. But she didn't move; she just nodded.

"You're shivering," he observed and rubbed her hands vigorously to warm them. "Where did you go just a moment ago? It looked like you had seen a ghost."

"A memory," she answered with a dry throat.

He glanced at the flames of the hearth before turning back to her. "A memory that has something to do with the fire?"

Taylor nodded, but was unwilling or unable to tell him further.

"A memory that has to do with your mother?"

She jerked as if he had slapped her, and she almost rose, except he pushed her back down.

"I know she was burned," Slane said softly.

Taylor attempted to rise, but this time Slane shot to his feet and braced his hands on either side of the chair, trapping her. There was something akin to panic racing through her veins, clenching her insides, telling her to flee.

"It was a long time ago, Taylor," Slane coaxed. "It's time you tell someone about it."

Taylor looked away from him, unable to meet his eyes.

There was one way she could escape his hold. "Where's Elizabeth?"

Slane cupped her chin and Taylor felt bolts of lightning rock her body. He gently lifted her gaze to meet his. "I sent her on to Castle Donovan."

Alone. They were alone. Was he a fool? Or did he really believe his honor could protect him? His thumb stroked her cheek, tracing her cheekbone. Taylor felt her heartbeat quicken.

Slane's gaze dipped to her lips. Tingles followed his eyes' caress, and Taylor held her breath, afraid to move, afraid that he would remove his hand from her chin. She instinctively licked her lips as if that would hide them from his view.

Slane swallowed hard. He was so close that his breath fanned over her face, smelling faintly of sweet ale. His hand glided over her jaw and down her neck to rest on her shoulder.

She wanted him to kiss her. She desperately wanted to feel his lips against hers. But she couldn't move. She was caught in the spell of his eyes, his touch.

And then he was leaning closer to her, moving so close that their noses almost touched. He cleared his throat and opened his mouth as if he were about to speak, but when she lowered her gaze to them, they closed without issuing a word. Her blood hammered in her ears; her entire body trembled with a want she had never known before.

A log cracked in the fire and sparks shot out from the hearth.

Suddenly, he grabbed her shoulders tightly, his fingers digging into her skin. "I'm an honorable man," he ground out between his teeth. "I have given my oath."

Taylor opened her mouth to speak. She wanted to tell him it was all right. She understood. She knew what kind of man he was. But no words came.

He dipped his head and Taylor closed her eyes, anticipating the kiss. But then he shoved away from her with a growl. "It wouldn't be enough," he snarled. "Not with you." And Slane stalked up the stairs to his room without a single glance back at her.

Taylor sat for a long moment with her eyes shut tight, willing him to return, willing the feel of his fingers from her skin. But neither came true. When she opened her eyes, the room was empty. Her gaze was drawn to the lone shadow on the wall, surrounded by the swirling, dancing light from the fire. She watched the light surround her and a shiver shot through her body. With a sigh, she stood and headed back to her own room.

As soon as she stepped through the door, she unsheathed her sword and laid it on the bed. She paced for a moment, unnerved by the feelings that Slane unleashed in her. Then her gaze was drawn back to her sword.

The full moon shone up at her, the bright orb reflected in the polished silver of the blade. She knew she should pick it up. She knew she should practice and prepare for the battle with Slane. But part of her didn't want to. Part of her wanted him to defeat her.

No. She couldn't surrender to him. She knew she had to fight him with everything she had. Just as Jared had taught her.

She reached out and grasped the sword's handle, staring down at the clear reflection in the polished blade. Her eyes were ringed with sadness; there were lines of misery about her mouth. She had never looked so lonely and lost in her life.

This face, this image, staring back at her was not her. She was stronger than that weak thing with the tragic eyes. Taylor's hand tightened around the pommel. She knew what she had to do.

CHAPTER
TWENTY-FIVE

"Are you certain you're all right?" Slane panted, glancing at her wounded side.

A large orange moon gazed down at the clearing, showering Slane and Taylor with golden light as their swords clanged in the night.

"If you're afraid to fight me, you can surrender now," Taylor retorted.

Slane felt a smile ease across his face and he couldn't wipe it away. A sense of pride filled him as he watched Taylor handle her blade. She obviously had put the last week to good use.

She feinted left and then swung right with amazing speed. He blocked the blow, but had to move quickly to do so. She really was very good. Much better than he had expected. Only a trained eye could see how she favored her left side. She was not as strong as he was, but she was quicker. Like a sleek little cat. Her green eyes even seemed to glow in the night.

In the midst of battle, her face flushed with a radiant glow. There seemed to be such life coming from her, as if she thrived on the conflict. Then he realized suddenly that most of her life had been a battle.

Taylor arced her blade over her head, and when Slane moved to block it, she brought her weapon down and in. Cursing, Slane had to spin out of the way to avoid the move. Damn, but she was fast! She continued after him, raining down blow upon blow.

Breathing hard, she paused, circling slowly to her left. Suddenly, she lunged to the right. But when Slane moved instantly to block her blow, she pulled back. A soft, rich laughter bubbled from deep in her throat, mesmerizing Slane.

"You're taking this rather seriously, aren't you?" Taylor wondered.

"I believe what I'm fighting for is important," Slane responded, pushing aside the warm feeling her chortle had sparked in him to concentrate on their battle.

"You should really learn how to relax," Taylor advised.

"And you should learn not to—" Slane drove his sword toward Taylor in a tight arc—"talk so much when you're fighting."

Taylor met his blow with the ease of a trained fighter. She stepped in close to him, casting him her most beguiling smile. "But that's how I win my fights," she murmured in a husky voice.

Slane pushed his blade forward against hers, moving his body toward her. "Not all," Slane growled, his voice barely above a whisper. He pushed harder and she was forced to retreat a step.

But then she halted, pushing against his blade and lifted those damned full lips toward his. "Do you love Elizabeth?"

Startled, he almost stumbled back, but righted himself instantly. "We are to be wed," he replied. "Does it matter whether I love her or not?" Her parted lips drew his gaze. Her mouth looked so soft, a velvet pillow to rest his own weary lips against. "Honor and duty are not as fickle and fleeting as love," he managed to add.

"There's no such thing as love," she spat with sudden bitterness. "I was just wondering if you were foolish enough to believe in it." She shoved him off. Her blade glistened in the moonlight as she pulled it back, then swung forward, the sword slicing toward his head.

Slane raised his sword, gripping the handle tightly, and took the brunt of the strike, grunting as the surprising power behind her blow sent a jolt through the muscles in his arm. He redirected her swing to the side, forcing her blade down toward the ground, pinning the tip of it against the earth. The sweet smell of her breath fanned his face as she glared up at him. He pushed her blade away and took a step back.

Taylor straightened up. "She'll make you a fine wife," she said. Her face was a mask of composure, but her chest rose and fell with her quick breaths.

Slane watched with a growing burning in his loins as her breasts strained against the fabric of her tunic with each glorious breath. It would be so easy to slide his blade through the cloth and shred the last remaining barrier between his hungry gaze and her tender flesh. Slane snarled, pulling his gaze away. The thought enraged him because it had come so easily. So damned easily. He swung his blade hard toward her, the air itself screaming as the silver metal cut violently through it.

She lifted her blade to block the blow, but as Slane's

sword connected with hers, Taylor fell beneath the brutal weight of it. She landed on her bottom with a cry.

Slane's eyes widened in shock. He hadn't meant to hurt her! "I'm sorry, Taylor," he said quickly and reached out a hand to her.

She pivoted on the ball of her foot, lashing out with her opposite leg. It smacked into his knees, sweeping his legs out from beneath him. He tumbled to his back. Taylor lurched forward, placing the tip of her blade to his neck.

Slane frowned at the triumph he saw in her green eyes, the sparkle of amusement that glittered there. "That was dishonorable," he observed.

"I like to win," she said, a grin stretching across her lips. "Yield to me," she urged.

A muscle tightened in his jaw and his eyes narrowed. She pressed the tip of the sword into his skin. His lips thinned as he muttered, "I yield."

Slane stood in the darkness of the common room, watching Taylor eat. At least her appetite had returned, and then some. She ate ravenously, as if it were the last meal she would see for a while. Her long dark hair shimmered in the flickering light of the hearth, thick waves of black falling over her back as she bent over her porridge.

She had beaten him! he thought for the thousandth time. And she'd wasted no time in accepting her triumph; he had already glimpsed the packed bag on her bed when he went to find her for dinner. She was ready to leave. He clenched his teeth and turned away from her. It shouldn't bother him. She had beaten him dishonorably! She had tricked him. But it did bother him. Immensely. Not because he had lost *to* her. He even begrudgingly admired her ingenuity beneath his anger. But because he had lost *her*.

He had promised he would say nothing when she left. That was the wager. But he had not counted on losing! Even left-handed, he was a match for the best swordsmen. He had had no doubt in his mind that he would defeat her.

But she had continued to taunt him with her body and the fiery looks from those bewitching eyes! She had distracted him with her infernal chatter! It was no wonder he had lost!

No fight with her could ever be fair. She would always have him at a disadvantage with her soft curves, the siren song of her voice, the eternal emerald depths of her eyes.

Slane threw back his head and took a long drink of ale. He stared at the reflection of his face in the shiny surface of the liquid. His eyes looked haunted, possessed by the image of a woman he could not have. And should not want! He looked up at the cause of his anguish.

Taylor opened her mouth to take a bite of bread. As he studied her lips—the fullness of them, the cherry sweet redness of them—her innocent look seemed to turn wanton. And then blatantly seductive. Even though he was standing in the back of the room, her mouth filled his vision as if she were sitting but mere inches from him. His gaze traveled up to her cheekbones, marveling at the delicate roundness of them, the hint of color that gave them such vibrant life.

Then she turned to stare right at him. Her eyes drew his gaze on, forcing them upward, locking them into a tight stare. For a long moment, he lost all sense of who he was, where he was. Her emerald gems shimmered, priceless jewels buried in the treasure of her face.

Suddenly, he was on his feet, stalking toward her. He would end this charade. How could she think of leaving his protection? How could she think she would survive one day out there alone with Corydon's men and Richard's mercenaries looking for her—especially after what had happened last time?

As he drew near, his shadow fell over her like a dark storm cloud. He towered over her for a long moment, staring at her inquisitive eyes with fierce anger burning through his body. He opened his mouth to order her to stay by him, to stay at his side . . . but stopped cold. He had lost. He had given his word that he would let her go.

Taylor kicked out the chair her foot had been resting on and Slane fell silently onto it.

He could do nothing but stare at her. At the way her hair tumbled about her shoulders in clouds of curls, the way her deep green eyes seemed to see into his soul, reading and understanding. Then her lids fell over her eyes as she looked down at her mug of ale.

"It would be safer for you to stay," Slane finally said quietly.

A grin tugged at her lips. "I knew you couldn't resist."

"I'm not trying to stop you," he insisted. "I just think you should consider your options."

She lifted her luminescent eyes to him. "I have."

"Hmm," Slane mused. "You'd rather take your chances with a dozen trained fighters looking to kill you or who knows how many mercenaries looking to kidnap you. Kill. Kidnap. Kill. Kidnap. Maybe even both." He looked at Taylor. "You're right. An easy decision to make."

An amused smile twitched the corners of her lips. "I'm going to miss your humor, Slane." She lifted the mug to her lips, taking a long drink; then she slowly set it down again on the table. But this time, she did not look at him; she turned to stare at the back wall.

A sudden agony swelled in his chest. "You don't have

to go." His hand reached out to wipe her hair from her face. Her locks parted, like the softest curtain in the world, as he moved her hair aside to see the flawless skin it hid. "Taylor." His voice sounded thick to his own ears. She didn't look at him and he suddenly needed to see her eyes. He needed to gaze at them one more time.

She rose quickly and moved for the door. Then Slane was out of his chair just as quickly, calling desperately, "I don't want to see you hurt again."

"You won't," she whispered.

Slane caught her arm, but she wouldn't turn. She wouldn't lift her eyes to his. Slane reached around her and placed his hand on her shoulder, turning her to face him. Taylor kept her head bowed before him, her black mane tumbling riotously about her head. He cupped her chin and forced her head up until her eyes met his.

The pain he saw there tore at his soul. It was a different kind of hurt—not like the kind he had seen when she was physically wounded, but like the kind he felt in his own heart. He crushed her to him, wanting to take the pain from those eyes so he could remember her as the vibrant, glowing woman she was. He brushed his cheek against hers, disheartened as the lavender smell of her floated to him. He tried to memorize the feel of her against him, the soft curves of her back, the feel of her hair against the back of his hands, the way her cheek lay against his shoulder.

She pulled away slightly and turned her gaze to his. Her lips were close to his; her breath fanned his face. He had never pleaded for anything in his life. Until now . . . "Taylor, please . . ." he begged.

Taylor tried to take a step back as she shook her head, but his fingers tightened convulsively around her arms, refusing to relinquish their hold. She opened her mouth to speak, but a sudden fear filled Slane. He didn't want to hear her stubborn words; he didn't want to hear her reasons for leaving.

Desperate, he pressed his lips to hers to silence the words. The touch of her wet lips sent a surge of longing shooting through his body. The innocence of her kiss tugged at his conscience, begging him to release her before it was too late. But wasn't it already too late?

He parted her lips with his tongue and drove deep into the recess of her mouth, plundering the sweet inner sanctity with a need that he had never known before. He tasted her, trying to get enough of her to last him a lifetime. Her tongue swept his, meeting, battling. He held her along the length of his body, afraid that if he let go she would flee. Longing lashed his soul. He wanted her as he had never wanted anything before in his life. If she would but say the word, he would go away with her, forsaking all else.

At that realization, his body stiffened and he broke away. What was he doing? But as he looked into the depth of those sea green eyes, he knew exactly what he was doing. He was saying good-bye to a woman he admired, a woman whose courage surpassed even his own.

She studied his face for a long moment, those bewitching eyes taking in every taut line, every clenched muscle, until he was sure she could see the battle waging in his soul.

He couldn't turn his eyes away from her, even knowing what she was doing to him. Even knowing how she was tearing him apart.

Finally, she stepped back. And without saying a word, she turned and continued up the stairs. He watched her every move like a hungry wolf. She didn't once look over her shoulder.

Slane wanted to throw his head back and scream and scream.

She would be gone by morning. When he awoke, his life would be back to normal, as if she had never entered it. But somehow, he knew it would never be the same again.

CHAPTER TWENTY-SIX

It was time to leave, Taylor knew. Time to leave Slane. As it had been a moment ago, a half hour ago, hours ago. But the feel of Slane's hard body pressed so intimately against her own, the feel of his lips against hers, made her long to feel more of his caresses. How could she go when every one of her senses was telling her to stay? How could she stay when her mind was telling her to run and never look back? She stopped pacing and sat heavily on the bed beside her packed bag. "Damn," she muttered, her feelings swirling inside her. Her brain felt ready to explode. She dropped her head into her hands, grimacing at her indecision. She had never been this confused before.

She rubbed her temples and bemusedly shook her head. What would Jared think of her now? she wondered. At the thought, her back straightened and drew her up.

She slowly dropped her hands from her face. *Jared. I've come this far to avenge my friend's death,* she thought. *And now I'm running away into the night like a frightened child. How can I abandon him like that? How can I allow his death to go unpunished?*

Then why have I wanted to leave so badly? Her gaze shifted to the open window. The moon struggled to give light to the world below it, but a haze of clouds blocked its feeble efforts, leaving the night dark. The haunting image of Slane pressing his moist lips to Elizabeth's cheek speared Taylor's mind. The pain she felt in her chest was as immediate as it had been the day that she had witnessed the scene. She slowly dropped her gaze to the dark floor. She didn't want to be hurt. She should put as much distance between her and Slane as she could, forgetting everything: the possibility of a paying job, free food and board, avenging Jared.

She knew now that a simple heated glance from Slane's blue eyes or a seductive grin from his lips could make her forget everything. That was why she had not left yet. She was afraid Slane would be waiting in the common room for her. Waiting with his worried blue eyes. Waiting with his strong arms. Waiting with his dangerous lips. She was sure if he kissed her as he had before, she would never leave his side. And deep down inside, she knew she didn't want to leave Slane. She wanted to stay with him. Maybe, just maybe, he would forsake Elizabeth and take her in his arms again. . . .

But she knew he would never break his vow. His honor. His oath. She was afraid now that her longing for Slane was clouding her judgment, giving her too much of a reason to stay. After all, couldn't she avenge Jared's death on her own? Did she need to accompany Slane to Castle Donovan? Of course, it would be easier to have Slane pay for her meals. And she could seek his brother's help against Corydon. And what of her father? He would be at Castle Donovan waiting for her. Could she see him again, after all these years, just to be with Slane a while longer? She slouched her shoulders, her long black hair cascading over her face onto her lap. She didn't care about seeing her father. All she cared about was Slane. She didn't want to leave him.

Then what is the problem? she thought. *Don't go. You've never given a rat's ass about anyone else. Why start now? If you want to stay, to hell with Slane's reputation, to hell with his honor. Stay. Do what you want, just as you've done for the last eight years.*

But that was the problem. The wanting. She didn't know what she wanted from Slane. And she didn't know if, when she figured it out, he would be able to give it to her. But she knew she had to find out. She had to know what it was about him that made her feel so . . . so much like a woman.

She rose to her feet and moved with determination to the door, throwing it wide. She was avenging Jared's death, after all.

Taylor stalked down the empty hallway, hurrying before she lost her nerve. Slane was paying for her food and board, after all.

She reached for the door handle to Slane's room and almost pulled back, afraid. Her heart pounded furiously in her chest. Afraid of—

I'm not afraid, she told herself. *Of anything.* She shoved the door open and stepped into the dark room. She heard the rustle of movement and then the familiar *swoosh* of a sword being drawn. In the torchlight spilling into the room from the hallway outside, Taylor saw the polished blade pointing at her throat. But somehow that didn't frighten her as much as facing the blue eyes that shimmered in the darkness.

She wet her lips. "I'm staying with you," she announced.

After a long moment, the sword lowered from her neck, dipping back down into the darkness whence it came. The room was as silent as a chapel.

"I'll accompany you to Castle Donovan," she clarified, wondering if he heard her. Finally, she took a step backward before turning away from him and leaving the room, closing the door behind her.

Slane dropped heavily onto the bed completely and utterly stunned, staring at the door. Had that been Taylor who had just stormed in here, announcing she was going to Castle Donovan? Or had he finally fallen asleep and dreamed it? A glorious, wonderful dream.

No, she had had a change of heart. She was going to Castle Donovan after all!

But why the sudden change of heart? he wondered. What was in it for her? She did nothing if there was not some profit to be made. But he quickly realized with a widening grin that it didn't really matter what her motives were now. She was going with him! She would be safe with him. No mercenaries would capture her. Corydon's men would never get their hands on her. Suddenly, his sense of jubilation died and was quickly replaced by doubt.

But she was also coming to Castle Donovan to be with Richard. To be his brother's betrothed.

A strange sense of melancholy filled him at the thought. Richard's wife. He couldn't imagine it. Richard would never tolerate her sarcasm. He would never appreciate her wit. He would never see her beauty. Like Elizabeth, Richard would see the mercenary, the wild hair, the callused hands. He would never see the way the blue streaks highlighted that rich hair; nor would he appreciate the skill with which she wielded her weapon. No. Richard would view her sarcasm as disrespect, her humor as insolence. Slane scowled. Was he delivering her to safety? Or was he putting her in greater jeopardy than she was already in?

He should tell her. He should tell her the real reason why he sought her. He had told her a portion of the truth. But not the entire story. Not the part about her father betrothing her to his brother.

His gaze lifted to the door. But if he told her, she would never go to Castle Donovan with him. She would never be safe.

Taylor sat in the common room with her back to the hearth, watching the shadows cast by the flickering flames dance over the walls around her own dark silhouette. She couldn't help but wonder if she had done the right thing in staying with Slane. She shrugged to herself. What was done was done.

The sudden hiss of the fire burning behind her woke her from the hypnotic trance of the twisting shadows on the wall. She pushed the blanket from her shoulders and wrapped her hand around her mug of ale. She started to raise it to her mouth and froze—

How could she hope to compete with Elizabeth? Compete? She wasn't trying to compete! She finished bringing the cup to her lips and drained it. Her emotions were all ajumble inside her. She had to work them out. She had to sort out what she was feeling. But how could she do that when so many of the feelings were new? Taylor rose and turned—only to find a man with a twisted nose and dark eyes standing before her. Over his shoulder, she saw another man a foot behind him.

Taylor stepped to the side to move around him, but the man moved to block her path. She was in no mood to deal with this and briefly thought of kneeing him in the groin. But she was sure Slane wouldn't approve. "Pardon me," she murmured and again attempted to step around him.

Again, he blocked her path, and this time his friend moved up beside him. "We saw ya over here and thought ya might like some company," he all but drooled.

Taylor clenched her teeth. "No, thank you," she replied.

"Ah, manners," the twisted-nosed one said.

"Ya can tell she wasn't bred in the streets," the friend added.

"I'm afraid we insist," the twisted-nosed one said, grinning.

So much for pleasantries, Taylor thought. Sarcasm curled her lip. "What you two *gentlemen* don't understand is that I don't keep company with the likes of you."

"What's wrong with us?" the twisted-nosed one asked.

"You should bathe more often," she answered.

"Are ya insulting us?" the friend wondered.

"No," she lied. "I'm just trying to give some friendly advice."

"You're givin' us advice?" the friend asked. "Let me give you some. Keep your big mouth closed and yer pretty legs spread. Hey, Simon?"

The man called Simon chuckled deep in his throat.

Taylor's eyes narrowed slightly. She planted her legs wider apart. "Like this?" she wondered innocently.

"Wider," Simon coaxed.

"You mean this wide?" Taylor swung her leg up and into Simon's chest.

As Simon flew backward from the force of Taylor's kick, the friendly man dived for her, but she easily sidestepped the rush, pulling her mug out of his path. He crashed into a table behind her. "I'm afraid I don't do requests," she said, placing her foot on Simon's throat.

She caught a quick movement on the stairs and glanced up. Like a dark angel, he appeared, a shadowed visage emerging from the blackness. "Slane," she whispered, just before Simon's friend's fist connected with her jaw, sending her spinning to her hands and knees, her mug flying through the air, its contents spilling across the wooden floor.

Taylor watched from the floor as Slane's sword whistled to life, slashing through the air, striking flesh, spilling blood. It only took a moment before the two men lay dead at his feet.

The innkeeper and his daughter had scrambled away to safety once the fighting began, so now only Slane stood near the lifeless husks of the two thugs. He clutched the sword tightly in his hands until his knuckles turned to alabaster.

Then Slane spit on the corpses.

Taylor slowly rose to her feet as he grabbed a rag from a nearby table and wiped his sword clean, resheathing it once its silver surface shone again. He turned a murderous gaze to Taylor and she almost flinched, but kept her composure.

"Are you all right?" His words were gentle, in stark contrast to the lethal look in his eyes.

Taylor nodded.

Slane rose to his full height and turned to face the

innkeeper and his daughter as they peered out from the kitchen doorway. He pointed at Taylor. "This woman is with me. If I even see you or your patrons looking at her the wrong way, you'll get the same lesson I gave that scum."

Shocked at the intensity of his rage, Taylor lifted a hand, absently rubbing her cheek. In his own strange way, she supposed he had just defended her honor . . . if she had any left. She approached Slane, surveying the carnage. "I could have handled them myself, you know," she said. "And they might still be alive."

"They deserved no less than they got," Slane replied. He closed his eyes. After a long moment, he slowly opened them. He put his fingers to her cheek and Taylor felt her heartbeat quicken at his touch. In his deep blue eyes, she saw his anger, concern, and apology.

Taylor grinned slightly. "I've had worse."

Slane smiled gently. "That you have." He glanced at the innkeeper and his daughter huddled together. When he turned back to her, Taylor knew as Slane did that they couldn't stay here any longer.

"It's time to move on," he announced quietly.

"And just when I was beginning to like this place," she murmured.

"Get your bag and I'll pay what we owe," Slane said softly, "and a few extra coins to take care of those slugs." He jerked his head at the two dead bodies on the floor.

Taylor nodded and moved to the stairs. She knew they had to leave. Word would get out, and quickly, of a woman and a man, both wielding weapons. Corydon would send men. And she couldn't fight to her full capacity yet. Not the way she used to. Her side still ached from the swordplay with Slane.

By the time she returned with her belongings, their bill

was paid and Slane was climbing the stairs to collect his things. "Hey, Slane," Taylor called up to him.

Slane turned to glance at her over his shoulder.

"Life would be pretty damn boring without me, don't you think?"

CHAPTER
TWENTY-SEVEN

After a full day of traveling, Taylor was grateful to finally get off her horse. She tethered her steed to a tree near a stream and arched her back, reveling in being able to stretch. She had grown soft sitting at the inn. She needed more exercise to work her muscles.

She turned her eyes to the slight hill before her. They were drawing closer to Castle Donovan. And as they drew nearer, her uneasiness grew stronger.

Taylor cast Slane a glance. He was patting his steed as it drank from the stream. The sun was setting and the fading golden light seemed to be stretching its fingers to touch him one last time. Taylor was captivated by the reined power in his hand as he ran it over the horse's neck. She had seen him wield a sword with unabashed strength, but to see him do something as simple as pat his horse took her unaware. She found her gaze traveling the length of his body, from his strong shoulders to his slim waist, to the leggings curved so lovingly over the muscles in his thighs.

Suddenly, he turned and locked eyes with Taylor. She blanched and then whirled to stare at the clearing to their right. She felt heat suffuse her cheeks and quickly moved into the clearing, toward the slight hill that edged it, away from Slane.

When she topped the rise, she felt her stomach drop. There before her stretched the most beautiful lands she had ever seen. Vales of trees dotted the green pastures. Rolling hills filled the landscape, lush green grass carpeting their mounds. A sparkling blue lake peeked from behind one of the slopes.

God's blood, she thought. *I didn't realize we were so close.* She felt tension knot her shoulders as a tidal wave of memories crashed about her.

"Taylor?"

At Slane's voice, she jumped and turned to face him.

The grin that he had approached her with disappeared as concern furrowed his brows. "Are you all right?"

"We're coming to Sullivan lands," she said with a nonchalance she didn't feel.

Slane nodded. "You knew we had to go through them to get to Castle Donovan."

Taylor turned back to the lands that stretched before her. She had known, yes. But somehow she hadn't been prepared. For years she had avoided these lands, steered clear of anything to do with them, refused to take any work that would even bring her close to them. And now, standing on the threshold of her old home, she felt a fierce anxiety seize her. She had to get away from these lands, from these painful, haunting memories.

She turned to do just that and came face-to-face with Slane.

Gently, but firmly, he set his hands on her shoulders. "It's all right, Taylor," he soothed in a rich, melodic voice.

Taylor wet her lips and looked around as if at any moment her father's men would spring forth from the surrounding trees and spirit her back to Sullivan Castle.

Slane cupped her chin and forced her to look at him, to look deep into his eyes. "I won't let anything happen to you," he whispered. "I promise."

His touch, his sincere look, calmed her, but his words erased her fear. He was a man who lived by his word. His oath. His honor. She knew he meant what he said. She leaned forward, resting her forehead against his shoulder.

His arms swept around her, encompassing her in the safety of his embrace.

Smoke and flames, hazy memories lingered at the edges of her mind. Taylor turned her head to the side, resting her cheek on his shoulder. Tears burned her eyes from the smoky cloud of those remembered flames. She fought the images, fought them back, refusing to see them again. Refusing to acknowledge their effect on her. Those memories were long gone now. It was over.

She broke away from Slane's embrace, moving away from the comfort and healing it offered, down the rise toward the horses.

"Taylor!" Slane called.

She halted, but didn't turn. Her insides trembled for his touch, his comfort. She was afraid to turn. She was afraid that she wouldn't be able to resist the lure and solace he offered. She was afraid of him . . . of falling in love with him.

"Smoke!"

She whirled to find him pointing toward Sullivan lands. Memories of smoke and fire resurfaced instantly in her mind's eye. She began to shake. It couldn't be. There couldn't be smoke. There couldn't be fire. That had happened years ago. Trembling, she turned her back on him. "I don't care," she announced coldly.

"You don't care?" His large strides brought him to her side as she reached the horses. "Maybe you think you don't. But you really do. This is your home!"

"It used to be," she snapped. "But it's not anymore."

"But you're the heir! Your father—"

"I don't give a damn about my father!" Taylor hollered. "Not after what he did."

Slane's scowl deepened. He moved to his horse and pulled himself up into the saddle. "Someone might need help," he said as if that were all the explanation he need give.

Taylor's angry glare clashed with Slane's furious stare. Finally, he reined in his horse and spurred the animal toward the rise.

Taylor watched him go, small puffs of dust kicking up from the horse's hooves as he sped away. Then his form disappeared over the hill, and anger boiled in her veins. Who the hell did he think he was? Going off to rescue every damned person in trouble. What if it was a trap! It would serve him right! Then where would his damned honor be?

She stared after him for a long moment. "Damn," she muttered and swung herself onto her horse.

The moon was high in the sky when Taylor finally caught up with Slane just outside of the village. But Slane sitting eerily motionless in his saddle wasn't what caught her attention. It was the village. All around her the houses lay in crumbled blackened ruin, victims of the fire's deadly wrath. Smoke still smoldered from most of the buildings. She sat there, blank, amazed, and very shaken. Her hands convulsively tightened around the horse's reins.

Slane urged his horse slowly on through the main street of the village.

Without a sign from Taylor, her horse moved forward. Waves of trepidation swept through her as her gaze focused on the skeletal remains of one smoldering ruin . . . the house that Mrs. Mulder had lived in. She had made the best apple tart in the lands, and Taylor used to come see the old woman every day in the summer to get a taste.

Taylor tore her gaze away from the burnt-out shell, and her gaze locked on Farmer George's house. Smoke rising from a charred, blackened beam swirled into a ray of moonlight. Long ago, Taylor had sat in that very room of the house, playing damsel in distress with Farmer George's son, Jeffrey.

She ripped her stare away only to find her gaze centering on the DeLuca house. Her friend Julie had lived there. God, she hadn't thought of her for . . .

Her horse drew closer to the still glowing rubble of the DeLuca house. Julie used to come to the castle with her mother who worked in the kitchens. She and Julie used to spy on the knights and pick their favorite as they jousted, pretending they jousted for their honor. Julie . . .

Taylor's horse halted. The animal pawed the ground skittishly, sending ash into the air. Heat radiated from the shell of the home in waves.

A tortured dullness swept Taylor up in disbelief. What had happened? All around her was destruction. The village lay in smoking ruin, burned to ashes. The smoke stung her nostrils, its choking scent closing her throat. She wiped at her nose, desperate to rid it of the foul stench.

Her eyes scanned the streets for any survivors. But there were no signs of living people, no moans of the wounded.

There was only intense heat and an occasional crack of a burning piece of wood.

Unnerved, she pulled back from the blackened frame and her horse followed her command, backing away, tossing its head as if in objection to the sights reaching its eyes.

Suddenly, a charred beam splintered in two and crashed to the ground, sending a shower of glowing embers into the night sky. With a jolt, Taylor realized where she was, and desperate to escape, she spurred her horse. With a slight rear, the horse lurched forward down the road, racing past the ravished remnants of what used to be a thriving village.

As she raced forward, Sullivan Castle loomed before her, silently beckoning her with its lowered drawbridge. The arrow loops were empty, now just vacant slits in the castle's walls, looking more like knife wounds sliced into the stone than the defensive windows they were supposed to be. Once a vibrant center of life, she knew the castle was now a barren monument to the dead.

Taylor's gaze immediately settled on something dangling over the castle walls. She pulled back on the reins, bringing her horse to a halt. Beneath her, the animal pranced nervously. As she looked closer at the thing hanging from the wall, she realized she was looking at a human form. It was a man. A man dangling from a rope, hanging by his arms, the rope binding his wrists rising up the castle wall to disappear over its edge. Every instinct inside Taylor told her to run. To get out of the village, away from the castle. But she couldn't take her eyes from him. His clothing was in tatters, hanging in shreds on his body. His graying hair hung in sickly strands across his face. Suddenly, the man turned his head, groaning loudly.

Taylor heard the sound of hooves coming closer. "I'll cut him down," she heard Slane say from beside her.

Taylor swiveled her head to see Slane moving his horse over the lowered drawbridge and heading into the open gates of the castle. She turned back to the man, swinging her leg over her horse to dismount. She approached him, squinting. There was something about him. Something familiar.

The man groaned again, tossing his head. The damp strands of his hair clung to the blood on his face. There were slashes all over his body; his skin was dirtied with ash and soot. He had been tortured, she was sure. But by whom?

Suddenly, the man fell to the ground. He landed hard and fell forward onto his stomach. Taylor glanced up to see Slane looking down at her from atop the castle wall. He grimaced and turned away. Taylor shifted her gaze back to the fallen man and approached him. He was badly beaten and there was no telling how long he had hung there.

Taylor bent and grabbed his arm, pulling the man over onto his back. She froze, staring at the face. Even battered and bruised she knew that face. Her insides swirled in agony and contempt. Finally, she stepped away from him, her face a mask of loathing.

"Who is he?" Slane wondered, emerging from the castle.

"My father," she whispered.

CHAPTER
TWENTY-EIGHT

Slane bent beside the fallen man, putting his ear to his chest. The faintest tremor of a heartbeat drummed softly against his ear. Slane lifted his head and placed a hand near the man's lips. Faint whisperings of air hit his hand at regular intervals. He lowered his hand and shifted his gaze to the man's closed eyes. "Lord Sullivan?" he called.

The man groaned and his eyes slowly worked themselves open to the merest slits of life.

"Who did this?" Slane demanded.

Lord Sullivan opened his mouth, but no sound issued forth.

Slane turned to Taylor. The night's wind gently lifted the wispy curls of her hair and placed them back over her shoulders delicately. Otherwise, she had not moved. She stood like a granite statue, watching through cold eyes. "He's dying," Slane hissed, furious with her inactivity.

But even with his admission, she didn't move to her

father's side, didn't kneel with tenderness and weep. "He's your father," Slane reminded her, shocked at her coldness.

"Taylor?"

Lord Sullivan's broken voice turned Slane's attention back to the man. His eyes had widened to pools of deep brown. His gaze moved past Slane to lock on Taylor with a renewed vigor, a wish granted. But the joy and happiness Slane saw for a brief moment on the old man's face faded.

Slane turned back to Taylor. She hadn't moved. Hadn't even batted an eye. *God's blood!* Slane thought. *What is wrong with her?* He stood and moved to her. "He's your father!" Slane whispered harshly. "Go to him."

But she didn't move. She never turned to look at Slane; she only glared at her father with such condemnation that Slane was taken aback.

"Taylor," her father pleaded. "I've finally found you." He lifted an old, trembling hand to her, his fingers outstretched, grasping for something. "Forgive me, child."

Taylor stiffened, her jaw clenching, her eyes narrowing.

"Forgive me," he begged.

Slane waited, as did her father—waited for the words that could heal them. Slane turned to look at her, urging her to forgive. She parted those lips, but the word that came from them was not one of absolution.

"Never," she snarled.

The old man's hand clenched into a fist and dropped to the ground.

"Taylor," Slane exclaimed. "He's dying. Let him go in peace."

"And what of my mother?" Taylor snapped. "Did she die in peace when those flames ate her skin from her body? Did she?"

Lord Sullivan groaned. As Slane turned to him, his eyes rolled into his head before his body sagged to the earth and he sighed his last breath. Slane knelt by his side, placing a hand near the other man's mouth. But he knew Lord Sullivan was dead. He placed a hand on his chest, saying a silent prayer for him. His final request had gone unfulfilled. He had not been given the forgiveness he had sought. After so many years, so much pain . . . Taylor could have let him die with honor, in peace, but she knew nothing of honor, nor of love.

Slane whirled on her, glaring up at her in disbelief, as if she were some dark goddess deaf to the desperate pleas of her subjects. "He's your father! And he is dead! Now you will never know his love. Never. Why? Why not forgive a dying man his faults?"

"Why should I," she demanded, "after what he did to my mother?"

"He wanted your forgiveness, Taylor! Now he's dead."

"Good," she snapped. "He deserved it. He killed my mother with no regret, no remorse. He showed her no mercy. Not even when I asked him for it. He refused to listen to *my* pleas. And I begged him—I *begged* him not to hurt her. I begged him not to take her away from me." Tears rose in her eyes. "He wouldn't even let me say good-bye to her."

Slane saw the shimmering sadness fill her eyes, but he felt such an incredible rage at her insensitivity that he couldn't stop himself from clenching his fist and taking a threatening step toward her. "He was your father!" Slane roared. "He gave you your life! You've cursed him to a horrible death that he can never escape! You could have given him one moment of peace with three damn words! Just three words, Taylor!"

Taylor did not retreat under his approach. She stood her ground. "Did he forgive my mother?" Taylor hollered back. "He murdered her! He took her life by burning her at the stake! What more horrible death is there? I'll give him no peace. Let him rot for what he's done to me. To her!''

"Listen to you!" Slane cried. "Listen to what you're saying!"

But she wasn't listening. Her voice broke as she tried to speak. "You don't know what it's like to have your mother taken away from you! I'll never forgive him. Never!''

Slane lowered his voice. "Don't you see, Taylor? Don't you see what you just did?" Slane waited to see the ugly realization dawn in her teary eyes. But the realization never came. "You have abandoned your mother forever." Slane paused. "You've chosen to make your father's rage and hatred your own. You now have his cold heart beating in your chest, not your mother's."

Taylor began to shake her head, to deny his words, but she halted, frozen in disbelief. Her mouth opened in silent denial, but her voice choked on the agony of his revelation. The pain of what she had become overflowed her lids, slipping down her face. She stood, trembling, her entire body shaking with misery.

Slane opened his mouth to speak, but suddenly Taylor whirled, running to her horse. In one fluid movement, she pulled herself onto her steed's back and was off.

"Taylor!" Slane hurried to his horse and quickly mounted. "Taylor!" he cried out again at her fleeing back, but he knew she would not stop. She was riding like a woman possessed, her hands cracking the reins again and again, her hair flying wildly out behind her. He spurred his horse forward, snapping sharply on the reins, demanding the beast ride as fast as it could go.

Taylor continued to charge ahead, racing toward a nearby forest, and then vanishing into its deep shadows.

"Taylor, stop!" Slane cried, following her into the thick trees.

He knew she was an expert rider, but he also knew she was not concentrating, not thinking where she was going. Slane watched her horse leap a fallen tree and felt his own heart leap as she teetered precariously for a long moment before righting herself. He had to catch up with her.

Slane urged his horse deeper into the thick expanse of trees, dodging fallen trunks, ducking beneath attacking branches. He saw Taylor's horse stumble and he spurred his horse on. His heart twisted inside of him, knowing the agony she must be experiencing. Knowing that he had inflicted it on her. But she had to see the truth!

He knew he would have to catch her if he wanted to stop her. Blood pounded in his ears; the wind rushed by him. His horse cleanly leapt another fallen tree and he found himself racing just behind Taylor, bursting into a small clearing.

Just then a dark shadow fell over Slane, obscuring the moonlight. He looked up to see a huge wall of trees filling his vision on the opposite side of the clearing, a mass of hard trunks and jagged spiked branches that were impenetrable for a horse.

"Taylor!" Slane screamed.

CHAPTER TWENTY-NINE

Slane spurred his horse hard and the animal surged forward. He lunged for Taylor, extending his hand as far as he could. Wrapping his arm around her waist, he yanked her sharply from her horse.

Taylor pushed backward, struggling against his hold, and toppled both of them from Slane's horse. They hit the ground hard—she landed on her right side, Slane on his back. He winced at the sudden pain in his back, but it disappeared just as quickly as it had arrived.

Taylor tried to roll away from Slane. "I don't think so," Slane told her and grabbed her wrist, yanking her back to him.

She pounded on his shoulder, trying desperately to break free of him.

He forced her legs down with the weight of his body and crawled on top of her, pinning her flailing arms to the ground at her sides with his hands. "Enough!" he roared into her face.

To his surprise, she stopped struggling, stilling her efforts at escape. He gazed down in wonderment at her broken face, shocked and guilt ridden by the tears that covered it in a sheen of sorrow.

She stared up into his eyes with such misery that it shattered his soul. A broken sob escaped her full lips. He wanted to take all her agony away. He wanted to touch her pain and erase it. He wanted to heal her broken soul. He rubbed his fingertips against her cheeks, tracing her cheekbone, wiping her tears from her skin.

She parted her lips to inhale a shaky breath and Slane's gaze was drawn to her mouth. She was so lovely. And so hurt. He dipped his head and pressed his lips to her quivering mouth to comfort her. Only to comfort her.

But something happened he had not planned on. A jolt rocked him as his body came instantly alive. It was as if he were feeding off her vibrancy, her need . . . and found the same need within himself. He pulled back to stare into her eyes. They were swollen from crying, but there was also something else, something hidden deep within them. Something that called to him. Something he could not deny.

A fiery urgency filled his body and he felt himself being swept up in an inferno, into a blazing fire of need that could only be quenched by one thing. Slane bent his head to Taylor's lips, reclaiming them. He needed her just as much as she needed him. He wanted her more than he'd ever wanted anything in his life. And this time, he would not be denied. Her mouth parted and he tasted her fully, exploring the sweet recesses of her mouth, feeding off of her delectable lips. His manhood grew strong beneath his breeches, bulging against the cloth, aching to explore the dark hollow that lay but a few inches beneath it.

Blood pounded through his mind as his lips swept hers. His consciousness seemed to ebb and then flame brighter than ever. He felt more alive than he had ever felt. He felt every inch of his body pressed intimately against hers, his chest pressing against her breasts, his bulge pressing intimately against her core. His blood surged through his veins, burning like molten lava. He released his hold on her and she immediately put her hands on his arms, refusing to relinquish the moment.

Instead of pulling back, Slane dipped his hand to cup her breast through her tunic, encircling it with his fingers, massaging it with his thumb. Her flesh was firm and full, filling his hand.

Taylor gasped and Slane kissed her again, driving his tongue deeper into her mouth, plundering the recesses, exploring every part of her mouth. Her hands moved from his arms to his back, tracing the coiled muscles with light strokes.

Slane slid his hand across her neck and dipped his fingers beneath her tunic, almost ripping it in his hurry, in his craving, to feel her flesh. When his fingers encircled the delicate, sensitive rise of her breast, he felt her arch toward him, gasping for breath. Her knees came up at the sides of his body, her womanly core pressing tight against his manhood. Slane dipped his head to her neck, tasting her skin, wanting her with an urgency he had never felt for anyone else.

Taylor moved her hips against his. She responded to his caress with a deep groan that inflamed Slane's already combustible senses. He slid to the side of her body, pressing kisses down her throat to the tip of her tunic. He moved his hand out of her clothing and over her flat stomach, across the planes of her belly, to the bottom of her tunic, which had gathered dangerously close to her womanhood. He moved his hand to the bottom of the cloth, feeling a heat emanating from beneath the fabric of her leggings as his fingers touched the very edge of the tunic. Then he dipped his hand lower. He touched the inside of her thigh, letting one finger roam close enough to her womanhood to feel her shudder. The smell of her raw lust permeated her leggings and he let the sweet aroma fill him, let the intoxicating scent of her possess his senses.

Slane moved his hand up to the top of her leggings. She placed a trembling hand over his, halting his movement. Confused, he looked into her eyes.

"You don't know what you're doing," she whispered in a husky voice.

His confusion vanished and a dark grin came to his lips. "I know exactly what I'm doing," he whispered in a silky voice before his hand slipped inside her leggings. He moved his fingers closer to the wetness of her womanhood and touched the soft curls of hair that kept her pearl hidden. Her womanly hair caressed his fingers with whispery, silky softness as he moved through them, easing his way toward the moist petals of her womanhood. He reached the delicate folds and parted them. And then he touched the precious jewel that lay hidden beneath. The sweet sound of her gasping breath, the gentle curve of her arching back, did indeed show that he knew exactly what he was doing.

Taylor couldn't have stopped him if she wanted to. But the only thing she wanted was more of him, more of his touch. Shivers of pleasure peppered her skin and passion pounded through her veins as he expertly stroked her to heights of rapture.

Slane removed his hand from her womanhood and was

surprised and gratified to hear a groan of objection. Slowly, he began to undress her, lifting her tunic up over her flat stomach, past her slim rib cage and over her breasts. He bent his head to the mounds, worshiping her flesh with light kisses. He eased the tunic over her head without taking his lips from the peaks of her breasts. His tongue swirled over the rosy tips, across the hardened pebbles of her nipples.

Taylor gasped, her mind swirling end over end, her world tilting on its axis.

Slane's lips returned to claim Taylor's, buffeting them until she was breathless. His hands skimmed the sides of her body to her waist and tugged down her leggings. His kisses traveled over her throat and down to the valley between her breasts as he pushed the leggings from her body.

When he had freed her body of her clothing, he gazed down at her with adoration. She was the most beautiful woman he had ever seen. Quickly, he yanked his shirt from his torso.

Taylor watched the unveiling of his glorious body. Like a curtain being swept aside, his tanned chest was revealed, gleaming like bronze in the rising sun light. Muscles lined his exquisite frame, and more planes of muscle contoured his stomach. She had never seen a more handsome man. When he slid his leggings from his legs, she marveled at the stark power in them.

He leaned over her, holding himself above her with his hands for a long moment, simply gazing down into her eyes. She reached out to him, running her hands along his arms, his shoulders and into his hair.

He lowered himself to her, and Taylor inhaled sharply as his chest touched her bare breasts, the peaks tingling with pleasure. Then his body covered her like a warm blanket. She felt something touch her most intimate core and knew what it was. She opened her legs, trying to feel him against her, to be closer to him.

Slane almost exploded at her invitation. His member lurched forward and found a hot wetness waiting for it. She wanted him as much as he did her. He groaned softly at the realization. He reached down and touched her core again, opening it. She raised her hips and he eased himself into her.

He felt her stiffen and stopped, pulling back to gaze at her face. Could it be? he wondered. Could she be a virgin? He kissed her lips with a powerful hunger, one close to starvation, and then trailed hot, wet kisses down her neck. He caressed one of her breasts with teasing feather strokes until she relaxed again.

He slid the rest of the way into her, penetrating her completely.

She gasped and thrust gently, tentatively. He answered her plea and began to move. Slowly at first, and then their tempo increased as she matched his moves, thrusting against him. A swirling ecstasy built inside her, until she thought she could take no more. He touched her breasts, kneading, squeezing, and kissed her neck with hot liquid caresses. Her desire rose to peaks of pulse-pounding passion, swirling past the stars to a heaven she had never known existed. Then he kissed her lips with a fierce possessiveness that sent her exploding toward the heavens. Shattering into a million twinkling lights, she lingered in those heavens for a long moment until she fell toward the earth like a shooting star, burning like a fiery inferno. Finally, she lay still beneath him, breathless.

Slane stared down at her in disbelief. He had thought she was beautiful before, but that was nothing compared to the vibrant creature that lay beneath him. Her cheeks were rosy and bright, her breath now easing from her lips in a sweet rhythm of contentment. She was more than he could have possibly imagined. She was everything he could ever want. And with that one thought, he lunged into her, again and again until his own world erupted in a rapture to rival hers. He stiffened, releasing his seed into her, holding her tightly, binding them body and soul.

Slowly, reality penetrated his mind. He felt the night's breeze cooling his heated skin. He heard his horse whinny in the distance. Birds clattered somewhere to his right. But mostly, he could feel Taylor's breasts crushed to his chest, her flat stomach pressed to his, his manhood sheltered in her warmth. Slowly he withdrew from her, rolling onto his side.

Taylor didn't want to open her eyes; she was sure it had all been a dream. She felt . . . safe somehow. It was silly and ridiculous but she felt sated and warm and . . .

She opened her eyes. The blackness of the night sky had burned away, replaced by the red of the rising sun. She felt the soft grass beneath her back, heard a soft whinny, and turned her gaze. In the distance, Slane's horse stood, eating the grass.

She turned to look at Slane. He was staring at her with a small grin on his face.

"What?" she asked defensively.

"You're beautiful," Slane whispered.

Taylor was unprepared for the honesty in his voice. She felt the heat rise in her cheeks and had to look away from him.

His low rumble of laughter shook her body. "You don't take compliments too well."

"Sorry. That wasn't something Jared taught me," she retorted, grabbing for her tunic.

But Slane was quicker. He snatched it off the ground and moved it out of her reach. "And did he teach you how to kiss like that?" he wondered in a strangely dark voice. "Or how to respond to a man's touch like that?"

"Of course not," she said, lurching for her tunic.

Slane easily moved it out of her grasp. "Then someone else taught you?"

"No," she said, dropping her hand. Her eyes got a faraway look to them as she remembered. "There *was* one man, or rather boy, who came close. But I just didn't trust him." She snorted. "It's a good thing I didn't. He was a liar and a thief."

"There were no others?" Slane wondered.

Something in his voice pricked her nerves and she lifted her head. He hadn't known! He had thought she had slept with other men!

Slane scowled. "I'm . . . You've never . . ."

Taylor shook her head slowly. He'd regret what he'd done now. He'd turn away from her. "No. There was no one before you." She steeled herself against his rejection.

But there was no rejection. His look softened with tenderness. There was possessiveness in his stare, and something else—something she didn't recognize. A crooked grin curved his lips and he leaned forward to plant a kiss against her cheek.

She lifted her eyes to lock gazes with his. He was so close to her that she felt the heat of his breath fan her lips. He reached out to her, drawing her to him, engulfing her in a tight embrace.

Shocked, Taylor couldn't reciprocate. She let him hug her, feeling the warmth of his body seep into her own. She felt the caress of his cheek against the top of her head.

Finally, she wrapped her arms around him, holding him tightly, nervously, as if she was afraid he would vanish and she would be alone again. They sat that way for a long moment, the glow of the morning light reaching out to touch their entwined bodies.

An ache filled Taylor, starting in her chest and encompassing her entire body. She had a feeling, a strange feeling, that this would be the last time she and Slane would ever be together. She pulled back to gaze in his eyes, stroking his hair, touching his face, trying to memorize this moment. She had never felt anything like this in her life. She wanted to stay with him, be a part of his life.

"I have to bury your father," Slane whispered. "You don't have to go back."

"I'll go with you," she said.

Slane touched her cheek softly, then bent and kissed her lips. He held her tunic out to her.

Taylor took it and slipped it over her head. Slane pulled on his leggings, and Taylor donned her own. She reached for a boot, but cast Slane a look over her shoulder. He was staring at her with a serene look. She straightened and looked askance at him. But then, the look was gone and Slane was smiling, reaching for her.

The horse whinnied in the distance as Slane chuckled, pulling her against him, kissing her neck. But every instinct in Taylor flared to life. She went as still as a rock.

Slane eased his hands from her. "What is it?" he wondered.

Taylor listened hard, but there was no noise. The birds, the forest around them was still, silent in warning.

"Slane," she cautioned, her gaze searching the trees around them.

Slane followed her gaze. He stood, pulling her up beside him, holding her protectively by his side.

Every instinct in Taylor's body told her to get her weapon. Her stare shifted to Slane's horse. *Where the devil is my steed?* she wondered. Her sword was on her horse! She scanned the clearing, but there was no sign of him!

She moved toward Slane's horse, but Slane caught her wrist. "What?" she asked, lifting her gaze to his. But he was staring at something directly before them.

She swiveled her head to see a line of black-clad men heading toward them. Some held bows and arrows aimed at them; others clutched swords. She froze as she spotted one man walking ahead of the rest. He was dressed all in black, his dark cape swirling out behind him in the breeze, looking like a bat's wing. An ugly, gleeful smile filled his thin lips and his dark eyes.

"Corydon," Slane snarled.

CHAPTER THIRTY

Hatred burned in Taylor's veins as she stared at the man dressed in black. She scanned the ground for a weapon of some sort, but there was nothing. Not even an old log. Here she was, face-to-face with Jared's killer, barely clothed and completely unarmed. She watched Corydon approach with narrowed eyes. Then she suddenly jerked forward toward him, her fist drawing back to strike.

Slane immediately grabbed her raised wrist and pulled her protectively to him, placing his body in front of hers to shield her from Corydon's lascivious gaze and her own impulsive actions.

"He killed Jared!" Taylor hissed.

"It will do you no good to get yourself killed," Slane snapped back.

Only then did her gaze shift to the archers to see their strings pulled taut, their arrows targeted on her chest.

"I have been looking for you forever, my dear," Corydon

said to Taylor. "What a joy it was to finally come upon you here." He chuckled lustily. "What an absolute pleasure. Your little love notes were quite helpful. I was so disappointed when they stopped."

Taylor moved to step around Slane, but he halted her, seizing her wrist in his fingers.

Corydon glanced toward the smoldering castle. "When you disappeared, I had to come up with another plan."

Slane's gaze followed Corydon's; then disbelief and contempt curled his lips. "It was you," Slane hissed. "You burned the village and the castle."

Taylor felt ice freeze her blood. The utter destruction and devastation she had seen was Corydon's doing. Not only had he murdered the only true friend she had ever had, but hundreds of innocent people as well.

"I knew you of all people would come charging to the rescue, bringing our lovely prize with you." His dark gaze shifted to Taylor. "Here I was ready to lay siege to the castle and wait for you to arrive when all I had to do was knock and convince your poor old father that you were my prisoner." Corydon chuckled softly, running his black-gloved hand over his mustache.

Taylor's back slowly straightened in dread. Surely, her father would not have been stupid enough to fall for such a ploy. . . .

"I must say, I was rather surprised at how much you meant to your father. Had I realized how easy it was to gain control of Sullivan Castle I would have done it much sooner."

"You bastard," Slane whispered. "You killed helpless people!"

Corydon shrugged his black-caped shoulders. "I only burned the village and the castle to get your attention. Rebuilding is simple compared with finding one woman.

A woman who was far too dangerous to let escape. The heir to Sullivan lands couldn't be left to roam the country-side . . . or join forces with one of my enemies, eh, Donovan? Now stand aside and let me have my prize."

Remorse and despair washed over Taylor. Even though she had tried to put her lineage behind her and forget her past for the last eight years, it rose like a specter to haunt her. Her noble position was the cause of all this death and destruction. It was because of her, because of who she was, that so many had lost their lives.

"She means nothing to you now! Her home is burned. Her father is dead."

"But she is still alive. She poses a threat," Corydon said. "Besides, she might be worth much more than I could have possibly hoped. Look at the way you're protecting her. And the romp the two of you just had. Why, one might think *you* had feelings for her."

Taylor saw Slane stiffen, saw his hands tighten to balled fists. She placed a hand on his shoulder, trying to calm him. "It would do no good to get yourself killed," Taylor whispered to him.

But her words had no effect on him. His muscles bunched beneath her fingers, refusing to release the anger and tension that knotted them tightly.

Slane studied Corydon for a long, tense moment. The two nobles stared each other down, their dislike for each other clearly visible in the mutual disdain etched into their features.

"Corydon. I've a proposition for you," Slane finally said.

Corydon held up his hand, stifling his laughter. "Please don't bore me with 'take my life instead.' "

"Not quite," Slane said. "A fight. You and I."

Corydon straightened, his dark gaze snapping to Slane. They locked gazes for a long moment.

"To the death," Slane added.

Taylor's heart lurched.

"It's what you want," Slane urged.

"A fight you say?" Corydon echoed thoughtfully.

"Right here. Right now. Me against you. If you win, you get Taylor and I will be dead. If I win, we'll go free."

"Slane," Taylor gasped, fear gripping her heart.

At Corydon's hesitation, Slane added, "What's wrong, Corydon? Are you afraid?"

A slow smile slipped across Corydon's lips. "This is an opportunity too good to pass up. Very well. I accept your challenge." He turned away and began to remove his cape.

Slane turned to Taylor. "No matter what the outcome," he whispered to her, "you take off for those woods. Do you understand?"

"No," she gasped. "Don't do this. You don't have to."

Slane lifted his eyes to hers. "What other option do I have?" he asked gently.

Taylor stared into his blue eyes. "My honor isn't worth defending. It's a losing battle."

"I don't give a rat's ass about your honor right now," Slane said, smiling softly. He ran a finger along her cheek. "I'm defending your life." Their gazes locked and held. Then Slane turned away to look at his horse, to look for his sword.

That was when Taylor saw Corydon approach, his sword raised high! "Slane!" she warned.

Slane shoved her hard out of the way. Taylor recovered quickly, rolling to her side to see Slane duck Corydon's swing and move away from the deadly blade.

"He doesn't have a weapon!" Taylor shouted.

Corydon stood over Taylor, an amused glint in his gaze. "He said right here, right now."

"You have to give him a weapon! What kind of fight would it be without one?"

Corydon turned back to Slane. "The best kind, my dear. The kind where I win."

Slane cursed himself for being a fool. He should have seen Corydon's trickery coming. He knew the man couldn't be trusted. But Slane would have done anything to give Taylor a chance to escape. Now he faced his most dreaded enemy, half naked and weaponless.

Corydon approached slowly, confidently, a taunting grin stretching his thin lips. "Your weapon is well out of reach. Surrender to me now and I'll make your death quick."

Slane's eyes narrowed. He glanced at Taylor to see her rising to her feet. She was so small and fragile compared to Corydon. He would never let Corydon get his hands on her. Just the idea of Corydon *thinking* about touching Taylor made Slane savage with anger. He couldn't lose this fight. Taylor's life depended on it.

Corydon swung and Slane sidestepped, barely avoiding the sharp blade. He had to concentrate on the battle before him, not on Taylor's escape. He focused his effort and his gaze on Corydon. If he could only get the sword from Corydon somehow.

Corydon feinted left and swung right. Slane easily avoided the move. Slane dodged the blows until Corydon arced one toward his head. Slane stepped into the swing and grabbed Corydon's wrist, stopping the strike midswing.

Slane held Corydon off, his muscles aching and straining against Corydon's pushing. Suddenly, Corydon slammed his foot down on Slane's bare toes. Slane grimaced and shoved off Corydon's arm, backing quickly away from him, doing his best to ignore the flaring pain in his foot.

He glared at Corydon's dark face. His toes pounded

with agony, but Slane pushed the pain from his mind. That had hardly been honorable.

And then an idea formed in his mind. An idea that bordered on dishonor. He remembered the move that had won Taylor victory over him in their battle.

Slane managed to avoid Corydon's swings until just the right moment, until Corydon thrust at his chest. Slane pretended to stumble as he backed away from the blow, falling to the ground on his bottom.

Corydon lifted his sword high over his head for the finishing blow. Slane pivoted on the ball of his foot, lashing out with his opposite leg. But instead of swiping Corydon's leg cleanly and neatly from beneath him, as Taylor had done to him, his foot slammed into Corydon's knees, toppling him like a tree . . . straight for him!

As he fell, Corydon managed to point the tip of his sword downward toward Slane, but his aim was slightly off, and the tip dug into the earth a mere inch from Slane's face. Corydon's weight pushed the weapon deep into the ground.

Slane raised his fist and punched Corydon in the face and then the stomach. When Corydon rolled off of him, Slane shot to his feet, pulling at the sword to free it. But it was firmly lodged in the earth.

Corydon caught him from behind, wrapping his arms around Slane's shoulders, pulling him from the sword. He spun Slane around and delivered two blows to his stomach. Pain exploded through his gut and Slane doubled over. When Corydon followed with a stunning blow to his face, Slane fell like a rock.

But he recovered quickly, pushing himself from the ground, shaking his head, trying to clear his vision. When his eyes focused, he saw Corydon trying to pull the sword from the ground. He was moving it back and forth like a saw in his attempt to free it from the earth's clutches.

Slane struggled to his feet and dove at Corydon, shoving him from the weapon. When Corydon turned, Slane plowed two blows into his face, followed by an upper cut to his chin, which sent the noble sprawling.

Slane turned and pulled hard at the sword. It slid reluctantly from its sheath in the earth. Slane whirled just in time to find Corydon throwing himself at him. The outstretched blade greeted Corydon, impaling him through the stomach.

Slane stood for a long moment, staring at his enemy. He gripped the sword tightly, watching as disbelief spread across Corydon's face. After a moment, Slane stepped back, releasing the handle of the sword.

Corydon's hands convulsed around the handle of the blade lodged deep in his abdomen. He glanced down at the sword once and then back at Slane. He fell forward to his knees, a trickle of blood seeping from the corner of his mouth.

Slane looked up, over Corydon's head, to see relief in Taylor's eyes. He lifted a hand to wipe the blood from the corner of his own mouth as he stepped around Corydon to join her.

"Kill them," Corydon ordered in a ragged voice. "Kill them both." Corydon pitched forward to the ground and then was still.

The archers lifted their bows and pointed their deadly arrows at Slane and Taylor.

CHAPTER THIRTY-ONE

The archers pulled the strings taut, taking aim. Slane grabbed Taylor's arm and pulled her behind him, preparing to take the first barrage of arrows.

Suddenly, shouts echoed from the forest behind the archers! The bowmen turned in time to see a garrison of riders erupt from the depths of the forest, brandishing swords. The riders swept through the archers, cutting them down like weeds.

Slane quickly scanned the field to see more than one of the archers still taking aim, still intent on fulfilling their master's last order. He pulled Taylor down, dragging her to the ground, covering her with his body. Several arrows *whooshed* overhead.

Beneath him, he could feel the ground tremble with the pounding of hooves and booted feet. All around them, Slane heard the thunderous roar of horses, shouts of dying men, the *clang* of an arrow striking chain mail. A smattering of dirt splashed into his face and he glanced up to see the shaft of an arrow embedded in the ground not five inches from his cheek.

Taylor squirmed beneath him, but he refused to let her rise until he knew what was happening. He lifted his head, his gaze scanning the riders in the distance. A few had broken off from the main group to chase the remaining archers, who were fleeing toward the cover of the forest. The rest of the riders were engaging several black-clad fighters.

Slane pushed himself up, allowing Taylor to rise. She climbed to her feet, brushing long strands of hair from her eyes. "Who is it?" she wondered.

Slane didn't answer. He knew their colors well. He actually knew some of the men, recognizing them as they came closer. He stood as one of the riders moved forward and approached him.

The large warhorse pawed the ground before Slane, clumps of dirt spraying Slane's bare feet. Slane gazed up into the rider's black eyes. But the rider's gaze was not on Slane; it was on Taylor. "Is this her?" the rider asked.

Slane's gaze remained on the rider, narrowing at the way the rider's gaze swept Taylor with unbridled lust. "Yes, Richard. This is Taylor," he said, an obvious distaste twisting his lips.

Finally, the rider's stare shifted to Slane. "Well done, brother," Richard acknowledged. "With this deed, you are released from service to me."

Slane felt Taylor's look snap to him. But he didn't dare acknowledge her right now. He would explain things to her later. He would make everything right again. "How did you find us?" Slane asked Richard.

"Elizabeth had the forethought to tell me you might be in danger," Richard explained, stilling the prancing horse beneath him. "As soon as I knew where you were coming from, I rode out to greet you."

Slane grunted. *More likely rode out to lay claim to Taylor,* he thought.

"And it seems lucky that I did," Richard said, gazing around at the carnage in the clearing.

"Yes," Slane acquiesced. "It was, indeed, lucky." He shifted his stare to his brother. "Corydon is dead."

"Dead?" Richard asked, shocked.

"Yes," Slane said without any emotion. He felt dead inside now that Richard was here. Now that his brother would take Taylor from him. "I defeated him in battle."

"This is turning out to be a most wondrous day," Richard said happily. "Well done, brother. We shall have a feast upon returning to Castle Donovan. To celebrate your triumph"—his gaze shifted to Taylor, his eyes small and dark, like a snake's—"and mine." He held out a hand to Taylor.

Something close to panic swept through Slane.

Taylor stepped away from the outstretched hand, and Richard's jovial expression immediately turned dark.

Slane knew his brother was used to women obeying him without question. He stepped forward. "She has her own horse to ride," Slane defended.

"Oh?" Richard wondered, his gaze searching the clearing. "Where? Where is her horse?"

Slane cast a glance at Taylor. She was staring at him with such complete desolation that he felt it in his soul. He wanted to take her into his arms and whisk her away. Instead, he pointed to his steed in the distance. "There," he said.

Richard looked at him with disappointment and Slane felt a feeling of victory surge inside him. "Very well," Richard said. "She may ride her own steed."

Slane turned his back on his brother, hiding Taylor from his view. "Go with him," he whispered, hoping that this once she wouldn't object.

She lifted her lids to reveal those luminescent gems shimmering with uncertainty.

"I'll speak with you later at the castle," Slane promised, brushing her chin with his forefinger. He was rewarded with a transformation. Her eyes lit with tenderness and a grin splashed across her full lips. She nodded and stepped around Slane, moving toward the horse in the distance. Slane watched her with a growing anxiety as she took the reins of the horse and pulled herself up.

When Slane turned around, his gaze met the suspicious eyes of his brother. Slane raised himself up to his full height, meeting his brother's stare. He knew that he could no longer fight the feelings he had for Taylor. They were stronger than he was. And quite frankly, he didn't want to fight them. Now he simply had to set things right. He had lost no honor yet.

Castle Donovan rose before Taylor like a mountain. A strange, unsettling feeling wavered through her as she shifted her gaze to Richard. He was staring at her, as he had been the entire ride to Castle Donovan. A feeling of entrapment strangled her like a rope every time she looked at him. She didn't like him. She didn't like his dark, shifty eyes or his abrupt manner and curtness with those around him. No, she did not like him. Not one bit. Why, he didn't even look like Slane!

She glanced over her shoulder, hoping to see Slane, but there was no sign of him. She still felt a flush of excitement when she thought of his kisses, his touches, the tender way he had made love to her. She looked forward to feeling his skin pressed to hers again, feeling his lips against hers. And that was the one opportunity Castle Donovan offered to her. To be with Slane. She refused to think of what the future might hold. She refused to think beyond Castle Donovan . . . for now.

The horse's hooves clattered over the drawbridge, jarring her. She was entering the castle. The dolt beside her was still staring at her as if she were some sort of prize. Now that her father and Corydon were dead, why was she so important to him? Why was he staring at her with such triumph?

She glanced sideways at him. His small black eyes glared at her like . . . well, like a snake's. She couldn't quite shake the feeling that at any moment he would strike. Angry with her uncertainty, and the trepidation she was feeling about this Richard, she turned her head to face him, gazing directly into his eyes. "You got a problem?" she wondered.

The smile disappeared from his face. His eyes widened with fury, his teeth clenching. Obviously, he wasn't used to being spoken to in such a way. But now that Slane had killed Corydon, now that Jared had been avenged, she didn't need Richard's help any longer, so she didn't much care what he thought.

He leaned toward her. "Obviously, you have a few things to learn," he murmured, "like *respect*." He straightened up in his saddle. "I will teach you."

Taylor snorted her disgust and disbelief as they entered the gatehouse to the inner ward. *What a pompous ass,* she thought, turning her head to study the castle. It was a large fortress, housing many small merchant buildings. They rode until they came to the apartments. Taylor moved to dismount, but Richard caught her arm in a painful grip, stilling her movement. "You follow your lord," he instructed.

Taylor nodded, and when Richard released her arm, she couldn't help adding, "If I see him, I'll do that." She swung her leg over the side of the horse.

She didn't need to look at Richard to feel his fury. He dismounted quickly, his eyes burning into her.

"M'lord!" a child shouted.

Richard turned his glare on the small boy, and the child skidded to a halt, bowing slightly before turning and racing back into the keep.

Taylor stared at Richard, her eyes slanted in dismay. *What kind of lord frightens the children so much that they back away from him with wide, fearful eyes?* she wondered. *How can terrified peasants possibly be productive?*

Richard stormed into the keep, leaving Taylor standing alone in the ward. Taylor watched as people scurried from Richard's path. One woman carrying dirty clothing bumped into a plump man in her hurry to move out of Richard's way. Her basket went flying through the air and landed on the ground, spilling over onto its side. The clothing tumbled out onto the ground.

Taylor's eyes shifted from the scattered laundry to the path Richard had taken. The bowels of the castle were dark. A feeling of impending doom settled around her shoulders as she approached the door. She had to go in. She couldn't very well wait for Slane in the middle of the ward.

She had no sooner stepped into the grim darkness than she was grabbed by the neck and slammed hard against the wall. Richard shoved his face near hers, snarling, "You will show me the respect I am due as your lord and your future husband, is that understood?" His fingers tightened around her neck until she gasped for breath.

She tried to pry his fingers from her neck. But he

squeezed his grip until she couldn't breathe. She fought wildly, trying to kick and fight her way free.

"Is that understood?" he demanded.

One conscious thought formed in her mind. Free, she had to get free. She clenched her fist, ready to smash him in the nose. But her vision waned as darkness edged in. She lifted her fist with the last ounce of her strength.

She heard his voice from far off. "Is that understood?"

Richard finally released her and Taylor fell to one knee, clutching at her neck, gasping for every painful breath she could take.

A satisfied grin curved Richard's lips as he towered darkly over her. "Anna," he called.

Taylor turned her head to see that at least five peasants and servants lurked in the shadows, trying to escape their lord's attention.

"See Lady Taylor to her room," he commanded.

Husband, Taylor thought numbly, finally hearing his declaration.

One of the women stepped from her place, bobbing a curtsy to Richard.

Richard turned to leave, but paused and added, "And make sure she wears some suitable clothing."

Taylor's breathing slowly calmed, and her heartbeat regained its regular pace. *Husband,* she thought again; what the hell . . . ?

"Lady?"

Taylor shifted her gaze to Anna. She was a young woman, fifteen perhaps, with brown hair and eyes.

"This way," she said, moving toward a stairway.

Tears entered Taylor's eyes. *There must be some mistake!* she thought. How could Richard think he was to be her husband? Why would he want to marry her? What did she have to offer him? It came to her suddenly in a moment of clarity. A dowry. If Richard was so desperate for gold, would he agree to marry her in exchange for a wealthy dowry? But why hadn't Slane told her? Didn't he know? And with her father dead, who would pay it? Unless . . . Taylor slowly stood, using the wall as support. Now that her father was dead, she was the sole and rightful heir to Sullivan Castle and Sullivan lands. Is that what Richard was after?

Taylor whirled to glance desperately at the large double doors behind her. Two guards stood lounging just inside the doors.

Anna gently took her arm. "This way, lady," she coaxed.

Taylor took one step, then another, allowing Anna to lead her. Slane would come. He would tell her that it had all been some sort of mistake. That he knew nothing of Richard being her husband.

But even as she thought this, she couldn't stop the feeling of betrayal that snaked around her.

CHAPTER
THIRTY-TWO

"You don't have to marry her," Slane told Richard. As soon as he had returned to the castle, Slane had immediately sought out his brother and found him in his solar, poring over his ledgers. Slane was amazed at how long Richard could look at the pitiful numbers he found there, as if he were expecting them to double before his very eyes.

Richard glanced up from the calculations that lay before him to lock eyes with Slane. "What in heaven's name are you talking about?"

"You don't need her dowry. You can let her go."

"Let her go?" Richard exclaimed, throwing himself back in his chair in exasperation. "Have you lost hold of your senses, brother?"

Slane scowled and stepped forward. "Richard." He planted his hands on the desk and leaned forward. "Corydon is dead. The threat of invasion is gone."

"There is always a threat of invasion. Corydon was just one fool in a sea of many. I still need knights to guard my castle."

A prickling feeling started at the nape of Slane's neck, crawling along his skin like a poisonous spider seeking a choice spot to sink its fangs into. "You don't want her any more than she wants to be your wife."

Richard shrugged. "I imagine a wife will be something of an inconvenience."

"She doesn't want to marry. Let her go," Slane encouraged.

Richard scowled. "Who cares what she wants or doesn't want. What is important here is what I *need*."

Slane felt his blood simmer. "Richard, you don't *need* her."

Richard waved his hand impatiently at Slane. "I need her dowry just as much as before."

"If the dowry is all that you're after, take the lands and be done with it. She wants no part of them."

"She is heir to those lands. I want no question of legality. Those lands will be mine rightfully and by marriage. With much thanks to you. Did I tell you how proud I am of you? I knew you of all people wouldn't fail me. All those other worthless mercenaries." Richard curled his lip in a grimace of disappointment. "But you! Ahh, brother. I knew I could depend on you!"

Slane crossed his arms over his chest, glaring down at his brother. "I bumped into a few of those worthless mercenaries," Slane said stiffly. "And one of them almost killed Taylor."

"A pity. But as fate would have it, you came along. Well done, brother. Well done," Richard said. He stretched his arms high above his head, groaning softly, then rose to his feet.

Slane watched him for a long moment, hating his brother in that instant for his coldness and viciousness. "Where is she now?"

"We're going to celebrate your successful mission. You'll join me, won't you?" He brushed past Slane.

Slane grabbed Richard's sleeve and spun him around to face him. "Answer me. Where is she? Where are you keeping her?" Slane demanded.

"For now, she is in Mother's old room." Richard leaned toward him, pulling his shirt from Slane's grasp. "In your travels with her, you must have learned much. Tell me, how did you keep from gagging and binding her?"

Slane felt rage pulse through his veins. "She is a very opinionated creature," Slane agreed. "But that is not the way to treat a woman."

Richard snorted. "She is impudent and needs the strong arm of a man." His eyes gleamed with expectation.

Slane's gaze narrowed. "Richard, you think everyone needs your strong arm."

Richard shrugged slightly. "What works is hardly worth changing."

"I think, in Taylor's case, you might think differently." Slane turned toward the door. "She doesn't take well to beatings." He paused with his hand outstretched for the doorknob. "You will not release her?"

"I never had any plans to release her," Richard answered. "You knew that."

Slane's jaw tightened. He was a fool for bringing Taylor here. What could he have possibly been thinking? But he knew what he was thinking. He had thought to pay the debt he owed to his brother so he could get on with his life. He now realized just how wrong he was.

"Ahh," Richard said, his face lighting with a grin. "All this talk of marriage has you missing your own beloved.

Well, I've kept you from her for far too long. She is probably waiting for you in the Great Hall."

Slane threw the door open, his thoughts not on Elizabeth at all. He had to see Taylor. He had to make sure she was all right.

"Why don't you dine with me and my betrothed," Richard suggested.

Betrothed. Slane froze, stiffening at the way Richard said the word. As if Taylor were some sort of possession.

Richard brushed past Slane without looking at him.

Slane hesitated for only a moment. He didn't like the way Richard was commanding him. He didn't like the sly look in his brother's eyes. He was up to something. But Slane knew he had no choice but to play Richard's game. He was lord of the castle and his word was law—a law that Slane had taken a vow to uphold despite his current misgivings.

Despite Anna's pleading, Taylor had chosen to remain in her leggings and tunic. Now she ignored the stares of the guards and the curious looks of the peasants as she sat in the Great Hall. She lifted the cup of ale that had been set before her and drained it.

She looked around the room. All the peasants were reveling, eating their fill. The guards lounged in chairs, squeezing the maids' bottoms as they scurried by to fill empty mugs with ale. A juggler performed in the middle of the room, tossing bags of beans round and round in his hands. Dogs barked in excitement, running from table to table to pick up the fallen scraps of food from the floor.

From Taylor's view at the head table, the Great Hall looked to be ordered chaos. She couldn't help but think that this was all wrong. She shouldn't be here. This was some sort of mistake. Her gaze scanned the hall, continually moving to the large wooden double doors at the rear, where she awaited the one person she trusted to explain what was going on.

Slane had said he would return. The thought had no sooner crossed her mind than two men strolled in through the double doors. Taylor's heart skipped a beat, even as trepidation gnawed at the edges of her consciousness. Forcing herself to be calm, she leaned back in the chair.

Wife. The dark, ugly word crept into her thoughts again. *Wife.* Why hadn't Slane told her? Surely, he didn't know, or he would never have brought her to Castle Donovan. Not after what they shared.

As Slane and Richard approached, Taylor couldn't help but notice the strong gait, the charisma, the pure power with which Slane entered the room. He was stunning to watch, easily the most handsome man in the room.

She failed to notice the dark scowl that crossed Richard's brow as he approached.

Slane's gaze locked with hers. There was something in his eyes that sent a vibration through her body, sent hope soaring within her heart.

As they rounded the table, Taylor stood to greet Slane. The smile that filled her soul reached her lips in a grin. She suddenly knew that everything would be all right.

But then Richard stepped in front of Slane. His blow struck her across the cheek and sent her reeling back onto her chair, the force of it knocking her and the chair to the ground.

"Taylor!" Slane said and leapt over the chair to kneel at her side. He helped her to a sitting position. "Are you all right?"

She nodded and the movement drew his gaze to her neck, where Richard's handprints had now turned to dark purple bruises. She watched Slane's eyes widen with disbelief and then fury. When he lifted his gaze from the bruises to her eyes, pain and guilt dulled his usually startling blue eyes. His jaw tightened and his fists clenched as he rose slowly to face his brother. "Damn you, Richard."

Taylor's cheek stung, but it was nothing compared to the unease that spread through her. She reached out to stop him. "It's all right," she said.

But Slane didn't hear her.

Richard's face was a mask of disgust. His eyes locked on Taylor in a disapproving scowl. "I told you to change out of those men's clothes," he warned. "I am lord here. You will learn to obey me. Or face the repercussions."

Slane's fist tightened convulsively and he drew his arm back. Taylor was on her feet instantly. She leapt at his arm, catching his elbow, preventing him from fulfilling his swing.

"No, Slane," she urged. "I'm not worth it. Think about what you're doing." Still, he battled with her, trying to shake free of her grip. "How can I leave if you're locked up?" she whispered.

Slowly, Slane stopped his struggle and lowered his arm.

Taylor felt a sigh fill her body. She felt Richard's gaze shift from her to Slane and back again. She saw the disbelief that widened his eyes. A grin notched her lips. "I don't take well to authority," she explained, releasing Slane. "Maybe someone had better explain that to you."

Richard's jaw tightened and he stepped forward, raising his fist.

Taylor stood unflinching, knowing that Slane would intercept Richard if he attacked. And he did. He caught Richard's hand in his downward arc.

"No woman speaks to me thus," Richard snarled, "especially not my future wife!"

"Then perhaps she's not right for you," Slane hissed, pushing his brother away from Taylor.

Taylor felt her hope die. There was no surprise in Slane's voice, no shock on his face. He *had* known! He had known all along Richard intended to marry her.

"Regardless of whether she's right for me, I will marry her. And she will learn her place," Richard said harshly.

A sinking feeling in the pit of Taylor's stomach pulled her down into an abyss of despair.

"You would be wise to learn your place, too," Richard snarled at Slane and whirled, storming off through the Great Hall.

The room had gone quiet. Now, as Richard passed, mumbling started low and then grew.

Slane lifted a finger to Taylor's neck and ran it along the length of the bruises. "I'm sorry," he whispered.

Taylor opened her mouth to ask the truth of him. All she needed was an explanation. A reason for his silence. Why hadn't he told her?

"Darling!"

Taylor and Slane turned. As Taylor saw Elizabeth approaching, a gnawing dread filled her, a feeling worse than when Richard had vowed to marry her. Suddenly, she couldn't face Slane. She couldn't look up at him and see the joy in his eyes at seeing Elizabeth. She didn't want to see his disloyalty.

Elizabeth threw her arms around Slane. "Darling, I'm so glad you're all right!"

A tightness closed Taylor's throat and her vision blurred. She had believed with all her heart that Slane would make things right again. She had trusted him. *Fool!* her mind roared. *All this time, he's done whatever it would take to get you to Castle Donovan . . . to his brother.*

No! her heart cried. *It can't be. He . . . he kissed me. He touched me.*

Her eyes locked with Elizabeth's over Slane's shoulder. There was such confidence in Elizabeth's brown eyes that Taylor felt her hopes being dashed on the stones, cracking into a thousand shards.

She brushed past Slane, moving toward the door. She willed away the tears she felt burning her eyes. *How stupid I've been!* she thought. *I know how treacherous nobles are. But Slane . . .*

She remembered the tender way he looked at her, the gentleness of his touch. He had treated her like no else before.

She banged into a knight and his ale sloshed across his tunic. He turned dark eyes to her, but she didn't even falter in her hurry to flee the Great Hall. She practically flew through the open wooden doors. But once out of the room, she halted and glanced over her shoulder to see Slane still speaking earnestly with Elizabeth.

Taylor saw the way he held her hand, the earnest way he gazed into her eyes. She whirled away from the heart-wrenching sight.

Taylor rushed to the inner ward. Her teary gaze scanned the morning rush of people. Panic rose up inside her. She felt trapped and imprisoned. She had to get out of there. She had to escape. She took a step forward and then another.

But suddenly, she came to an abrupt halt. What good would it do to run? Richard would send men after her. Perhaps even Slane. No. Slane's debt was paid, Richard had said. He was free of Richard . . . and of her. But the men would come. The Corydons. The Magnuses. The nameless, faceless mercenaries of her nightmares. She would never know a moment's peace. She would always be looking over her shoulder. That was no way to live. She was done with that.

Jared would have told her to stand and fight.

Taylor straightened her shoulders, angrily wiping at the tears that wet the corners of her eyes. *I'm not running any longer. Richard is the cause of my plight. And he will be the end of it.*

With a new resolve, she turned and headed back into the castle in search of Slane's brother.

CHAPTER
THIRTY-THREE

Slane fought back the urge to call after Taylor as she fled the Great Hall; he fought back the urge to race after her and pull her into his arms and shield her from all the horrors his brother had brought upon her and was yet to bring upon her. The feelings he felt for her grew stronger every time he saw her, every time he stood near her. And now the emptiness he felt in his heart when she was not with him, when he couldn't smell the essence of her or hear the melody of her sweet voice, grew deeper and darker. It was a gaping hole in his soul that needed to be filled. And Taylor Sullivan was the only one who could fill it.

"Slane darling, are you all right?"

Slane turned to Elizabeth and realized that he knew what he had to do. But he also knew that it wasn't going to be easy. He took Elizabeth's hands in his own. "We need to talk," he said quietly.

"What is it?" she wondered.

"Come on," he whispered, leading her out of the Great Hall and into a small antechamber.

Her brows furrowed. "Have I done something?" she wondered, her lips curving downward.

He rubbed the back of his neck thoughtfully. He didn't want to hurt her. Yet, he knew she would be hurt. "Elizabeth," he began.

She grasped his hand tightly. "I'm sorry for whatever it is I've done."

"No," Slane said and there was agony in his voice. He slid his hand from hers. He saw the confusion in her large brown eyes. "You've done nothing." And that was the truth. "I can't lie to you, Elizabeth. I just can't . . ." He raked a hand through his hair. Then he sighed and drew himself up with resolve. "I wish to continue our friendship—truly I do. But I cannot marry you."

"What?" she managed to gasp.

"I don't love you," Slane told her gently.

She fell back onto the seat near the window. "You did," she whispered, her voice barely above a whisper.

"No. What I felt for you was a great fondness. I felt protective. But I was never in love. When my father ordered us to wed, he never asked me for my approval."

"Nor was I consulted," she agreed.

He knelt before her, desperation washing over him. "Then you know how I feel."

"No," she retorted. "It's true that I didn't love you at first. But you're kind and gentle, and I can't see myself marrying anyone else. I don't want to!"

"That's not love," Slane insisted, rising, pacing before her. "Love is this feeling that you would give anything for another. You would climb to the moon and steal the stars from the sky if she asked it. You want to shelter her and protect her, yes. But it's more than that. When you walk into a room, she is the first one you look for. Her laughter brightens your day, and when she is hurt, you are, too. It's the warm feeling that fills your soul when she is near. A mere touch of her hand sends you to your knees with wanting." He turned to Elizabeth and saw her lidded eyes, her back as straight as a board. She knew.

"You love someone else," she stated.

Slane heard the mixture of pain and resentment in her voice. He met her stare and nodded.

"It's that girl. It's the Sullivan girl."

"I'm sorry, Elizabeth. I'm sorry to hurt you like this. But you're a bright, beautiful woman. Your father will find someone more deserving than I."

"She's betrothed to Richard, Slane," Elizabeth argued. "What future will there be for the two of you?"

Slane remained quiet. This was one of the many questions he had asked of himself. He just didn't know the answer yet.

"I'll wait for you," Elizabeth proclaimed.

Slane shook his head patiently. "It isn't fair to you," he said kindly. "And I won't ask that of you. I won't have you do that to yourself. You must continue with your life."

"You'll come back to me," she said softly. "When you can't have her, you'll come back."

"Please, Elizabeth," Slane said. "For your own good, find another lord who will look after you. Find another husband."

Tears entered her eyes and Slane turned away. He paused at the hallway. "I'm sorry this had to happen to you, Elizabeth. I truly did not mean to hurt you."

"Your honor!" she exploded in a husky, tear-filled voice. "How can you break your word?"

Slane felt his back straightening. "That is why I am

telling you. So you are not disgraced. I am leaving your honor intact.''

"What about *your* honor?" she pressed.

"It was my father's word that I would marry you. Not mine," he said and rounded the corner, leaving her alone in her misery.

It was for the best, he told himself. He couldn't be married to a woman he didn't love. It wouldn't be fair to her. He was sure he had done the right thing.

Taylor moved back into the castle, formulating what she would say when she confronted Richard. She noticed two guards near the doorway as she entered. One was shuffling his feet, staring down at them as if inspecting his boots for some defect. The other guard was staring directly at her, his hand resting on the hilt of his sheathed sword.

Taylor's eyes narrowed. She had seen these same two guards near her room and when she had first entered the castle. They were following her! Ah, God! She closed her eyes in exasperation. If she hadn't been so distracted, believing Slane would get her out of her current predicament, she would have noticed these two imbeciles immediately.

She moved up to the two men. As she approached, the one staring at his shoes looked up. She could see the reluctance in his gaze. He didn't want to be doing this. She smiled at them. "How you doing, boys?" They exchanged uneasy glances and Taylor continued. "Where is your lord?"

"I believe he is in the solar," the one who had been looking for the defect in his boot answered.

"And where is that?"

They gave her directions, and she set off, noticing that

the guards trailed her at a short distance, making no effort to be discreet.

Taylor moved past the Great Hall and couldn't help but glance in. Her steps faltered as she noticed that Slane and Elizabeth were gone. A squeezing pain tore through her chest at the thought. She felt an overwhelming grief well up inside her. *Who am I kidding?* she wondered. *He belongs with her. In her world. He is a lord. A knight. He could never fit into my world. And I don't want him to,* she told herself firmly.

But she knew that was a lie.

She took a deep breath, steeling herself against the waves of grief that coursed through her. Slane had manipulated her, even going so far as to make love to her to get her to Castle Donovan. To Richard.

She forced herself to take a step. And then another. All her life she had depended on Jared. It was time she depended on herself. She concentrated on the confrontation that was coming. She was good at concentrating. She could focus on a job and bury her feelings. She had for eight years.

Then why was her throat closing? Why couldn't she push her pain aside?

She followed a set of spiral steps upward, taking one laborious step after another. She thought of Slane's smile, his touch, his protection. She had become accustomed to them. She even looked forward to seeing his warm blue eyes. She wondered if he knew how they sparkled in the moonlight. Other images and feelings crowded her thoughts. The glorious golden wave of hair that crowned his head. His strong, masculine features. The chiseled lines that held soft lips within their ruggedness. The feel of his body, his hot kiss.

She faltered in the middle of the stairway, gripping the

wall for support. *God's blood!* she thought. *I have heard women talk of these things. Ridiculous women. Women who professed to be in love. But there is no such thing as love, so I thought for sure these were nothing more than the expressions of lust. But it's such a strong feeling! The strongest feeling I have ever known,* she realized. *Can lust be so invigorating and paralyzing at the same time? Or is there more to my feelings than some animalistic urge to share another night of love with Slane?*

She heard the clang of armor in the stairway below her. The guards. She began to move again. Her hands trembled; her mouth was dry. *No, no,* she told herself over and over. *This isn't possible. There is no such thing as love. It's merely lust. Nothing more. A physical need. Nothing more than that. Please let it be nothing more than that.*

She reached the top of the stairs and took a deep breath to steady her confused emotions. It didn't work. Her hands continued to shake, and the last drop of moistness in her mouth evaporated into nothingness. She began the slow walk down a long, unfamiliar hallway.

Had Slane run through these hallways as a child, laughing, chasing his brother? She cursed him quietly. How could she hope to stand before Richard and denounce their betrothal when all she could think about was Slane? Slane—who was betrothed to another woman.

The thought of Slane touching Elizabeth as he had touched her, stroking her, kissing her lips, sent agony spearing through her body like an arrow. She began to pace to try to clear her mind. Was she a fool? How had this happened? She prided herself on her detached feelings, on the carefully hidden emotions that she had buried long ago. How could she have let a noble find them? How could she have let a noble *release* them?

Anger and humiliation churned within her. She forced the feelings of humiliation aside, but kept the anger strong, nursing the rage until it threatened to burn her very thoughts. *It was your fault! You needed someone after Jared's death. And you latched on to the first man around. Fool! Idiot! You should have known what you were doing.*

She continued down the hallway, now moving with determined steps. *Well, this is one situation I can remedy.*

She stopped at the last door and lifted her fist to knock soundly on it. After a moment of silence, Taylor impatiently lifted her fist again and pounded on the wooden door.

When no one answered, she pushed the door open and entered the room.

It was dark, but her eyes adjusted quickly to the dim lighting thrown by a single candle on a nearby table. The blanket on the large bed caught her attention as it shifted and twisted, turning like some great beast. She took a step toward it and finally made out two forms beneath the blanket.

"This had better be worth it," a growl warned from beneath the fur pelt blanket. Richard poked his head out from beneath the fur. The scowl of anger on his face was replaced by shock, and then a dark smile shadowed his lips. "Darling," he said.

The form beside him, still hidden beneath the blanket, groaned.

"Not you, you stupid woman," he murmured.

A head emerged from beneath the blanket beside Richard, and Taylor was momentarily shocked to see that it was Anna, the servant girl who had escorted her to her room when she had first arrived. Then Taylor shook her head in dismay. She raised her chin and looked Richard squarely in the eyes. "I think it's time to put an end to this farce," Taylor stated.

"Farce?" Richard echoed. "I can't say I know what you mean."

"This betrothal. This proposed marriage," Taylor explained. "A farce."

"There is no farce where a profit is to be made."

"I won't marry you," Taylor said.

Richard sat up in the bed, a frown curving his lips. "I don't think you have a choice."

"I'm leaving," she added as if he hadn't spoken.

Richard grinned. "You can't leave. I won't let you," he said simply, matter-of-factly.

Taylor felt her stomach bottom out; she knew Richard's word was law here. But she pressed on. "You can't keep me here."

"If it takes locking you in the dungeon, then I'll do it," Richard said darkly. "Your father promised you to me. And I plan to honor his last wish."

Taylor's jaw clenched. Her mind worked furiously. She wanted to rant and rave and demand to know why in heaven's name he would want to marry her. "I guess this is the start of a wonderful marriage, eh, Richard?" she finally spat.

Richard's lips twitched. "If you only knew."

"And everyone will be happy. You, lying in bed with her. Me, standing here wanting to rip your head off. Slane . . ." But her voice broke with such anguish that she couldn't continue.

"Yes. He will be happy, too," Richard continued for her. "Slane had much to gain by bringing you to me. He owed me a great debt—one that he hated to have hanging over his head. I restored his precious honor when Father would have disowned him. But by bringing my lovely wife to me, he has finished repaying his debt. He is free of me now. He can marry Elizabeth and be happy. Very far from here."

Taylor's chest contracted painfully. Slane *had* manipulated her. Deceived her. And she had fallen into his trap.

He had said whatever he could to get her here. After all, how could a man of honor make love to her when he was betrothed to another woman? "I won't stay here," she whispered hoarsely.

Richard rose from the bed, the blanket falling away from his nakedness.

But Taylor didn't notice. Not even when he approached her. Her mind was locked in battle with her heart. Slane couldn't want her when he had Elizabeth. Elizabeth was beautiful and caring and noble. Slane had lied. But how could he fake those looks, those touches and caresses? There was no such thing as love, Taylor knew. And now she realized she had just learned another painful lesson. There was no such thing as a knight of honor. They were both horrible, deceitful myths that women clung to. But in the end, Taylor knew all women only came to know the dark nature of their illusion.

"You have no choice," Richard said from close beside her. "You are on my lands now. In my castle. You are mine to do with as I please."

Sorrow gripped Taylor and she couldn't focus her thoughts. Her mind kept saying, *He lied, he lied.* Her heart continued to argue, *He couldn't have, he couldn't have.* She was lost in a limbo of confusion.

Richard gently gripped her hand and guided her toward the door. "Come, dearest."

Taylor violently ripped free of his hold. "Don't touch me!" she snapped and rushed out of the room, moving down the hallway past the amused, scornful eyes of the guards.

She tried desperately to tell herself that Slane hadn't lied to her. But the evidence was irrefutable. She had seen him with Elizabeth since their return. She had seen their embrace.

What had she expected? Tears flooded her eyes in an onslaught of anguish. *There is no such thing as love,* she told herself again. *Then why do I feel as though I'm dying of love?*

Hands grasped her shoulders and she looked up through blurry vision to see the two guards staring down at her.

"My lord has suggested we escort you to your room," one of them explained.

Taylor saw the determination in the grim set of their mouths. Even in her daze, she knew they were going to lock her up. She was a prisoner. She was Richard's possession now.

She nodded, but then swung around and pulled one of the guard's swords from its sheath! She faced them with desperation, a fear gnawing at the pit of her stomach. She was in too deep, and she knew it. There would be no escape. Not from Richard, and not from the feelings Slane had aroused in her. The only thing she had left, the only thing she had ever been any good at, was fighting. She brandished the sword before her, waving it from side to side as if warding off some sort of evil.

The guards looked at each other and then the one who still had his sword drew his weapon.

She would have laughed had she been her old self. She would have escaped in the blink of an eye. She would have told them they didn't have a chance, talked them out of fighting her. She knew they didn't want to fight. But she wasn't her old self. She felt the tears trickling from her eyes, even as she fought to control them. Her vision wavered.

"We don't want to hurt you," the guard told her.

Taylor lifted her arm and wiped her cheeks and eyes clear. *And I don't want to hurt you,* she knew she would have said. But her throat was closed so tightly the words were strangled before she uttered a sound.

She lunged forward and the guard easily parried the blow.

As their swords connected, her survival instinct took over. She felt a semblance of her old self flare to life. She attacked instinctively, driving the man back with blow after blow, clearing a way to the stairs. She whirled and dashed for the spiral staircase, skipping every other step until she reached the ground floor. She bolted from the stone stairway and into the hallway just outside the Great Hall. The corridor was crowded with villagers and merchants and mercenaries and guards, all heading from the Great Hall, and she had to push her way through the throng of bodies.

"Stop her!" a voice shouted from behind her.

She pulled up short, scanning the faces before her. A man with a red beard looked at her with beady eyes. A fat merchant pointed a finger at her. A noblewoman screamed and stepped behind a guard. They were all enemies, all untrustworthy. Someone grabbed her wrist. She tore away and surged forward, running through the corridor. Somewhere to her left someone laughed.

And then far down the hall, she saw him towering a head above the rest, his blond hair wavering in a breeze. Despite the distance, she even thought she saw the sparkle of those blue eyes. And then behind him, Elizabeth emerged.

Taylor felt a raw and primitive grief overwhelm her so intensely that it was a physical pain in her chest. She almost doubled over.

And then she felt hands on her shoulders, her arms. The nameless masses that were her enemies, pulled her back, but she fought them, kicking and struggling. The sword was wrenched from her grasp. Somewhere, someone was screaming.

The hands and weight on her shoulders shoved her

down, down. She still struggled, but the overwhelming force was too much to fight. Defeated, she was shoved to her knees.

A cry of anguish resounded through the corridor. And with a jolt, Taylor realized that she was the one who was screaming.

CHAPTER THIRTY-FOUR

Slane watched in utter horror as Taylor was pushed to her knees and whisked from the corridor. He rushed forward, shoving people from his path to reach her side. He raced down the aisle, skirting curious peasants and alarmed nobles. A hound dashed in front of him and he almost hurdled the dog, but it hurried out of his way.

He skidded to a halt at the end of the hallway. Glancing right, he spotted the last of the group of soldiers moving up the spiral staircase. There were at least seven men all guarding one woman. The thought was ludicrous! He found himself racing after them before he consciously decided to do so. His heart beat frantically, his mind replaying Taylor's anguished cry again and again.

When they didn't stop at the second floor, but continued to the third floor, he knew where they were taking her. His mother's old room. Panic struck him. Was she hurt? What were they doing to her?

He reached the door just as a soldier was shutting it. He pushed the other guards aside and slammed his fist on the door, halting the soldier's movement. He shoved the door open. And then stood motionless in the doorway for a moment, horrified at what he found.

Taylor sat on the edge of the bed, hunched forward, her hands clasped in her lap, her long black hair hanging over her face, obscuring it from his vision. His little wildcat was trembling.

"Taylor?" he murmured, approaching her.

"Stay away from me."

The snarl froze him in his tracks. Slane didn't know whether to take her in his arms or to leave her alone for the moment. "What happened?" he asked.

There was a long moment of silence before Taylor answered, "You got what you wanted. You manipulated me perfectly." Her voice was so quiet that he wasn't even sure if those were her words. A sob shook her body. "How perfectly you played me the fool."

"Taylor," Slane protested, her words ripping a hole through his heart. He lowered himself to his knees before her. "I never lied to you."

"You didn't have to," she whimpered in a cry that spilled from her soul.

Slane glimpsed the agony on her face, the tears that sparkled like gems on her cheeks. He wanted desperately to touch her and promise her that everything would be all right. He lifted his hand toward hers, but she shifted her body, moving away from his touch. The trust she had put in him had somehow been taken away and he felt devastated. "Taylor," he whispered desperately, "I don't understand. What did I do? I've done—"

She lifted her eyes to lock with his. Disbelief and anguish glimmered in those deep green orbs. "You brought me here, knowing I was to be his wife. And you didn't even tell me."

He knew she was right as soon as the words left her lips. He had known all along that he should have told her. But somehow, it hadn't seemed important. At first, he had merely wanted the mission over. But then, as he traveled with her, he was afraid that she would not accompany him to Castle Donovan and some mercenary would find her . . .

The thought of her death, because he had no doubt she would fight to the end, was more agonizing than telling her the truth. So he had let her believe that her father wanted her returned, let her believe that she could join forces with Richard to avenge Jared's death. But still, he should have told her. He should have allowed her to make her own decision. Now she would never trust him again. All his life he had lived by a code of truth, of honor. The one person he wanted to have faith in him would never believe him again. Not even if he told her that the sun would rise every morning. The thought staggered him and he rose unsteadily to his feet. "Taylor," he said, "I will do everything in my power to make this right."

"Don't bother," she retorted. "You've done quite enough already."

Slane stared hard at Taylor for a long moment, words refusing to come. Not knowing what else to say to her, and unprepared for the torment her rejection caused, he turned to the door and opened it, departing from the room in silence.

Three guards stood outside the door, all raising their eyes to him when Slane emerged. They quickly looked away from his scowl, finding interest in the lint on their tunics, a crack on the wall, the dirt on their boots.

Slane forced himself to walk down the hall, concentrating on each step as he felt his insides crumbling. He had not considered the disastrous consequences of his deception. *Deception? Yes,* he admitted to himself. *Deception.* That was exactly what it was. He had deceived Taylor, led her to believe something that wasn't altogether the truth. And now he felt as though his world were breaking apart. He had not lied to her!

No. He had not lied. Her father had, indeed, wanted to speak to her and make amends. Her father had gone to great lengths to get her back, to redeem himself, even promising her in marriage to Richard.

Slane entered the spiral staircase and stopped. He leaned his forehead against the cold stone wall. *God's blood, what have I done?* He had twisted the truth until it fit his mission, not telling Taylor the most important part. The part that would change her life forever. He felt his heart aching until he thought it would explode in his chest.

He lifted his hands to either side of his head. Taylor— a woman who gave her trust very frugally, if at all—had given it to him. And he had betrayed her.

He pounded the wall with his fists and groaned. He had betrayed the one woman who meant more to him than anything in the world. The one woman he was willing to give his life for. He had hurt her. Deceived her.

He lifted his head and resolve filled his thoughts. It was time to undo the wrong he had done.

Slane rapped hard on the door. When no one answered, he knocked again, more insistent.

"Damn!" A voice hollered from the other side of the door. Then the door was flung open and Richard stood before him, naked and furious.

Slane pushed past him.

"Come in, brother," Richard said sarcastically.

Slane heard the door close behind him. The moment he entered the room, he saw Anna bent over the side of the bed, her naked bottom sticking out toward him.

"Care to take a turn?" Richard asked.

"Get rid of her," Slane said.

A smile lit Richard's face. "Debtless you are a force to be reckoned with." Richard snapped his fingers. Anna was at his side instantly. "However, I think I'll keep the wench here for when we're done."

Slane clenched his teeth tightly; his eyes narrowed.

"What troubles you, brother?" Richard wondered, moving back to sit on the side of the bed, pulling Anna next to him. When she slid her hand down his stomach toward his manhood, he pushed her away from him, commanding, "Be good. You're in the company of a man who is betrothed, after all."

"I am no longer betrothed," Slane said.

"What?" Richard gasped. "But it was father's last wish!"

Slane turned his back on Richard and moved toward the window.

"What happened? Did she find some flaw in your honorable nature?" Richard probed.

Slane threw open the shutters, letting the bright sunlight into the dark room.

Richard groaned and shielded his eyes.

"I don't love her," Slane said.

Richard guffawed. "Love has nothing to do with marriage! Or I would be marrying a lusty little girl like Anna here and not that man-woman." He dipped his fingers between Anna's thighs and she squealed in delight. "Imagine! A woman with a sword! It's obscene."

Slane clenched his fists tightly and slowly turned to Richard. "Just why *are* you marrying Taylor? Her father is dead. There is no more dowry!" Slane heard the desperation in his own voice. He silently cursed himself. He had to be stronger. He had to stay in control.

Richard's gaze rose from Anna to Slane. "No, there is no more dowry. A shame. Now instead of a mere dowry, all of Sullivan's lands and all that the treasury holds will be mine. Curse my rotten luck, eh, brother?" Richard grinned coldly at Slane. "I would be a fool to let her slip through my fingers. And I'm not a fool."

"Castle Donovan is wealthy. Its lands are rich and fertile. Surely by next spring—"

"The treasury is depleted. I need her gold. And I need it now."

"There is plenty of food for the winter. What could you possibly need her gold for?"

"I need it to pay my knights," Richard said simply.

"I'll lend you the gold for that," Slane insisted.

Richard scowled and slowly rose before his brother. "If I didn't know better, I'd think you didn't want me to marry her."

Slane couldn't meet his brother's gaze. He returned to staring out the window, looking over the lands, studying the distant village.

Richard shrugged. "Besides there are other things that I've grown accustomed to. Do you know how expensive silk is? And my women like little baubles from France occasionally. And there is the dolphin that I so love." Richard smacked his lips.

And then Slane understood. Richard was going to ruin Taylor's life because he liked to eat dolphin at feast time and to give his wenches trinkets and new dresses. Slane clenched his teeth. "What will it take?"

"For what?" Richard wondered.

Slane turned to him, his jaw tight. "To free her."

"To free her?" Richard echoed in confusion, standing

before his brother. "She isn't a prisoner. She's to be my wife. There is nothing to free her from."

"I'll give you the gold you need for your knights' pay," Slane continued as if Richard hadn't spoken. "What else will it take?"

"That will deplete your years of savings. Surely you can't be serious."

"What else will it take?" Slane demanded.

Richard studied Slane's face. Slane tried desperately to keep it blank, but he had never been good at hiding his emotions. That was the trap he had fallen into with his father. His father had known Slane didn't want to marry and so had betrothed him to Elizabeth. Now Richard would read his feelings and use them against him.

"I want nothing from you. I want her," Richard said dismissively. He turned from Slane and began moving over Anna.

Slane's hand shot out and grabbed Richard's arm. "I'll give you my servitude. I'll give you my gold. Just let her go."

"Good Lord, Slane. Get ahold of yourself," Richard said, attempting to ease his arm free.

But for a long moment, Slane wouldn't release Richard's arm. He held it in a tight grip as their gazes locked and clashed. Finally, Slane released his hold.

"This isn't like you, Slane," Richard baited him. "Don't tell me you sullied my bride's honor while you were supposed to be guarding her for me."

Slane turned away from his brother.

"She'll be a dutiful wife, I'm sure," Richard went on. "She'll make a fine after-dinner morsel. I'll train her in the most vigorous of ways. She'll part those creamy thighs for me. I'll train her to open her mouth wide—"

Slane whirled on Richard, fury burning in his orbs. He recognized the trap too late.

But Richard simply smiled. "Guard well your lust, dear brother. Willing or not, she is my betrothed."

Slane's anger refused to abate. He tightened his fists until his nails bit into his palms.

Anna reached up to pull Richard against her. Richard obliged willingly.

Slane turned and left the room, his fury irrational, his anger fierce. He paced before Richard's closed door for a long moment, trying to bring this tidal wave of anger under control. Richard had no respect for the unique woman Taylor was. He wanted a dutiful wife—a wife he could cheat on with every woman he could get his hands on while she waited patiently for him in his bedchamber. Well, Taylor would wait for him all right, but it would be with a dagger.

Slane's jaw clenched. All for his damned dolphin and petty trinkets!

He wanted to cry out at the injustice of it all. He wanted to beat Richard until he freed Taylor. But mostly he wanted to return to Taylor and tell her of his success in talking Richard into freeing her. But he couldn't.

He leaned against the wall, agony spearing his body like a knife wound. He couldn't let Richard marry Taylor. But how was he going to stop his brother?

Taylor sat forlornly in the dark room. She hadn't moved from the bed since Slane had left, her hands still clenched in her lap. *What a fool I've been,* she thought for the hundredth time. *How could I have trusted him so completely? All he wanted was to get me to Castle Donovan to marry his brother.*

And he did anything and everything he could in order to do it. Including making love to me.

Suddenly, the door opened.

Taylor lifted her head in time to see Elizabeth quietly close the door behind her. She was holding a candelabra in her hand. A fierce anger filled Taylor's body at the sight of Slane's fiancée.

"Get out," Taylor snarled.

Elizabeth raised startled eyes to her.

Taylor's back straightened. "I said get out," she repeated.

"I'm here to help you," Elizabeth said, taking a tentative step into the dark room.

"To help me prepare for my marriage to Richard?" Taylor demanded, rising to her feet. "I don't want your help."

"I can help you escape."

Shock rocked Taylor. Escape? She tried to read Elizabeth's eyes, but they were shadowed in flickering darkness. A choked laugh escaped Taylor's throat. Another noble to trust. Another noble to deceive her. To lead her to her death. "No, I don't think so. But thanks anyway."

"You're refusing my help to leave this castle?" Elizabeth wondered, aghast.

"I knew you were quick," Taylor retorted.

Elizabeth raised the candelabra higher, illuminating the surprise on her face. "Then you're a bigger fool than I thought." She turned toward the door.

Taylor turned her back on Elizabeth to face the shuttered windows. "You must love him very much." She was horrified that she had spoken the thought aloud. She didn't want to hear the answer. She prayed Elizabeth hadn't heard her.

But Elizabeth had. "Yes, I do. I love him very much."

"How do you know?" Taylor couldn't stop herself from asking.

There was a long moment of silence before Elizabeth spoke. "He's the first person I look for when I walk into a room."

Taylor's chest squeezed tight until she could barely breathe.

"His laughter brightens my day," Elizabeth continued.

Taylor's eyes stung with tears.

"A mere touch of his hand is heaven."

Taylor stood rock still as her insides crumbled. She heard the door open and close and knew Elizabeth had left. But not before her words had destroyed her.

CHAPTER
THIRTY-FIVE

Slane sat in the Great Hall for the remainder of the day, trying to figure out how to help Taylor. But everything he thought of led to a dead end. He thought of petitioning the king on her behalf. But her father had willingly betrothed her, had signed and sealed the official document with his own hand. Slane would stand no chance of winning that battle. He thought of bringing Taylor a weapon and fighting their way out of the castle. But the thought was ludicrous. Innocent men would be killed.

Taylor's tormented visage continued to materialize before his mind's eye. Her sagging shoulders, her dull green eyes. He ran a hand through his hair and his own shoulders hung in defeat. He had done it to her. If only he had told her the truth! If only he had given her the option of deciding for herself. But he hadn't. He had imprisoned her just as surely as Richard was doing now.

"Slane?"

He lifted his head to find Elizabeth standing at his side. "You look dreadful," she whispered, bending to kneel at his side. She touched his arm. "Is there anything I can do to help?"

Slane eased his arm from her grip. He began to shake his head, but then lifted his gaze to her thoughtfully. Could she free Taylor? he wondered.

But then he thought of the guards that Richard would have posted around Taylor. And he knew there was even less chance of Elizabeth helping Taylor. And he didn't want her to. He didn't want to be indebted to her. Slane shook his head. "No. There's nothing you can do," he admitted.

Slowly, Elizabeth rose before him. "Very well," she said. "Will you join me for dinner?"

Slane lifted incredulous eyes to her. Didn't she hear him when he said he could not marry her?

Elizabeth shifted slightly and glanced down at her folded hands. "We can still be friends," she said softly.

Slane wanted to kick himself. She was a woman of incredible heart. How could she forgive him after everything he had done to her, everything he had put her through? He stood and took her hands in his. "Of course we can be friends. I would enjoy having dinner with you." He smiled at her. "Thank you for understanding."

Halfway through the meal, Richard joined them. Every muscle in Slane's body tensed as his brother took the seat beside him.

"It's good to see the two of you talking again," Richard murmured to Slane. "Perhaps there is hope yet."

"Elizabeth and I have come to an understanding," Slane admitted.

But Richard didn't hear him. His eyes scanned the back of the room. "Now where could my betrothed be?"

"Perhaps she finds your company . . . not to her liking," Slane suggested.

Richard turned dark eyes to his brother. "And pray tell, what do you mean?"

But before Slane could reply, a low murmur reached his ears. It began in the back of the Great Hall and spread like fire. Then the talking and laughter ceased abruptly as all eyes turned to the double doors.

Slane raised his gaze . . . and found himself breathless.

Taylor was approaching the head table, flanked by two guards. But Slane didn't even see the two guards. He was entranced by the vision that Taylor presented in a shimmering deep green velvet dress that conformed to her breasts and hips like a second skin. The dress flared out just below her hips to conceal the long, shapely legs Slane knew were hidden beneath. Her luxurious black hair was combed into soft curls, which hung about her shoulders like dark clouds.

This woman wasn't the Taylor he knew. She had somehow been transformed into a lady. A lady who would fit into Elizabeth's world. Doom settled in the deep recesses of Slane's heart. Had Richard extinguished her fire already?

Slane felt a pushing on his shoulder and realized a second later that it was Richard pushing him back into his seat. Without his realizing it, he had somehow risen from his chair at the sight of Taylor.

"She's stunning," Richard murmured as Slane sat. "I never could have imagined it."

Slane turned burning eyes to Richard. He didn't like the tone in Richard's voice. Then he sank deeper into his seat, a hopeless feeling overwhelming him. Richard was to be Taylor's husband. He had every right to desire her.

Still, Slane could not stop from clenching his fists.

Taylor approached the head table and moved around it to her seat beside Richard.

Slane couldn't take his eyes from her. She was gorgeous. He had known she was beautiful, but now, dressed in a gown that accented her feminine attributes, Slane realized that the word didn't do her justice. His mood darkened and he slouched lower in his chair.

He felt a hand on his shoulder and turned to see Elizabeth gazing at him sympathetically.

"My dearest," Richard cooed, and Slane turned his gaze back to Taylor.

She took the seat beside Richard. Richard's hand brushed her cheek and she didn't even flinch. Slane closed his eyes as his jaw clenched. Had Richard beaten her indomitable spirit already? Had he forced her to become what she loathed?

"Slane," Elizabeth whispered, "care to escort me back to my room?"

Slane heard her words, but couldn't reply. He opened his eyes and they focused instinctively on Taylor. She sat only two seats away from him, with Richard a formidable barrier between them. His brother carved a piece of meat from the bone on his plate and held it up in his fingers to Taylor's lips.

Every muscle in Slane's body tensed. She would never accept his brother's meat. She would never open her mouth for him. Richard would be outraged. He would raise his fist and Slane knew he would be forced to intercede. . . .

But when Taylor delicately bit the meat in half, Slane's eyes widened in disbelief. He shot to his feet, prepared to . . . prepared to do what? he asked himself. His clenched fists fell slack at his side. He felt defeated. He felt powerless. But mostly he felt lost. He felt a wretchedness of mind that he'd never known before. He turned away from Taylor and found Elizabeth standing before him.

She placed her hand on his arm and he let himself be escorted from the Great Hall.

Slane returned to the Great Hall much later that evening. He sat alone before the hearth, the flickering fire doing nothing to warm his cold spirit. A mug of ale dripped from his fingertips as he slouched forward in the chair, his head hanging over his knees.

Why? his mind kept asking. Why hadn't he told her? Why hadn't he told her the truth about bringing her to Castle Donovan?

He ran a frustrated hand through his hair. Because he would have lost her. *And now?* he demanded silently of himself. *You've lost her now, too.*

Desolation consumed him. He would give anything to right this situation, to have Taylor at his side again. Instead, it seemed she had accepted her fate. Taylor was a master at survival, he knew. Had she come to the realization that she was to be Richard's wife forever? Was she simply surviving the only way she knew how? Slane knew he should be grateful. Many, many people would prosper from the union. The castle and lands would continue to be protected. The people would be safe.

But he didn't give a damn about the people. Not when he couldn't have Taylor.

Hopelessness threatened to sweep him into an abyss of despair, but Slane fought the swirl of dread that tugged at his heart and his mind. He knew there was some way to make this right. He knew there was an answer somewhere. All he had to do was find it.

He glanced down at the mug of ale. And sitting here

drinking himself into a pitiful stupor wasn't going to give him the answer he was seeking. He stood, tossing the mug aside, and turned.

That was when he saw it. The glimmer of steel in the darkness just outside the large double doors. A scowl creased Slane's brow. *Armor?* he wondered. *No. I know that flash.*

He drew his sword and headed toward the double doors.

CHAPTER
THIRTY-SIX

Taylor stared out at the night sky. The darkness was sprinkled with small twinkling diamonds, but none of their shine touched her soul. When Slane had left the Great Hall with Elizabeth, Taylor felt a loss so complete and so devastating that she had almost been unable to control the tears that burned her eyes. Rejected. Betrayed. But she vowed that even her pain would not stop her from her plan. Not even if Slane came to her proclaiming his love. *Love,* she thought, and images of Slane holding her in his arms, touching her, kissing her began to form in her mind, but she quickly pushed the word aside and the images vanished.

She turned from the window and approached the door, stopping only long enough to retrieve the candelabra from the table. She opened the door and peered outside. The guard standing sentry outside her room spotted her immediately and straightened up.

Only one guard, she mused. *Richard fell for my ploy. He must think of me a willing lamb.*

Taylor moved a step out into the hallway. She had purposely donned the sheerest nightdress she could find. It conformed to her curves, just barely veiling the dark nipples of her breasts. "Excuse me," she called to the guard in a soft voice.

He took two steps toward her, eyeing her with suspicion. And an obvious aroused curiosity.

Taylor leaned back against the wall. "I . . . I'm not really used to this sort of luxury," she said softly. When the guard didn't reply, she continued. "I'm quite lonely." She shifted her position, straightening her shoulders so that her breasts jutted slightly. The guard's gaze instantly dropped to her offered charms. "I'm not used to being alone at night." His gaze rose to hers and Taylor knew that she had won by the simmering look in his eyes. "I was wondering if perhaps you would join me?" She eased the door open with her foot, holding the candelabra higher to illuminate the doorway.

"Well," the guard hesitated. "I don't think I should. Lord Richard said to stand guard—"

"Oh, you'll be guarding all right, but you won't be standing."

He stared at her with incredulity in his eyes. "You're my lord's betrothed!"

"He enjoys an occasional tryst with other women, does he not? He knows I have a desire to do the same with men I find attractive. Lord Richard and I have an . . . understanding." Taylor stepped closer to him, being sure her breasts brushed his arm. "Besides, I won't tell if you don't."

With a quick look down the hall, the guard stepped past her and moved toward the room.

Taylor struck swiftly, bringing the candelabra down hard on the back of his head. The flames flickered as the hard metal struck the guard. The man staggered, and when Taylor hit him again, the candles wavered and went out. He fell to his knees and toppled forward. Taylor glanced left and right down the hallway, the torches burning on the wall revealing nothing but an empty stone corridor. She grabbed the guard's arm and pulled him into the room.

She quickly seized a small bundle of clothing and boots she had hidden beneath the bed earlier in the day. Then she knelt at the guard's side and her hands searched over his torso until they reached his waist and his sheathed weapon. She eased it from his scabbard and rose to her feet, moving out the door and down the hall. She reached the stairway undetected and quickly descended the spiral steps. The stones felt icy cold against her bare feet. Her blood pounded through her veins with every beat of her heart, but she continued on through the darkness until she reached the bottom of the stairs.

She glanced left and then right toward the large double doors that led to the inner ward. A step closer to freedom. Here, too, the hallway was empty and every muscle in Taylor's body tensed. It was a trap. It had to be! It was too easy.

She moved cautiously out into the hallway, her ears alert to every noise, her eyes seeing everything. She sneaked toward the door, toward freedom, creeping past the open door to the Great Hall, pausing to glance in, dreading the possible sight of servants scurrying about. But it was as quiet as the rest of the castle. She saw only a group of peasants huddled together not far from the hearth against a wall, nestled together in sleep for warmth.

As she reached the large double doors leading out to

the inner ward, her hand gripped the pommel of the sword tightly. Suddenly she heard a noise and froze. She recovered quickly and whirled, bringing her sword up. Another sword met her swing. But it wasn't the shiny silver blade that captivated her.

It was his eyes. The bluest eyes she had ever seen.

Slane stood before her, holding his weapon crossed against hers. Shock filled her for a long moment and she could do nothing. She knew that she should run him through. She knew that she should cut his traitorous head from his neck.

But she couldn't. She could only stare at his blue eyes and remember his kisses, his caresses.

"Taylor," he whispered and straightened, drawing his sword from hers.

His voice sent tremors racing down her spine. And still she couldn't move.

"Lord Slane!"

The voice jarred her and she turned her head to see five soldiers racing down the hall. She recognized the guard she had hit over the head. He was holding a bloodied towel across his crown. Her eyes returned to Slane, beseeching.

But Slane glanced from her to the men.

"Well done," one of them said, nearing.

Slane glanced at his sword and then back at Taylor.

Taylor clutched her weapon so tightly that her hand shook. Her eyes watered, blurring her vision.

"She hit Anderson over the head," one of the soldiers said, "and tried to escape."

The soldiers quickly moved to surround her. Taylor's eyes narrowed. She would never give up without a fight. Never. Her knees bent slightly.

"Don't," Slane called.

And again, her body responded to his call. She glanced at him, taking her mind off the guards for the moment.

"Taylor, put down your weapon," Slane ordered.

But she refused to let go of the only thing she could trust. The sword. She blinked furiously, trying to clear her eyes of the tears. "Traitor," she hissed, pointing the blade at his neck.

Suddenly, Slane lunged forward, knocking her blade aside with his own, and pinned her body tightly against the wall with his. She squirmed for a moment and he pressed his body harder against hers, trapping her against the wall. Her agonized gaze locked with his determined stare.

"You can't win," he whispered.

For a long moment, they stood that way, Slane looking down into her eyes with a softness in his gaze, Taylor staring back with hurt and anger. But the anger was at herself. For ever trusting him. For believing him. She should have known better. She should have seen through his soft looks.

He stepped back and two soldiers took her arms. She felt the sword being wrenched out of her grasp. It felt like her heart being torn from her chest. She lifted her chin, hoping that it wasn't quivering as much as it felt. The soldiers led her away. She glanced back once, but it wasn't to look at Slane. It was a last glance at the double doors.

And her freedom.

CHAPTER THIRTY-SEVEN

Slane couldn't move. Frozen in the moment, he watched the guards lead Taylor away, back to the room. It had all been a game, her dress, her behavior, a facade to deceive Richard so that she could escape! A slap on his back jarred him.

"Well done, brother," Richard congratulated, his dark eyes on Taylor's retreat. "Why, if it hadn't been for you, she would have escaped."

Guilt weighed heavily on Slane's shoulders as Richard's words rang in his ears. She would have escaped. *She would have escaped!* He wished she had cut him down. He had inadvertently prevented her escape. This was all his fault. And he could not let the mistake go on. He turned full face to Richard. "You have to set her free, Richard," Slane proclaimed in a voice that brooked no argument.

Richard turned startled eyes to Slane. For a long moment, neither said a word nor moved.

Suddenly, Richard began to laugh. "You must be out of your mind! I'll not free her. She is mine."

"She is not yours, Richard," Slane said possessively. "She is a woman whose life you will destroy if you force her to marry you. You *will* set her free."

"I think not, brother," Richard answered stiffly. "You presume to know much of my betrothed. Perhaps too much. If you were any less than the honorable man you are, I would be suspicious. I mean, after all, the two of you were alone for a long while."

"Yes," Slane whispered harshly. "And I took the time to get to know her."

"How well, brother?"

"Well enough to know that what you're doing is wrong." Slane's fists clenched, and he faced Richard with all the rage and fury and frustration that pounded through his blood at the injustice.

"Did she seduce you?" Richard demanded.

"No," Slane growled.

"Then what? Tell me, Slane. I've never seen you this passionate before."

"I am defending a woman who has no one to defend her," Slane said righteously.

Richard peered into Slane's eyes as if he could see through to his soul. "This has nothing to do with honor, does it? Tell me, Slane, did you lie with her?"

Slane swallowed hard. He could not lie to his brother. And yet he could not tell him the truth. But his silence was answer enough.

"I thought so," Richard whispered.

Slane was surprised at the nonchalance of his brother's reply. Any other man would be furious at being cuckolded. But Richard didn't seem to care. Not one bit.

Richard shrugged slightly. "I figured she would not

come to me a virgin, but I must say I'm a bit disappointed that it was my own brother—"

"It had nothing to do with you."

"Nothing to do with me?" Richard retorted. "She is my future wife."

"I will not allow you to do this," Slane proclaimed.

"Not allow . . . ?" Richard all but roared. His black eyes were wide with incredulity. "I am lord here, brother." His voice steadily rose in pitch. "Lest you forget! I run this castle! *I am lord!* You will follow my every command. Do my every bidding. This is *my* castle, Slane. Not yours."

Slane's eyes narrowed as he met his brother's rage head-on.

Richard's breathing slowed and his voice lowered, but his face was as red as a beet. "Is this disrespect how you repay me after everything I've done for you?"

Slane could no longer keep his anger inside. After he had spent years bowing to his brother's whims, the festering resentment would not be buried any longer. "Done for me? You've done nothing for me, except make me your slave!"

"I defended you before Father. You would have been disowned if it hadn't been for me. You would have been disgraced. I risked my inheritance for you!"

"I've repaid that debt and more. I've come to your rescue a dozen times. This castle is only standing thanks to me! God's blood, I'm the one the villagers turn to in time of need. You are lord in name only!"

"Get out," Richard snarled. "Get out of my castle and never dare to show your face here again."

A chill black silence engulfed them as they stared at each other. Slane straightened up, dread cresting over him like the tip of a huge wave. What had he done?

"Get out!" Richard commanded. "You'll never see her again. She's mine."

Slane stood for only a moment longer staring at his brother's coal black eyes; then he whirled and disappeared out the door, Richard's scream echoing in his ears: "You'll never see her again! I promise you. *Never again!*"

Taylor sat on her bed as the two guards left her room, closing the door behind them. Slane. It had been Slane who captured her. Slane! Of all the soldiers, of all the servants, of all the strangers who could have thwarted her escape, she had never thought it would be Slane. But why not him? Why not that traitor? Tears rose in her eyes at the thought. But how could he be a traitor if he was never on her side to begin with? She pulled her knees to her chest, trying to comfort herself, trying to find some semblance of the person she had been before. But she felt hollow and lifeless. And so very alone.

Suddenly, the door burst open and she lifted her head in surprise to see Richard standing in the doorway. His chest rose and fell with his rapid breathing. His brown eyes were wide with fury. He stormed up to her and grabbed her arm, hauling her to her feet. "Slut," he hissed. "Prefer my brother over me, eh?"

He yanked her roughly to the window, pointing to the courtyard below. For a moment, Taylor thought he was going to hurl her out the window, and she braced her palms against the cold ledge. Instead, he gripped her arm, pinching her flesh.

"Well, say good-bye to your lover," he snarled.

In the pale moonlight, it was hard to see anything in the courtyard, but finally Taylor's gaze locked on a rider moving through the middle of the inner ward, rushing beneath the walls of the gatehouse. Instinctively, she knew who it was. She knew it was Slane. Stunned confusion washed over her, disorienting her. Where was he going? He fled the outer ward, riding hard toward the outer gatehouse. A guard scrambled to get out of his path.

He was leaving her.

"Marry me," Richard barked.

Slane had told Richard about their night together, and now he was leaving her to her fate. Taylor felt coldness spread through her. "No," she answered, her gaze still locked on the dark rider speeding through the night.

"He's gone. You have no one. Marry me."

She felt his fingers digging into the flesh on her arm. With the pain, a flash of her old self returned. "I don't think so," she replied.

She watched Slane ride beneath the gatehouse, emerging onto the road that led away from the castle. Away from her.

When next Richard spoke, his words cut through the air like the blade of a sharp sword. "If I can't have you, *no one* will. You will marry me or burn."

Taylor turned to face Richard, not really sure he had spoken the damning words. His lips were curled into an ugly sneer. His eyes were narrowed to pinpricks of black light. His fists were clenched tightly. But strangely, it wasn't Richard she saw. It was a man with dazzling blue eyes. It was a man with golden hair that cascaded to strong shoulders. It was a man she couldn't have. A man who didn't want her.

She lifted her chin in the face of Richard's threat.

With a roar of rage, he flung her to the ground. "I shall enjoy watching you burn," he proclaimed. "And then we will see who is lord here." He stormed from the room, slamming the door behind him.

Taylor stared at the door for a long moment. The

wooden planks wavered before her eyes. *Burn.* She remembered the pounding drums announcing the execution. She remembered the dark smoke, rising like spiraling clouds into the dawning red sky, like crooked black fingers scratching at the sun. She remembered the screaming, the horrible screaming.

And she began to tremble.

CHAPTER
THIRTY-EIGHT

All night, Taylor lay on the bed, curled up into a ball, staring at the shaft of moonlight that shone into her room. But she didn't really see it. She knew she should be thinking of some way to escape the stake and the flames, or perhaps how her life had taken such a drastic turn, or at the very least how she had gotten here.

But her mind refused to focus on anything other than Slane. She remembered the way he had touched her, the gentle stroke of his hands, the caress of his heated lips against hers. The way his smile warmed her entire body. At least the morning's light would bring an end to her misery and pain, an end to the tormented longings for something she could not have. . . .

Flames flared around her, their heat singeing her cheeks until she had to turn away. Her mother stood in the flames, her mouth wide in a silent scream. Suddenly, her mother dissolved, her skin melting from her bones. Horrified, Taylor jerked away. But she couldn't move her hands. She couldn't move! She looked down at her feet to see the fire swirling around her ankles. She looked up to see Slane's face in the fire, distorted by the shimmering heat. He bent to Elizabeth, who was standing in the fire beside him, and pressed a kiss to her lips.

Taylor sat up, a scream frozen on her lips. Her eyes darted right, then left, struggling to focus. Her mind swirled with panic, struggling to remember where she was. It took a moment to realize that there were no flames biting at her feet; only darkness surrounded her. The shaft of moonlight had moved across her floor and Taylor realized that she must have dozed off.

She looked down at her hands and saw that she was shaking with a ferocity that shocked her. But it was not the flames that frightened her anymore; death had been a constant threat for years. No, it was her intense feelings for Slane. They clouded her judgment; they swirled through her mind like foggy vapors. She couldn't eat or think. Her mind seemed to want only to concentrate on him. In the face of death, he had become more important to her than her own life.

She stood and paced the floor, trying to work off some of her anxiety. But with each step she recalled his smile, his eyes, his hair, his powerful gait.

She wanted to scream at the unfairness of it. She wanted to cry for the loss. But mostly she wanted to be held in his arms.

Jared would strongly disapprove of the way she had let him through her defenses. After all his training, it would end for her the same way it had ended for her mother.

The irony wasn't lost on her. *Maybe you can't escape fate,* she thought. *Maybe it's a Sullivan curse.*

Taylor returned to the bed and sat down. Mother. Lord, she hadn't allowed herself to really think of her for years. She wished her mother were here. What would her mother say? To have faith? That Slane would return to rescue her? That she should have followed her heart from the beginning?

She knew that was not true. There was no such thing as love—she was sure of it now. Only torment. Only pain. Only death. Slane would not return for her. He had Elizabeth. And he had something that she could never hope to overcome. He had his honor.

She must have drifted off to sleep again, for when she opened her eyes, Anna was seated on the bed beside her. The girl lifted a white cotton tunic from her lap and reverently laid it beside Taylor. Anna smoothed out the garment and stared at it for a long moment.

Taylor watched the girl's brown eyes. In them, she could have sworn she saw sadness and despair.

"Do you want me to help you?" Anna wondered, shifting her stance slightly.

Taylor was silent for a long moment, her mind refusing to function. And then she realized the meaning of the white tunic, the bleak significance of it. It was to be her final garb. Her burning clothes. She turned her gaze back to the garment on the bed, a simple, undyed piece of cloth.

Silently, Anna stepped forward. She reached toward Taylor and untied the ribbons at the back of her nightgown. Taylor sat motionless on the bed as the girl removed her gown and then slipped the white cotton tunic over her head. The cloth was course and chafed her skin. Taylor glanced down at the white tunic, knowing that it would soon lose its purity, would soon turn into black, smoldering tatters.

Would soon burn.

There was a soft knock at the door and then a man's voice asking, "Are you ready?"

Taylor's eyes shifted to the open window. There she saw that the sky was blanketed with gray clouds that were only now turning pink with the rising sun. *Rising sun? Taylor* wondered. *It can't be dawn already!*

But in defiance of her thoughts, the drums began in the distance, their melodic pounding filling the air, filling her ears, drowning out everything but their dark, beckoning rhythm. A panic seized Taylor and she glanced around the room in horror. This wasn't happening. This couldn't be happening.

Anna squeezed her hand and helped her to her feet with a gentle hand beneath her elbow. "It's time," the girl said softly.

Yes, time, Taylor thought. *Time for me to die.* Taylor looked into Anna's eyes, searching for the strength to see her through this. Instead, she found sympathy. Taylor had always despised sympathy, especially when directed at her. But now she didn't have the energy to berate the girl.

Anna pulled Taylor's hair away from her face and tied it back. When she was finished, she stepped before Taylor and smiled grimly.

Taylor turned to the door. It took all her courage and strength to walk to it. She reached out to the handle and found that her fingers were trembling. She curled them into a fist.

Anna reached around her to open the door.

One of the four guards standing outside the door in the hallway stepped forward.

Taylor couldn't move for a long moment. She swallowed hard and bolstered what little courage remained. She took a deep breath and moved forward.

The hallways were empty as the four guards led her through them. The guards' footfalls echoed in the vacant corridor, their booted feet clanking on the stones with each step. Most of the castle's inhabitants were probably in the courtyard, ready to watch the burning, Taylor guessed.

Burning. My burning.

They descended the spiral stairway in silence. When they emerged into the first floor hallway, Taylor halted at finding it was remarkably crowded for so early. One guard urged her forward with a shove. As they moved down the hallway, a strange silence spread through the corridor as one by one all eyes turned to her. They weren't waiting for her in the courtyard. They had all come together to get a final glimpse of her before . . . before . . .

Taylor raised her chin. This she was used to. People staring and casting judgment. But somehow she couldn't stop her hands from trembling. The guards led her through the large wooden double doors into the inner ward. She halted just outside the doors, shocked at what waited for her at the bottom of the steps.

A caged wagon. They thought she was some sort of an animal. Or were they afraid she would try to escape? She knew she should. But how? Her gaze traveled upward to the battlements and walkways. Armed guards were staring at her, pausing in their patrols to gaze at the doomed prisoner.

She would have no chance against all these men. But that had never stopped her before. If only she had her sword. Better to go out fighting than as a helpless prisoner.

At one time, that thought would have propelled her into action, but now she could barely muster the strength to take another step. She glanced over at a guard, seeing the sword at his waist safely encased in its sheath. *Just reach for it,* a voice inside her urged. *Grab it and cut him down.* She felt her fingers coming to life, felt her hand begin to move. But just then, one of the guards shoved her roughly forward toward the wagon, and the moment was lost.

The wagon master, a small man dressed in a simple brown smock and matching leggings, opened the cage as she approached and waited near the cart. She paused again before the open door of the cage to glance at the man. His protruding belly looked obscene on a man with such a small frame. He smiled a humorless grin at her and gestured into the cage.

Taylor hesitated, but a rough shove from one of the guards pushed her into the wagon. The door closed behind her and she had a moment to scan the inner ward, to let her gaze roll over the sea of blank faces that watched her with grim eyes. The wagon master mounted his seat, took one final glance back at Taylor, then lashed the horse. The wagon jerked forward and Taylor had to grab one of the bars to keep from falling.

The cart was escorted by four armed men on horseback. Taylor saw their eyes searching the shadows of the castle as the cart moved forward, their hands resting on the hilts of their swords. Taylor wanted to laugh. But her throat was dry. What were they looking for? she wondered sarcastically. Robbers?

The cart moved quickly through the inner ward. She had entered Castle Donovan of her own, foolish free will. And now she was leaving a prisoner, sentenced to death. Taylor glanced back at the keep. The castle's inhabitants were racing after the cart, shouting with excitement, pointing in her direction, urging others to follow; no one wanted to miss the great burning.

The cart moved forward with a jolt that almost threw her to her bottom, but Taylor recovered quickly, righting herself.

As they neared the outer ward, Taylor heard the murmuring thunder of hundreds of voices. They moved beneath the inner ward gatehouse and she saw a huge crowd. It appeared as though the entire village had turned out to witness her execution.

As the cart grew closer, the crowd became quiet. Women standing next to their children scowled at her. Farmers and their sons glared at her. Alewives and breadmakers sneered at her.

"Harlot!" a voice shouted from the silence.

The crowd swayed, moving as one giant being, surging left and right, murmuring agreement rippling through it. Suddenly, something struck the cart, spraying her with a warm wetness. She blinked and pulled away from the side to see the splattered remains of a rotted cabbage on the bars. She glanced down to see that the cabbage was splashed across the front of her cotton tunic.

"Slut!"

Voices joined the others, rising to a chorus of insults and slurs that all mingled into one steady drone of contempt.

The wagon drew closer to the center of the outer ward.

But as Taylor raised her gaze to the center of the courtyard, her ears grew deaf to their shouts. She no longer heard the redheaded woman screaming vile words at her. She no longer heard the butcher threatening her life as he swung his knife through the air. She no longer heard the mud-streaked children laughing at her. She only saw the pole—the pole that stood like a beacon in the middle of the ward. Dread and desperation shot through her.

Something else hit the cart, splattering her face with something, but she barely felt it. She couldn't tear her gaze from the pole. Panic welled up in her. She was going to die. Tears entered her eyes, but she blinked them back with resolve. *I won't give these vermin the chance to see my fear,* she vowed.

The cart came to an abrupt halt, knocking Taylor to the straw-covered floor. She quickly stood and watched the guards dismount and move to the door. The wagon master climbed down from his seat and hurriedly moved to the cage door, opening it.

The crowd surged forward but the guards pushed them back.

One of the guards reached in and pulled Taylor from the cage. The crowd lurched forward again, and for a moment, Taylor was trapped in a sea of bodies. She couldn't move, couldn't breathe. All around her, voices screamed, condemning her. The guards hollered back. The drums continued to pound.

The guard holding her arm jerked her forward, pushing and shoving his way through the crowd, his grip on her wrist unrelenting as he pulled her toward the pole. As she drew near, she saw two peasant men stacking branches around the back of the pole. To her right, Taylor saw a man dressed from head to toe in black, holding a torch. Was that one of Corydon's men? her confused mind quickly wondered. No, Corydon was dead. The man standing before her was the executioner. Her executioner.

Fear seized her as her eyes locked with his. Was he smiling beneath that black hood? Then someone pushed her from behind, propelling her forward. The other three guards emerged from the crowd to surround her in an impenetrable wall of flesh.

The guard holding her wrist pulled her up to the pole.

He whipped her around to face the crowd and yanked her hands savagely behind her back, behind the pole. Taylor felt the course rope being lashed across her wrists, binding them tightly, cutting into her skin.

The crowd jeered at her. "Burn! Burn! Burn!" they chanted, their voices filling the square.

The guard finished binding her hands and bent to her feet, wrapping a second rope around them, binding her firmly to the pole. Then he stepped out from behind her. He nodded his head at someone off to the side, then stepped back as the two peasants began to stack the branches at her feet.

She watched the peasants for a moment, feeling strangely detached. She turned her head to the side and— a dark, horrid face filled her vision. Richard now stood at her side, the smug, satisfied look on his face giving him an evil countenance. She suddenly realized she was staring at the devil himself.

Taylor clenched her jaw and looked away from Richard. She lifted her gaze to the sky to see the glow of the sun beginning to peek over the horizon.

The two peasants quickly backed away from the stack of wood. Suddenly, the drums stopped, the last drumbeat seeming to take forever to fade into the distance. An eerie silence spread over the square.

Taylor swiveled her gaze toward the executioner as a strong wind swirled around her. He stepped forward and Taylor's stare was drawn by the bright flames of the torch he carried. The flames seemed to sway toward her, eager to begin their duty. Taylor's body instinctively tried to pull away from the deadly fire, but her bindings held her firmly.

The executioner stopped just before the dry branches at her feet and turned to look at Richard.

"Burn her," Richard commanded.

The executioner touched the torch to the branch at her feet. The branches crackled and popped, erupting immediately into hissing, spitting flames.

Taylor watched the fire spread from branch to branch, watched the hungry flames eat away at the wood, already feeling the heat of the blaze penetrate her feet. She tried to lift her gaze to the silent crowd, but the hypnotic movement of the flames held her eyes captive. The flames continued to hiss at her, condemning her to her fate, confirming what she already knew.

There would be no escape.

CHAPTER THIRTY-NINE

The flames reached for Taylor's feet, its tendrils weaving and snapping through the air, hungry for her delicate flesh. The intense heat rising up from below attacked Taylor's face, threatening to smother her. She turned her head away from the scorching flames, but the heat still assaulted her. She felt a scream rising in her throat, felt a howl of terror begin to surface, but the heat battered her face in intense waves and it took every last bit of strength she had just to take a breath. The hot air burned in her lungs.

Terrified, she tried to shift her body away from the hungry flames, away from the hellish heat, but the fire surrounded her, trapping her in its deadly embrace.

Then something moved out of the corner of her eye, a large shadowy shape; she turned and lifted her head to see what it was. Through the most intense part of the flame, through the core burning deep blue, she saw a vision. Slane wavered before her in the heart of the fiery inferno, towering over her like some god. She remembered her dream and thought for sure he would bend to kiss Elizabeth's lips, consigning her to her doom.

Then she noticed the reason for his superior height. He was on a horse. For a moment, complete confusion washed over her and she thought the heat from the flames was eating away at her sanity. What would Slane be doing here? He was gone.

Suddenly, the magnificent vision raised his arm and struck out with his sword, cutting the flames in two, pushing the burning sticks from Taylor's feet. Was this a dream? Taylor wondered. Was she dying? Then Slane bent behind her and she felt her hands being cut free, then her legs. What was he doing here?

One of the guards rushed forward, and Slane whirled, cutting him down with one stroke. He turned quickly back to her and scooped her up into his powerful arms, positioning her on the horse before him. She couldn't take her eyes from his face. His glorious, wonderful face!

What was Slane doing here?

The horse circled once and Slane's gaze seemed to take in everything. As if from far off, Taylor heard the clashing of swords, the screaming of people. Then the extraordinary vision of a man captured her with his gaze. He couldn't be real after all, could he? Not with glorious hair that defied the flames with their brilliance. Not with that powerful physique that dared deny the flames its prey. His stern eyes softened as they alighted on her. "Are you all right?" he asked.

The only response she could muster was a nod.

The grin that formed on his lips warmed her spirit and ignited her soul. She felt the blood begin to surge through her veins. But only when he bent and pressed a quick kiss to her lips did she come to life. She felt her heart beating wildly in her chest, felt her senses flaring to life, felt her soul being reborn. Were these really Slane's arms that were around her, embracing her, holding her on the horse?

She glanced around with widening eyes, as if seeing the courtyard for the first time, and took in the raging battle around them. Richard's men were locked in combat with other men, who wore no heraldry. Her gaze moved across men clashing swords, men fighting hand to hand, men dying. A loud, cracking noise startled her and she turned to see the pole that once held her captive erupting in flames, the fire hissing angrily now that its victim had escaped.

Slane spurred the horse and it moved toward the outer gatehouse and freedom.

Taylor looked back to Slane, finally noticing that he was dressed as a commoner. She still couldn't believe that Slane had come for her. She sat, dazed, staring at his handsome face. Suddenly, a scowl darkened his features and Slane brought the horse up short.

Taylor twisted her head to see that five guards were running from the door of the outer gatehouse to bar their escape.

Slane's hand tightened around her stomach as he engaged the first knight. He swung his blade mightily down at the attacker, knocking him to his knees with one blow. But before Slane could even land a second blow, another group of knights dashed beneath the gatehouse to race toward them.

Beyond the outer gatehouse, Taylor saw the drawbridge beginning to rise. They were going to be trapped inside the castle!

Cursing, Slane yanked harshly on the horse's reins. It reared slightly and turned, racing back through the inner ward, deeper into the castle. The growing wind whipped Taylor's hair wildly about her head.

Taylor looked up to see flames reaching into the dawning sky. A strong gust of wind had pushed the fire toward a merchant's cart, which had been foolishly positioned too close to the pole. The fire had quickly leapt to the wagon, engulfing it within seconds. Now the flames grew fast. People began to panic as the wind lashed the fire, spreading it from roof to roof. Already, five buildings were ablaze. People rushed to and from the well in the middle of the inner ward with buckets of water in their hands. But Taylor could see that their efforts were useless. The fire had spread too fast; it was consuming everything in its path. The fierce wind snatched some of the flames and lifted them, depositing them on the nearby roof of the blacksmith's shop.

A gust of wind hurtled a burning, broken piece of wood at them. Slane yanked hard on the reins and the horse swerved. The enflamed wood just barely missed them, landing in a nearby pile of straw, igniting it immediately. Above the screams and calls for water, the fire crackled and raged. Suddenly, a man burst out of the blacksmith's shop, his clothes aflame, his tortured cries of pain filling the courtyard. He dropped quickly to the ground, rolling in the dirt, but the fire had already consumed too much of him. Taylor watched with wide, terrified eyes as he screamed one final time and then lay unmoving in the dirt.

The castle might have escaped the ravages of the plague, but she knew it would not escape this epidemic of murderous fire and flame. Like dancing children, the flames raced across the roofs.

Taylor looked back to see a group of five soldiers chasing them, their swords drawn. Suddenly, she felt Slane tense. She turned her gaze forward to see two more soldiers waiting for them at the entrance to the upper ward, their swords drawn. Slane and she were trapped!

Slane kicked the horse hard and it lurched forward, charging through the inner ward, bursting into the upper ward. The two soldiers waiting there slashed at the horse as it emerged. The horse went down, toppling to the ground, but Slane grabbed Taylor around the stomach from behind and dove, rolling away from the horse as it plummeted to the ground head first.

Bruised and battered, Taylor managed to look up to see the two soldiers rushing toward them. Slane was already on to his feet, greeting them both with the edge of his sword. He held the two men at bay, expertly blocking their attacks and counterattacking with deft strikes of his own.

Taylor climbed to her feet, looking around for some sort of weapon to help Slane. Instead, she saw the flames leap the wall that separated the wards and catch on the thatched roof of the meat stores building. It was as if it were following her, searching for her. She watched the bright fire for a moment, transfixed as it ignited the dry roof quickly, sending sparks and angry flames shooting high into the early morning sky. Within moments, the fire was a raging inferno, spreading quickly to the building beside it. Moving toward them. Moving toward her.

"Slane!" Taylor screamed, raising her voice to be heard above the sudden din of the monstrous blaze. Her eyes burned from the bright flames and smoke, and she suddenly had difficulty seeing. She blinked her eyes quickly, trying to force them clear of the blinding smoke as a sudden panic flared through her. The fire blinded her! "Slane!" she cried out again.

She felt a hand grab hers and pull her, forcing her to quicken her pace. She rubbed at her eyes and they teared up from the stinging smoke. Finally, tears wiped across her

eyes, clearing her vision. She looked up to see Slane kick
a soldier away from them. He pulled her on, and they
raced toward a door leading to the upper ward walls. The
heat intensified as they entered, and Slane slammed the
door closed behind them, giving them a moment's respite
from the torrid air outside. He paused, glancing around
the small, dark room; then he grabbed a large barrel and
pushed it in front of the door. He whirled, grabbing her
hand again, and raced up the stairs. Taylor had to take
the stairs two at a time to keep up with him.

When they emerged on the walkway, smoke instantly
assailed them, reaching for their mouths, their noses. Taylor covered her mouth with her hand and stumbled back
away from the deadly clouds, but Slane pulled her on
through the fog of smoke that billowed up over the walkway, guiding her toward one of the two towers that bordered the rear of the castle.

They ran inside the tower and Slane shut the door.
Taylor leaned against the wall, breathing hard, looking
around the small room. She looked down to see the smoke
slink under the door, oozing across the floor like some
shapeless mass. She knew behind the smoke, behind this
mindless scout, its master followed. She looked away from
the approaching cloud to see stairs leading up to the look-
out. There was another door kitty-corner from the first
one, leading to the walkways that rimmed the castle walls.
Taylor moved for the door, but Slane grabbed her hand.

She turned to him and froze. She felt as if she were truly
seeing him for the first time since he had rescued her from
the burning. His noble face—his wonderful, exquisite
face—was smeared with soot and sweat. He stood tall and
proud beside her, a strong warrior.

He had come back for her. The thought surfaced, but
she did not want to dwell on it, fearing that if she did he

might vanish and she might awaken to the smell of burning flesh and find herself still strapped to the pole, still a meal for the hungry flames. *Please don't let this be a dream,* she thought.

"Are you all right?" he asked softly.

She noticed the concern in his glimmering blue eyes and grinned slightly. "This is a fine rescue, Slane Donovan," she said lightly.

He shrugged his shoulders. "It isn't what I had planned."

Taylor lifted a hand and placed it on his cheek. The warm flesh of his face sent a welcome rush of heat throughout her body. He was real. He was no ghost. He was no specter born of a fevered dream. "Thanks for coming."

Slane covered her hand with his own. "I wouldn't have missed it."

Impulsively, Taylor threw her arms around Slane, pulling him tightly to her, crushing him to her heart. "Slane, oh, Slane," she whispered into his shoulder, the dark horrors of her escaped fate still haunting her thoughts.

Slane gently disengaged from her embrace. He brushed a lock of wild hair away from her eyes. "We have to get out of here," he softly reminded her. He pressed a kiss to her palm and then moved toward the door. He flung it open and stepped onto the walkway.

Taylor followed him and together they raced across the walkway. Slane paused to glance over the wall. Far, far below, the still waters of Lake Donovan looked black in the early morning light. Above them, dark clouds blanketed the sky, holding the dawn captive. Slane glanced at the door that led to the other tower just before them and took a step toward it.

Suddenly, the door burst open.

Slane halted and readied his weapon. Taylor wished she

had a sword. She wished she could fight at his side. She strained, standing on her toes to see over Slane's shoulder. Then a figure materialized, a mere black shadow in the swirling smoke; then a dark shape seemed to form out of the darkness, giving the shadow substance.

Taylor gasped as Richard stepped from the south tower, emerging into the pale light.

"Back so soon, brother?" Richard said.

Taylor placed her hand on Slane's shoulder and felt his muscles harden into stone. She tried to pull him back the way they had come, but he didn't budge.

Disdain filled Richard's curled lips, his narrowed eyes. "After everything I've done for you. I've tried to help you. I even convinced Father to give you Elizabeth."

"I won't watch you burn her," Slane said simply.

"You don't care if you ruin me then?"

"If it's her gold you want, take it and be done with it."

"It's gone far beyond that, dear brother." Richard approached, and for the first time, Taylor saw the glint of the sword in his hand.

"I won't fight you," Slane said.

"You've disgraced me. You've humiliated me. You've betrayed me. You stole my betrothed. You even slept with her!"

"I didn't intend to do it."

Taylor's heart dropped. She had known all along that Slane had believed their lovemaking to be a mistake, but to hear him say so hurt. Hurt very much. She dropped her hand from his shoulder.

"For a man who considers himself a knight of honor, I find your actions most dishonorable, don't you?"

"No," Slane said, looking away. "I never meant to betray you."

" 'Oops, sorry. I just slept with my brother's future

wife,' " Richard snarled. "Is that how it was? Then what do you call it? What could you possibly have been thinking?"

Slane shook his head. Taylor stepped away from him and he swung his gaze to her. Conviction straightened his back, as if simply looking at her were enough. He turned back to his brother. "She was not meant for you. I knew that she could never be happy as your wife. I knew that ultimately she would refuse you."

"She had no say in the matter."

"She did. Because she is Taylor Sullivan. Because she's the bravest, noblest woman I have ever met. She would have fought you every chance she got."

"Oh, so now it was all to protect me? Make any excuse you like, dear brother. It doesn't change the fact that you are a liar and a cad."

Slane stood protectively before Taylor.

Taylor watched Slane's jaw clench with resolve. She saw his eyes narrow with determination. But she knew that deep in his heart the anguish and the heartache were tearing him apart. She bowed her head. She knew in that moment that she would do anything for him. Anything to erase his pain. Anything to restore his honor. "No," she said. "I seduced him. It's my fault." She lifted her gaze to meet Richard's.

"No," Slane said softly. "No more lies." He gently cupped her chin and turned her face to his. "I love you. Very much." He looked back at his brother, dropping his hand. "And if she'll have me, I intend to marry her."

Joy exploded inside Taylor, filling her with a warmth she had never known existed. She was blissfully happy and more alive than she had ever been in her entire life.

Richard visibly shook with his fury. "Not while I'm living," he shouted and rushed forward, his sword raised high.

Just then, a wall of fire suddenly erupted over the walkway behind them, exploding upward from the flaming roofs below, its scorching fingers reaching hungrily for Taylor, its crackling flames ecstatic at finally having found her!

CHAPTER FORTY

"Slane!"

Slane heard Taylor's shout of alarm as he raised his sword and his brother's blade clanged into it. He instantly knew the cause of Taylor's warning shout; he could feel the heat of the flames clawing at his back. He parried Richard's first two blows, knowing that he couldn't give ground. He couldn't give way. Not with the fire at his back. He had to take the offensive, to drive Richard back. It was their only chance. But Richard attacked relentlessly, forcing him on the defensive.

Within moments, Slane found himself standing side by side with Taylor. He chanced a quick glance at her. Through the smoke, he saw her looking behind him with widening eyes. The heat grew stronger, intensifying all around him. The air seemed to be getting thicker as it grew hotter. He could hear the flames feeding behind him, snapping and crackling and hissing as they devoured everything in their path. He quickly pulled Taylor to him and turned back to face his brother just in time to—block a strike that was headed straight for his head! When their blades crossed, Slane grabbed Richard's arm.

"Give her to me," Richard snarled.

"Never," Slane retorted and pushed his brother back.

Richard stumbled, but quickly righted himself in time to dodge Slane's attack.

The flames closed in behind them, drawing closer and closer. Slane felt the approaching inferno at his back, driving him forward. He looked for Taylor, hoping she was staying close to him, relieved to see that she was. Richard took advantage of his momentary distraction and struck, bringing his blade down toward Slane's chest and then slicing quickly upward. Slane fell, his sword flinging high into the air, the flames dancing in its shining reflection as it spun over the walkway and disappeared into the fire below.

Richard stepped forward and towered over Slane.

"No!" Taylor cried.

Richard's gaze rose to Taylor before he raised his weapon for the finishing blow. "Oh, yes," he answered.

Then, Slane pivoted on the ball of his foot, lashing out with his opposite leg. His shin smacked into Richard's legs, catching him off balance. Richard's knees buckled and he tumbled toward the inner edge of the walkway. Slane saw his brother hit the rim of the stone wall and teeter on its edge. Slane lunged forward to catch him, but his fingers grabbed air.

Richard fell from the walkway, plunging into the raging fire burning in the courtyard below, his tortured scream quickly drowned by the incessant roar of the flames.

Slane stared over the side at the bright flames for a long moment. The heat smothered his face in stifling waves.

His brother was gone. Dead. He didn't feel the grief he knew he should feel. Or should he? In the end, Richard had turned out to be an enemy, not the brother Slane had always thought him to be.

Slane lifted his gaze to Taylor.

Taylor launched herself into his arms and Slane caught her, holding her tightly. The wind whipped around them, fueling the inferno that was growing ever stronger. The fire's angry howl rang loudly in his ears. But he didn't want to move, didn't want to let Taylor go. She was his now. He had fought and sacrificed everything for the woman he loved.

Finally, Slane stood, pulling her with him. He held her tightly against his body, refusing to let her go, relishing the feel of her arms around him.

It was Taylor who pulled back slightly. "We have to get out of here," she said.

Slane nodded in acquiescence. He took her hand and began to walk toward the south tower, their only avenue of escape. But then a gust of wind spiraled the flames from below up and over the walkway, trapping them between its hungry arms!

Slane pulled back from the fire. He glanced at Taylor to see the glow of the flames highlighting the fear on her face. *No,* he thought. *This can't be. I can't have rescued her just to be killed by this cursed fire!*

Flames stretched their greedy fingers toward the walkway they stood on, forcing them back to the outer wall. Slane looked up, but no magical rope appeared, no flying carpet to spirit them away. He looked from side to side, but the hungry fire waited to engulf them everywhere he turned. Then he followed Taylor's gaze to the water of Lake Donovan glistening in the morning light like a beacon.

"Can you swim?" Taylor wondered, then pulled herself

up the wall. She balanced precariously and reached down to help Slane up. He had no sooner stepped onto the wall than the flame bit at the walkway, eating away at the wooden platform that they had been standing on mere seconds before.

She clutched at him as the wind swirled around them, threatening to push them back into the flames. Slane clutched her hand tightly in his, partly for balance, partly in uncertainty.

Slane gazed into those bright green gems for a long moment, hoping that they would both make it through this.

Then something crossed Taylor's features, an understanding, a longing, a fear. Were those tears that made those green gems sparkle? She took one last glance at the flames, at the fire that had forced her into a life of hardship and misery. Slane could see the fear seeping from her face, replaced by a determination and a force of will that he had always known to be the strength of Taylor Sullivan.

She turned back to face him, a soft grin on her lips. "Last one to shore buys the ale," she said and launched herself off the castle wall.

Slane's heart lurched into his throat as he saw her soaring through the air, dropping hard and fast toward the water below.

Then he jumped right after her and felt himself falling through the air. As he plummeted toward the glistening water, he saw Taylor strike the surface and plunge beneath the waters. It seemed like an eternity that he waited for her to emerge. But she didn't. He hit the water feet first with a sharp jolt to his legs, then plunged beneath the surface. When his downward momentum stopped, he used strong strokes to bring himself back to the surface. He broke through to the air, taking a deep inhale. He quickly glanced around the lake, searching for Taylor. But the surface remained quiet except for his splashing.

"Taylor!" he hollered.

Fearful images built in his mind. What if she hadn't made it? What if . . . ? Frantically, he dove, searching the water for her body. But it was too deep. He couldn't reach the bottom. When he broke through the surface again, he was breathing hard. "Taylor!"

Then he heard a distant splashing. He turned and saw her swimming toward the shore. Relief coursed through him and joy bubbled in his heart. He started after her, but knew that she would make it well before him.

Each stroke brought him closer to the shore until finally he pulled himself out of the water and collapsed on the grassy bank. He turned over, gasping hard. The rising sun struggled to emerge from the clouds. Finally, it peeked out, momentarily blinding him. But then its radiance was obscured by a shadow. He opened his eyes to find an angel standing above him. Or was it a devil? A smile stretched across his face. "You'll do just about anything for an ale, won't you?"

Taylor shrugged. "When I'm thirsty, I will."

It was good to hear the levity in her voice. It was even better to see happiness shine in her eyes as she gazed down at him. She sat beside him, pulling her legs up to her chest. "Was what you told Richard the truth?"

Slane boosted himself up on his elbow, trying to look into her eyes. But she was looking down at her toes, which peeked out of the hem of the execution dress she wore. "You know it was. Every word of it. I don't lie."

Taylor lifted her gaze to him and there was confusion in her eyes. "Why would you want to marry me?"

Slane smiled. "Who else would leap off a castle wall with me?"

But Taylor wasn't smiling. She was looking down at her toes, wiggling them nervously. "I don't know how to be a wife. I'm a mercenary. That's all I know."

"I would have you no other way," Slane said sincerely. God's blood! Didn't she realize how exciting she was? How beautiful and intelligent?

She planted her feet firmly on the ground. "I have nothing to offer you."

Slane took her hand in his, drawing the gaze of her emerald eyes. "You have everything. You are all I want. You are perfect the way you are." She cocked her head doubtfully and Slane grinned. "I love you."

"You must have hit the water pretty hard," she said.

"Why else would I have come back to save you?"

"It's in your blood," she offered. "Knight of honor and all that."

"I know what I want, Taylor. I think the problem is you're having trouble accepting it. You thought no man could want you."

"Well, that's not entirely true. I knew there were men who could want me. I just never knew one of them could be you."

"I didn't come back just to rescue a damsel in distress. I came back because I want you to be my wife."

Taylor's sharp gaze probed him; then she puckered her lips in thought, raising her eyes to the sky. "Lady Taylor Donovan." She giggled and the sound warmed Slane's heart.

"But there is one condition," Slane said seriously.

Taylor shifted her gaze to his.

"I desire complete and utter devotion. I would have it no other way."

"That's an awful lot to ask," she mused.

For a moment, Slane's heart sank. Then he saw the

mischievous look in her eyes, the slight curl of her lips. "Where would you take a mercenary to live?" she wondered.

Slane stood and offered her his hand. "You can't go back to Castle Donovan. You're still an outlaw there."

Taylor grasped his hand and he pulled her up. "I'm an outlaw in many towns," she observed. She cast a glance into the distance. A stray beam of sun had broken through the clouds, shining down on a green hill. "I think it's time to head home," Taylor said. "To Sullivan Castle."

Surprise rocked Slane, and then pride. He gently ran a finger along her cheek. "You've conquered all your ghosts," he said with admiration, wrapping an arm around her waist to pull her tight against him. "It will take a lot of work. A lot of dedication."

Taylor stroked his cheek, gazing into his eyes with affection and tenderness. She kissed his lips lightly, brushing hers along his with a feather-light stroke. "We will rebuild. It's time to start a new life, to stop looking over my shoulder."

Slane nodded. "I agree," he said, running a hand through her wet hair.

"Then I will give you what you desire." Taylor stared adoringly into his eyes, all the mischief gone, replaced by genuine sincerity. "I love you, Slane Donovan."

The words spoken from her lips ignited a powerful response in Slane. Elated, he pressed his lips to hers, encircling her with his powerful arms. Then he pulled back to gaze into her wondrous eyes. "I knew it," he said.

"Pretty arrogant, aren't you?"

"And why shouldn't I be?" Slane asked. "I learned from the best."

Taylor played with a lock of his wet hair, curling it around her finger. "For all these years I believed that there was no such thing as true love. What a fool I've been. There *is* such a thing. And it saved me, Slane. You saved me. Not only from the stake, but from my past as well."

"Isn't that what a knight of honor does?"

"That, and he marries poor, helpless mercenary girls."

A large crash from the castle made both of them turn and look. The fire was dying, its flames withering, its deadly heat fading. The crackling flames spit one last venomous hiss before becoming nothing more than a mute whisper.

Taylor stepped away from Slane, facing the dying beast. She stared at the fading fire for a long moment, feeling a sense of triumph.

Slane stepped up behind her, wrapping his arms around her waist.

And Taylor knew peace for the first time in eight years.

Put a Little Romance in Your Life With
Fern Michaels